SAVAGE MEMBRANE

a cal mcdonald mystery

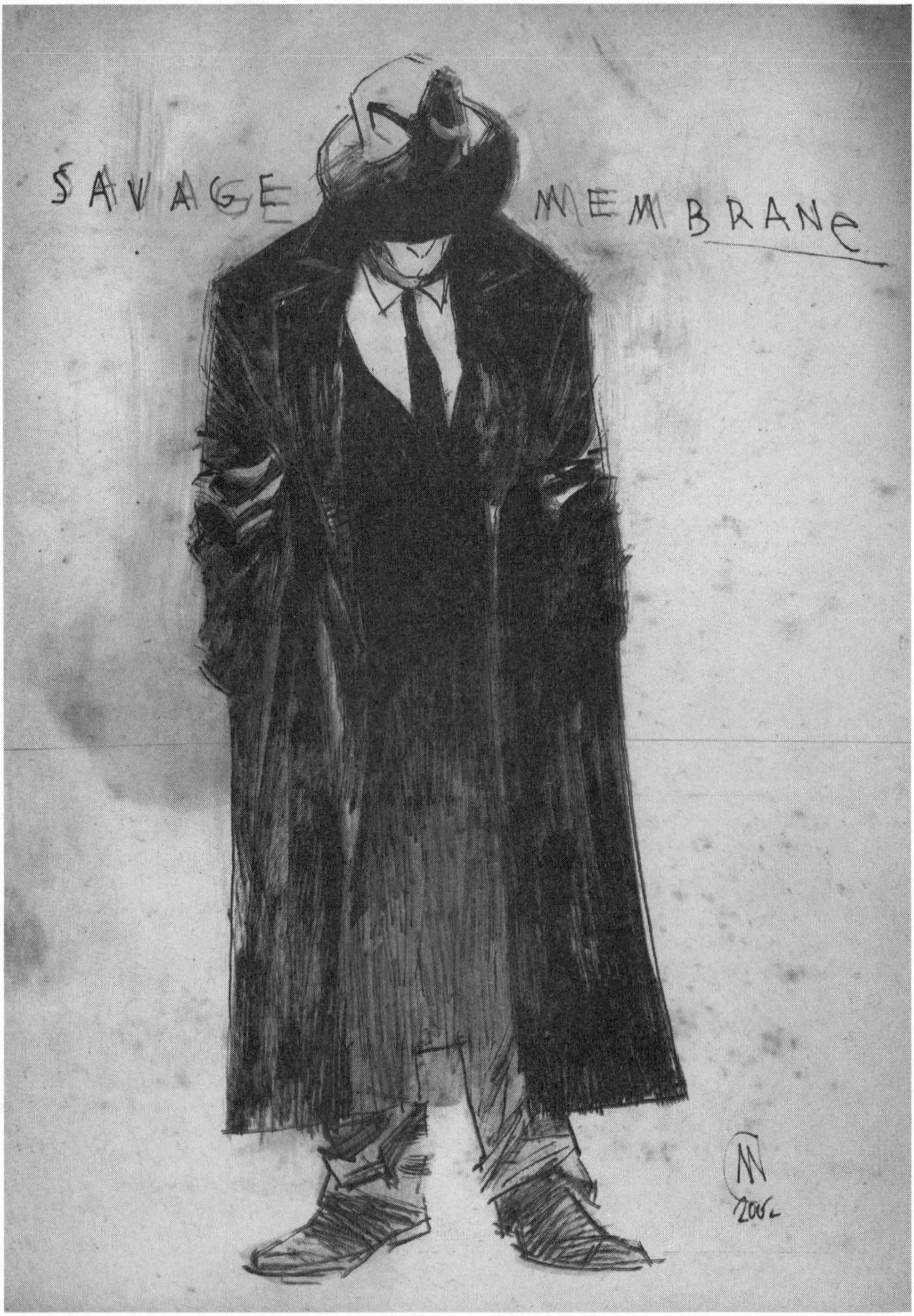
SAVAGE MEMBRANE
NW
2006

SAVAGE MEMBRANE

a cal mcdonald mystery

Written by
STEVE NILES

Illustrations by
ASHLEY WOOD

IDW PUBLISHING
san diego
www.idwpublishing.com

Savage Membrane:
A Cal McDonald Mystery
is © 2002 Steve Niles
Artwork © 2002 Ashley Wood
All rights reserved.

Book design by Robbie Robbins
Edited by Kris Oprisko

Published by
Idea + Design Works, LLC
2645 Financial Court, Suite E
San Diego, CA 92117

www.idwpublishing.com

ISBN: 0-9712282-3-X

05 04 03 02   4 3 2 1

Manufactured in Canada

IDW PUBLISHING is:
Ted Adams, Publisher
Kris Oprisko, Editor-in-Chief
Robbie Robbins, Design Director
Alex Garner, Art Director
Cindy Chapman, Designer
Beau Smith, Sales & Marketing
Lorelei Bunjes, Website Coordinator

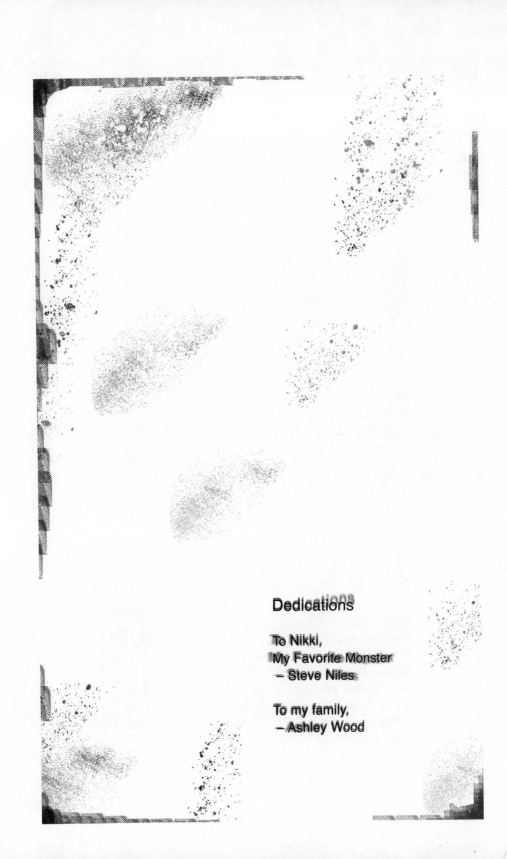

Dedications

To Nikki,
My Favorite Monster
— Steve Niles

To my family,
— Ashley Wood

CHAPTER

1

IT WAS THE NIGHT AFTER HALLOWEEN.

I had vague memories of crashing a costume party with a couple of ghouls I know. I started drinking. After that I draw a blank, but I'm sure there was trouble—there always is. Besides, I could feel a hell of a fat lip throbbing and my hands were cut and bruised with the unmistakable indentations of human teeth across my knuckles. I'd hit somebody and somebody had hit back. That didn't bother me so much. I was always hitting and getting hit. What I found disturbing was my empty shoulder holster. My .38 was gone.

I was face down in my apartment, experimenting with the adhesive properties of vomit and hardwood floors, when, of course, the phone rang. It sounded like a hammer against a steel barrel inside my skull. I groaned and peeled my face from the floorboards. My stomach lurched. It didn't like the idea of being moved very much but the phone was ringing incessantly. It was six at night so I had to get up anyway, but I didn't like being nagged. Wiping my face with one hand, I snatched the receiver violently from the cradle, choking the brain-rattling ring in half.

"McDonald Investigations. What d'you want?" I barked. My voice was gravel and phlegm.

The voice on the other end blurted, "Cal. I got something down here you might want to see."

It was Blout. Jefferson Blout is a big, bad ass cop from the precinct I worked in for all of a year. That is, before I was asked to leave as a result of a drug test. Evidently traces of alcohol, marijuana, and crank were found in my blood. Traces, hell! At that time I was practically sweating the stuff. They didn't need to check my blood, they could've just sucked on my arm.

Blout stuck by me when everyone else on the force had turned their backs. He knew why I did all the drugs, and why I still do sometimes. He knows what these eyes see. Christ. Believe me, if every time you turned around some fucked-up monster was coming down on you, you'd stay wasted too.

You see, I have this knack. Call it power, talent, what you like. I call it a curse. A fucking pain-the-ass.

It's like this. Some people attract love or money and some—I think I'm one of the few—attract the bizarre. Always have, ever since I was an eight year old kid living in the 'burbs. That's when I found my first corpse.

I'd been tooling around the woods, playing with sticks and crap, when I came over an embankment near the creek that ran parallel with my house. There it was, tucked in the mud and leaves like a big, naked pea-pod. I saw its feet first, then the torso. And that was all, because that's all there was. It was headless.

Maybe that was when things clicked, when my fate was set in stone. I wasn't scared, though—more like enthralled, so much so that I didn't bother to call the cops for over an hour. All I could do was think about the headless man. Who was he? Who killed him? And why had they taken his head?

Somehow, I knew instinctively that the head wasn't in the area, and when the cops arrived I told them my theory. They laughed, patted me on the head, and said I'd make a great detective.

That pretty much set the tone for the rest of my life: bizarre crimes, laughing cops, and me in the middle. Like I said, I'm a magnet for the weird, so I did what the cops told me all those years ago and became a detective. Now I really get on their nerves.

Anyway, Blout's supported me, helping with cases and sometimes with bail. I've tried to return the favor whenever something strange comes along that normal police investigations and procedures can't touch. And believe me, they hate to admit when they need help—especially from the likes of me.

There was this case a few years back where body parts of young boys and girls were being found all over the place—tragic, but not altogether uncommon. What was odd was that the limbs and other body parts hadn't been crudely chopped off, the norm in a hack-and-slash case. Instead, they were removed with almost perfect surgical precision. The killer took his time with these kids, lots of time. Even weirder, the parts were rubbed with strange oils and exotic herbs. The cops waited almost six months before they came to me. If not for Blout's insistence, they may never have.

Once they showed me everything, I knew immediately that we were dealing with something of voodoo origin. The herbs and oils were commonplace in Haiti and New Orleans, even certain parts of New York. But the surgical accuracy behind the removal of the limbs had me stumped until a day or so later. I was walking through an alley on the way to the corner liquor store, when I spotted an illegal chop shop—a garage where stolen cars are cut up for parts. It hit me like a ton of bricks, or better, a ton of bloody body parts.

I suggested the cops check the Feds' files for plastic or transplant surgeons of Haitian descent from the New Orleans area that had been fired in the past five years and had relocated to the Washington DC Metropolitan area. Second—and this even creeped me out—hit the files for stalking investigations on the Internet, specifically cases involving adults seeking teenagers.

On a hunch, I told them to check out a guy I'd seen on the news, name of Francis Lazar. He headed an organization that actually believed young children, and I mean young, were capable of physical relationships with adult men. The organization was called ManChildLove. I remember when I saw Lazar on CNN I quickly lost track of what he was talking about and concentrated on his eyes. In them I saw mania. The guy was a sick, twisted freak hiding behind his rhetoric.

Bottom line, boys: keep your eyes peeled for one or two twisted fucks with a penchant for teens, home surgery and voodoo.

Sure enough, everything I told them involving the case fell into place. The cops, with the help of the Feds (who love to come in right at the end), located one Dr. Polynice, formally of New Orleans and fired from his post for "unusual practices with cadavers". In his basement, the authorities discovered the good doctor's very own teenage chop shop and Voodoo Lounge. After checking phone and mail records, it was found that the doctor had been shipping large crates all over the States. Before each shipment, a call was made from the Doctor to MCL spokesman Francis Lazar.

Connection made, target hit. Bull's-eye. Dr. Polynice's network was collecting innocent teenagers, murdering them, rearranging their body parts into unidentifiable corpses, and reanimating the patchwork cadavers with forgotten voodoo zombie rituals. And it gets worse, if that's possible. The bastards were selling the jigsaw kiddies to ManChildLove members. What those twisted pricks did with them I'll leave to your imagination.

It took me less then a week to solve the case after the cops had jerked around for six months because they couldn't stretch beyond their own perception of the world. How many kids could've been saved if they'd called me sooner? That's the question I couldn't shake.

In the end, more than sixty people were arrested from DC to San Diego and charged with crimes ranging from murder to kidnapping to necrophilia. Arrested were members of MCL, lonely, disturbed women and one or two well meaning but extremely misguided couples unable to adopt or procreate.

Throughout the trial, the subject of reanimation was never brought up, nor were the zombie teens ever shown, talked about, or presented as evidence. They just disappeared, victims for all time. Nobody wants to believe in Frankenstein, but they will believe that someone mail-ordered corpses for sex.

Soon as I heard Blout on the phone this time, I knew something strange was happening. Something the cops couldn't handle using conventional methods.

"What is it? Emergency? 'Cause if it ain't, I got a lot of throwing up to do."

Blout laughed. "Yeah, I heard about last night."

I didn't want to let on I had no idea what happened at the Halloween party, so I returned the laugh and said, "It was a great party. I had a good time." I laughed again. It was one chuckle too many.

"You have no idea what happened last night, do you?"

I paused as long as I could. "No."

There was an awkward silence that happens every time Blout and I come too close to personal talk. He went on.

"You going to come down here or not?!"

I belched. Bile boiled in my throat. "Yeah, yeah, give me a couple minutes to clean up."

"Please do."

He hung up before I could retort. Bastard.

CHAPTER

2

I TOOK OFF MY FILTHY CLOTHES

and used them to wipe up the area where I slept, then threw them out the window into the alley. It would be easier to get new stuff than to pay to have vomit, blood and God knows what else cleaned out of them. I drew all the shades, lit a smoke and strutted around the apartment naked until I found myself standing in front of my half shattered, full-length mirror. It'd been a long time since I'd looked at myself. What a mess; a maze of scars covered my body. I looked like a scarification fanatic, except they do it on purpose. I got mine quite unwillingly, the result of years and years of getting the shit kicked out of me.

I shook my head. Only thirty years old but you'd think I was in my late forties. Christ, fifties even! Standing there naked, I realized I looked as much like a monster as any I'd fought. I laughed a breathy, gasping-for-air laugh. Yeah, fucking hysterical.

I turned towards my trash covered desk, head pounding. My guts were twisting so I pulled open the bottom drawer where a bottle of Jim Beam greeted me. It went down hard and connected with the craving in my bloodstream, making me queasy. The sick retreated before I returned the bottle to the drawer. Hair of the dog wins another in a long series of battles.

Kicking a trail through ankle deep trash, I made my way to the bathroom, figuring I could catch a quick shower and shave and get down to the station within a half hour.

Just then I heard a sound from the other side of the shower curtain. Someone (or something) had shifted. I reached for my gun, but all I got was a handful of armpit. I had no weapon and I was naked, so I began to ease out of the room.

The curtain flew open and I screamed. A huge, dark figure stood in my tub. "Ahhhhh!"

"Hey Cal, when did you wake up?"

It was Mo'Lock; sometime partner, reluctant friend, full-time ghoul. A ghoul of the lurking variety. My heart was pounding so hard I thought for sure I would die right then and there.

Yeah, I see all sorts of shit. Ghouls are actually one of the more common monsters around. They can be found all over the world, mostly in urban areas. They are the purest form of the undead, and actually the most harmless. Way back in the Middle Ages, ghouls were known for eating flesh and lurking in graveyards, but they came into their own around the turn of the century when they realized they didn't need flesh or blood to survive.

While the world was living through an industrial revolution, ghouls began a revolution of self-discovery. They were dead, cursed to live forever in a twisted form of their former human self, but they didn't need anything to survive. They made peace with the human race and began a hundred-year process of acclimating themselves into human society.

These days you can find ghouls everywhere. They tend to favor service industry jobs because they like the hours. Next time you pass a road crew, take a second look. I guarantee there's a ghoul among them. The same goes for postal workers and a wide range of people you probably never look at twice.

Most people would be surprised how often they're in contact with the dead. All
in all, ghouls are pretty low maintenance—that makes them all right in my book.

I met Mo'Lock on one of my earliest cases and he's been glued to me since.
He has an annoying habit of creeping around, but I can't get too mad. That
would be like blaming a cat for being hairy.

A slit of a grin appeared on his stark white, bony face. "You forgot I was here,
didn't you?" He looked a little too pleased with himself.

I took a deep breath. "Get the hell out of my bathroom. I got a call from
Blout. Something's up."

The ghoul stepped out of the tub with long, sweeping, puppet-like motions.
Two strides and he was standing outside the bathroom facing me. He looked
me up and down like a ten cent peep show.

"Do you know you're naked?" He seemed to be genuinely concerned.

I slammed the door in his face. It hit him, and he fell to the floor cursing. He
was very tall and thin, like a bone rail. Getting himself off the ground was a
major pain. Teach his dead ass to mess with me. Maybe it would be a good day
after all.

I showered, shat, shaved and dressed before returning to my desk, where the
ghoul was emptying his pockets onto the blotter: mace, a lock-blade knife,
handcuffs, and a pair of short spiked steel knuckles—an inexpensive, but nasty
cousin of the brass knuckle—covered the stained desktop.

"Hey, don't go dumping your shit on my desk!"

"This is your 'shit'. I took it from you at the party after your episode with
the alien," he said, "Besides, I do not have any 'shit'."

He wanted me to see the bloody smashed mess the door had made of his
nose, but I just stared at him. His busted nose wasn't any big deal, it'd heal
before we got to the precinct. The undead have amazing healing capabilities.
He just wanted some easy sympathy.

"Officer Blout called again while you were in the shower. I took a message,"
Mo'Lock said as he lifted a piece of paper off the desk. "He said, 'If you don't
get your fat, lazy-fuck, bastard-self down to the station immediately, you can
kiss my black ass.'"

I loaded the stuff Mo'Lock had been holding for me into my pockets.
Six-thirty p.m. and I was ready to start my day. When I headed for the door,
Mo'Lock lumbered behind me. I stopped.

"You coming?"

"Do you mind?"

"No, not at all. You got cash?"

"Yes."

"Let's grab a cab."

The ride to the station was the usual bit of the bizarre that I've come to expect. The driver was of Mo'Lock's ilk, and the two of them gabbed on and on in a tongue that sounded foreign, but was simply regular English spoken at unbelievable speed. It's fascinating for about thirty seconds, then it works your nerves to blunt nubs. Moments like these made me wonder what the hell I was doing riding in a cab with a couple of the living dead. It was the eternal question—why me?

CHAPTER

3

AS A RULE, I DETEST POLICE DEPARTMENTS,

but I really hate my old precinct. Aside from the stares and nasty comments thrown my way as I pass, the place has a smell that sets my memory reeling. Walking the halls, I'm always reminded of the worst times.

The year I graduated from the Academy, for instance, was a long, shit-pile of a year. I became a cop, then lost my family and nearly my mind. In the space of twelve months, my mother and younger sister were killed by a drunk driver and my father, Ben McDonald, went berserk and cut the driver's throat outside the courtroom. As usual, I couldn't do a damn thing about it because I was so loaded on smack.

My father was charged and he responded by

hanging himself the night before his hearing. I discovered the body. I'll never forget the image of his corpse swinging back and forth, the sound of the rope creaking against the rafter beam, rhythmic and maddening.

All my life I tried my damnedest to be normal. I ignored the dark fringes of the world that crept toward me and if something got too close, I stomped it dead and turned my back like nothing had ever happened. Monsters? Nope, didn't see them. Werewolves, aliens, demons and freaks? Just keep on walking. Don't look.

The Police Academy was an attempt at normal existence, but even there I should have known it would be impossible. I could never hide or live a normal life. No matter how hard I try, I always seem to land right in the middle of Freak Central.

The Academy was no exception.

It turned out that the place was built on a goddamn burial ground. Of course, the dead decided to have their revenge the week I arrived. It was a blood-bath of possession, sacrifice and the living dead. I don't mean living dead like Mo'Lock, bloodless ghouls who can function and think; these sons-a-bitches were mindless, kill-crazy zombies.

The place turned upside down. Everyone panicked except me. The one benefit of my life is that I'm never surprised. I've had the crap scared out of me a few times, but I never panic. That day, I fought my way through the relentless invasion until I reached the little room used as the Parish. I convinced the priest, who I found hiding in his confessional, to follow me to the basement where I told him to bless the water main. It took some convincing, and a slap or two, but eventually he agreed.

It was in the bag. I manned one of those riot control hoses and hosed the place down with a half million gallons of high octane Holy Water. The dead and possessed withered and melted, screamed and let loose the innocent. In the end, only a few dozen were dead and nobody except me and the priest knew what happened. Well, at least that was the official stand. The Academy closed and moved to a new location a year later. Chickenshits.

Still, I refused to give in, to acknowledge the supernatural regions of life. To hide, I took more and more drugs, more and more drink, anything to blur my vision or dull my senses. It was a miracle I lived, let alone graduated. But I did, and everything was going great for awhile. I even made the effort and kicked drugs. It was hard, very hard, and not just because of my physical and emotional addictions. The more I stayed sober, the more horror I saw: strange things peering around corners, voices whispering in my ear in the dark. But I had to make an effort, had to make some sort of a stand against the darkness that threatened to overtake me.

I was absolutely straight the day of my graduation from the Academy. My family was there (it would be several weeks until the drunk driver entered our lives) and though nobody said outright, especially my dad, I knew they were proud.

At one point he caught me alone near a crowd of rowdy graduates. He shook my hand and in a very low tone said, "You look good, son. Nice job."

He used the pretense of the graduation to congratulate me on kicking drugs, but it was better than nothing. Then in the crowd I saw a stranger moving quickly through the crush. He moved with a confidence you don't see in a normal person. I couldn't take my eyes off him, even though my father was talking to me. He broke through the crowd, and as he passed he looked at me and raised his hand. Then I saw his palm and the strange scar burned into its center. A pentagram, the mark of the beast. I started to go after him, but stopped. I wasn't going to give in. The darkness would not consume me. I forced myself to look away. When I looked back, the stranger had disappeared into the throng of graduates.

The next night I had dinner with my parents. I stayed sober despite the sight of the man in the crowd. It had been eating at me all night, though, because he seemed to take pleasure in taunting me. I knew what the man really was—a pentagram on the palm was the sign of the werewolf.

The dinner was nice despite my preoccupation. They were happy about me becoming a police officer and my new-found sobriety. Nobody said it in so many words, or any words at all, but they buzzed around, smiling at nothing, and there was a general air of peace that had been absent for a long time. My little sister Stephie suckered me into playing Nintendo with her after dinner and we wound up playing for hours. Finally, after I'd received countless ass-kickings, my dad asked that we turn off the game so he could see the news. I pretended to be disappointed, but it was a relief.

Everything came crashing down when the television flickered to life. The lead story on the news was a gruesome, extremely bloody multiple murder. To our horror, we found out the murders had happened nearby. A family was having a small party celebrating their daughter's graduation from the Academy. Details were sparse, but at some point the party came under attack—twelve people were slaughtered.

My stomach began to tighten. I needed a drink, a pill, something. Anything to stop the feeling rushing over me.

"...details are sketchy but police are telling us that this shocking tragedy seems to be result of some sort of... animal attack."

I was numb, sick. I felt responsible for the deaths. I had the killer in my sights and let him go.

I suddenly felt panicked and had to get out of that house. I hastily thanked my mom for the dinner as the whole family pleaded that I stay. I remember looking back as I got into my car and seeing my parents standing in the doorway. They weren't waving. They just stood there watching me, knowing I was about to leap off the wagon. They were right—I went on a binge that would've shamed Keith Richards.

It did the trick. I felt nothing but the buzz of alcohol and painkillers in my system. Above all, I saw nothing.

Three weeks later, a drunk driver took my family. After that, and after I found my dad swinging by his throat, I was gone. I remember nothing from the last half of my year as a cop save for loads of crushing pain. It was then that I faced my fate, spit on it and kicked it in the balls.

I was so much of a mess that my sergeant demanded I take a drug test. The results were bad. They didn't just ask me to leave the force, they kicked my butt and threw me bodily from the station.

It was the final straw. Still, I didn't care. I laid in the gutter until I had the strength to stagger to a liquor store. I was beaten down, twitchy and paranoid. Faces stared, some dumbly, some seemingly loaded with malice. I had lost it all. Soon I would come apart at the seams, or if I was lucky, just collapse and die.

Then it happened. I was walking, swigging rotgut, alongside a small shadowy park off Fifteenth Street, just short of Mount Pleasant. It was a dark moonless night, yet when I glared into the park I could see clear as day. I saw the figure of a man looming over a woman. At first I thought they were making out, and I began to turn away to get back to feeling sorry for myself. Then I saw the moist glimmer of fangs.

Vampire.

I tossed the bottle, smiled and cracked my knuckles.

I ran into that park feeling every ounce of the pain in my chest, every loss I'd suffered and most of all, the hatred I felt for the horrible luck I had. I channeled the rage into my body, feeling strong, sober and clear-headed. In reality, I was out of control, drunk and over-confident.

I attacked the vampire with such ferocity that the bloodsucker seemed frightened and tried to get away. From me, a mere human! In that moment, I gave up trying to run away. If the dark wanted me, it had me.

I ripped the head from the vampire's shoulders with my bare hands, pissing on the fate that was handed to me. This was my life. I had arrived.

And that, to make a short story long, is why I hate going to the precinct. It reminds me of my family and the sorry state of my life.

Blout was waiting for us outside the door of the coroner's lab, chewing on a big sloppy cigar. Normally I dislike cigar smokers, but he pulled it off. Blout was a large, wide-framed black man in his early forties, very dark and tall. In fact, he was almost as tall as Mo'Lock. He always wore dark suits that made him all the more imposing, making me feel small and unimportant in his shadow.

He looked pissed—pretty much his natural state—and none too pleased that I brought the ghoul along. Nobody could quite figure out who or what Mo'Lock was. He definitely made humans uneasy, but he always wore a suit and tie, so they assumed he was okay. Funny what you can pull off with a decent suit.

Blout stood up and looked straight into my eyes. Mo'Lock was ignored with clear, obvious disdain.

"What'd you bring him for?" Blout asked in his low, rumbling voice. He stood close. I could smell the minty stink of his menthol shaving cream and the fast food taco he had for lunch.

I shrugged. "He's my assistant. Might be able to help."

Blout shoved a big finger close to my nose. "Just keep him the fuck away from me. Got it?"

I showed him two palms. "Okay, no sweat. What've you got?"

Blout bobbed his head sideways, indicating the door of the coroner's lab. "In here."

The lab was cramped, bare of equipment, and dark. There were only two lights; a small desk lamp and a bare bulb dangling above the examination table in the center of the room.

There was a body on the table, head and chest cut open. The scalp had been sliced, and the flesh from the top of the head peeled like an orange. The face of the dead man was wrinkled and folded down over itself. It would have been comical if it weren't so disgusting. The ribs were sawed clean away so there was a tidy viewing window to examine the cavity. I could see the internal organs had already been removed for examination. The heart and liver were in steel trays and next to them was an array of bloody saws and surgical tools. An autopsy had recently been completed.

I stepped up to the table. The body was male. By the looks of his overgrown hair and the haggard, leathery look of his skin, I assumed he was homeless. That is, of course, when he was alive. He was dead now. Homeless and lifeless, what a raw deal.

Mo'Lock stayed behind me, close to the exit, but slowly edged toward the corner where there was the least amount of light. Blout moved to the other side of the table. He looked down at the body and sighed. He didn't have much of a stomach for an experienced cop. When he looked up at me I was screwing a cigarette into my mouth. His expression went from disgust to irritation.

"Don't smoke in here, Cal. Christ, you know better."

I put my lighter back, leaving the unlit cigarette in my mouth. "Yeah, I wouldn't want to give the stiff cancer," I said. "What's the story?"

"John Doe, homeless. He was found last night stuffed in a drainage pipe that used to dump into the old reservoir near the DC/Maryland border."

I could see no reason why I was needed. Dead bums weren't my forté, and not the least bit strange. I chewed on the unlit cigarette like a piece of beef jerky. "What's the cause of death?"

Blout smirked. He thought he had one on me, as though the answer were so clear, so obvious. "Try opening your fucking eyes. You notice anything missing?"

I scanned the body again, stopping at the head. I leaned down and squinted into the open skull. Inside it was a clean white, as though the cavity had been scrubbed and bleached.

"I'll be damned," I said, and stood up straight.

"You see why I wanted you to come down."

From the other side of the room, Mo'Lock emerged from the shadows.

"What is it?"

Blout and I spoke at the same time.

"No brain."

The autopsy was conclusive: the skull was completely empty. There was no blood, no matter, and x-rays showed there were no breaks in the skull whatsoever. The brain stem was there, untouched, as though there had never been anything attached to it. The official coroner's report called it brain death, but isn't brain death when you're still alive but a vegetable? How can something that isn't there be the cause of death? I'd like someone to explain that one.

The strange thing was, I'd seen this before. Blout knew it.

"Remind you of anything, Cal?"

I nodded. This time Blout kept his mouth shut.

Mo'Lock walked right up to the table. He stood so close I could feel the cold of his flesh, his annoyance evident. "Excuse me, but I'd like to know what's going on."

I was staring at the floor, my head swimming in watery visions of distant memories.

CHAPTER

4

IT WAS ONE OF MY EARLIEST CASES,

during a phase when I was doing some pretty hard drugs. I was still a mess from what had happened with my family. It had been only a few months since I'd been thrown off the force, but I decided to go into business for myself —what did I have to lose? The way I figured, if weird shit was constantly getting in my face, I might as well get paid for it. I managed to throw together enough cash to get the apartment that I use as an office, and soon after began getting a few cases.

Most of them were simple, basic demon possession or hauntings. Other jobs were total fakes, people who thought their neighbors were Satan worshipers, vampires, and werewolves. Sometimes they were, but mostly they weren't. I didn't tell them that, though—I needed the cash. I had rent to pay and a bad habit to feed. Actually it was more difficult to cheat people than it was to deal with supernatural problems. I hated to lie, but cases involving the unnatural are pretty hard to find. It's tough making a living off something people refuse to believe exists. Things have to get way out of hand before they seek help.

That's what happened the day a guy named Edgar Cain developed a bizarre and dangerous ability. The police, at wit's end, were forced to turn to me.

Edgar lived in a huge, four-hundred unit apartment complex. He was a lonely man, keeping to himself and hiding in his apartment for weeks on end. He was employed as an accountant for a company that did telemarketing and was thus able to work from home. It cut him off completely from contact with others, insuring his solitude. All that loneliness right smack dab in the middle of a tower of humanity was the catalyst for Cain's ability. Over the years I've found loneliness to be the source of many bizarre crimes and unnatural behavior.

One morning, residents of Cain's complex started to drop dead. Just like that. Bam, they're dead. By noon the body count reached seventy-five. And like the current stiff lying before me, their brains were gone. Not broken, splattered or spilled. Gone.

All the while, Edgar Cain grew inside his apartment. With each death, Cain's brain increased in size and so did his skull and head. Somehow, he was absorbing the brains of everyone around him. With the brains came their intellects, memories, and ideas. In his own horrific way, Edgar Cain undid years of loneliness by making a community inside his enormous, growing head.

That was the point where I came in: scores dead and a giant head going berserk on the top floor of an apartment building. The cops had come to the right guy—it had me written all over it.

Of course, I was wasted that day, but this time it would work in my favor. I didn't know it right away but Edgar couldn't absorb my brain because of the tremendous amounts of narcotics swimming in my blood stream. When I marched off the elevator with a shotgun, there was nothing he could do to stop me.

But I didn't just run in shooting. First I tried to reason with him. He ranted on about becoming one entity, one life, making loneliness impossible. Blah, blah, blah. After the speech, he attacked me and went airborne. The fucking head could fly! I tried to shoot him but only managed to blast his skinny little leg. He hit me hard. We went out the window, and just like that, we were flying over the city, a thousand feet up. I was clinging to his hair, ears, an open wound, anything to stay on while I punched and kicked at the wailing head.

Then I remembered the syringe in my pocket that I had shot up with earlier. I used that very syringe to stab out Cain's eyes and bring him crashing to the ground. He exploded in a massive spray of tissue and bone-chips, which conveniently broke my fall. A perfect ending—I was alive and there was nothing left of the head.

CHAPTER

"END OF CASE. UNTIL THIS," I FINISHED.

I looked from Mo'Lock to Blout and then to the body. "I thought it was a simple case of spontaneous phenomenon, but if it's happened again..."

Blout shook his head, "What the hell's spontaneous phenomenon?"

"I made it up," I said, "It means something that's never happened before."

Blout raised his hands. "You can't make up case descriptions!"

"Sure can," I shot back, "I just did."

Blout was about to blow his top. The fact that I smiled didn't help.

"There has to be a source." Mo'Lock said, moving the conversation back on topic.

I rubbed my eyes. "Exactly."

Blout looked at Mo'Lock's pale flesh and deep sunken eyes. The ghoul bothered him in a way he'd never admit. To even entertain the thought of the walking dead would drive a normal person over the edge. For a cop like Blout whose entire existence is grounded in fact, the truth would kill him.

Blout started to say something, but before he got it out, the door of the lab was knocked open by someone pushing a cart. It was a young woman with a serious face and hair pulled in a tight bun wearing a dark blue coroner's office windbreaker. On the cart was a bagged corpse, and behind it another.

"You Blout?" she demanded as much as asked. "On the John Doe case?"

Blout nodded quickly, flustered as a third and fourth cart were rolled in. "Yes to both questions," he said. "What the hell's going on?"

The woman handed him a clipboard. "We've been trying to reach you. Beat cops found a dumpster full of bodies alongside the water treatment plant near Georgetown. Sign please."

Blout grabbed his head and shot me a look. "All homeless?"

"Near as I can tell." She stopped for one quick moment as she caught a glimpse of Mo'Lock and was out the door.

In the hall, they had begun to line the walls with carts and bodies. There wasn't any room left in the lab.

Seconds turned into minutes at Dead Body Central. We all did a lot of head shaking, muttering and heavy sighing. Everywhere we looked was a cart and body-bag. The place was a cadaver parking lot. I waited for Blout to say something, but when at last he spoke, it was anti-climatic to say the least.

"I better get back to the office to start sorting this shit out." He eyed me sharply from across the table. "Got any ideas?"

"A few. I think the first thing I should do is get ahold of the Edgar Cain files. Can you get them for me?"

Blout shook his head. "Whoa, whoa, whoa! Don't go running off on one of your tangents. That was a nice story, but I need to investigate on planet earth first."

"Would it hurt you to humor me before it's too late just this one time?" I said and smacked his shoulder.

Blout muttered something under his breath, then, "Give me an hour."

"What about Cain's phone records?"

"Oh, come on, Cal. Why do you want phone records? You know what a bitch those are to get." Blout looked irritated.

"Just a hunch. I'll fill you in if anything pans out."

I turned to Mo'Lock. "One thing's for sure, if John Doe was found outside a drainage pipe and this crowd was near the treatment plant, we got one place we have to check out."

The ghoul bobbed his head. "The sewers."

"Right. Grab some of your buddies and check it out."

"I'm on it."

Out of the corner of my eye, I saw Blout shudder as the ghoul left. I chuckled.

"That freak gives me the creeps," Blout said with a little extra gravel in his throat.

"Be glad he's on our side. You'd cry like a baby if you knew what he was capable of," I said. "Besides, he's saved my ass more times than I care to admit, so in my book that makes him a lifetime pal."

"The two of you make a lovely couple. Let's get out of here. These stiffs got a meeting with the butcher."

Right on cue, the Medical Examiner came in with a couple of her assistants following like little blood-thirsty ducklings. I was halfway down the hall when Blout stopped and went back to the door.

"Wilson? Would you mind starting with the head examination first? I need to know what you find."

"Sure. It's your show."

Blout caught up with me as I was heading out the front door. "Hey Cal, want your gun back?"

I stopped outside, bit the inside of my lip and turned. Blout was grinning. My stomach sank. "You have my gun?"

He nodded slowly.

"You were at the party?"

"After the police were called in."

I threw my hands up in the air. Fuck it, I had no idea what I'd done. The jig was up. "Okay, you got me! What the hell happened?"

"First," he said reaching into his coat pocket, "here's your piece. Try to hang on to it."

I took the gun and put it into the empty holster. "Go on. I can see you're enjoying the shit out of this."

"Well, it seems you took it upon yourself to break some kind of world record for most drinks consumed in an hour—"

"Skip the embellishments."

"You got blind, piss-drunk, and seemed to forgot it was Halloween and you were at a costume party. Evidently, you spotted this dude in a real convincing alien costume and you... went... nuts." He rolled the last word off his tongue by touching it to his teeth, causing an irritating hiss.

"Did I hurt the guy?"

"Oh yeah."

"I didn't shoot him or anything, did I?"

Blout shook his head. "No, no. Luckily your buddies disarmed you while you were getting riled up. All you managed to do was smash a forty gallon punch bowl over his head and beat him with a table leg. It wasn't pretty."

I slapped my hand over my eyes. "Is he pressing charges?"

"I'd be expecting a large lawsuit in the not too distant future."

I waved off the whole mess. "Fuck it. I don't care. I'll think of something." I started down the front steps. The night air was breezy and the first hint of cold tickled the surface of my skin. Fall was in full swing.

"Let me know when you find Cain's case file, and about the autopsy results."

Before the door closed I heard Blout laughing, saying "I'm on it," in his best Mo'Lock impression. It was horrendous.

Walking back to my apartment I snagged a pint of rotgut from the liquor store and swigged. The bottle was empty by the time I reached my building, and I was feeling fine. A little bleary, but better.

I reached for the door handle but it wouldn't budge. I gave it another tug. Nothing. It was stuck.

"Goddammit."

After one last yank I leaned in and inspected the door closely. The space between door and frame was clogged with hardened opaque crud. Some punk had super-glued the door shut. I was about to curse everyone under thirty, when I suddenly stopped. There was a sharp noise over my shoulder—a click.

The small hairs on my arms stood on end. Instinctively I dove sideways. At that exact moment, the door exploded in a hail of automatic gunfire. I hit the ground hard and rolled, but the barrage followed me like a swarm of angry bees. I rolled as fast as I could and jumped to my feet, diving for cover into the alley. Not fast enough: I felt the sting of a bullet graze my shoulder.

Then, as suddenly as it began, it was quiet again. I was laying in a pile of rancid garbage and pigeon shit, bleeding and trying to stay as still as possible while a car screeched away. When I ran to the curb a smoke cloud from the tires still hung in the air. I could see the car ahead and a figure hanging out the window, throwing away the gun. He was wearing a ski mask, no gloves, and wrist-bands. I reached for my revolver, but the shoulder wound tore wider and stopped me cold.

The street looked like the set of *The Hound of the Baskervilles*. Smoke was everywhere. I pushed through the haze towards the receding car until I found the gun lying in water and leaves. I don't know a hell of a lot about guns but I was pretty sure it was an Uzi. That in itself was scary enough. To top that off, painted along the side of the gun were the words, "Cal McDonald".

Venturing a guess, I'd say it was meant as a threat. Rank amateurs. That out-of-control hail of bullets could have just as easily hit me as not. Some warning. And writing my name on the weapon? That was just plain stupid.

Then I noticed the entire door to my building was gone, blown completely apart. At least I could get in now.

My shoulder was bleeding, but not bad. I'd be able to sew it up myself.

CHAPTER

BLOUT SENT CAIN'S FILE TO MY APARTMENT

by courier. No phone records, and the rest I already knew. The evidence list, though—that I found fascinating. Most of the stuff was pretty standard, but I was surprised to see that an accountant who worked out of his home owned no calculator, computer, fax, or answering machine. His life seemed oddly devoid of modern conveniences.

About ten minutes after the courier dropped by, Blout called with the preliminary autopsy results. The heads of the first three victims were empty and sparkling clean. I was sure the rest would turn out the same. What did surprise me was what Blout said next.

Some of the corpses had been dead for more than five months.

I was getting the unsettling feeling this case was going to be a bit more difficult than my usual day-to-day monster-in-the-closet case. As far as I knew, Cain was the only loon to suck brains telepathically, and that ability died when I killed him. This was something new, something bigger, and something much, much deadlier. I wasn't sure if that case had anything to do with this one, but it was all I had to work with. I needed to establish a timeline of Edgar Cain's activities the day he started absorbing people's brains.

"By the way," I said into the receiver as I reached for the bottle, "someone tried to turn me into a greasy smear outside my apartment earlier. I got the gun. Can I drop it off for dusting and ballistics?"

Blout sounded amused. "Any idea who it was?"

"Zip. All I saw was a dark '65 Mustang, speeding away with three people inside."

"Why don't you run down here in a little while? I'll run the weapon, and we can grab some food and talk about the case. Suits upstairs are nervous that the press might catch wind and turn the thing into a circus."

"Give me half an hour. I took a slug in the shoulder. I gotta stitch myself up." I took a big swig of Beam.

"Christ, Cal. Go to the fucking hospital!"

I swallowed. The burn felt great. "No. I've been there a thousand times this month. It's nothing. I'll take care of it."

"Fine," was all Blout had to say. He hung up.

I chuckled. "What a granny."

I removed my dress shirt and did some sewing.

By eleven o'clock that night, I'd polished off the bottle, popped some speed and was at the station with the gun. The precinct was quiet. The only two people in the front office were me and the desk sergeant, an old-timer named Potts. He plastered a fake welcome smile across his bored, withered face.

"I'm here to see Blout."

Potts made a face like bile had just shot the length of his throat, picked up the phone and paged Blout.

I was about to take a seat when the front doors banged open. Two uniforms came in, noisily hauling an unruly who looked to be drunk and disorderly. I knew one of the cops, Dan Stockton. He was a major prick, disliked by more people than just me. He was pissed because he was still in uniform while everybody else made detective or better, bitter because he knew he was a nasty fuck that everybody hated, but mostly because it was just his nature. He was what you'd call a bad egg.

Stockton let his partner take the prisoner, and stopped—facing me. He was way too close. I was torn between a short lecture on personal space and jamming the cartilage in his nose through his brain.

"Well, well, if it isn't Cal McDonald," he sneered. "What the hell are you doing here? This is a police station, not a junkie detective station."

He stepped even closer. I stood my ground.

"I got plenty of business here, Stockton. And all of it's none of yours, so why don't you just back off," I growled, curling my mouth into a nasty scowl.

Stockton's eyes blinked and stuttered. I'd got him. He wasn't so sure I'd back down. I could tell he was searching for something snappy to say, but all he could muster was, "Why should I back off?"

"Because I have an aversion to halitosis," I shot back.

It was a dud. He didn't get it. Instead of being offended, he was confused.

"What?" he sputtered.

I sighed. "Bad breath." I was disappointed that the fire had puttered out. But Stockton snapped and went for his baton screaming "Motherfucker!"

I backed away fast and threw my bag down. If I was gonna fight a cop in the damn precinct, I didn't want to have a loaded Uzi on me. They'd just love that.

Stockton had his nightstick at the ready, violence flaring in his eyes. He could beat the crap out of me and get away with it. He was a cop, after all! If I fought back, he could slap me with charges and a free beating. I didn't give a shit. I had every intention of mopping the joint with the nasty little prick's face.

Before any blows could be exchanged, Blout came out of a side door. "Stockton, what the hell are you doing?!"

In the end, I was relieved there weren't going to be any punches thrown. I would have come out on the losing end of that particular stick any way you looked at it. Cops don't look kindly on flatfoots beating on uniforms in the hall of the precinct.

"Get the hell out of here," Blout spat.

Stockton gave me a nasty look and promptly left. It wasn't over. Blout was looking at me, pissed again.

"Do you think you could stay out of trouble for two seconds?"

I shrugged. "I'm willing to try," I said, picking the bag off the seat. "Here's the Uzi someone tried to kill me with."

Blout laughed a jerky, breathy laugh.

We left the Uzi with the lab to dust for prints and run ballistics, and left the precinct at around eleven thirty. Blout was hungry, but I had other plans.

CHAPTER

7

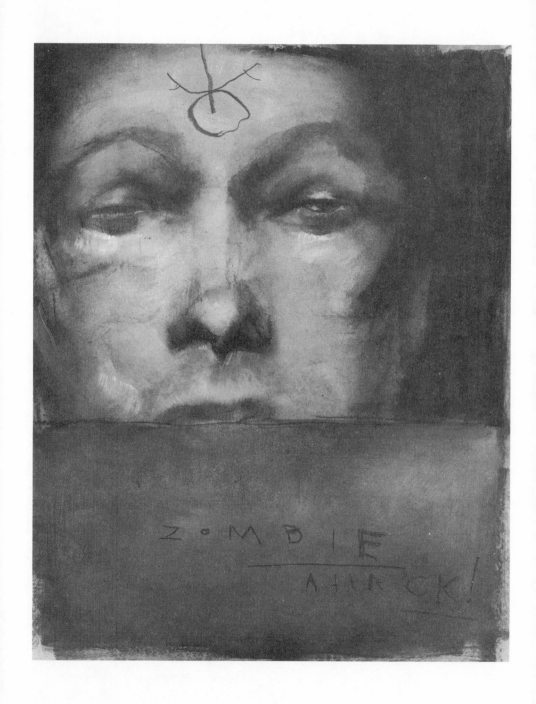

BY MIDNIGHT WE ARRIVED AT THE

deserted apartment complex where Edgar Cain had lived. The place couldn't have been creepier. The street lights were dead, but it didn't matter since four looming high rises would block out any moonlight. The way the buildings were laid out gave the impression that the architect had simply thrown blocks into the air, and the way they landed was how the apartments were built. It was planned chaos that created shadowy corners, blind spots, and black canyons even the bravest thug would be wise to avoid.

The complex was called Whitney Green. In some ways it could be compared to the gigantic, soulless projects in New York and Chicago, with two major differences. It was condemned, for one. But what made it ominous was when you looked around Whitney, you saw nothing. No graffiti, no gang signs. No homeless, no squatters. Not so much as a broken window since the day Cain slaughtered the tenants with his mind. The compound imprisoned the troubled memories of over a hundred dead.

Nobody, not even the lowest of lows, dared penetrate its boundaries for shelter. It was truly a haunted place.

Blout was not at all pleased to be there.

"This is ridiculous, Cal. There's nothing here!"

We each had a flashlight. I flashed mine forward into the pitch dark courtyard leading to unit number four, Cain's building. My footfalls echoed around our ears. Behind me, Blout's breath was heavy and labored.

"I have to make sure. I got a feeling something's here. Something that can help us." I said, and started walking away from Blout. "I'm going in. You can stay here if you want."

Blout didn't need to think it over. "Just wait up, goddammit."

The flashlight did little to light our path once we were inside the building. The darkness had a texture like smoky tar that seemed to fight the light, only allowing it to penetrate a few yards ahead of us. I was looking for the staircase.

"This is crazy. Why don't we come back during the day?" Blout whined behind me.

My light landed on an exit sign above a red steel door. "Because you can find things at night that aren't there during the day."

"Listen to yourself, McDonald. You're nuts!"

I ignored him. Some people need to whine when they're frightened. I know I do. "This way," I said, guiding him to the red door as I gave it a shove.

Inside the stairwell a gust of rotten air greeted us. An echo gave voluminous dimension to the corkscrew tower as we stepped inside. The door creaked shut slowly and closed with a small but definitive click. Blout swallowed. Like it or not, we were in.

"Which way?" he asked.

"Up," I said. "Cain's apartment. Top floor."

I took the first step. Then, above us, we heard a door slamming.

I jumped back. Blout threw himself against the exit door.

"W… what the fuck was that? Wind?" Blout hissed. I could hear the dry crack of his throat.

"Probably not. Come on."

Hearts pounding, we went up the first flight, then the second and third. By the fifth floor we were both calm.

Bang!

This time it came from below us. My eyes had adjusted somewhat and I could see that Blout was covered with sweat.

"You okay?" I whispered.

"No," Blout croaked. "You realize that in high rises like this, it isn't really the fourteenth floor. It's the thirteenth."

"Yes, I thought of that."

"Does that figure into your case?"

"Everything does." We had reached the eleventh floor. I stopped and pulled a flask out of my jacket, took two short swigs, and offered it to Blout.

He grabbed it, took one mini-swig, washed it around in his mouth and spit it out. "Christ, what is that crap?!"

"You heard of 'premium'? That's 'sale'." I took one more drink and then pushed on.

Cain's floor was as I'd left it years before—completely destroyed. The walls and ceiling were ripped away. Plaster and tile littered the place, forming piles of dusty white. At the far end of the hall I could feel a breeze coming through the hole we'd made when we went airborne. I could see the shattered wall and the dark blue, star-flecked sky that filled the vacant space.

Exactly halfway down the hall was another hole where Cain had smashed through from the inside of his apartment. That was where we stopped.

"This is it," I whispered and shot Blout a glance. He was looking behind him and wasn't listening to a word I said. "Blout?"

He turned. "What?"

"In here. Cain's apartment."

The hole was large enough so that the two of us walked through side by side. For me, walking into the apartment brought a rush of memories. Because of the massive amounts of drugs I was on at the time not all of my memory is available for recall, but standing in this room where so much violence had taken place brought it all back to me.

Cain had first attacked me when I was still several floors away. His strange power pulled at my brain, but he couldn't take it. The pain was unbelievable, like nothing I'd experienced before, like fingernails grinding along the base of my brain. It made a migraine feel like pure pleasure. Cain pulled, pushed, tugged and squeezed my brain. I was so determined, or so wasted, that I kept moving until I was standing square in the doorway.

I had a shotgun trained on the floating head, but it wasn't afraid. I remember that we spoke.

"Why won't you leave me alone?"

"You killed all those people."

"I didn't do it," he said. "Didn't really kill them. Only absorbed their brains. They were unhappy, all of them. Leading empty, pointless lives..."

The floating head paused, and swayed. I shot off one of his legs, and he hardly noticed.

"...like everyone else." He went on, "I simply combined them into one big pointless life."

Then Cain stopped talking and attacked. The fight wasn't over until I stabbed his eyes out high above the city and sent him crashing to his death.

"Cain had no remorse," I said.

Blout was at the window shining his flashlight along the shattered frame. "What was that?"

I shook my head. "I remember Cain talking like he did the dead a favor by taking their brains."

"He was a homicidal maniac. You were expecting logic?" Blout said. Then, as though suddenly annoyed, he turned off his light and raised his arms. "Would you please tell me what I'm supposed to be looking for?"

"Not really sure. I just needed to come here... to feel it."

"Well, are you done feeling it yet?"

"Look, Blout, I don't knock your methods. Don't knock mine."

I was getting pissed. I turned off my flashlight and waved him over to my side of the room. "Let's take a break."

As we pulled up boxes and sat, I took out my pack of cigarettes and the flask. I swigged and handed it to Blout. Before drinking he held it up to the moonlight coming through the window.

"Checking for germs?"

"No, just seeing if there was any left." Blout said and this time took a big-ass mouthful and choked it down. "Ahhhhh ahh! Damn, that's awful." He coughed, then took another pull.

I smiled, thinking how odd it was that the two of us tolerated each other. We couldn't have been more different. He was successful, together and completely on the up-and-up. And me? I was in as much, if not more, trouble than I was in my teens. What a pair we made.

"You know, you have a name that should be in a Frank Capra movie. *Jefferson Blout Goes To Washington*." I displayed the marquee in the air with my hands.

Blout laughed. "Yeah, Capra made a bunch of films about black cops."

I took a drink and swallowed hard. "Can I ask you a question?"

Blout just shrugged. The last mouthful was his.

"It's what, two, three o'clock in the morning. Doesn't it bother your wife that you don't come home?"

Blout looked away and sighed. "Jessica left me last month. So yes, I guess it did bother her."

"Shit, I'm sorry. I wouldn't have brought it up if—"

"It's all right. We were married a long time, a lot of good years. I don't have any regrets." He was fumbling in his coat. His hand came out holding two of those jumbo cigars he smokes. "Want one?"

I was about to agree when I had an idea. "I'll be right back."

I got up and darted to the right where there was a small efficiency kitchen. I opened the refrigerator and smiled. I love it when hunches pay off.

"What've you got there?" Blout asked at my back.

I turned and showed him. "I present to you, one six pack of the finest ten year old Black Label for our consuming pleasure. Warm, of course."

I planted the six pack on the floor between us, broke one from the ring and gave it to Blout in exchange for the cigar. When I popped open my beer, it foamed. I took that as a good sign.

Blout was staring at his can. "Is this safe?"

"Only one way to find out." I swigged and was surprised to discover that it tasted as crappy and watery as a new Black Label.

Blout sipped, testing. Finding it normal, he swigged away.

"What about you, Cal? Why haven't you ever settled down? I've seen you with some young women that weren't completely out of their minds."

"Thanks," I laughed. "The way shit comes flying at me, it's impossible. Nobody can take a life like that, and I wouldn't wish it on them."

"Come on. You're exaggerating. It can't be that bad."

I looked him square in the eyes. "My best friend is a fucking ghoul. It's that bad."

Blout stared at me for a full minute before he spoke. His voice lowered. It was serious time. "It really boggles me that you buy into all this crap."

"When a brick lands on your head, you start believing in bricks or you get your skull bashed in." I paused, feeling a speech coming on. "Don't you see, Blout, nothing is true if you don't believe, but if you do believe, really believe, you can create the impossible. The power of belief—Braaappp!—is a potent force."

Blout opened his second can and tossed me one, but I was already on my third. "Then explain this. How come you're the only one who ever sees all this spooky bullshit? Can you tell me that? I never see any of it."

"It's right there in front of you. You just don't accept it. I see it because I believe. Ain't it the shit?" I stopped and gave a smirk. "But mostly because you're not looking. You've seen it. I've seen you see it."

"Bullshit."

I looked around at nothing in particular. "Maybe, maybe not. Ignorance is bliss, right?"

I stood. This conversation could only turn ugly. It was time to get back to work. I looked around the room. My eyes were more or less adjusted to the cool light of the moon. I could make out the corners and some muddied colors.

Blout stood as well. "So what aren't I looking for now? I know you're after something here."

"I'm trying to figure out where it began. Where was Cain when people started to die?"

Blout perked up. I'd finally given him something to work with. "In the report it said that the deaths started early, before noon."

I snapped my fingers. "The bed."

It was in the farthest corner from the front door, away from the window. The bed itself was crushed.

"It started in the morning. Cain started absorbing early and grew until the bed couldn't support the weight."

Blout had moved to the foot of the crushed bed, where he stood pushing debris away with his feet. "What do you make of this?"

I stepped to the end of the bed where Blout was looking down at the floor. There was a pentagram carved into the floorboards. I flashed my light on it as Blout kicked away more of the plaster and dust. Carved around it, smaller but no less prominent, were several other symbols: a Star of David, a pyramid, a cross and several that were so badly carved I couldn't venture a guess.

"Well?" Blout said. "How does this fit into your conductor theory?"

I shrugged. "It doesn't, but it doesn't discount it either," I replied, lamely trying to cover my ass. "It just means Cain wasn't getting his security deposit back"

Blout didn't laugh. "I'm outta here," he said and headed for the exit hole.

"Blout, wait. Just one more thing."

I got his attention. He stopped and turned. "One more?"

"One more, then we get breakfast."

"What is it?"

"I want to check out the basement."

"See ya."

I chased Blout halfway down the stairwell. He finally stopped on the ninth floor, not because I was pleading with him to stay and help, but because we were both horribly out of breath.

"You ask too much, Cal."

"I know, but you want to solve this thing, right? You've got a morgue full of people who died under very strange circumstances. It stands to reason that the solution is going to be as strange as the crime."

Blout laughed. "You're the only person I've ever met that talks in circles and comes out makin' sense."

"Basement, then breakfast?"

"Deal."

We started back down the stairs to check out the basement, but somebody had other plans. All at once, above and below us, the sounds of doors opening and slamming filled the stairwell.

Slam!

"What the hell is that?!" Blout yelled. The sound was deafening.

Slam! Slam!

We both had our guns drawn, cocked and waving at darkness.

Slam! Slam! Slam!

"Screw the basement!" I screamed. "Let's break for the first floor and get out of here!"

We got nowhere. I heard a rasping sound, and stink passed beneath my nostrils, making me gag. Then a board hit me flat on the back of the head and I went down hard, feeling my neck doused with hot blood. The hall was filled with attacking bodies. Blout was yelling and firing off rounds, but I couldn't do anything to help him. I was being beaten on every inch of my body.

There were so many attackers I couldn't breathe. When I gasped for air, all I got was a lung full of dusty, death-like stink.

I fell, gagging and trying to go limp, but there were a dozen fists and two dozen kicking legs waiting to meet me. It was too dark in the stairwell to see our attackers, and I was being hit too much to focus. The last thing I remember was hearing Blout screaming my name. As I began to lose consciousness, I reached out for support, but instead my right hand fell upon what could only be a face. I scratched where the eyes should have been but my fingers found nothing but dry empty sockets.

Then, mercifully, everything went black.

CHAPTER

I WAS OUT COLD, DRIFTING IN A

state that would have been pleasant had it not been forcibly induced by a beating. I had a vague awareness of being dragged, surrounded by loud static noises, heat, flame and smoke. Voices barked and grunted, and as time passed I felt the presence of fresh air. Then more screaming and a sound that could have been the pounding of feet on concrete.

It all ended with a jolting blast of pain erupting in the back of my skull. I woke to the sights and sounds of the chaos I had been distantly experiencing while unconscious. It wasn't what I expected.

I saw daylight, early morning daylight. I was on my back, lying in the parking lot of Whitney

Green surrounded by emergency medical personnel. They were looking down at me, poking and prodding my body, and talking like I was an idiot. I tried to sit up, coughing, pushing them away. Every millimeter of my person hurt. I felt broken ribs, a multitude of bruises and a gaping gash on the back of my head.

"Get off me!" I yelled at the medics, and stood with great effort. It was then that I saw what had happened.

Cain's apartment building was an inferno. From the ground floor to the roof, fire tore away the structure. Flames shot from every window. Smoke billowed thick into the clouds overhead. Stopping the blaze was useless. The best bet was to contain it, and judging from the lackadaisical efforts of the firefighters, I guessed that was the plan.

Let it burn, let the haunted halls crumble. I'm sure that was what everyone was thinking. Erase the horror once and for all. I could see it in the eyes of the onlookers—they were watching a monster die.

I shook my attention away from the fire. I had to find Blout so I headed toward the nearest squad car where I found some medics working on a nasty swelling beneath his left eye. When he saw me, his eyes went wide. I had a pretty good idea what a bloody mess I was.

"Jesus H. Christ, Cal! Are you okay? My God, they really worked you over!"

"It's a karma thing, no doubt." I touched the back of my head. My hand came back soaked with sticky red. "Can I get a goddamn bandage here?!"

I finally allowed a pesky medic to bandage me up. They wrapped my ribs and put in a couple of butterfly stitches, including a few in the bullet graze that I'd stitched earlier. They doused each wound with antibiotics, which hurt worse than the damn beating, then finally backed off.

Meanwhile, Blout gave a very abbreviated report to his captain.

"...there was every reason to believe we had a connection between the bodies discovered early yesterday and the events that took place here ten years ago. We decided to check it out, but instead came across a bunch of crackheads. They attacked us, and I guess that's who set the fire."

Luckily, the Captain was too concerned with the arriving TV crews to notice the huge holes in the story. He wasn't even looking at Blout during the last half of the spiel.

"Um, okay... I want it on my desk by this afternoon," the Captain said, and was gone.

Blout rolled his eyes in my direction.

I winked, blew him a kiss and re-split my lip doing it. "Fuck!"

All I wanted to do was get back home. I needed to shower. I needed to sleep. But before that, I needed many drinks and smokes. Unfortunately, Blout wasn't finished. I tried to walk away from the rapidly burgeoning media circus when he came stomping up behind me.

"What the hell happened in there, Cal? How'd we get out? Did you do it?"

I kept on walking. "Last thing I remember was being in the stairwell getting the shit kicked outta me."

"Cal, stop. We'll take my car."

I fell behind him as we walked. He was asking too many questions too soon. My head was spinning and I guess his was as well. After all, he wasn't used to this kind of thing.

I caught up to him at the car. It was one of those bland blue jobs that looked like a giant matchbox car. "Is this thing for undercover?"

"Why?"

"Wouldn't fool a blind man. Why don't you just write 'COP' on the doors."

Blout wasn't amused. "I'll inform my superiors."

I got in. Blout stared ahead with a sleepy blank stare and then turned to me. "Any idea what we just got out of?"

"I'd bet that our attackers were also our saviors."

"What?! That makes no sense. What possible purpose would that serve?!"

"A warning, maybe," I said as the car jerked and rumbled to life, "possibly a diversion. All I know is those things could have offed us easily, and didn't. Hell, they could've just left us inside. But they did destroy the building. We were close to something, that's for sure."

We pulled out of the lot, waved on by a uniform guarding the exit, and drove for a while without saying a word. I sat there feeling every cut and bruise throb, and thought of morphine. I missed it, but I wouldn't fall into that trap again. I'd have to settle for some percocet or something equally tame. Fuck.

CHAPTER

9

AFTER A LARGE AND MUCH NEEDED DINER

breakfast, Blout dumped me off at my place just short of noon. I felt bad for him—while I was planning to lapse into a painkiller-induced coma, he had to go back to the precinct and do paperwork.

Blout caught me looking at him as I pushed open the door. "I'll call you if anything happens," he said. "Get some sleep."

I slammed the door, then leaned down to the open window. "Let me know how the ballistics and crap turned out on that Uzi."

"Will do."

He pulled away with a screech and was gone.

As I turned toward my building, I noticed the door hadn't been fixed, just boarded up. It was a sloppy, erratic job with dozens of holes and jagged slits and it sure as hell wouldn't keep anybody out. Pull one nail and the whole job would fall apart.

Even worse, there was a little man in a suit waiting right beside the boarded door. He had a stained manila envelope tucked under his stubby arm. No doubt about it, he was here to serve me papers.

I thought briefly about running, but he'd seen me, and really, what would be the point? Sooner or later those little rat bastards manage to slip you the notice. So I just walked right up to him, stood a little too close, and stared down at him.

"A...are you Mr. Calvin McDonald?" The little weasel shook and broke a sweat.

I leaned in. "Yes."

As cowardly as the creep looked, he was quick. Without saying a word he crammed the envelope into my hands, scurried sideways and was walking away toward a hot little sports car when I heard him say without a shake in his voice, "You have been served."

I didn't open the envelope. I rolled it and shoved it into my back pocket, pulled the door open and went in. Everything hurt, as three flights of stairs painfully tugged, pulled and stretched each gash and bruise. And I don't mind telling you, I bitched and moaned every step of the way.

I stopped cold on the last step. My place was the first door on the left and I could see the door from where I stood. It was open. Just a crack, but open just the same. I took out my piece, planted my back against the wall and began edging along the flaking plaster until I was right beside the door. I held my breath so I could hear over my raspy, pained breathing. There was movement inside, drawers opening and closing, paper rustling. It didn't sound like a shakedown. They don't close drawers.

"Mo'Lock? Is that you?" I said low, almost a whisper. Ghouls have excellent hearing.

There was a second of complete silence. I lowered the gun at the crack in the door. Another second passed.

"Yes, it's me, Cal." The voice was Mo'Lock's unmistakable low rumble.

I jammed the gun back in my armpit and stepped through the door. The ghoul was at my desk, bent over, looking for something. He straightened and I saw that he was filthy, almost completely covered with grime and soot.

"Are you looking for a moist towelette?"

Mo'Lock bobbed his head. I'd confused him. Any sort of modern reference tends to throw off a guy who's been dead for over a hundred years. "Well," he said "something of that sort. I didn't want to muss up your cloth towels."

"Ah, go ahead. Just leave one for me."

That was all the ghoul needed to hear. He turned and trucked out of the room while I gingerly began removing my jacket and tie. Lastly, I kicked off my shoes and untucked my shirt and threw the envelope on the floor. I retrieved the bottle from the desk and several quick swigs later began to feel fuzzy and light. To add to the haze, I threw down a couple of painkillers. By the time the ghoul came back all clean and sparkly, I wasn't feeling a goddamn thing.

"So what happened? Did you find anything?"

Mo'Lock stepped up to the front of the desk and bent forward. "I assembled a couple of my friends as you asked—"

I interrupted him. "Please, for God's sake, sit down. You make me crazy."

The ghoul did as I asked, which brought him to just above eye level.

"My friends and I went to the drainage pipe where the first body was found. But first, I searched the area where the dumpster was located. We found an entrance to the sewer, but didn't go in. It was too small and smelled terrible. Instead, we doubled back to the larger drainage pipe and entered." He nodded at the end of the speech, as though some point had been made.

I shook my head. "And that's how you got dirty?"

"Let me finish."

"Sorry."

"After walking through the pipe for an hour, we came to an intersection. I believe it was somewhere below Dupont Circle." The ghoul spoke slowly and carefully, rolling out each word for maximum effect. Sometimes his speech patterns reminded me of a drunk trying to sound sober, but with an air of elegance that belonged only to the undead.

"Dupont? That's like five miles from the drainage pipe!"

"Yes, I'm aware of that. Anyway, that was where we found the hole."

I sat forward. "Hole?"

"Yes, and it was not city work, I can tell you. The pipe had been cut with a blow-torch and was very uneven, like the cutter started out trying for a circle, but settled for a square."

"Where'd it go?"

"For the first several yards it went east, maybe north-east."

I nodded. "Toward Whitney Green." I took another drink. My gums were numb and my scalp felt like it was swarming with ants.

"Possibly, but after those several feet the tunnel turned into an incline, and after that there was an unexpected drop... straight down."

I was getting a little impatient. At times he could be too efficient. "Did you go down?"

Mo'Lock looked away. "We had no choice... we slid."

I laughed. "And you got dumped into the pit!" I was feeling good.

I offered the bottle to the ghoul as peace offering. He waved it off. "No, thank you."

"Come on, it won't kill you," I urged.

He looked back toward me. "No, it won't kill me. It tastes bad."

The drink and drugs were making my thoughts wander. "When was the last time you ate or drank anything?"

He thought about it for a second. "Just a little over a hundred and ten years. Not counting the occasional mouthful of rainwater."

"Or a chunk of that guy's neck! Remember that?!" I was having fun. It was the best I felt all week. You gotta love painkillers.

Mo'Lock stuck out his tongue. "How could I forget? That tasted very bad."

We fell silent for a moment as Mo'Lock worked the memory of biting that guy through his mind. I lit a smoke. "So, you and your buddies fell in the pit..."

Mo'Lock looked up slowly. "It was a short fall into another tunnel. We found that it went in two directions, so we split up. I went east by myself. The other two went west."

"What was the tunnel like?"

"Big, wide. I'd say twice the size of the drainage pipe," he answered, then continued. "I walked for a while. Didn't see much of anything. The tunnel was clean and quiet, like a spotless mining shaft. Very odd."

I laid my head on the desk.

"Then I started coming across exits. They were above me, and near as I could see they were normal manhole covers with these strange clamp locks welded to them. You know, like on preserve jars. There was one about every five hundred yards."

Tunnels and exits heading toward and away from Whitney Green. A web.

Something solid was beginning to form, connections were being made. I just wasn't exactly sure where it all led.

Mo'Lock went on. "After another hour I began hearing noises ahead of me. I walked faster until I was running. The noises got louder as I got closer. At first it was just a banging sound, then voices."

I raised an eyebrow, but stayed head-down on the desk blotter.

"As I got closer to the voices and the banging, the tunnel was no longer smooth. It was rough dirt with rocks, rats and trash everywhere. It was when I stopped running that I heard your voice."

That got my attention. I raised my head. "My voice. You heard my voice? Are you sure?"

"Yes, and Blout's as well. You were arguing. It was high above me and there was an echo."

I nodded for the ghoul to continue his story.

"I moved cautiously toward the sound of your voices when suddenly it changed to yelling and screaming. I thought you and Blout might be under attack so I ran, but unfortunately I was blocked by a large steel door. I pulled and kicked at it, but it was too strong. So I did all I could. I listened."

"Meanwhile, I was getting my ass kicked."

Mo'Lock ignored me. "A short time later a thunderous stampede came from the other side of the door. There was a great grinding noise, and then the door unlatched and flew open. I was face-to-face with your assailants. At first they didn't see me, but when they did, they started screaming and crying, cowering against the wall. They were terrified of me."

"What were they? Did you get a good look?"

"Undead of some sort. Nothing I'd ever seen before. They were mummified, dried skin tight against their skulls, with empty eye sockets."

I nodded. "That's them."

"I approached one that was near me. It screamed and carried on. I didn't mean to, but in trying to calm the thing, I accidentally grabbed a necklace that was around its neck, and it came off." Mo'Lock stopped talking and looked down at his feet. "It was terrible."

I didn't say a word. He'd go on when he was ready.

"The thing just turned into dust at first, but then it liquefied and became blood. Just like that, there was a pile of clothes soaked in blood." The ghoul shook his head. I guess it was a little too close to home for him.

"What happened next?" I urged.

"Chaos. The other things started running away, back the way I'd come. I was about to give chase when I remembered you were somewhere on the other side of the door. As I started through, I was overcome by black smoke and intense heat. I tried to push on, but it was too much. I ran to one of the sewer covers. It was melted shut, so I had to break the concrete to escape. I could see the building on fire, but when I saw you and Mr. Blout were all right, I came back here."

"Did you say you broke the concrete?"

"Yes."

"With what?"

"My hands."

"You can break concrete with your hands?"

"If need be."

I smiled, recalling when I first met Mo'Lock. He was just your standard ghoul doing what ghouls do best: lurking in the shadows, wandering the earth soulless and aimless. He'd helped me out on a case because he thought I was a monster as well. He said it was a vibration I gave off. Sort of the supernatural equivalent of a butt sniff.

When I met him, he barely spoke. Now he could recount events as well as any detective I'd ever known. Better, really, with his heightened senses and all.

"What about your two partners and the necklace you nabbed?"

"I haven't seen them since. I'm a bit worried." He fumbled in his pocket and then held up an object. "This is what I pulled from the neck of your undead attacker."

He held up a simple homemade necklace. I took it from him. It was a plain strip of brown leather with a pendant attached, a small glass vial. Inside was what I took to be blood. That seemed to go along with the ghoul's description of what had happened.

"Amulet?" the ghoul asked.

I shook my head. "More like a talisman. Amulets protect, ward off evil and things like that. Talismans make things happen."

I held it up to the light, turning it in my palm. No inscriptions or marks of any kind. Nothing that told me what it was, or where it originated. I had two facts; the object was a talisman, and the wearer had been a reanimated, mummified corpse. Its origins could range from Haitian voodoo priests to Egypt or South America. Every culture had some sort of reanimation ritual, but which one fit the tiny vial?

It was just another mysterious piece to the puzzle. I still had no clue what the big picture was.

I held the vial up to the bulb of my desk light again. I wasn't sure, but there seemed to be something else inside, floating in the blood. Probably a clot or a maggot.

I stared at the vial and shook my head. When I looked up to say something, Mo'Lock was gone. He was pinned against the wall, staring out the window—trying not to be seen from the outside.

"What is it?"

The ghoul turned to me. "Are you aware that someone is watching the apartment?"

"Dark colored sports car?"

"Yes. How did you know?"

"Lucky guess." I swallowed a huge mouthful of whiskey.

CHAPTER

10

I TOLD THE GHOUL TO SHUT THE BLINDS.

I'd had enough for the week. Some downtime was needed or I was going to fall apart. The vial was stashed in a compartment inside the top drawer of my desk. It would be safe there until I wanted to deal with it. I took another percocet, stood from the desk and zig-zagged over to the couch. It was buried in trash. I cleared it off with a swipe of my aching arm, while Mo'Lock watched me curiously.

After I had the couch cleared, I opened the closet near the unused kitchen. I dug around in there until I found a small black and white television which I put on a chair in front of the couch.

Lastly, I went to the fridge and snagged a six pack, grabbed the ashtray, whiskey, and smokes. Then I did something I hadn't done for years. I just sat my ass on the couch, turned on the idiot box and stared like a goon.

"Ahhhhhhh," I moaned in relief. Each and every wound on my body purred and tingled. The painkiller was working its magic.

I immediately began to nod off. Mo'Lock shuffled his feet, bored. I suggested that he check out whoever was watching the apartment, and he was out the door.

Then the phone rang. I started to answer it, but decided to let the machine get it. After the tone I heard Blout's voice.

"Cal, are you there? Pick up."

I shook my head and yawned.

"Well, listen. The test on the Uzi came back. Whoever shot at you had no fingerprints. They were burned off. The rest of the test came back empty. They couldn't trace the weapon."

I started into the bedroom, but Blout went on.

"Another body matching the others was found. This time it wasn't some homeless guy. It was a history professor from George Washington University."

I ran over and picked up the phone. "I'm here! What kind of professor was he?"

"Like I said, history... uh, it says here something about folklore and myth. Sounds like he might be a friend of yours."

"Where was his body found? Sewers again? Because—"

"No, get this. The guy had been in a bad car accident about six months ago and lapsed into a coma—"

Lucky stiff, I thought.

"—and he stayed that way until this morning when he was found dead. When they cut him open, no gray matter, nothing."

I stretched and felt some of the butterflies tighten. I was close to passing out. "Look, Blout, we found dick in that apartment. Can you find out what happened to Cain's personal belongings? I noticed on the evidence list there were some books I'd like to take a look at." I yawned right into the receiver.

"Have you slept yet?"

"Nope."

"Neither have I. What say we check in with each other tomorrow?"

"Sounds good."

I dropped the phone into the cradle, turned, reeled into the closet I call my bedroom and was out cold before I hit the mattress.

CHAPTER

11

I WOKE UP ON THE FLOOR THE NEXT

morning. I was groggy, but felt pretty good. It was Sunday, just before eleven a.m.—an eighteen hour sleep. Eighteen hours of drug-induced, body-healing bliss. But soon enough my thoughts turned to the case. Something had been eating at me that I needed to check out.

Mo'Lock was waiting for me in the office. I had locked the apartment door and the front door and he had no key, but he still managed to get in somehow. I never asked how and he never offered the information. In the past, I would have been startled, but I was beginning to get used to it. It was just another ghoul thing, another of the seemingly endless talents acquired by those caught between life and death.

"Morning Mo'," I said, doing a bee-line to the desk. I called Blout at the precinct. After a couple of holds and transfers, I got him on the line.

"Something's been bugging me," I said.

Blout didn't say anything, waiting for me to get on with it.

"Medical autopsies aren't usually performed on John Does and homeless, are they? Why were they performed on the one we got?"

Blout wasn't impressed. "Well, the first one looked like he was thrown in the ditch. Possible homicide. The dumpster full I think you can figure out."

"But my point is, usually medical autopsies aren't performed on homeless found dead, are they?"

"Not if it looks clean," Blout said. "Dental records are checked for identification and then cause of death is determined. Most of the time there's no reason to open the chest, let alone the head."

"What about senior citizens who die of natural causes in retirement homes and hospitals?"

"Same. What are you getting at?" Blout sounded a little upset, possibly because he thought I was ahead of the game and holding out.

"What about people who die of a chronic illness—AIDS, cancer and the like?"

"There's no reason to do an autopsy. The cause of death is presumed known by the circumstances of the illness." Blout paused. "Look, are you going to tell me what this is about, or am I going to have to hang up?!"

"It's just that I think we should consider the fact that deaths like these could have been going on for awhile, months or even years. We just lucked out because whoever or whatever is behind this got sloppy." I was pleased with my coherent argument. "Is there any way we can get confirmation?"

Blout sighed hard. "I think you've got something there, but it would be next to impossible to find out. Usually John Does are cremated by independent funeral contractors. The rest could be anywhere. Besides, I can guarantee there's no way I'd get clearance to exhume any bodies."

I thought about that for a second. "I think it's enough that we consider the chance that this might have been going on for awhile. Maybe a very long while."

"I agree," Blout responded reluctantly. Maybe he was doing the math, like I had. The possible body count was daunting.

Blout went on. "Cain's personal belongings are stored in a warehouse next to the sixth precinct. I told them to expect you, so bring some I.D. and leave your freaky friend home."

"Thanks. Anything else?"

"No."

We hung up without good-byes.

The ghoul was standing by the window as usual. He was pulling up the shade I had asked him to close yesterday. Without looking my way, he spoke. "I tried to check out the subjects watching you, but when they saw me coming, they drove away."

"Did you get any kind of look at them?"

"There were three of them. They appeared to be fairly young, late teens, maybe early twenties. Two male, one female. What I found odd was that they all were wearing wrist bands and scarfs of some sort around their necks."

"Ascots?" I laughed. "No accounting for taste."

Mo'Lock's brow wrinkled as he squinted out the window. "Well, I'll be."

"What?"

"They're outside the apartment again." The ghoul said and looked my way. "One of them has a rifle."

"What the fuck are they doing?!" I started toward the ghoul and the window. Enough was enough.

Mo'Lock went on, "He's pointing it up here and—"

Blamm! Blamm! Blamm!

The window shattered and the ghoul's upper back exploded in three places. He flopped in the air like a marionette cut loose, then collapsed hard to the floor. I threw myself against the wall. Mo'Lock was spread eagle on the floor. No blood seeped from the three big holes in his shirt.

"You okay?" I reached out with my leg and gave him a little nudge with my foot.

"I'm fine," the ghoul said from the floor. "Don't kick me."

Nobody shoots my friends, even if shooting them doesn't hurt. I was pissed. I dove past the shattered window and grabbed my pistol off the desk. I was out the door before Mo'Lock could get to his feet. Taking the stairs by twos, I was outside in time to see the three fashion casualties getting into their Mustang. I wasted no time in raising the gun, and quickly squeezed off a few shots.

"Freeze, you sons-a-bitches!!"

My first shot shattered the back window of the car. The second and third went stray. The last three were anybody's guess. A thirty-eight caliber crap shoot.

The Mustang's rear tires spun. Burned rubber wafted across my face as I ran up to the curb, but the car was already gone, speeding away down the street and very nearly hitting a commuter bus. That would have been perfect, but they steered clear. For the second time, they had gotten away with shooting at me. But this time there was a silver lining. There was blood on the sidewalk. At least I'd hit one of the bastards.

It was then that I realized I was standing in the street holding a smoking gun—wearing only my boxers.

CHAPTER

12

THE SIXTH PRECINCT
POLICE EVIDENCE

warehouse was little more than a bunker sitting in a corner of the parking lot. It was a flat, one story building made of cinder blocks and those god-awful green glass cubes. The chain-link fence surrounding the warehouse had rusted barbed wire running along the top, but it and the fence were in such bad shape they would probably crumble at the slightest touch, and besides, the gate was open. The steel door of the warehouse was protected by a large but far from unbreakable padlock—nothing that couldn't be snapped with a decent crowbar.

Point being, it would've been easier to bust into the joint than go through all the usual procedural bullshit, but I did it anyway. I knew they had my name and didn't want to get Blout in trouble.

A uniformed flunky unlocked the door, removing the padlock with a lazy yank, then handed me a large ring with one key dangling pathetically from it like a tiny hanged man.

"Lock up when you're finished. The boxes are alphabetical by last name of victim or perp. If you want to take anything, clear it at the desk," he drawled and walked off, lazy and slack-jawed.

I watched him walk away. He was more dead than any zombie I'd ever encountered. "Thanks a lot, sparkles," I muttered. I was pretty sure he didn't hear.

The big metal door gave me a little trouble at first. I had to push against it with my bum shoulder, but that wasn't enough. So this was the master security system, I thought. How diabolical. The hinges were rusted, so I resorted to kicking. The first two kicks did nothing but send shooting pains up my leg. The third did the trick. The door swung open, sending a of cloud of dust billowing into the air.

I coughed and fanned my arms through the soot. The warehouse was dark and smelled of grime, mothballs, and that smoky smell you can only get from old books. I let the door swing shut behind me while I fumbled for a light switch. The low-ceilinged rectangle filled with brownish-yellow light. The place was jam-packed to the roof with rotting cardboard—a total mess.

I doubted anyone had been in here for a long time. I was equally sure the place had been ransacked, with anything even remotely of value stolen. That happened all the time with police evidence. There are cops who use these warehouses as their own personal K-Mart. Luckily, I was looking for books. I was willing to bet that the type of cops who stole police evidence weren't big readers.

The evidence had been stored in alphabetical order as the flunky had said, but only in the most general sense. There were letters of the alphabet painted on the walls, like an underground parking lot. I was amazed at the idiocy of the system. Fortunately, the boxes themselves were labeled, but it was still going to be a major pain in the ass. I took off my jacket, rolled up my sleeves and set about digging into the area around the letter "C".

It took over an hour for me to locate five small boxes labeled as Cain's property. All of the seals were broken, but it didn't look like much had been stolen.

I sat down near the door encircled by the boxes, lit a cigarette and took out my flask. After a long satisfying gulp, I dug into the clutter.

I found something curious as soon as I saw the first book title. The rest were much the same. It seemed Cain and I had some shared interests. There were editions I owned myself, titles like *Monsters, Myths and Folklore*, *The Big Book of Spells*, *Modern Witchcraft*, *Ceremonies of Haiti*, and *ESP and Telepathy Today*.

Each of the books were littered with papers marking spots in the pages. On several of the papers, Cain had written notes. It was better than I could have imagined, a friggin' Clues 'R' Us. It seemed odd that the original investigators didn't take notice, but I assumed any further probing might have brought out facts the authorities would rather not know. Besides, who was I to point fingers? I dropped the case as soon as we smashed into the pavement.

The first book I looked over was *ESP and Telepathy Today*, an outdated and sensationalist volume published by a company specializing in books on Bigfoot and UFOs. The paperback was packed with black and white photos and crude drawings that claimed to prove the existence and validity of telepathy, telekinesis and ESP. There were photos of people floating in the air with no visible supports (obviously airbrushed), a man with horned-rimmed glasses and a goatee straining to lift a person with the power of his mind, and that sort of crap.

I actually found myself enjoying flipping through the junky, dog-eared book, just like when I was a kid. True or not, these books had a kind of charm about them that I still found fascinating. Cain seemed to have been especially interested in a section of the book showing a man bending spoons with mind power. The pages were marked and several photos circled, but nothing seemed overly important, so I closed the book and shoved it into my coat pocket.

Next was *The Big Book of Spells*. Most of it was clean except for a chapter on voodoo which Cain had highlighted and underlined almost completely. The text was very simple, obviously intended for young readers with overwritten, dramatic passages and outright silly chants purported to evoke the spirits. Cain had circled several of the spells in red.

Early in *Monsters, Myths, and Folklore*, Cain had marked off a two-page spread discussing the Egyptian god Anubis, the jackal-headed god of death. He was often associated with the creation of the art of embalming and was sometimes called the conductor of the dead.

Most of the underlining seemed to revolve around gods of death, reanimation, and resurrection. When I came across the last marked page, the pieces began to fall into place. The passage described the Norse legend of the Yimir. On the edges of the text, Cain had scrawled the words "the first giant", and had underlined "legend says that the clouds are made from the brains of the Yimir". At the bottom of the page he had written down incantations from the voodoo book. Next to some of the spells were page numbers.

I opened the spell book Cain referred to and turned to the indicated pages. The underlined section read "in voodoo, the brain is the seat of animate spirits."

On a Post-it note stuck to the page, Cain linked the passages:

> *The brain is the seat of the animate, the soul of all spirits.*
> *Clouds are made from the brains of the Yimir.*
> *The Yimir was the first giant.*

> *The mind is the soul.*
> *The heart is life.*
> *Never shall they cross.*
> *Never will we die.*

I had no idea what the hell this all meant, beyond the fact that it was pretty clear he'd been obsessed with witchcraft, voodoo, and resurrection. I began to rethink my earlier deductions about spontaneous phenomenon: there may be a source other than Cain, and he may have even created it, but Cain was dead, definitely dead. I had sat covered in his splattered remains. There was nothing left of him that could even be collected. That final fall we took together had reduced him to a pool of splattered, slimy slop.

I found what I came for. Not a lot of answers, but a whole lot of clues, and one or two flimsy concepts. I threw the books back into the boxes, keeping all the scraps of paper for myself. Before I left, I rummaged through the boxes one more time.

Good thing too, because I came across something interesting. It was a pair of brown corduroy bell-bottom pants. The fact that somebody actually wore them was amazing enough, but in the back pocket I found Cain's wallet, complete and untouched. The pocket had been snapped shut with those little pocket snaps that they only use on kids slacks. Thank God for small miracles and inept police work. I did wonder how the cops could have possibly missed the wallet, but the reason became immediately clear. There was a skid mark the size of New Jersey that started on the inside of the pants and seeped all the way through to the outside. I dropped that foul shit and prayed my hand hadn't gone near the stain.

Inside the wallet there was, briefly, seventeen bucks. I found Cain's driver's license, but the photo didn't ring any bells. The only time I'd seen him, his head was huge, features stretched and distorted. When I felt along the inside seam of the wallet, I felt a small hard object sewn inside. The seam tore easily and a tiny manila envelope fell out. It hit the cement floor with a muffled clink.

The envelope had the Riggs National Bank logo stamped on it. Inside was a key on a tiny cardboard tag, "G454" written on it. I couldn't help but grin.

CHAPTER

13

IT WAS SUNDAY, SO GOING TO THE BANK

was out of the question. Instead, I had another plan. I called my apartment, and after a few rings, Mo'Lock picked up. In the background the TV was blaring so loudly that I could hardly hear the ghoul say hello.

"For Christ sake, Mo'!" I yelled. "Turn down the TV!"

I heard him drop the receiver. Fuckin' ghoul.

The noise cut off abruptly and a second later he was back on the line. "Yes, Cal. What is it?"

"How're you doing?" I asked, "Gun wounds alright?"

"All healed up, but I need a new shirt."

I grinned. "I got a plan. It looks like we've got a little down time on the brainless case, so I thought we could go after the gun happy punks who shot you."

"They're outside again. A little farther down the block, but I can see them."

"Persistent little bastards, aren't they?"

"And not too bright, I'd say. Tell me the plan."

He sounded more like a cop than I ever did.

"Simple, get a couple of your friends together. Not a crowd, just one or two—"

The ghoul cut me off. "Since the disappearance of the last two volunteers in the tunnel, I don't think anybody will be up for another mission."

"They're goddamn dead already! What the hell have they got to be scared of?!" I was pissed, and a little embarrassed. I couldn't even get dead guys to help me.

"That's just it, Cal. They have nothing to be afraid of, but they are afraid. We still have gotten no word from the last two and nobody wants to go down there to find out why."

"Pussies. When I get the chance, I'll do it myself. Right now, let's just stop these punks before they get lucky and put a slug in my brain. Are you with me?"

Mo'Lock sounded insulted. "Of course."

"I need you to distract them. Walk by the windows, rustle the shades. I don't care what you do, just keep 'em looking at the apartment. When you see some action, come down and give me a hand."

"I'm on it."

It took me a few minutes to walk from the Dupont Metro station to the street where I lived. I stopped about three blocks back, careful to check everything in my line of vision. Since it was Sunday, the streets were deserted. If bullets started flying, I didn't have to worry about bystanders.

Everything was clear. When I was a block away, I flattened myself against the wall of the building to my left. If Mo'Lock was right, my ascot-wearing would-be assassins were right in the courtyard, near the entrance.

I took out a can of mace and my favorite blackjack. I wanted them alive, if possible. Well, at least one of them. For questioning. If they were working for someone else, I needed to know who it was. If they were operating on their own, I wanted to find out why. After that, I was just going to beat the living crap out of them for fun.

I peered, one-eyed, around the corner. They were there, all three of them, staring up at the window of my place. I started moving around the corner, edging slowly so as not to catch their attention. I made the mistake of following their gaze and almost laughed out loud.

Mo'Lock was thrashing wildly from window to window. It looked like he was doing a super-charged dance of the veils. I forced myself to look away and focus on the perps.

They wore the same clothes as the day before, with one exception—the female had a bandage around her head. I could see a spot of blood where one of my shots must have grazed her.

I crept up until I was right behind her, but she turned quickly. The look on her face when she saw me was reward enough, but I popped her anyway. One swipe with the blackjack and she hit the ground like a wet tea-bag. Her two buddies spun around and I was in trouble instantly. Caught with no room to move and no time to reach for my piece, I did what seemed to be the only thing that made any sense.

I screamed for the ghoul to back me up.

"Mo'Lock!"

Yelling stalled the two boys for half a second. I was about to mace them to hold them at bay while I awaited tall-dead-and-ugly, but the sight of their faces made me hesitate. They were beyond strange, like plastic or wax, but very, very pretty. Like models straight out of a glossy advertisement, every feature was carved perfection. I began to realize who these oddly beautiful teens might be.

One of the lovelies broke my reverie by pulling a small silver pistol. The look on his face was anything but attractive as he lowered it and fired. I dodged but the bullet hit the exact spot of the first bullet wound, an unbelievable bull's-eye. To describe the pain would be impossible. Suffice to say, I screamed.

The kid never got off a second shot. Mo'Lock had arrived via the window. He was on the armed kid like stink on shit, a flailing angry marionette, hitting the shooter while kicking the other male, the only blonde of the three, in the lower back. Blondie hit the ground, and I followed up with a smack from the blackjack, hitting him square in the mouth. His teeth blew apart like china tea cups, raining on the street with a hundred gentle tinkles. It was incredible.

Mo'Lock was out of control. He had the kid over his head. I wanted to say something, but it was too late. The ghoul threw pretty boy through the Mustang's windshield and the brief skirmish came to a sudden and resounding halt. All we needed to do was get the three of them up to my place for a little chit-chat. I grabbed the girl and toothless and left Mo'Lock to deal with the one wedged in the windshield.

The trio slept for awhile, giving us time to tie them to chairs after patching them up. Mo'Lock played nurse, applying cold packs and bandages to their bruises. As they began to stir, I removed their ascots and wrist bands. What I saw underneath, just below the neckline of their shirts, cleared up a mystery I had been trying to resolve for years and confirmed the hunch I got when I first saw their faces.

Wrapping all the way around each of their wrists and throats were very faint but visible stitch scars—scars from where the body parts had been grafted together by Dr. Polynice at the request of Francis Lazar, founder of ManChildLove. Tied to chairs in my apartment were the mail-order Voodoo Love Teens, kids that those two creeps had created. I'd broken the case wide open and sent Lazar, Polynice, and all those involved to prison, including anyone who had ordered a love slave, but not a trace of the teens had ever been found.

Until today.

I stared at their chiseled features. If you looked very closely you could see faint signs of plastic surgery. It was very important to Lazar and the good doctor that the love dolls could never be traced to the original victims. Their entire bodies, including their heads and facial features, were a jumbled mish-mash of dissected, murdered young men and women, complete with burned off fingerprints and brittle teeth.

The teeth were a nice touch—you've gotta admire attention to detail. Fake teeth meant no dental records. They must've used porcelain for that perfect white color. Evidently, being smacked in the mouth with a blackjack wasn't in the plans.

Windshield was the first to come around. He shook his head, blinked, and blew his dark hair away from his eyes which were a deep, unnatural navy blue. They locked on me immediately. The look was pure hatred.

"You got a name?" I asked, indifferent to the boy's glare. I was standing with one foot up on a chair, interrogation style.

"Randy."

I was surprised. The kid gave up his name easily. I suspect that was part of the conditioning they went through before they were sold off. Nobody likes a difficult love doll.

The whole thing made me sick to my stomach, and it wasn't just me.

Mo'Lock seemed uneasy around the kids. He muttered under his breath about tormented souls before retiring to his corner and staring out the window. I didn't have that luxury. If I didn't do something now, these damn kids would never stop coming after me.

I got on with it. "You know who I am?"

Randy nodded, with his glaring blue eyes fixed on my face. "Cal McDonald," he said. "You took my father away... took away all our parents. Took away Lazar and everybody!"

I shook my head and paced a small circle. This was going to be tough. "What your 'parents' did was wrong, not to mention illegal and highly immoral. Lazar was a bad person who had to be stopped."

"He never hurt anyone! He took care of us when nobody else would, and he found us homes!"

The other two had begun to stir. The female was muttering and her head swayed side to side.

This was going to be difficult. Very, very difficult. The kids probably had no idea what they were or where they came from. I had to be careful. Mo'Lock turned to me and shrugged his wide bony shoulders, offering me no help. I couldn't determine whether the ghoul couldn't or wouldn't. He seemed edgy about the whole thing, edgy and distant.

I paced a little, then went back to Randy and stood in front of him holding my hand on my chin.

"Can you tell me how old you are, Randy?"

The kid dropped the glare and thought about the question.

"I think... yes, I'm sure. I'm five years old." His face lit up with pride.

I shook my head. "Don't you think you're a little big for a five-year-old."

Randy looked at me, incredulous to my query. "No," he said, "all of my brothers and sisters are five."

By now the other two were conscious and listening. Neither had the rage in their eyes that Randy had. Just the opposite, actually. They seemed scared of me. I counted myself lucky for that. It meant if I could get through to Randy, the others would most likely follow. I scrambled for questions.

"Can you tell me how you were born?"

The boy looked at me like I was the dumbest thing he'd ever laid eyes on. All three smiled, enjoying their little in-joke.

"In the lab," Randy said sarcastically, "Where else?"

Blondie and the girl suppressed laughter.

I nodded. Lazar and Polynice had done a real job on these kids. They had no concept of the real world, just the twisted reality created for them. In desperation, I looked at Mo'Lock again—I was out of ideas. "What do you think, Mo'?"

"They are very scary, Cal. Do you realize between the three of them, they share the fragments of over one hundred tormented souls."

"Fucking-A. What we can do? How can we make them see what's really happening? They don't even know what they are!" I could hear the desperation in my own voice.

Mo'Lock turned and stared at the three teens who were whispering to each other, seemingly unaffected by the fact they were tied up.

"They're not stupid, Cal. Show them the file, the articles, the whole mess. Let them see for themselves."

He was right.

I told Mo'Lock to untie Randy's arms so he could flip freely through the files, but to make sure his legs were secure. I didn't want the little punk running off on us. Meanwhile, I ransacked the file cabinets for everything I had on the Lazar case.

While I was rooting around, I glanced over and saw Randy staring fascinated at Mo'Lock. Mo'Lock met the kid's eyes and did something that was all too rare for a ghoul, and truly gave me pause. He smiled. Slight, but distinct. His dead lips parted, curving slowly upwards. His eyes, usually stone cold, opened wider and brightened.

I was a minority in the room. The others were cousins in a very large and odd clan—the family of the living dead.

When I'd gathered all the Lazar/Polynice files, I dropped them in Randy's lap. He no longer glared at me. In fact all three seemed much less hostile. They were like putty, instantly impressionable, easily swayed. Nonetheless, I wasn't about to untie anybody until after they'd read the files. I had no idea what the reaction would be, but it was reasonable to assume a violent one.

All eyes were on Randy. He began reading the police report, slowly scanning the pages. At first he seemed calm seeing the photos of the men who had created and sold him for a profit. He almost had a look of love in his eyes.

But as he began to soak everything in, his features hardened. Word after word, paragraph after paragraph, page after page had a visible affect on him. He began to shake as pages turned. Finally the tremors were so bad he could no longer hold onto a file. I stood by uncomfortably. Mo'Lock rocked foot to foot behind me. There was nothing we could do but wait for the reaction, the inevitable explosion.

When it came it was fast and loud. Randy's eyes began to well. He looked up at me first, then shot quick glances at Mo'Lock and I, eyes overflowing with tears. It was as if his soul were bleeding out his tear-ducts.

"Who am I?" he asked.

For that, I had no answer... but Mo'Lock did.

Mo'Lock stepped past me, stopping close to the weeping boy. The other two had started crying as well, but I doubt they knew why. Fuckin' puppets. Mo'Lock got down on one knee and addressed his distant cousin.

"You are many people and many souls. You are bound by the bodies that have been assembled for you. There is no changing this. You must accept what you are... as I have."

Randy stuttered and stammered before finally collecting himself enough to speak. "You... you're like us?"

The ghoul nodded. "In a sense. I too used to be mortal, but then I died. Though my soul departed, I remained. Now I am undead. What happened to all of you was brought on by the magic of a conjurer, and now you too are undead. Trust me when I tell you... being dead is not at all a bad thing to be."

He spoke in such a confident manner, oddly poetic in a scary sort of way. His voice was soothing, gently guiding the zombie youth to the realization that although they were created from evil they did not have to follow its twisted course. That was the great lie to which too many monsters, past and present, had fallen prey.

They were quickly convinced, maybe because they were made that way, maybe because we offered them an alternative future. I wasn't about to question it, though. I'd expected much worse.

I was still uneasy, but Mo'Lock assured me they were okay now, so I reluctantly loosened their bindings. Sure enough, they'd been defanged.

Randy introduced the others. Blondie was Scott, and the girl was Miriam. I shook each of their hands as they apologized for trying to kill me.

"Don't sweat it." I said. This whole situation was fucking surreal. I grabbed the bottle from my desk and took several large mouthfuls until it was empty. I hadn't eaten, so I felt instantly buzzed.

Twenty minutes passed without anyone saying a word. Mo'Lock and I realized the poor kids had spent so long tracking me down that they had no other experience whatsoever. The three of them sat there, free of the ropes, but with no reason to stand and nowhere to go.

"What do we do now?" Randy said.

Maybe it was only a drunken brainstorm, but I had an idea. I weaved out of the room and came back a minute later with the Yellow Pages. I tore a page out and handed it to Randy. He was confused at first, but a smile soon grew across his lips.

"What do you think?" I asked.

He showed Scott and Miriam the page. They all smiled.

Miriam looked at me. "That would be fun. Do you think we can?"

"I think you'd be perfect."

The beautiful voodoo teens were absolutely giddy. Mo'Lock was confused.

"Mo'Lock, how much cash do you have?"

He shrugged. "Couple hundred."

"Can you get these guys set up someplace? One of your ghoul flophouses or something?"

Everybody was happy. Mo'Lock agreed to leave with the trio and find them a place to crash, but after ushering the group out the door he popped his head back inside as I was taking a seat at the desk.

"What was on that page, Cal?" he asked peering around the door.

"Modeling agencies. I figured once they healed, they'd clean up pretty good as models," I said. "Always attractive. Never age."

He mulled it over for a minute, then nodded. "Good going, Cal. Good for you," he said and was gone.

I admit that I felt pretty damn good after that. For once I didn't have to kill something to solve a problem. It's not often in my line of work that there's a happy ending. I celebrated with a Vicodin, a pop of crank and a big sloppy gyro I had delivered, along with a huge, heart-stopping pile of cheese fries.

CHAPTER

14

THE GOOD FEELINGS LASTED FOR AS LONG

as it took the phone to ring—four blissful days. Then on Thursday Blout called and broke the spell.

"Big trouble!" he yelled. I'd never heard him so agitated.

"Calm the fuck down! What's up?"

"Tourists are dropping like goddamn flies down on the Mall. We've got ten down in Natural History and the 911 switchboards are lighting up! I'm heading down there."

Christ, I thought, it was just like Whitney Green all those years ago. "Here we go again. I guess whatever is behind this is up to steam. Listen, do you have any painkillers or some liquor there with you?"

"Yeah, sure... why?!"

"Do me a favor, before you go down there, have a drink or a pill or sniff some glue. I don't care, just do something that clouds your mind. It won't take you if your brain is damaged."

"Please, Cal, shut the fuck up. I called for help."

He wasn't buying it. "Think of the dope as a kevlar vest for your brain."

Blout paused. For once he didn't argue. "Whatever."

I told him I had an errand to run, that it was important to the case and that I'd be down as soon as I could.

Speed and a pot of black coffee got me to work making some changes on Edgar Cain's driver's license. I altered the expiration date and popped in my photo. Kid stuff really, and when the job was done it looked damn convincing. There'd be no trouble at the bank.

As I was about to leave, Mo'Lock came through the door.

"Good," I said, "I'm glad you're here. We got bad news."

"I know. My brothers and sisters are fleeing the city. There's a major disturbance. Any leads?"

"Leads I got. Answers, not a one" I rubbed my face. "Everything points to Edgar Cain, but—"

"He's dead," Mo' said and then, "He *is* dead, right?"

I looked up. "That's the one thing I am sure of. There was nothing left of him, not enough to even collect for evidence. The fire department had to wash the gunk off the streets with their hoses..."

I stopped. If my head could have turned into a jack-ass head, it would have. Mo'Lock finished my thought.

"Into the sewers."

I rubbed my eyes. "Why do they always go in the sewers."

CHAPTER

15

I HAD WHAT I THOUGHT WAS A DECENT PLAN,

but first, I had to get to the bank. I had a pretty good hunch what was in that safe deposit box, and we'd need it to survive what was to come. After that, there was no avoiding it. The ghoul and I had to go down into the sewers.

Mo'Lock and I agreed to meet at the drainage pipe a few hours later. After he left, I checked to make sure I was properly armed. Fuck yeah, I must have weighed an extra ten pounds with all my extra baggage. I made sure I had the safe deposit key and the talisman Mo' had found.

As an extra precaution, I slipped a small leather case that I kept for years into my sock.

Everything was in place. I was as ready as I'd ever be. But before I could get out the office door, I had company.

Dan Stockton, that huge prick of a cop, standing there blocking my exit, with two other uniforms behind him.

I motioned to push past. Stockton blocked my way.

"I don't have time for this shit, Stockton. Get out of my way. We can fight later." I made another move, he countered. This time he held up a folded document.

"This ain't personal," Stockton said, waving the papers in my face. "This is straight up official. I've got a warrant for your arrest."

I stepped back. All three pressed forward. I could see that the two back-ups were taking out their batons. One had handcuffs ready for me.

"Arrest? What the hell for?!"

Stockton smirked. "You had a court date yesterday with some guy you pummeled on Halloween, and you were a no-show. That, my asshole friend, is against the law."

"Moving a little fast, aren't they?" I said.

Stockton's smirk widened to an outright obnoxious grin. "That's the personal part. I did the paperwork myself."

"Gee, thanks."

The scene froze while everybody waited for something to happen. I made it happen by bolting for the door. I broke the blue-boy wall, catching them off guard. Stockton made a stupid choking sound as I brushed past, as though he couldn't believe he'd lost control of the situation. Idiot.

I was at the door, almost to the hallway. Once there, I could really haul ass. "I told you I don't have time for this sh—." That was that.

For the second goddamn time in under a month, I was knocked cold.

CHAPTER

16

I WOKE IN A SMALL ROOM THAT REEKED

of body odor and cigarettes, handcuffed to a loop in the wall. I was kneeling, facing the loop, with my back to the rest of the cramped room. The only way in or out—a heavy, industrial-strength door—was behind me. The brick walls were spotted with traces of blood that had been lazily wiped off and covered by a thin coat of off-white.

Standard interrogation procedure. They wanted you to see the blood so you'd start shitting yourself before they even hit you. I'd been through it before, but had a bad feeling about this. Something felt very wrong.

My wrists were bleeding from the cuffs that supported most of my weight and the back of my head stung from where Stockton had planted his nightstick. It made me think of those kids and how I'd walloped them with my blackjack. I was about to feel bad about it when the door behind me opened. I didn't twist around to see who it was. I already knew.

"Thought you'd never wake up," Stockton said behind me.

"Gotta get my beauty sleep."

I heard him shut the door, then a hard clack as the lock slipped onto place. "You're gonna go out smart assin', huh?"

Go out? What the hell was he talking about? I mean, we didn't like each other, but this was out of left field. Years of unfriendly snips, the occasional fisticuffs was one thing. This was beyond bitter dislike. This was nuts. I began to feel scared for the first time in a long while.

"You know, Stocky," I said. "This kind of thing is frowned upon these days. I could sue." I was half telling the truth, half fishing. I heard my voice shake.

He grabbed me by the hair and jerked my face around to his. He was red-faced and spitting. "Not if you're dead, funny man!"

"Have you considered an anger management course?"

That was the last thing I remember saying. The next twenty minutes were a blur of kicks and punches. Stockton was good at it. He knew all the places to hit and just how hard to strike for maximum pain. I just went limp and tried not to make a sound. I figured even a raging psycho like him would get sick of beating on a wet sack of mud after a while.

But he just went on and on until my face was puffed like a bloody bunt-cake and my body was tender to the touch. What amazed me even as I was being beat was his skill at keeping me conscious. He wanted me awake, and awake I stayed. Finally he tired of hitting me and pulled a blade from his back pocket.

I spat a wad of thick blood. "Come on, Stockton. You made your point."

He ignored me. "You ever hear of hamstringing? It's supposed to hurt a lot."

I shivered. Nobody walks after having the backs of their knees sliced. If he truly meant to hamstring me, I was through.

Luckily, I have a merciful angel that watches over me. That angel happens to be a big cop named Jefferson Blout.

My eyes were nearly swollen shut, but I heard him come crashing into that room like a diesel. I had the pleasure of hearing Stockton give a little baby yelp right before Blout shattered his jaw with a roundhouse punch that would have made a Viking weep. It was beautiful.

When it was all said and done, I was banged up pretty good, but I could still walk. Blout talked me into going to the hospital where I got a couple dozen stitches and a jumbo band-aid or two. I made sure to whine until the doctor ordered some painkillers, so in the end I came out okay. Shit, I'd gone through a lot worse to get drugs before.

Blout was waiting for me outside.

"So how the hell did you know Stockton had me dragged in? " I asked. His appearance had been nothing short of miraculous.

"A rook tipped me off. He wasn't too keen on losing his badge so Stockton could waste some lousy gumshoe."

"Thanks."

"His words, not mine." But he enjoyed telling me. I could see it in his face.

"So what's the word on the deaths at the Mall?"

"Not as bad as I thought. Eight, maybe nine."

"Skulls?"

"Clean."

I nodded. "It's revving up for the big strike."

Blout rammed one of his cigars into his mouth and lit it. "What are you talking about now?"

"What we're dealing with here played it safe for a few years. It plucked the brains out of people who never went through full autopsies, like chronic cases and the elderly. Then it moved on to the homeless."

I paused and lit a cigarette of my own.

"Now it's getting up some speed and hitting tourists, and soon it's going to bust loose and then... the whole city's fair game."

I thought Blout was going to bust my chops, but instead he shook his head. "Christ. What are we dealing with here? Do you have any ideas at all?"

"It's Cain," I said.

"The dead man?"

"The dead man."

"You want to tell me how?"

"Would it matter?"

Blout thought about getting pissed, but he didn't have the strength. He just nodded a sad little nod and bit his lip.

As we got to Blout's ugly car, he gave me back all the stuff the cops

confiscated—gun, blackjack, fake ID and safe deposit key. Asshole held back
two items, though, wanting answers before he'd hand them over. I was in no
shape to fight, so I'd play his little game.

He opened one of his big hands, revealing the leather case I'd stashed in
my sock. It was my old friends: syringe, spoon, and smack. I couldn't believe
Blout had retrieved it for me. In the other hand he clutched the talisman
Mo'Lock had ripped off the tunnel zombie.

"Where do I start?"

"How about the works?" Blout said. "Don't tell me you're doing shit again."

I shook my head and spoke, praying my voice didn't slur from the
painkillers. "Remember what I told you? That last time I dealt with Cain? It
didn't absorb my brain because it disliked the pollution. I just have it on me as
a precaution. I swear." My hand was raised like a boy scout, and I tried to force
a brown-nose smile across my beaten, puffy face.

He seemed satisfied enough and tossed me the case. "Thought you'd say
that. Only as a last resort, you got it?" he said. Then he held up the talisman.
"And this?"

"Mo'Lock found it in the tunnels beneath Whitney Green." I looked down
at the ground.

"Tunnels beneath Whitney Green? Hmmm, I don't recall you mentioning
anything about tunnels," he spoke in mock tones of mystery. Then he screamed,
"YOU FUCK!" and rammed his palm right into my wounded shoulder.

I yelled out.

"What else aren't you telling me? Goddammit, Cal! Stop keeping me in the
dark! What good am I if I only know half the story?"

I looked up, rubbing my shoulder. "Sorry. I'm not used to letting cops in on
this kind of stuff. I think you'll recall what happened the few times I did. I got
laughed right off the case."

Blout took a couple of angry puffs off his log of a cigar. "Well that was them,
this is me. Cough it up."

He was right. Where would I be if he hadn't informed me of the mysterious
deaths when he did? I told him everything I knew, about Mo'Lock and the
crusty tunnel zombies who had attacked us, and about the missing ghouls. I
filled him in on Cain and what I found in the evidence room. When I was
finished he tossed me the talisman.

"What about this, then? How does that fit it?"

I looked at the charm. "Considering the thing wearing it turned into a pool of blood when it was removed, I'd say it's a resurrection talisman. Black magic, voodoo maybe. I can't say for sure."

"Did you notice something floating in the liquid?"

"Yeah, but I couldn't make it out. Probably a piece of bone." I stuffed the charm into my pocket considering the issue closed and moot.

"It's an Egyptian symbol," Blout said plainly.

"Huh? How'd you know?" I was stunned.

"My wife collects all kinds of that ugly crap. The house was full of it. The living room looked like friggin' King Tut's tomb. That shit was gone the moment she left."

I had to laugh. "Any idea what it means?"

"The perp shops at the same place as Jessica?"

"Now who's the smart ass? So what we're left with here is a mix of black magic, monsters and myth, voodoo of several varieties, and now Egyptian symbols. That's the oddest, because the Egyptians weren't into reviving dead. All their ceremonies revolved around surviving the afterlife. Even this talisman's a little bit this, a little bit that—a goddamn potpourri of evil." I scratched my aching head. "Oh yeah, and we have a giant brain-sucking head that should be dead but somehow isn't."

I needed to get moving to clear my head. With all the time wasted getting the crap beat out of me, I'd have to hustle to meet the ghoul at the drainage pipe. I told Blout to drop me off at Riggs while he went on to meet Mo'Lock and tell him to wait until I arrived. Blout wasn't thrilled with the plan.

"No way," he said. "I'm not going near that freak without you. I'll check the box. You take the car to the pipe."

I tried chiding him. "Are you scared?"

He pulled the wheel extra hard on a left turn, slamming my head against the window frame. "I wouldn't call it scared, punching bag. More like creeped out."

"Splitting hairs." I gingerly touched the swell of bruises on the side of my face. "Besides, you might not like what you find in the box." I tried to sound ominous, but I came off more like Bob Barker. My mouth was too swollen.

Blout gave out a quick breathy laugh. "I'll take my chances. And to be on the safe side, I won't look inside until I meet you back at the drainage pipe."

"They are not going to let you walk out of the bank with the whole safe deposit box." I started laughing, knowing full-well what was coming next.

He turned to me. A big toothy grin was spread across his face. "Wanna bet?"

CHAPTER

17

BLOUT SCREECHED UP TO THE CURB

in front of the bank. He got out with the car running, keys dangling in the ignition. I scooted across the seat and pulled the door shut. Instead of charging into the bank as I'd hoped, Blout stood there shuffling his feet. It didn't take a brain surgeon to see he was nervous with me behind the wheel of his butt-ugly car.

"Are you okay? For driving, I mean. What did they give you back at the hospital?"

I let my head bob out of control. "I'm phhhhine! Don't worry about a phhhhing!" I fell against the wheel, sounding the horn for a good thirty seconds. Fun, but we were losing time. "Seriously. We've got work to do. I'm fine and I'm late."

I floored it, leaving Blout breathing exhaust. When I glanced back, he was flipping me off, both hands raised above the smoke. I laughed, but the seriousness of the situation began to sink in. I was through joking for the moment.

I glanced down at the dashboard and saw one of those cheap plastic stick-on digital clocks just above the ashtray. If the clock was right, I was over half an hour late. Mo'Lock would wait, that much I could rely on. He had the patience of a dead man.

I drove carefully, taking the back streets past Dupont Circle straight up Connecticut Avenue until I was near Embassy Row. Once I was clear of the major urban areas I pulled over and parked in front of a liquor store. Not only was I shaky, but a headache had begun creeping up on me, moving around like a probing flashlight beam. In the liquor store, I purchased two pints of rotgut—one for me and one for Blout.

In the car I popped a couple of pills from the hospital and washed it down with the booze. It occurred to me it might not be safe to mix the two, but I figured the results would become apparent soon enough.

It took about ten minutes to arrive at the old reservoir off Wisconsin Avenue. From the street it looked like a small lake, but when you got close you could see a cement bottom and surrounding fence. Problem was, it took eight minutes for the mystery of mixing drugs and alcohol to be solved. It wasn't good. I was dizzy, my head was reeling and I couldn't feel my teeth.

I steered the car around the chain-link fence and cruised along the elevated access road, raising roostertails worthy of a *Dukes of Hazzard* episode. The drainage pipe was far from the main road and more or less hidden from public view. In my drugged haze, I'd let the car drift to where the shoulder dropped away from the road surface. I took a sharp right to bring the car back parallel with the pipe while jamming on the brakes, but it was too little too late.

The big car skidded over the edge sideways, jumped and began to turn over. It rolled with me trapped inside being flipped and flopped around like socks in the dryer. With a sickening crunch all motion ceased as I arrived at the drainage pipe. The car came to a halt on its roof a few yards short of the pipe's entrance. Totaled, crushed like an accordion. Blout was going to kill me!

I was pinned, but could hear voices outside. It was Mo'Lock for sure and, from the sound of it, he'd found some backup. And there I was, the big leader, trapped in a borrowed car that I had driven into a ditch. What an entrance.

I was relieved to see that neither of the bottles had gotten smashed in the crash. The talisman, however, hadn't been so lucky. My pants had a dark sticky wet spot seeping through the pocket.

I kicked at one of the back doors while Mo'Lock pulled from the outside. Finally I was able to crawl free into the hazy daylight.

Mo'Lock's big pale face was right there. "Is this Mr. Blout's car?"

"It was."

"He's going to kill you."

I ignored the comment as I dusted myself off, noticing the volunteer army Mo'Lock had assembled; the frankenteens Scott and Miriam and a large ghoul I'd never met. The unknown ghoul was huge, with wide shoulders, big hands and a head that looked like a cement block with slits for eyes and a dark flat-top.

Mo'Lock did the introductions. "Cal, this is Hank Gundy. He's offered his services. I'm afraid all my brothers and sisters refused."

I shook the behemoth's hand. "You're not a ghoul?"

Gundy shook his head. "Not ghoul," he said. "Hank a creep."

I shot Mo'Lock a quizzical look.

He waved me off. "I'll explain later."

I swear, there are more varieties of monster than there are insects. Even with all my years of dealing with the shit I still don't know them all.

I turned my attention to the teens. "Thanks for coming," I said. "Where's... um, Windshield?"

"Randy," they both said.

Miriam smiled. "He got a gig!"

Not really wanting to hear more, I ushered everyone to the tunnel mouth. Mo'Lock had outlined what he knew of the plan—the layout of the tunnels and the static he'd encountered—and I filled them in on the rest. The teens seemed to understand everything, but Gundy kept looking around distracted. It didn't matter. I suspected that if and when there was trouble he'd know what to do.

"I don't know what we're going to find down there. All I do know is that it involves many, many forms of witchcraft and dark arts, so be ready for anything. Most important of all: if anybody's head starts to hurt, drop back."

Mo'Lock edged up close as I finished my instructions. "Do you see them?"

I whispered back out of the corner of my mouth., "Yup, been there for the last 10 minutes."

Just inside the tunnel, where light stopped and darkness began, stood a wall of empty-eyed zombies.

"We've got some company." I pointed them out to the rest of our crew.

Scott stepped forward. "Those are the things that attacked you?"

Mo'Lock and I both nodded.

I took out my gun, an unreturned police issue 9mm, and aimed into the crowd at head level. Although I was wasted, my aim was steady as I squeezed off two quick bursts. One of the zombies' heads snapped back violently, and his body quickly fell to the ground like a rag doll. The others went wild, moaning and beating on each other. They wouldn't cross into the light, but wouldn't retreat either. Then the one I shot stood back up with a big chunk of skull missing, only seconds after the gunfire's echo had faded.

I turned to Mo'Lock and Gundy. "This looks like your kinda job."

Mo'Lock led Gundy inside and pointed, making sure the big guy was looking. "See those necklaces they're wearing?"

"Around stinky man's necks?"

"Yes?"

Gundy nodded.

"You and I are going to run in there and grab as many as we can. It kills them. Got that?"

Gundy sharpened at the prospect of violence. "Got it. Hank take necklace. Stinky man die."

"Let's go," said the ghoul.

They charged into the tunnel, leaving me and the frankenteens behind to watch and pray. It took only seconds for them to hit the zombie wall. From my vantage point, it looked like a riot had erupted: I couldn't even make out the shapes of Mo'Lock and Gundy as the crowd consumed them. Amidst the furor, though, I heard sounds that hinted at some level of success. There was a distinct slopping and sloshing sound of thick liquid being spilled. Those things were going down in gobs of blood.

Problem was, there seemed to be too damn many of them. I got panicky and pulled my gun out again, edging into the tunnel along the wall. I began shooting into the crowd, thinking it served as a distraction if nothing else.

From inside the tunnel, we heard Mo'Lock shout, "We could use some help in here!"

I was glad to oblige, but Miriam and Scott didn't share my eagerness. They were scared stiff. I ran into the tunnel without them, itching for some payback. I planned to blast first, then tear away their talismans before they could recover. I started shooting as I ran, but my heel hit a thick dark puddle and sent me sliding top speed into the thick of the fray. Through it all, I'd never stopped firing.

I clamored to my feet, but they were on me instantly. I remembered their dry, crusty touch from the stairwell. That time they'd blindsided me. This would be different.

I let them kick and punch at me. I didn't care. All I wanted was a handful of leather, a sliver of glass in my palm. When I had it, I yanked. Time after time, I'd hear a satisfying yelp followed by the sound of hot stew hitting the floor, then I'd grab for more. It was like flushing away the enemy, one of the most satisfying fights I ever had.

I hardly noticed when it was over, with the last dozen or so zombies retreating into the inner depths of the tunnels. Suddenly there was pin drop silence. I looked around. Mo'Lock was nearby with two fistfuls of necklaces, Gundy was behind us. In one hand he had necklaces, but the other held a leg. I looked down and saw we were up to our ankles in liquified zombie blood. It was fucking disgusting.

We left the tunnel to gather ourselves as Mo'Lock giddily enthused about all the souls that now had a chance to be free.

It took a moment before we noticed Gundy wasn't following. When we turned, the big guy hadn't moved an inch, hovering on the razor's edge of shadow and light.

"Gundy? You okay?" I yelled.

I could see his big face even at a distance. His expression was like a baby about to cry. He dropped the leg and placed a big hand to his head.

"Head hurts," He said.

And that was that. Big Hank Gundy dropped dead where he stood. I didn't need to see his cracked-open skull to know the brains were gone, completely empty save for the thick curl of steam that slowly snaked from the empty skull cavity.

"Fuck," I said.

We'd wait for Blout before we made our next move.

CHAPTER

18

I WAS PISSED ABOUT GUNDY'S DEATH,

if that's what you can call it—I never did find out exactly what a creep was. I hadn't even known the guy for ten minutes and now he was a stiff.

I told the frankenteens to get the hell home. I wasn't going to risk the kids, not after all they'd been through. Luckily, it took little convincing. They wanted to leave.

Like that, my pathetic army was cut in half. It was just me and Mo'Lock again. No one spoke, so I took the time to smoke and have few drinks. I fished the leather case out of my sock, unzipped it and stared at the contents.

"What's that?" Mo'Lock asked. He shambled through the dirt and sat next to me.

I zipped the case and tucked it back in my sock. "Backup plan."

Before he could ask any more questions, we heard a car door slam a short distance away. Blout was walking briskly up the dirt road with the safe deposit box tucked under his arm as the cab returned to the city.

He spotted his car laying upside down at the bottom of the ditch and slowed, shoulders slumping noticeably at the sight. I was afraid he'd drop the box but he clutched it tightly. I watched and waited, half expecting an attack.

"Nice parking space, asshole."

I apologized profusely, but Blout wanted none of it. He was focused on the task at hand, saving all his anger for a fresh new ulcer. For whatever reason, he'd been surprising me lately. Maybe he could sense some bad shit coming. I know I felt it.

The box under his arm was large, much bigger than the proverbial bread-box. True to his word, Blout hadn't opened it. He placed it down in the dust outside the tunnel, glanced inside at the aftermath of the fight and sat down on the ground with a grunt.

"Christ, my head is pounding," He said.

My head was hurting too, but I was still under the protection of a painkiller and alcohol cocktail. I handed Blout the pint I'd picked up for him. He took it and drank the thing down like sugar water. That should do the trick, I thought. If it didn't, I'd get him out of there, like it or not. Even if I had to knock him out, I was not going to have a repeat of Gundy. Not with Blout anyway.

Mo'Lock was shifting on his feet with an expression that I'd never seen before—discomfort. I doubted very seriously that the ghoul was constipated. It had to be his head.

I went to his side. "What's up, Mo'? How're you feeling?"

He looked at me. "I'm not sure... it's been so long, but I think I have a headache."

I took the other pint out of my coat pocket. I'd drank some, but most of it was still there. I forced the bottle into his big white hands.

"Take it. Drink," I demanded.

The ghoul looked at the bottle and grimaced. He shook his head.

"It can't hurt you," I said. "Better safe than sorry."

The ghoul was a sucker for clichés. He looked at the bottle like a boxer staring down his opponent. I guess I understood. It had been over a century since he had a drink and his first one was about to be some cheap rotgut.

I glanced over at Blout and saw his face was lazy and calm. His eyes were blood-shot and hooded. He had the look of a man with a poisoned brain—our best defense.

"AAAAAHHHHGGGHHHH!!"

Blout and I jumped, simultaneously pulling out our weapons, but it was just Mo'Lock. He'd swigged the entire bottle in one huge gulp and now stood swaying with wide, crazy eyes. I lowered my gun first and with my free hand slowly guided Blout's down to his side. He wasn't so sure there was no reason to shoot.

Blout and I stood by as the ghoul went through a series of shudders and twitches, until gradually the liquor slipped through his ancient veins and his dark-circled eyes reddened.

I waited a few minutes, then took the bottle from him. "How does it feel?" I asked.

"I feel stupid."

"Perfect."

I rubbed my head and looked from one bleary partner to the other. Blout was trying to find the end of a cigar and having a hard time of it. He'd chugged his entire bottle. Mo'Lock was pressing a finger into his forehead and sticking his tongue out in response to each touch. I sighed. Here we were, the city's heroes. We were doomed.

There was no use wasting any more time. I picked up the safe deposit box and headed into the mouth of the drainage pipe. When I turned, no one else had moved. They were just staring at me blankly.

"Well," I said, "Time to move, you buckin' fastards!"

With that they both shook themselves out of their individual hazes and followed me into the tunnel. Not one of us could walk a straight line.

CHAPTER

19

WE WALKED DEEP INTO THE TUNNEL,

sloshing through the remains of the zombie guards, until the entrance was a pea-sized dot of light behind us. I lit a cigarette and waited for our eyes to adjust to the pitch dark. When Blout's outline became clearer I could see he was agitated and nervous.

"When are you going to open that thing?" he asked, pointing at the box.

I shrugged. "We could do it now if you want. I've got a pretty good idea what's inside."

I felt the key slap against the side of my face and I managed to catch it before it hit the dirt. When I leaned down to feel for the keyhole, I was too ripped and had little luck. My hand clanked the key clumsily against the metal, finding everything except its target.

"You want some light?" Blout switched on his pen-light as he knelt down beside me.

"Thanks."

I found the lock and gave it a twist. The box opened with one quick flip, releasing a billowing mushroom of putrescence into the air.

Blout reeled away. "Aw Jesus!"

I covered my mouth and nose, but the odor was so strong it stung my eyes and forced me to back away from the box. After a second or two the mist cleared and the stench was reduced enough to make it bearable. We knelt and stared down at the throbbing contents of Edgar Cain's safe deposit box. At first glance, it reminded me of those old fifties ads for meat: the colors were too bright and the sheen looked greasy and unreal. But it *was* real, and it was alive.

A beating human heart.

The disembodied heart rose and fell as if it were still part of a person, still attached to arteries pulsing with blood. Surrounding the heart was a garnish of objects that ranged from feathers to bones. Symbols from a variety of regions and religions were scrawled on paper and wood. It was the same pattern as everything else.

I looked up to Blout. He couldn't take his eyes off the beating heart. Then he caught my stare.

"Is this what you expected?" he stammered.

"I had a hunch it would be something of this sort."

Blout looked back at the heart. "If this is Cain's heart, why don't we just destroy it?"

It was a good question, but not a safe option. Sometimes hearts are not only used to keep something alive, but also to imprison something or keep it in check. We couldn't be sure which kind this was.

"Cain may have put this heart here to protect himself from what was happening," I concluded.

"He didn't do a very good job," Blout said.

Mo'Lock raised a finger. "It could also work to our benefit to have the heart alive, if it is the heart of the killer. It would give us leverage. A hostage, if you will."

So it was agreed—the heart would keep beating for now. I locked up the box and we all headed deeper into the tunnel.

We walked on, deeper and deeper, and I cursed myself for not buying more liquor. I had no idea how long the effects of the alcohol would protect us, and finding out might mean dying. I thought about the leather case in my sock, but shoved the thought away. That was the last resort. Anyway, I still had seven painkillers. If the pain got bad enough I'd convince Blout or the ghoul to take one, like it or not.

I laughed darkly to myself, thinking that only I could stumble onto a case where excessive drug and alcohol use was the best way to stay alive. But here I was with a straight-arrow cop and a hundred-year-old ghoul, drunk in the sewers beneath the nation's capital.

Finally, after what seemed like hours, we came to the intersection Mo'Lock had described last week. I saw the crudely cut hole, definitely not the work of a pro. The edges were rough and jagged and we had to be careful stepping through.

Like the hole itself, the tunnel on the other side was rough hewn. The walls were rock-encrusted, the floors and ceiling uneven and craggy. Support beams appeared to be stolen phone poles and billboard posts, giving it the look of a derelict coal mine. It was very small and confined, and the threat of claustrophobia dug at me like a creeping itch.

As we walked along, the floor gradually began to decline, until the angle was so severe walking became difficult. We all leaned backward, trying very hard not to fall on our butts and wind up sliding out of control.

"Can we take a break?"

It was Blout, sweaty and out of breath. I was sweating too, my shirt soaked through. "Sure, but let's make it quick."

I wanted to ditch my coat, but needed the things in its pockets: mace, a lock blade, blackjack, a small back-up pistol, and several clips for the 9mm. If I tried to load all that into my pants I'd look like I shit myself.

"How's everybody's head?" I said as I slid down the wall, gripping protruding rocks until I was sitting.

"I'm okay," Blout said.

The ghoul nodded.

I told them I had the Percocet if they needed it, but both waved me off. I felt like a goddamn pusher.

After a minute's rest, Blout signaled he was ready to continue. As soon as I planted my foot for my first step, I fell and immediately began sliding. I held the box with one arm and with the other I grabbed wildly for anything that would stop my skid. Anything turned out to be Blout's pant cuff, and then we were both tumbling out of control down the slope.

The next moment there was nothing beneath us except absolutely black air. As we hurtled downward, all I could do was hold on to the box and brace for impact.

CHAPTER

20

THE FALL WAS SHORT BUT PAINFUL.

I landed with the box under my ribs and heard a loud crunch. Pain shot through my midsection like an electrical charge. I let out a scream that would have shamed Fay Wray. Broken rib for sure, plus I'd aggravated a couple dozen Stockton-inflicted wounds.

The next second I heard Blout hit the ground beside me with a short hard thud. At least his fat ass didn't land on me.

We both stayed on our backs, moaning. Blout was the first to try to get up.

"Are you okay?" he said as he stood, dusting himself off.

I stared up at the ceiling of the tunnel. "Just leave me here. I'll be fine in a day or two."

Blout thought I was kidding. He grabbed my arm and pulled me until I was sitting up. At that point we realized we were now in a huge tunnel, at least twice the width and height of the city's drainage pipe. Then we saw the box. When I fell on it, I'd crushed one side. The hinges had snapped and spilled the beating heart onto the floor. Blout shined the pen-light beam on the throbbing muscle. It was filthy with dirt, but still beating.

"Oops."

I gathered it up, wiping it clean with my shirt. Blout watch me tend to the moist hunk of meat with a look of total disgust.

"Maybe after we're done here, you can name it and keep it as a pet," he said and turned away.

I picked a few granules of dirt from one of the sealed arteries then tucked it back into the battered box.

Finally Mo'Lock appeared, landing feet first and seeming damn pleased about it. He had been there before, but I distinctly recalled that the first time he explored the tunnel he'd arrived on his ass, so his smugness rolled right off me.

"Which way did your buddies go?" I asked.

The ghoul looked slowly in both directions, then back again, and once more to be sure. "Whitney Green is east... that way," he said pointing. "They went west."

"Then west it is." I started to walk, but stopped when I saw Blout holding his head. "What's wrong?"

"It's nothing... just NHHHGHGH!"

The big man buckled and fell. Mo'Lock grabbed him by the shoulders, catching him before he hit the dirt. I could see the dark glimmer of blood running from both of the cop's nostrils.

I fumbled in my pockets for a pill. Blout was grimacing and shuddering. He was gritting his teeth so hard I could see the pressure was producing blood. It was seeping through the tiny seams between teeth and gum, filling the nooks and crannies with crimson red. Getting him to swallow a pill was going to be tough. I grabbed his face at the jaw and pinched hard, trying to get his teeth to part. It worked on the third squeeze and I jammed the pill in.

It was too late, though. Blout's eyes shot open. They were huge, blazing red with anger. It wasn't Blout—something had him. His body was suddenly animated beyond human capability. His arms flailed as though his limbs had no joints restricting their movement.

Without looking at him, Blout grabbed Mo'Lock by the throat and swung him off the ground, using the ghoul as a weapon against me. He slammed into me, sending the two of us flying hard against the wall.

Mo'Lock and I sprung to our feet and readied for the next attack, but none came. Blout was hanging there in the air, floating before us from invisible puppet strings. I saw blood droplets making mud beneath his feet. Whatever had him planned on killing him. Blood ran from every orifice; the tear ducts in his eyes, his mouth and nose, even from beneath his fingernails.

I stared, not knowing what to do. Something was inside him, manipulating his every move; pushing, pressing, possibly grinding his insides to a pulp. The heart jumped wildly in the box I cradled.

I whispered. "What has him, Mo'?"

"I don't know. I feel Blout and another presence."

Blout's bleeding eyes slammed shut tightly, then abruptly shot open again. His lips parted, allowing foamy blood and a long, lung-clearing hiss to roll out. Although his limbs continued to flail, they were non-threatening movements, like a cut-out paper doll blowing in the wind.

I pulled out the 9mm and aimed at the floating cop, with no intention of shooting—yet. Possessed or not, I wouldn't let my friend die without exhausting every last option. I had to wait and let the scene play out.

The noise from Blout's throat changed from its monotone hiss. It began to fluctuate and rise until peaking in a shrill shriek that echoed throughout the tunnel. Mo'Lock winced and covered his ears. Suddenly the noise cut off sharply and fell back to its steady, low hiss. Then, it spoke:

"Get away from this place."

It was a thick, sludgy voice, more like the ghoul's than Blout's. It sounded forced from the gut and past Blout's unwilling, unmoving lips. Only the jaw moved, seeming out of sync with the vocals. The sight reminded me of a strange ventriloquist act.

"Leave here at once and you will be spared!"

I laughed, couldn't help it. As scary as the situation was, the "Great and Powerful Oz" dialogue threw me. Maybe it was the break in the tension, but in that moment I concocted a plan.

The levitating body lurched. *"Get out while you still can!"*

I flipped the lid off the safe deposit box and scooped out the heart. I let the box drop to the ground, spilling the garnish of charms, stones and herbs. I held the heart tightly in my folded left arm and with my right pressed the 9mm into it. If this thing wanted cornball, I'd give it cornball.

"Let the cop go, or I'll let the heart have it!"

Nothing.

Mo'Lock was staring at me, eyes wide. "Cal, are you sure this is—" he whispered.

"Shut up," I hissed. "It might work."

I stepped forward and pressed the gun harder into the side of the heart and repeated my threat. This time I added a 5-second time limit and began the countdown.

Still nothing. I hesitated.

"Four... Three... Two... "

Finally, just when I thought my bluff had been called, Blout dropped limp to the ground. He began coughing and gagging, trying to catch his breath. His wide back heaved and arched as he fought to regain control of his body. He was free, but I knew what'd we'd seen might only be a small taste of the power of our foe.

CHAPTER

21

BLOUT WAS GROGGY AND AGITATED, BUT

very much alive. Although the bleeding had been horrible to see, he hadn't lost much blood in the end. It was just enough to achieve the desired effect—scaring the crap out of all of us.

"GHAA! What the hell was that?" Blout sputtered, trying to clear his throat. "I couldn't move, couldn't hear a thing... I was floating in tar."

I tried to help him to his feet, but Blout shook his head. He was still too weak. We all took a seat in the dirt again and ate more painkillers. All except Mo'Lock, who waved me off again.

"You sure?" I said, downing another myself. "How's your head?"

The ghoul nodded confidently. "I'm fine. There's nothing there, I'm sure."

Blout was looking more alert despite the pill. Slowly he came back to his old self. He snapped at me for staring and got annoyed with the blood caked around the various openings of his face. When he got around to re-lighting the cigar he'd dropped I knew he was close to a hundred percent.

I grabbed the box and stood using my free hand to wipe off the dirt that stuck to my pants. It was much more moist than it had been before, less crumbly and more like dough. Definitely doughy. Mo'Lock noticed the same, and was examining one particular wad of the stuff.

"You think we're near water?"

Mo'Lock shook his head slightly. "I don't think this is dirt. Feels like very rich soil."

"Great, we'll start an herb garden."

"I'm no expert, but I thought soil was usually found close to the surface, the top layer."

"Well, add it to the list of weird shit. If there's room."

I started walking on but stopped as Blout grunted and fell behind me. He was injured pretty bad. I began doubting whether he'd be able to continue.

Not that I was much better. With the repeated beating my body was taking, I was asking too much of the painkiller. It couldn't block out pain from injuries and protect me from invading psychic forces forever. Again I thought about the packet in my sock, but fought it off. Not yet, not yet.

We moved along the tunnel, shambling and weaving. The dirt beneath our feet gave in to our every step, adding an unfortunate suction effect that made walking harder. My legs began to ache.

I could make out the rough tunnel walls but not much else—it was just a long dark corridor leading God knew where. I was a little disappointed to see there were no cryptic inscriptions on the walls, no dramatic warnings or symbols to ward off enemies. Then when we came to a turn where I could detect a slight glow of light around the corner.

Blout was beside me. "What the fuck?"

I walked toward the glow, the others following. Blout had his revolver drawn.

The light was dim and yellow, most definitely not natural. It had the erratic blink of a bulb casting twitching shadows in all directions. We slowed as we neared the corner, taking each sticky step carefully. Just before we reached the source of the light, I stepped on something that crinkled.

I grabbed the object from beneath my foot. "You were right, Mo'."

Mo'Lock leaned over my shoulder as I presented an empty plastic bag. The logo was a smirking cartoon cow, with "Good Cow Top Soil" printed underneath. The ghoul grinned at me. I threw the bag to the ground and moved around the corner.

There were lights lining the hall, scores of naked bulbs hanging from thick bundles of power cords, but they weren't there to illuminate the path. They were grow lights. Countless plants completely covered the tunnel walls, crammed into every inch of space.

The variety of plants was unbelievable, but all were herbs and roots common to all forms of magic and voodoo. Some, like basil and coriander, were common cooking herbs that also had uses in the dark arts. Others were nastier: hemlock, a deadly poison, and a large cluster of the rare aconite plant, also poisonous.

I pointed at the cluster. "Greek legend says that plant came from the mouth of Cerberus..."

"... the dog that guarded the lower world," Mo'Lock nodded and felt the leaf of the plant next to its hood-shaped flower. "Another misplaced myth, a random use of legend and witchcraft."

I slapped his shoulder. "Now you're getting it."

"Not me," Blout spat. "Care to fill me in?"

I held my finger to my mouth. Blout was yelling, and I thought we'd better keep it down. We were close.

"It's been like this throughout the case, Blout. The voodoo charm with the Egyptian symbol, the writings in Cain's books crossing Greek legend with witchcraft, and now this. This plant's Greek origin fits the needs of the perp— to guard this tunnel—but..."

Mo'Lock broke in, "... in reality the plant is used for treating gout and rheumatism."

Blout shook his head violently. "I'm completely lost. Is our perp using stuff wrong because he thinks it's something that it isn't?"

"Maybe, maybe not. It all depends on what you believe."

Blout still didn't understand.

I tried my best to explain, "Some things exist whether we believe in them or not. Like the moon, or the sound of a tree falling in the woods, right?"

Blout blinked once and stared at me.

Mo'Lock took a turn. "But what if something that doesn't exist can be created simply because someone believes in it strongly enough?"

Blout looked from me to Mo'Lock.

"You see what we're getting at?"

"No," Blout said, "I must admit I don't."

Mo'Lock clapped his hands. "It's simple. The power of belief can create things which might not exist, granting them power and making them real."

Blout glared at the ghoul for a long time. "Let me tell you what I believe, freak job. I believe this is getting too damn weird, and after what happened to me back there, we need some back-up. That would be the smart play."

I said, "If you're getting scared, you're welcome to hang back and wait."

"Don't pull that kiddy crap with me!" Blout growled. "And I'm not scared."

Blout stomped forward. As we continued on our way our surroundings began to change. The tunnel narrowed and the plants thinned to one every several feet.

As Blout rounded a bend, I heard him retch violently and hurried to catch up. Our path was blocked. A pair of disembodied heads sat impaled on a two-pronged spike protruding from the soft ground. Based on the torn flesh and dangling veins at the neck, they had been violently ripped from their bodies. I didn't need Mo'Lock to tell me that these were his missing buddies, but he did just the same.

"It's them, Cal. It's them."

I began to raise my arm to the ghoul's shoulder but stopped when the heads simultaneously snapped open their eyes.

"Mo'Lock, is that you?" the left head said. Its voice was hollow, accompanied by a deep sucking sound that whistled through the open end of its neck.

We all took a step back. Blout was making the sign of the cross.

Mo'Lock recovered from the initial shock and quickly stepped towards the heads. "Tyus," Mo'Lock said addressing the left head, "what happened?"

Tyus blinked once and tried to wet his lips. It was futile. "We failed. Attacked by a mob of zombie hooligans. Please forgive us."

Mo'Lock placed his hand to his chest and for a moment I thought he would weep. "No. Forgive me. I should not have sent you. Where are your bodies? What did they do with them?"

The head on the right spoke. "They burned them before our eyes and set our heads here with a warning." The ghoul head turned his eyes to me. "The warning was for you, Cal McDonald. Stay away, or certain death awaits."

I shrugged and spat. "Whatever. Who gave you that message? Cain himself?"

Tyus spoke again. "It was just a voice."

"In our heads."

I looked at Mo'Lock. "Do you want to go back and get them to safety? Your call."

The heads spoke together. "We'll be fine. Go and stop this thing. This place stinks of death."

The right head made an effort to look past the ghoul and me. "I think your human friend could use some help."

Mo'Lock and I turned to find Blout out cold, spread eagle on his back. God, how I envied him. He'd get to sleep through it all.

The ghoul and I kept going, leaving Blout with the heads and the message that we'd pressed on. I sensed we were close as the heart beat hard inside the box. Whatever Cain had begun or become, it was soon time for a showdown. I was eager to get it over with. My only regret was that I'd miss the look on Blout's face when the heads gave him our message

CHAPTER

22

THE LONG CORRIDOR BECAME THINNER AND

thinner as Mo'Lock and I advanced. The lights here were spotty and dim, only a few every other yard or so to accommodate a plant here, a root there. Still, there was enough light to see that the end was a long way off. At least I could see no immediate threats. The only sounds were our own footfalls grinding in the soft, muddy dirt and the occasional drag and kick when one of us lost our footing.

The peace and quiet bothered me more than the action. It gave me time to feel my hurting body, each and every cut, scrape and bruise. I was a mass of pain and needed the distraction of motion. Without it, the pain was too much. I couldn't focus. It was then, I think, that my mind was first tugged away...

All at once, my head began to feel strange. It hit like a breeze, then a wave, building to the force of a wrecking ball. Not pain, not really, more like a creeping paralysis—like a stiff, aching joint. I had to stop. I was confused, unsure where I was.

"Cal, are you all right?" a voice said to my side.

I couldn't see anything. Was I home. Too late?

The voice repeated the question.

I covered my face in my hands. "Yeah, I'm fine Dad..."

"What?" Mo'Lock asked.

I felt his hand on my shoulder. "I said I'm..."

I blinked, shaking my confusion away as I dug in my pocket for a pill. The bitter crunch was a needed slap in the face. My vision cleared and I saw the ghoul standing there with a look of unmistakable worry.

"Stop that," I said, standing fully erect. "Fucking ghoul."

I walked away stamping my feet and used my tongue to pick at the jagged chunks of pill stuck in my teeth. Behind me Mo'Lock had a hand to his temple and a strained expression on his stiff white face.

"What's up?" I asked, but didn't slow my stride.

The ghoul kept walking brow raised. "I just had the oddest sensation," he said. "It was as though my brain itched."

"I'm tellin' you, take a fucking pill."

"No. The alcohol is still doing the job. I feel sufficiently bleary."

"Mo'Lock—"

"Cal. No. I can do this, and you've got a job to do."

He wasn't going to budge. It was that uncanny ability to stay focused. He didn't want me to worry or get distracted. No matter how badly I treated him, I was always his number one priority. I thought about it all the time. He could have any life he wanted, even travel the world if he so desired, yet here he was slopping through a subterranean voodoo pit with me—with not so much as a complaint.

"Cal. Up ahead."

Ten feet in front of us, a zombie stood frozen, legs bent and poised to attack, its empty eye sockets dripping oily maggots. One hand was braced on the craggy earth, the other fanned out with palm toward us.

"Shit. Only one?" I laughed.

I handed Mo'Lock the heart and started in, but the thing wasn't looking for a fight. I'd called its bluff. When I got within striking distance, it spun away and ran off into the darkness.

When I turned back to Mo'Lock to gloat, my stomach sank.

Hanging between me and the ghoul was the body of a man, swinging by his broken neck. I backed away, forcing myself to look up at the twisted face. Fuck if I hadn't seen it before. It was my father as I'd found him years before; blue-faced, bloated tongue sticking out grotesquely between tight lips.

I spun away, letting a cry escape, but a new obstacle blocked my way. I covered my eyes, but this only left my other senses open to attack.

"Calvin? Is that you?" The voice was soft and tiny. I remembered it instantly despite the years. Then I smelled baby powder and knew she was there.

I spread the fingers covering my eyes and saw her standing there as beautiful as the last day I saw her—my sister Stephie. Seven years old and so pretty, the image of my mother.

"Stephie! Yes honey, it's me… Cal." I heard my voice cracking. I was losing control. It's not her, I told myself. I clamped my eyes tightly shut and tried to speak, but before I could, Stephie's face changed from the sweet child I'd known to one filled with burning rage.

"Why weren't you in the car, Cal?" she spat. Crevices began to appear across her forehead, blood filling the hairline cracks. "You were supposed to be in the car. Me and mom waited, but you never came."

I shook my head hard and beat myself with my fist. The image before me flickered. "Get out of my head!" I screamed and struck myself again.

Stephie was falling apart. Blood ran from her face as it was raked to the bone by an invisible shattered windshield. She cried my name and called out to our father hanging from the rope. I slammed my head again and screamed, pulling my hair.

"Get out!"

As quickly as they'd come, the images disappeared.

"Fuck!" I slammed my fist into the tunnel wall. I was mad and needed a release. I thought I'd break my hand for sure, but the wall turned out not to be stone and rock at all. The soft red clay fell in a spray of chunks when my fist hit it.

"What now? Mo'Lock!"

"I beg your pardon, sir?"

The voice was the ghoul's, but distinctly different. The hoarse grumble was gone, the imaginary echo no longer there. It was a clear, proper voice. I took a closer look at him. He stood complete and upright, the rigid stance of a gentleman of long ago.

"What is this place? A mine shaft? Where are Caroline and the children?"

I stuttered. I didn't know what to say. It wasn't my ghoul that stood in the tunnel with me. It wasn't anybody I'd ever known.

"Oh, do speak up man! Where are my wife and children?"

"What year is it... sir?" I asked trying to sound polite.

The man was indignant. "Are you daft? It's December 15th, 1919," he spat, looking around the tunnel. "Now answer my question. Where are my wife an..."

He cut himself off and banged his head with his big bony hands. "NGGGH! Leave me... get out of my mind!"

It was Mo'Lock's voice, but it didn't last seven words.

The gentleman came back, but the pompousness was gone. This time his face was dreamy, unaware of his surroundings. His eyes were welling with tears.

"Caroline dear, I promise you the automobile is perfectly safe, perfectly safe."

I stepped toward the weeping ghoul. "Mo'Lock, are you..."

The gentleman became unsettled as I approached. "My... my name is Michael Locke. Can't you see that I've killed my family?"

That was all I could take. I hauled off and let the ghoul have it right in the side of the head. He reeled backwards and I saw his face change. We stood there silent as Mo'Lock wiped the tears away from his face, studying them before wiping his hands on his pants.

"Thank you, Cal."

I looked at him a long moment. "Looks like you and I share something."

The ghoul nodded. "We always have."

Now I really wanted to kill whatever was at the end of the tunnel. I wanted it to suffer, suffer like it made us suffer. I knew the pain Mo'Lock carried was as great as my own and that was fuel, baby—fuel that would bring this evil down hard.

Just then I noticed the place on the wall where a chunk of clay had fallen after I'd hit it. The naked patch was about the size of a jar lid, a glistening moist whiteness beneath the surface of the clay. It reminded me of the flesh of a floater, a drowning victim that has been in the water for days.

I gave the patch a prod with my index finger. It was cold, soft and clammy and caved at my touch. A shudder ran through my body, echoed by a soft roll that seemed to travel through the ground beneath our feet. I realized then why it reminded me of the flesh of a drowned person. It was human skin.

And unlike a floater, it was alive.

CHAPTER

23

I KICKED THE DIRT AT MY FEET AND

revealed another fleshy white patch. We were so busy trying to get to the end of the tunnel that it never dawned on us that the thing we sought was the tunnel itself. At some point we had entered it and never knew.

It was time to make a move before whatever Cain had become tried to get in our heads again. The surrounding blubbery wall gave me an idea. It was time to get drastic. I shot a look at Mo'Lock.

"Let's fuck this thing up."

I tried not to think about the clammy flesh surrounding us. The idea that we might be inside some gigantic monstrosity was too disgusting to consider. I pushed the thought out of my mind by retrieving the pouch from my sock. I pulled out the needle, spoon, syringe, and last, but hardly least, the packet of chunky white power.

I created a little torch out of some debris, stuck it into the dirt and lit it. Then I put the chunk into the spoon and spit on it several times. The drugs and saliva cooked over the candle flame until they melted. I filled the needle, pushing the plunger to clear out the air bubbles. A major overdose was on the way.

Mo'Lock knelt down beside me. "Cal, are you sure you want to do this? Aren't the pills working?"

I grinned and gave the needle a little squirt. "Who said it was for me? Let me have the heart. I'm gonna try a little voodoo magic myself... with a twist of smack."

I pinned the heart to the dirt with my left hand. The muscle began beating harder, fighting me. The walls and floor began to shudder and rumble. The thing was getting jumpy.

I wasted no more time. I raised the needle in my right hand and jabbed it into the center of the heart, emptying all but a single hit of heroin into the pulsing muscle. Instantly the heart fluttered and beat hard, then settled down to a slow, steady pace.

A low moan echoed through the tunnel like a powerful generator grinding to a slow halt. The sound came from all sides, even from inside my head for a flash.

I took what was left of the smack, enough to overdose an elephant, and stabbed the fleshy patch on the wall. I didn't know how big the thing was, so I couldn't guess how long the drugs would last, but I definitely wanted to err on the side of safety. The bellowing moan sounded again, louder this time. When the floor rumbled violently, I left the needle dangling from the wall, grabbed the heart and Mo'Lock and ran for the end of the tunnel.

At the tunnel's mouth, zombies blocked the path. Their empty eye sockets panned back and forth, waiting for us to come at them.

The ghoul and I slowed, but we didn't stop. When the zombies saw that we weren't going to turn back, they scattered, clearing a path for us. They were all bluff and wouldn't risk a fight, since we were aware of their vulnerability.

We entered a massive room the size of an aircraft hanger, but more square than rectangle. The walls were parts of many things; red clay, hard rock, and stone. Protruding everywhere, ceiling to floor, was bone-white skin, throbbing and moist. We moved into the center of the room, surrounded by fires tended by zombies. They kept their distance, cowering and shielding the talismans around their necks with bony hands.

Behind me, Mo'Lock was staring in awe at the fleshy room. There was a tangible energy in here I was sure he felt. It made every tiny hair on my body stand on end.

Familiar symbols covered every exposed surface, while altars occupied the lower halves of three walls. One I recognized as a classic voodoo altar, covered with dried blood and melted candles, copper pots overflowing with chicken feet. Another appeared more satanic, with a Hand of Glory—the severed hand of a suicide victim—placed in front of a goat's head. The third was a clean white table combining the symbols of the Jewish, Christian, Hindu, and Muslim religions.

But the fourth wall was where I found what we'd been chasing all along, the source of perhaps a thousand deaths. A thing that had once been a nothing, a nobody. A little man who decided to take whatever he needed to invent his own world. He created a reality by pick-pocketing the beliefs of the world and using it to recreate himself as a monster that fed on brains, the very source of the soul. By doing so, he'd made his own world.

It was an unbelievable testament to the power of belief and the ugliness of egotism and hatred. Why is it when humans tap into tremendous power, the first instinct for most is to take, to destroy? Before me was just another example of someone who could have been special, the greatest intellect on earth, but instead used his power to shed blood and sow terror.

I stared at the face in the wall—the face *was* the wall. It was gnarled by rock and stone, stretched by its own voracious appetite. It looked stupefied by the heroin flowing through its massive system.

It was a face I knew and suspected, but one I still couldn't quite believe I was seeing again.

This was the reason I did what I did. This was a monster.

"Hello Cain. It's been a long time."

CHAPTER

24

STARING AT THE ABOMINATION, MY

mind raced back to the aftermath of our last confrontation. I'd stood watching them hose off the street, the gooey pink gripping the asphalt, desperately fighting to hold its ground. But the hoses won in the end, and bit by splattered slimy bit, the last remains of Edgar Cain were washed into the sewers.

Unfortunately, Cain had a back-up plan. His heart lived on in the deposit box, and as long as the heart lived, so did he. After that, he had all the time in the world to perfect the powers of his abnormal brain, using his own strange blend of religion and magic. Finally he could populate his lonely existence, and eventually reanimate his own splattered, defeated form.

I scanned the room and saw pink-white flesh protruding everywhere from clay and rock. How deep was this fucking head embedded in the earth? How many lives stolen in their sleep? And that terrible force...

I had to remind myself that if I killed Cain once, I could do it again. This time, there would be no coming back.

"I wouldn't phink pho loud if I were yoo, Detective."

The face was speaking. And it sounded as though the drugs were working. He was trashed.

"Okay, then I'll say it out loud. You're going down, Cain," I said. "You've done enough killing for one lifetime."

Cain's eyes blinked sluggishly. "I'ph kilt no one. I absorbed the lonely... the ill... the hopeleph." He blinked again and smacked his lips trying to shake the effects of the drugs.

Mo'Lock stepped up beside my right shoulder. "Actually, Mr. Cain, you did far worse than killing them. You stole their souls, their essence. You took what little chance many of these people had for eternal peace."

The face guffawed. "Nonsense! You know nophing!"

I stepped toward Cain's face. "It's over. Face it, you're done."

My confidence infuriated the giant head even more, but he was too wasted to fully react. "W...why you... Do you know what you are dealing with?! I am the second giant! I could bend and break you with a single thought! I am the single biggest intellect in all the world! "

It was time to act. I held the throbbing heart out so that the face could see it clearly. "Recognize this?"

Cain's eyes widened. "How did you f...find it?"

I stepped back. "Brown corduroy bell bottoms. The key in the wallet. I just followed the corduroy road."

Cain wasn't as upset as I would have thought, but there was still serious worry in his eyes. Then he squeezed his lids tightly shut, and for a moment a dull image flickered in my mind. Stephie again, bloody and begging for help. This time, the image quickly faded.

Cain coughed, blinked and clamped his eyes shut again.

This time there was a suggestion, a lame imitation of my inner voice telling me to shoot myself. I shook my head and flipped it off like a bronco throwing a quadriplegic.

I tapped my right foot and bobbled the heart hand to hand. "Are you finished?"

I threw the organ to the floor. It flopped once, rolled and came to rest underneath Cain's chin. Now it was my turn to do the glaring. I stared it right in the eyes and waited for its worry to turn to fear. To speed up the process, I took out both of my pistols, the six shot in my left and the 9mm in my right.

Cain snorted. "I'ph grown beyond my heart. Go ahead."

"We'll see."

Cain's eyes met mine. Now tears welled in the stretched corners. "Please... don't..."

I sneered. "Kiss my ass."

I went into my best Two Gun Kid imitation, firing both guns from the hip and making that beating heart dance.

Cain screamed with the sound of a thousand voices.

The heart blew apart into a splattered mess of tissue and goo, a hundred bloody chunks. I kept firing until there were a thousand, reloaded and shot until I had to reload again. The heart was a grease mark when I finished. A crimson smear.

While I reloaded, I noticed Mo'Lock going berserk.

He had smashed one altar and was on to the next, using a steel candle stand as a weapon. Hit by crushing hit, he was destroying everything in sight.

"...please, stop... please!" Cain pleaded to deaf ears.

He screamed and begged and howled for help that would never come. Or so I thought.

Because right then, I heard three clicking sounds behind me. Mo'Lock and I turned in unison, raising our hands as we swiveled. It was a reflex. You always reach for the sky when you have guns pointed at you.

At the mouth of the chamber stood Randy, Scott and Miriam—the Frankenteens. Each held a M-16, and they all wore a look of condescending "I-screwed-you" pleasure that made my stomach twist in a knot so hard it

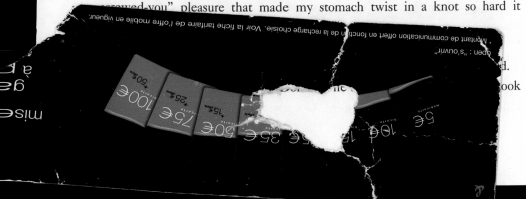

I glanced at the ghoul, utterly shocked at the sight of him. His eyes were wide, blazing. I'd seen him angry before, but this? This was different. It sent a chill down my spine.

I kept my hands raised. "I tried to help you kids. How was I supposed to know you were as messed up as Lazar." I pointed a thumb back towards Cain. "And I don't even want to know how you got hooked up with this loser!"

Randy twitched angrily and squeezed off a shot at my feet. Cain squealed. Randy shot again and this time he hit me right in the same goddamn spot he'd shot me the first time! I reeled back and screamed. It hurt like a bitch.

Scott and Miriam looked nervous.

"Mr. Cain contacted us," Scott said. "In our heads."

Miriam smacked Scott in the chest. "Shut up!"

Randy moved forward again.

"The next one goes through your head, McDonald!" He yelled and raised the M-16 as promised.

I didn't even see Mo'Lock take the gun out of the kid's hands. It was that fast. Then the ghoul stood over Randy, his face twisted in such a grotesque sculpture of rage that I hardly recognized him.

"You lied to me."

That was all he said before proceeding to dismember Randy limb from limb. He ripped the kid's arms from their sockets effortlessly. Skin tore with a rubbery snap and bones popped with a sickening crunch. In a matter of seconds, Randy was returned to the pile of miscellaneous organs and limbs he'd been in Dr. Polynice's Lab.

Then Mo'Lock turned to the other two.

They shot at him as he marched. He took the bullets right in the chest but kept on advancing steadily. After they'd been disarmed he tore them apart as he had their leader, without making a single sound. It was the most terrifying thing I'd ever witnessed in my life, and I've seen quite a lot, thank you. I was never happier to count Mo'Lock as a friend. Plus, I learned an invaluable lesson—never lie to a ghoul.

When he was finished, arms and legs were scattered all over the chamber floor. I could see Mo'Lock took no pleasure in what he'd done. Regardless, I gave him a nod. He paused and returned the gesture.

I looked up to Cain triumphantly. "Got anything else?"

Cain smirked, and the chamber began to rock.

Mo'Lock and I stood in place, dumbfounded. We were out of options. The heart was obliterated, but Edgar Cain still lived. He'd actually become powerful enough to do without his heart. Cain's eyes glowed with renewed malevolence as his wide lips parted and he spoke the words that were running through my mind.

"You are so screwed."

The walls shook, throbbing as the heart once had. Clay and stone loosened and crumbled, crashing down around our heads.

I rolled away from the falling debris, reloading the 9mm and revolver as I moved. I tossed a gun to Mo'Lock who just stared at it.

"What am I supposed to do with this?" A gigantic wedge of damp red clay landed at his side. He didn't even flinch.

"Just shoot!"

Cain's eyes spun in his head. "No!"

I raised my gun into the air and fired once. Above us the fleshy surface burst open as the slug impacted, and gooey pink matter spat out in violent, gushing bursts. I looked at Mo'Lock and he gave me an affirmative nod. We'd get out of this mess yet.

"Looks like this baby's about to blow," I said. "What say we help it along?"

Cain began screaming again, trying anything to distract me. When I felt him pulling at my brain, I shook my head, leveled the 9mm at his distended face and fired twice. The skin parted slightly where the bullet struck, but there was no blood.

Nothing.

But deep inside the head, the pressure was building, pushing at the small hole until it split and ripped lengthwise. Before I could react, a geyser of snotty pink goo shot across my face.

I dove, rolled to one knee and picked up one of the Frankenteens' M-16's, unleashing a blaze of automatic fire into the right wall. Behind me, the ghoul was shooting in dangerously random directions. Each shot brought forth a gusher of crude pink brain matter. The fleshy walls rumbled and shook, percolating like bags of boiling tar. And then the smell wafted into my nostrils. I gagged, my stomach lurching. The stench was worse than death, hot and thick, and impossible to ignore.

Cain was finally silent.

His forehead spit pink and gray, his eyes teared and saliva-soaked lips blubbered uncontrollably. I almost felt sorry for him. Almost, but not quite.

Mo'Lock and I met in the center of the room, dodging falling slabs of clay and rock. A growing roar rumbled ominously inside. On the ceiling and walls, tiny geysers of matter tore at the small holes, enlarging them.

I looked down at my feet and saw we were already ankle deep in fetid soup. Edgar Cain's eyes were closed, but tears ran freely through closed lids.

"Cain," I said. My tone was soft, almost a whisper.

The face opened its eyes.

I leveled the M-16, point blank, between his eyes. "In your next life, get out of the house more often."

I emptied the clip into his face, killing him once and for all. Unfortunately I also opened the brain matter floodgates. The gunk had now risen to our knees, and all around us the flesh walls were stretched to breaking. The evil was finally dead, but so were Mo'Lock and me if we didn't make tracks quickly.

Mo'Lock looked at me. "Got a plan?"

I nodded. "Run."

CHAPTER

25

RUNNING KNEE-DEEP IN THE THICK,

ever-increasing brain matter proved easier said than done. I could hardly move, let alone raise my legs above the slop. At least Mo'Lock had a height advantage. He used it to jump free of the current and gain about a half yard each time. I had to push my way through, which considering the shape I was in was no simple task.

By the time he reached the tunnel, I was still several yards behind. The head pudding was now waist high and the walls and ceiling threatened to burst. If it cut loose before I got to Mo'Lock, I'd had it for sure.

Lucky for me, the ghoul's loyalty was stronger than his own sense of self-preservation. When he saw I was having a hard time, he cut through the flowing gunk with relative ease, grabbed my wrist and headed back to the exit. The fact that he was dragging an extra hundred and ninety pounds with him had little effect on the ghoul.

Just as we reached the exit, the far wall split with a thunderous tear. A tidal wave of brain rushed into the room. Steam rolled off the bubbling surface, producing a new eye-searing wave of stench. It was like a slaughter house in August filled with rotten eggs, bad cottage cheese and just a hint of old foot. Mo'Lock gagged. I tried to draw air through my mouth, but it was little help.

At the exit, the streaming brains were causing a nasty undercurrent. One moment Mo'Lock and I were gripping the walls of the tunnel, the next we were swept away, riding the wild pink gunk. Behind us, I heard another flesh wall swell and burst, and the speed of the rapids pulled us along even faster. I tried to grab hold of the walls, but it was hopeless. We were moving too fast and it took all my energy to keep my head above the torrent. I figured the tunnel would fill and either rake our heads along the ceiling or simply drown us. Either way, it was looking mighty grim.

The surface in front of me bubbled, foamed, and broke. Stinking pink muck spattered, blinding me momentarily. When I managed to clear my vision, Mo'Lock was right in front of me, his sight seemingly unaffected by the fumes. He must have swam backward to find me. He threw his long arm around my neck, pulled me close and helped me stay above the current.

"Hang on!" the ghoul yelled.

"I'm trying!" I screamed back, "But I think I left my Palm Pilot back there!"

"Shut up and save your breath, Cal!"

We were traveling through the tunnel at three times the rate we had walked in. It was difficult to tell where we were, save for the fact there was now little more than a foot and a half of air separating us from the jagged ceiling. The thick current tugged and pulled at our legs, slamming us side to side against the tunnel walls. Mo'Lock did his best to hold onto me, but the constant pounding made the task next to impossible.

Twice he lost me, only to grab me again. The second time, I went under and got a mouthful of grotesque, gelatinous head pudding. I choked and almost swallowed. I thought I'd drown in the crap for sure, but somehow I forced the slime from my mouth, shut my eyes tight and held my breath. I thought I'd try to ride it out, hold on until the tunnel ended at Whitney Green. Maybe there the pink sludge would spill into the burnt foundation of the building and I would find air.

Then I felt a hand grabbing at my hair, followed by a painful yank that removed several clumps of hair. I gasped and gulped greedily—fresh air. Mo'Lock had pulled me to the surface. I spat and choked, trying to clear my eyes and ears.

"Cal!" The voice screamed.

It was Blout just ahead of us, sounding closer by the second.

I screamed. "Blout! Over here!"

"Up ahead, Cal! My hand! My hand! Can you see it?!"

I tried to focus through one eye. Ahead was the point where we fell into the tunnel. I could just make out a dark object swinging back and forth from the ceiling.

"See it?" Mo'Lock yelled at my ear.

"I think so." I blinked my eyes hard. The slime was stubborn and sticky. Finally I was able to make out the fuzzy outline of Blout's hand hanging down just yards from me and closing fast. "I see it!"

There was another surge of brains. We were thrown against the left wall of the tunnel and a second swell almost scraped our heads against the ceiling. Mo'Lock pulled me closer, then moved his hand to the back of my shirt and held on like a mother cat holds a kitten's scruff. I could see Blout's hand dangling from an unseen ledge.

Mo'Lock strained to hold me further above the pink and gray rapids. "Grab hold , Cal! Grab hold of his hand!"

Blout was screaming as well. He couldn't see us, so he had no idea I was about to hit. I hoped the sudden jolt didn't drag him over the edge.

"I'm here!" I warned. I saw his fingers flex and spread wide, ready to grab hold.

Another second, another swell of brain and our hands met. Blout had me. But Mo'Lock was slipping. I reached with my free hand, grabbed for his suit coat and got it, but the rapids threw and twisted him and the collar tore.

"Mo'Lock!" I cried out, dangling in the air.

Blout pulled me out of the torrent. As I hit dry ground I got a glimpse of Mo'Lock being taken away by the rapids. He flailed his arms and yelled something I couldn't make out. Then he was gone.

CHAPTER

26

I WAS ON SOLID GROUND. I ROSE TO

my knees and pounded my fist on the dirt. "Damn!"

Blout was right there beside me. "Christ, are you all right?"

I felt his hand on my shoulder, and swung my head around to face the big man. I was pumped. I must have looked like a rabid dog, but this thing wasn't over. I had to stay pumped or I'd drop like a rag doll.

Blout's slacks were wet from the knees down. He'd gotten himself out before the tunnel filled.

"How'd you get up here?"

He shook his head. "I didn't. I found a manhole back a ways. I climbed out there, doubled back and came here," he said, impressed with himself. "What the hell happened down there?"

"You don't want to know, trust me," I said. "But Cain's dead."

Blout jumped. "You sure this time?"

I nodded and started walking away. "It ain't over yet. We've got to get to Whitney Green." I stopped, and turned. "Did you get the heads?"

Blout shuddered visibly, but nodded. "I left them at the entrance."

"Thanks. You're a pal."

Outside the tunnel I picked up the heads. Blout had wrapped them in his jacket, and they were pleased to hear the danger had passed. I told them what had happened and they were as anxious as I was to rescue Mo'Lock.

"Mo'Lock's as tough as they come," said the head called Tyus. "I'm sure he's fine."

I wasn't so sure, but agreed anyway.

Blout stood by, watching me converse with the two disembodied heads with an air of absolute disgust. Then he went to his car to radio for backup. I heard him mention Whitney Green. I didn't like it. I had to get there before any cops did.

I ran to the road. Cars were whizzing by in pre-rush hour panic. I tucked the bundled heads under my left arm, and with my right waved to passing taxis. Blout was yelling as a cab screeched to a halt. I ignored him. I opened the back door of the cab and tossed in the bundle as Blout ran towards me.

I waved him off. "Wait for the backup. Meet me at the Green."

The driver was a ghoul as I'd hoped, so I explained the situation to him. He knew Mo'Lock and understood the immediacy of the dilemma. He burned rubber and we headed toward Whitney Green at seventy miles an hour. I introduced the heads as I unwrapped them, but the driver already knew 'em. Cozy community.

Ten minutes later we came to a screeching halt just outside the entrance of Whitney Green. I shot out of the cab without paying, leaving the severed heads behind. The driver agreed to take care of them. I didn't know exactly what that meant, but then again I didn't care.

"Just save Mo'Lock," he told me. "That would be payment enough."

I sprinted to the edge of the burnt pit that was once Cain's home. Now it was a huge hole, bubbling and foaming with slimy, surging brain matter. It spread out before me like a lake of frothy, stinking pulp. I scanned the surface for any sign of movement among the floating debris. There was nothing.

A horrible sinking feeling began to well in my gut. I felt panicky. Where the fuck was Mo'Lock?!

I could hear sirens wailing in the distance and closing fast. When the cops saw this, they'd do their best to cover it up, meaning I sure as shit didn't want to be there. I got panicky. Pacing the edge of the hole, I cupped my hands and began to yell.

"MOOOO'LOCK!" I hollered and repeated even louder, "MOOO'LOCK!"

From the shadows somewhere behind me, a figure shifted. "I'm not deaf, you know. I'm right here."

I spun on my heels. Mo'Lock stepped from the shadows, dripping pink slime.

I ran over to him, grabbed him by the shoulders, and shook him. "You crazy fucking ghoul! You scared the crap out of me!"

Mo'Lock smiled.

"Don't get the wrong idea, gruesome." I could feel the adrenaline fading quickly and all the pain beginning to return. "I just need someone to get me to the hospital."

CHAPTER

27

I DREAMT ABOUT TERRIBLE PAIN

shooting through my ass, and being chased by rolling dumpsters overflowing with decapitated heads. After that, I woke in a hospital room bandaged from head to toe. The blinds were closed and the room was dark. I could see my arm was in a support, dangling above my bandaged torso. Beside me I heard beeping apparatus that I suspected did little more than raise the per day rate.

My head was wrapped in bandages and gauze so thick that I could hardly lift it to see whether I was alone. I used every ounce of strength to raise my head off the pillow and was rewarded with the sight of a lumpy figure slumped in a chair next to the window. It was Blout, fast asleep.

With a great deal of effort I got my hand on the bed pan so comfortably rammed under my ass. I dragged it out to the edge of the bed where I let it fall to the ground. There was huge clanging noise. Blout shot to his feet, reaching frantically for his holster. I had just enough energy to chuckle. Then I passed out again. This time I dreamt of nothing, and that was fine by me.

I woke later and found Blout still in the room with me. He was asleep again, but now light seeped in at the corners of the closed shades. I dragged my head to the edge of the mattress and saw a mountain of crumbled fast-food bags and crushed coffee cups on the floor.

Christ. How long had I been out?

"Who do you have to fuck to get a drink around here?"

Blout stirred. When he stood I could see that he had a large, square bandage on the left side of his forehead. A spotty blotch of dried brown blood showed through. His hands were wrapped with bandages, but in a way that gave most of his fingers freedom to move.

"You ain't fucking me no more this week. I've had enough."

His face was stone. I waited for the explosion. Instead I got a big toothy grin.

"Welcome back, asshead." He slapped my leg. It hurt. "You had us scared for a while there. You know they had to pump your damn stomach?"

Then the big guy reached into his overcoat and pulled a small stuffed rabbit that had a "Get Well Soon" sign. "Here, I bought you this fuckin' bunny."

The bunny landed next to me, rolled and fell on its cute little face. I tried to sit up, but quit after a brief and futile attempt. "How long was I out?"

"I think it's a record for you. Almost four days. Today is the fourth day, but it's early."

"Damn." I was impressed. "Everything turn out okay?"

"Yeah, it seems there was some kind of weird spill at the burned out Whitney Green apartments. I called out the Hazmat crew and they gathered what they could, destroyed what they gathered and burned what was left in the pit." Blout had a big grin plastered across his face.

I snickered and felt my ribs throb. "What about the media?"

Blout laughed again. "You kidding? Chemical spills are the one thing that keeps their asses out of our business. Nobody knows nothing about nothing."

"But you're keeping the file open?"

"Damn right. I'm not about to report the case closed. I am not going to put myself in a situation where I have to explain what happened down there." He was shaking his head.

I grinned and pulled my arm out of the sling, trying again to sit up. This time Blout helped me and I made it. "What's the matter, Blout? Afraid nobody will believe you?"

"Exactly. I'll leave that crap to you."

I nodded. We both ran out of witty banter, and fell quiet. It was a little uncomfortable.

"It's over, isn't it, Cal?" Blout said, low and quiet.

I nodded. "Definitely."

"You're sure this time?"

I glared. "Absolutely."

Blout stuck his big hand out in front of my face. "That was real good work you did. Thank you."

I took his hand and shook it. There would have been another awkward silence, but the door was pushed opened by a scurrying male nurse, followed by the doctor. A heartbeat later, Mo'Lock lumbered in wearing a spiffy new suit.

Blout shot a look at the ghoul, then quickly back to me. "I've got to get going," he said and shook my hand again. "I'll check back before they let you go."

I thought Blout would go to great lengths to avoid Mo'Lock, but as he passed by the ghoul he gave him a slap on the shoulder.

Mo'Lock waited patiently while the doctor and nurse checked me out. When they had gone, he made sure the door was shut. He turned and tossed me a little stuffed rabbit much like the one Blout had given me.

"All my friends are comedians," I said.

Mo'Lock smiled. "Pull its head off."

"What?"

"Pull the head off."

I gave the bunny head a twist and pull. It came off with a pop, exposing the neck of a half pint of good stinky hooch. I grinned and looked up at the ghoul. "God bless you."

"I figured you'd have a bad case of the DT's when you woke up."

"Naw, they've got me pretty pumped full of juice. I don't feel a thing."

The ghoul stepped around to the foot of the bed and lifted my chart off the hook, scanning it with big, dead eyes. After a second, he let out a long whistle. "Four hundred stitches. That a record?"

"Yeah, I'm breaking them left and right. Where's my goddamn trophy? So what's been going on while I was in la-la land?"

The ghoul touched his hand to his chin. "Surprisingly quiet, really. The lawyer for the man who was suing you left a message with a new court date. I wrote it down."

"Great. Enjoying my apartment?"

"Yes, thank you. Landlord stopped by. He said he wants you to pay for the front door. He left a bill. The insurance co..."

I waved him off. "Okay, okay. What about work. I need some cash—a lot of cash—and I need it yesterday."

Mo'Lock stood at the foot of the bed staring at me for a moment, as if he was deciding whether or not he should tell me anything that might get me excited. Then he took out a small spiral memo book, flipped it open and began to read.

"We got a call this morning from..."

"We?"

"You got a call from a woman named Veronica Vanderbilt."

"As in the 'we-got-more-money-than-anyone-in-the-world' Vanderbilts?"

"The one and only." The ghoul went on. "She sounded very scared and would like you to come to the house as soon as possible."

I was feeling better by the second. "What's the skinny?"

"She has a teenage son who is acting very strange. Sleeps all day and stays out all night."

I shrugged. "Sounds like a teenager to me."

"This morning she said she found something in the boy's closet that alarmed her. She didn't want to call the police. She was too embarrassed, so she called you."

"What was in the closet?" I rolled my eyes, pretending I didn't see the answer coming up Main Street.

Together we said, "A coffin."

I nodded. "What'd you say my... our rate was?"

Mo'Lock grinned. "A grand a day plus expenses."

"Sounds good. Now help me out of this fucking bed." I tipped the headless bunny into my mouth and emptied it, then got shakily to my feet. There was no time to waste. We had a new case.

THE END

ACKNOWLEDGEMENTS

Special thanks to the following:

Ted Adams, John Lawrence, Ashley Wood,
Brian Holguin, Beau Smith, Robbie Robbins,
Kris (the slasher!) Oprisko, Terry Fitzgerald,
Mason Novick, Clive Barker, Jon Snider,
Don Murphy, Brad Gould, Brent Ashe,
Emek, Paul Lee, Mark, Dante and Geoff,
Ann Chervinsky, and my entire family.

Without their help, support and friendship
this book would have not been possible.

–Steve Niles

BIOGRAPHIES

STEVE NILES is the current writer of the monthly comic book HELLSPAWN and a new Image Comics series entitled FUSED! He has also contributed to several issues of SPAWN, SAM & TWITCH, and is co-writer with Todd McFarlane on the upcoming SPAWN 2 movie. Steve began his career by founding his own publishing company, Arcane Comix, where he published, edited and adapted comics and anthologies for Eclipse Comics. His adaptations include works by Clive Barker, Richard Matheson and Harlan Ellison. He has also written for Dark Horse Comics, contributing to titles such as DARK HORSE PRESENTS and 9-11: ARTISTS RESPOND.

Steve's latest project is the upcoming comic series 30 DAYS OF NIGHT from IDW Publishing.

Originally from Washington DC, Steve now resides in Los Angeles with his wife Nikki and their two black cats.

ASHLEY WOOD was born in Australia in 1971. An award-winning artist and commercial illustrator, his art is published worldwide on a monthly basis and he has participated in both joint and solo fine art exhibitions.

A Spectrum Award winner, he has also worked on numerous television and movie projects.

His work can be seen quarterly in the pages of IDW Publishing's POPBOT. IDW is also the publisher of Wood's first art book UNO FANTA: THE ART OF ASHLEY WOOD and the upcoming DOS FANTAS. Ash's first children's book IMPOSIBUS RHINOCEROS, GIRAFFE, AND GNU is written by T. Paula Louise.

POPBOT ONE

FROM THE PAGES OF UNO FANTA >> A NEW SEMI REGULAR SERIES
written and illustrated by ASHLEY WOOD

POPBOT number one

by ashley wood | IDW PUBLISHING | 2002

COMIC
ARTBOOK
CHICKEN SLICE

8.5X11> PERFECT BOUND> DUO TONE> 48 PAGES>
SEXY ROBOTS> BIG ROBOTS> SPINDLY ROBOTS> CATS> WARHOL> MORE

MATURE READERS

POPBOT BOOK TWO ON SALE APRIL 2002

UNO FANTA the art of ASHLEY WOOD
>>96 PAGES-FULL COLOR-HARDBOUND-W/DUST JACKET<<

N A M E >_____

ADDRESS>_____

C I T Y >_____

S T A T E >_____ Z I P_____

P H O N E >_____

E M A I L >_____

Send orders to:
IDEA + DESIGN WORK, LLC
ATTN: UNO FANTA - DEPT SM
2645 FINANCIAL COURT, STE E
SAN DIEGO, CA 92117

Allow 2 Weeks for Delivery - U.S. Orders.
Longer for International Orders.

Uno Fanta ™ and © 2002 Ashley Wood.
All Rights Reserved.

I T E M	QTY	PRICE	T O T A L
UNO FANTA **STANDARD EDITION**		$29.99	
UNO FANTA **LIMITED EDITION** with **ORIGINAL SKETCH**		$100.00	
SHIPPING: $5.00 for the first book, ADD $1.00 for each additional book. INTERNATIONAL orders: $15 for first book, ADD $5 for each additional book.		TOTAL	
		SHIPPING	
CA TAX (for books shipped to California addresses): 7.75% of total of books and shipping		CA TAX	
U.S. MONEY ORDERS ONLY **NO CHECKS ACCEPTED**		**TOTAL ENCLOSED**	

TO PAY w/VISA or MASTERCARD VISIT WWW.**IDW**PUBLISHING.COM

CARDINAL SINS

The card-play exploits of the monks at St Titus have a special place in bridge literature and their fame has now spread round the world. This collection of highly entertaining and absorbing stories from the monastery (where an ex-bookmaker friar makes a killing) includes a further hilarious interlude with the missionary monks and the celebrated bridge-playing parrot in the Bozwambi jungle. For good measure there is also a brief diversion to Medieval Nottingham where Robin Hood, Friar Tuck and a witch succeed in … it would be a Cardinal Sin to spoil your fun. You have no option but to find out for yourself.

'The fourth volume sees the authors at their best, wickedly funny . . . The principal feature that makes Reese's and Bird's efforts stand apart, more even than the entertainment factor, is the fact that the hands they use are of genuine interest.'

– Bridge Magazine

Humorous bridge fiction in the

MASTER BRIDGE SERIES

by Terence Reese & David Bird

MIRACLES OF CARD PLAY

UNHOLY TRICKS
More Miraculous Card Play

DOUBLED AND VENERABLE
Further Miracles of Card Play

CARDINAL SINS

***

by David Bird

THE ABBOT'S GREAT SACRIFICE

THE ABBOT AND THE SENSATIONAL SQUEEZE

HEAVENLY CONTRACTS

CELESTIAL CARDPLAY

ALL HANDS ON DECK!

BRIDGE OVER TROUBLED WATERS

***

by David Bird & Ron Klinger

KOSHER BRIDGE

THE RABBI'S MAGIC TRICK

CARDINAL
SINS

Terence Reese
&
David Bird

Weidenfeld & Nicolson
IN ASSOCIATION WITH
PETER CRAWLEY

First published in Great Britain 1991
in association with Peter Crawley
by Victor Gollancz
First paperback edition published 1996
Second impression 2000

This edition published 2011
in association with Peter Crawley
by Weidenfeld & Nicolson
a division of the Orion Publishing Group Ltd
Orion House, 5 Upper Saint Martin's Lane,
London WC2H 9EA

An Hachette UK Company

10 9 8 7 6 5 4 3 2 1

A catalogue record for this book
is available from the British Library

ISBN 978 0 297 86443 1

Printed and bound in Great Britain by
CPI Mackays, Chatham, ME5 8TD

The Orion Publishing Group's policy is to use papers that
are natural, renewable and recyclable products and made
from wood grown in sustainable forests. The logging and
manufacturing processes are expected to conform to the
environmental regulations of the country of origin.

www.orionbooks.co.uk

Contents

PART I

At the Monastery of St Titus

1

The Abbot's Forecast

"It's such a beautiful evening we might as well walk to the match tonight," said Brother Xavier. "It's only a twenty-minute walk to Hursley Village."

"I'll see you there, then," replied the Abbot, feeling for his car keys. "Knowing my luck, there'll be a gale blowing by the time the match is through."

The match, a local league encounter, was played at the thatched cottage of Mrs Port-Binding. This hand, early in the first set, led to interesting play at both tables.

Love all, dealer West

```
              ♠ 8 2
              ♡ J 9 8 2
              ♢ J 6 5 2
              ♣ 7 4 3
♠ A 9 3                      ♠ Q J 10 7 6 4
♡ 6 5          N             ♡ 10
♢ 10 7 4    W     E          ♢ K 9 3
♣ K Q J 9 2    S             ♣ 10 8 5
              ♠ K 5
              ♡ A K Q 7 4 3
              ♢ A Q 8
              ♣ A 6
```

West	North	East	South
The	Mrs	Brother	Mrs
Abbot	Stott	Xavier	P-Binding
No	No	No	2♣
No	2♢	No	2♡
No	3♡	No	4♡
End			

[7]

The two ladies bid to four hearts and it was the Abbot to lead. "Three hearts shows good values, does it?" he enquired.

"Well, she can't have that much," replied Mrs Port-Binding, laughing. "She would have gone to game with a good hand, wouldn't she?"

The Abbot blinked. "You don't play that three hearts is stronger than four?" he persisted.

"No, we're playing simple stuff, straightforward Acol," came the reply. "A raise to three is a limit bid."

Giving up the struggle, the Abbot led ♣ K. Mrs Stott laid out her dummy, headed by the two red jacks.

"Yes, nicely bid, Winifred," said Mrs Port-Binding. "Small, please."

With a studious air Mrs Port-Binding ducked the opening lead and won the club continuation with the ace. After peering at dummy for a few seconds, she drew trumps with the ace and jack. She then played a diamond towards her hand, finessing the 8.

The Abbot won with the 10 and exited with a third round of clubs, ruffed by declarer. Mrs Port-Binding now crossed to ♡ 9 and finessed ◇ Q successfully. Both defenders followed to ◇ A, so the contract was home. Mrs Port-Binding crossed to dummy's last trump and discarded a spade on the established ◇ J.

"Yes, my two jacks worked hard for you," observed the elderly Mrs Stott. "Well played."

"I was reading about that type of situation only last week," replied Mrs Port-Binding. "Some ancient book I found in the loft. 'The Experienced Game' I think it's called."

The Abbot raised his eyebrows. "May I enquire which particular learned point you had in mind?" he said.

Mrs Port-Binding was more than happy to explain. "Well, the contract was only in danger if you had ♠ A," she said. "Are you with me so far?"

The Abbot, wincing slightly, nodded his head.

"So, I made the assumption that you held that card," continued Mrs Port-Binding, peering over her spectacles. "And since you hadn't been able to open the bidding, that marked your partner with ◇ K. All I had to do was to duck the first diamond into the safe hand."

"Ah, into the safe hand," said Mrs Stott, reaching for the next board. "Very good. I think I've read something along those lines myself."

The Abbot felt there must be a flaw in Mrs Port-Binding's analysis. "But you might have lost two diamond tricks the way you played it," he said. "Then you'd have gone down even when ♠ A was well placed."

Mrs Port-Binding smiled at the Abbot and patted him on the hand. "But you're forgetting that ◇ K was *bound* to be onside," she said. "I'll lend you the book afterwards if you like. I have it upstairs."

The board was soon passed to the other room, where Lucius and Paulo were playing Mr Carver, a retired tax inspector, and his wife. This was their auction:

West	North	East	South
Mr	Brother	Mrs	Brother
Carver	Paulo	Carver	Lucius
No	No	2♠	3 NT
4♠	No	No	Dble
End			

Brother Lucius led ♡ A against four spades doubled, North signalling with the 9 and declarer playing the 10. It seemed unlikely that the strait-laced declarer would be up to a false card of the 10 from J 10 x, so Brother Lucius was inclined to place her with a singleton heart. In that case two tricks would almost certainly be needed in diamonds. The opening bid marked declarer with the king, but it was possible that Paulo had the jack.

At trick two Brother Lucius switched to ◇ A, followed by the queen. Declarer won with the king and picked up the trumps successfully. When ♣ A was forced out, though, the defenders were able to cash a second trick in diamonds. Four spades doubled was one down.

"We would have made 3 NT, I think," observed Brother Paulo. "No doubt they would lead clubs, but you can reach my hand in hearts to take the diamond finesse."

"True," replied Brother Lucius. "Four hearts our way is an interesting contract. It seems you can make it by leading ◇ J from dummy. That's covered by the king and ace, then you can lead a second round from dummy, ducking the trick to West."

Mr Carver smiled at his wife. "I'm not sure the girls will be up to a play like that," he said.

At the tea interval the monastery team found themselves unexpectedly adrift by 2 IMPs.

"What a feeble effort," declared the Abbot. "We should beat a team like this by at least 3 IMPs a board. They haven't the first idea about the game."

"Any more tea for anyone?" called Mrs Port-Binding, poking her head around the door.

The second half had not been long under way when at adverse vulnerability Mr Carver picked up this splendid hand:

♠ A 9 8 6 4   ♡ A K Q 10   ◇ A K Q J   ♣ —

Brother Lucius, on his left, passed. Mrs Carver passed and Brother Paulo opened one spade in the third seat.

Mr Carver stole a glance at Brother Paulo – the sort of look he would give a suspicious tax return. "*Two* spades," he said.

Brother Lucius passed and Mrs Carver studied her hand intently. These were her cards:

♠ 7 5 2   ♡ J 9   ◇ 7 3   ♣ A K J 8 5 3

Facing a cue bid, her hand was enormous. Horace would never forgive her if she didn't show some signs of life. "Five clubs," she said.

Mr Carver could not believe it. Two spades was forcing to game. What in heaven's name was Evelyn up to, jumping to the five level like that? "Five diamonds," he said, in a tone he had used in court on certain occasions.

"Six clubs," said Mrs Carver brightly.

"Six diamonds," persisted Mr Carver. Hands such as his arrived once in a blue moon. He had no intention of letting Evelyn waste it in some fatuous club contract.

Six diamonds was passed out. This was the complete deal:

North-South game, dealer West

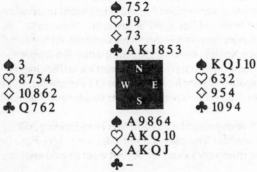

```
                ♠ 752
                ♡ J9
                ◇ 73
                ♣ AKJ853
  ♠ 3                        ♠ KQJ10
  ♡ 8754          N          ♡ 632
  ◇ 10862      W     E       ◇ 954
  ♣ Q762          S          ♣ 1094
                ♠ A9864
                ♡ AKQ10
                ◇ AKQJ
                ♣ —
```

The Abbot's Forecast

West	North	East	South
Brother	Mrs	Brother	Mr
Lucius	Carver	Paulo	Carver
No	No	1♠	2♠
No	5♣	No	5♦
No	6♣	No	6♦
End			

Brother Lucius led his singleton spade to the 10 and ace. Mr Carver inspected the dummy with a dazed expression. One small chance of a making the slam was to drop ♣Q doubleton. It seemed that the only other possibility was to endplay West. If West held exactly three clubs to the queen it might be possible to throw him in with the third round of clubs.

Mr Carver decided that this was the better chance. He drew trumps in four rounds, then crossed to dummy by overtaking ♡ 10 with the jack. He then cashed the ace and king of clubs, discarding two heart winners from hand. His original intention had been to exit with a low club now, discarding his remaining heart honour. The appearance of East's ♣9 changed his mind. "Jack of clubs, please," he said.

The ♣J drew East's 10 and Mr Carter discarded his last heart. Brother Lucius won the trick with the club queen and had to surrender the remaining tricks to the dummy. Amazingly, the slam was home.

Brother Paulo recognised a well played hand when he saw one. "Bravo, indeed!" he exclaimed. "My little joke in the bidding has exploded on ourselves, it seems."

Mr Carver, flushed with success, returned his cards to the wallet. "It was a fortunate lie of the cards," he said.

When the hand was replayed in the other room there were three passes round to the Abbot in the South seat. "Two clubs," he said.

Brother Xavier responded three clubs and the Abbot rebid three spades. When Xavier raised this to four spades, the Abbot thumbed through his cards uncertainly. Was he worth a further move? There was no law against Xavier having K x x or Q J x in spades, was there? "Five spades," he said, expecting Xavier to advance if he held good trumps.

Brother Xavier passed hastily and Mrs Port-Binding, sitting East, ventured a double. The play did not take long. Mrs Port-Binding scored three trump tricks and the Abbot went one down, conceding 200.

"Thank you for the double, partner," said Mrs Stott, updating her scorecard.

"We won't gain much on that one," observed Brother Xavier. "It looks as if one of us should have gone to 5 NT."

The monastery players were soon engaged in comparing scores for the final time.

"Minus 200," announced the Abbot when the critical board was reached. "One off doubled in five spades. Xavier gave me a positive. I could hardly let the bidding die in four spades on my giant hand."

"Yes, well, in our room we bid the spades first," said Brother Lucius. "Paulo opened one spade on a six-count!"

The Abbot gave an irritated shake of the head. "So now they kept low, I suppose," he grunted. "How very ill-timed."

"It had the opposite effect, actually," continued Brother Lucius. "It jockeyed them into six diamonds on a 4–2 fit."

"Really?" exclaimed the Abbot. "Thank goodness for that. Perhaps it wasn't such a bad effort, being in the third seat. Yes, I think I might have opened one spade myself."

"Six diamonds was cold, unfortunately," said Brother Lucius. "1370 away."

The door opened and in came Mrs Port-Binding, followed by her victorious team. "Eight IMPs to us, do you make it?" she chirped.

Mrs Port-Binding's arithmetic proved correct. After a few muttered words of congratulation the monastery team accompanied their hostess into the hall. "It was a thoroughly enjoyable match, Abbot," she said. "Now, are you sure you don't want to borrow that book? It's no trouble for me to get it for you." She opened the front door of her cottage. "Good gracious!" she said. "It's pouring with rain."

The Abbot reached for his car keys. "It would surprise me if it wasn't," he replied.

Brother Lucius is Outgunned

This year the St Francis of Assisi Swiss Teams was to be held at St
Titus. Some thirty-six monastic establishments had announced their
intention of entering and a notice pinned to the inner door of
Brother Lucius's cell offered the following odds:

St Titus	7/2
St Hilda's Convent	5
Bagshot Friary	7
Corpus Christi	10
St Michael the Divine	100/8
B'hood of the Five Wounds	14
20/1 BAR	
One quarter odds a place 1-2-3	
Rule 13 applies on any non-show	

The great day soon arrived and in the first round St Titus were
drawn against supposedly weak opposition from the Edgeworth
Friary in Sussex. This was an early hand:

Love all, dealer West

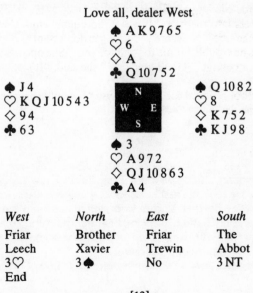

West	North	East	South
Friar	Brother	Friar	The
Leech	Xavier	Trewin	Abbot
3♡	3♠	No	3 NT
End			

Friar Leech led ♡ K against 3 NT and the Abbot viewed the dummy with little enthusiasm. He could doubtless shut West out of the play, but the lack of communications still made nine tricks a distant prospect.

Suddenly the Abbot spotted a chance. He allowed West's ♡ K to hold, contributing the 9 from hand. When West continued with another heart, the Abbot pointed a nonchalant finger at dummy's ♢ A.

"The diamond?" queried Brother Xavier.

"Unless my finger has developed a crook in it," retorted the Abbot.

Winning the trick in hand, the Abbot played ♢ Q. East won with the king and returned another diamond. The Abbot had no intention of finessing the 8 and risking a torrent of hearts. He faced his ♢ J and gave a satisfied grunt when the 9 showed on his left.

The run of the diamonds reduced East to five cards in the black suits but the Abbot took no risks in the end position, settling for the nine tricks that were on view.

Friar Leech turned towards the Abbot. "I thought you'd made a careless mistake there," he said. "But it seemed to work out quite well, throwing that ace away."

Friar Trewin, a tall thin man with a prominent Adam's apple, caught his partner's attention. "I was rather hoping that you would switch to a club at trick two," he said.

"I dare say you were," replied his partner, "but you played the 8 of hearts. I took it as a come-on."

The board was soon replayed at the other table. As might have been expected, the auction was identical:

West	North	East	South
Brother	Friar	Brother	Friar
Paulo	Fewkes	Lucius	Tackett
3♡	3♠	No	3 NT
End			

Once more ♡ K was led against 3 NT. Since West was marked with seven hearts, the pale-faced Friar Tackett saw no point in holding up. He took the first heart trick, then played ace, king and another spade. Brother Lucius won with the 10 and paused to consider his continuation. It seemed natural to return a diamond, but a further spade throw-in would follow and he would then have to concede ground in one or other minor.

Brother Lucius gave an almost imperceptible nod of the head as

[14]

the winning defence occurred to him. Yes, so long as declarer could be kept from his assets in diamonds there would surely be five tricks for the defence – two spades, two clubs and the diamond king. At trick five Brother Lucius made the apparently surprising play of cashing his remaining spade guard. Only then did he exit with a diamond to the ace.

Friar Tackett cashed dummy's two spade winners, then played a club to the ace. The ◇ Q followed, won by East's king. Brother Lucius's last three cards were ♣ K J 9. He exited with ♣ 9, giving declarer his eighth trick, then claimed the remaining tricks to put the contract one down.

"Yes, that was careful defending," observed Brother Paulo. "If you hold on to the spade queen you are endplayed with it. We can't stop nine tricks then."

"I did consider leading ♣ K," replied Brother Lucius. "A sort of Merrimac coup. It doesn't quite work, though."

Friar Tackett listened in amazement to this learned discussion. It was like having breakfast with the Pope, he remarked later.

Back at the other table the Abbot was in game once more.

North–South game, dealer South

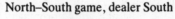

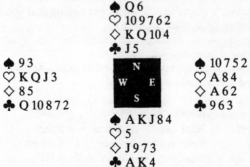

♠ Q 6
♡ 10 9 7 6 2
◇ K Q 10 4
♣ J 5

♠ 9 3
♡ K Q J 3
◇ 8 5
♣ Q 10 8 7 2

♠ 10 7 5 2
♡ A 8 4
◇ A 6 2
♣ 9 6 3

♠ A K J 8 4
♡ 5
◇ J 9 7 3
♣ A K 4

West	North	East	South
Friar	Brother	Friar	The
Leech	Xavier	Trewin	Abbot
			1♠
No	1 NT	No	2◇
No	3◇	No	3♠
No	4♠	End	

[15]

Missing the superior game in diamonds, the monastery pair came to rest in four spades. Friar Leech led ♡ K and smiled when his partner produced the 8. "I suppose you'll tell me that's not a come-on," he jested. "Well, I'm a simple fellow. I'm going to risk another heart anyway."

The Abbot ruffed the second round of hearts. Since the trump situation was tenuous he decided to embark on his side suit before playing trumps. He played a low diamond to the king, which won the trick. It still seemed right to persist with the side suit, so the Abbot continued with a low diamond from dummy. Friar Trewin went in with the ace and gave his partner a diamond ruff. Another force in hearts reduced the Abbot to three trumps and there was no way he could prevent East scoring a further trump trick. The contract was one down.

The Abbot reflected that he would have made the contract if East had not held up ◇ A. He would have taken a second heart force from East in hand, ruffed a club and attempted to draw trumps in three rounds. Despite the bad break he would then have been able to score two more tricks in diamonds before East could ruff with the outstanding trump.

"What induced you to hold up the diamond ace?" enquired the Abbot.

"Ah well, that's a standard position," replied Friar Trewin, his Adam's apple throbbing knowledgeably. "When you're sitting over a K Q 10 combination you have to hold up the ace once to give declarer a guess on the next round."

"But I *bid* diamonds," exclaimed the Abbot. "If your partner held the jack it would show on the next round."

"Perhaps it was silly of me, then," said Friar Trewin. "Could we have put you two down?"

Brother Xavier said nothing, but it occurred to him that the Abbot might have made the contract in more ways than one. He could, for example, have discarded a club on the second round of hearts. Then he could ruff the third round of hearts, draw trumps in four rounds and force out the diamond ace. East would have no heart remaining.

The last hand of the match was an obvious slam hand for the two North–South pairs.

Game all, dealer East

```
              ♠ A Q J 10 8
              ♡ A 6
              ◇ K 10 4
              ♣ K 10 3
♠ 9 6 5 2            N            ♠ 7 3
♡ K 10 7 4 2                      ♡ Q J 9 3
◇ 9 8 6       W        E          ◇ Q J 5
♣ 5                S             ♣ Q 8 7 4
              ♠ K 4
              ♡ 8 5
              ◇ A 7 3 2
              ♣ A J 9 6 2
```

West	North	East	South
Friar	Brother	Friar	The
Leech	Xavier	Trewin	Abbot
		No	1♣
No	2♠	No	3♣
No	4♣	No	4◇
No	4♡	No	4♠
No	5 NT	No	6♣
End			

The Abbot and Brother Xavier had an agreement never to cue-bid a shortage in partner's main suit. Brother Xavier could therefore be sure that the Abbot held the spade king. A Josephine enquiry revealed that one of the top trumps was missing, so the monastery pair stopped in six clubs. Friar Leech led ♡ 4, won by the ace in dummy.

Despite the annoying heart lead, prospects were excellent. A losing trump finesse would let the defenders in to cash a heart, so the Abbot's first move was to cash the ace and king of trumps. He was not pleased to see West show out on the second round. The contract would still succeed if East held three or more spades, since declarer could then dispose of his heart loser before reverting to trumps. The Abbot cashed the king and ace of spades and, mouthing a prayer, called for the ten. Friar Trewin observed this suspiciously. He pulled out the queen of clubs but finally replaced it and ruffed low. The Abbot could over-ruff, but he still had to lose a club and a diamond.

"Good lead, partner," observed Friar Trewin.

"I don't often lead from a king," replied Friar Leech excitedly. "I just thought this might be the moment."

Muttering some inaudible excuse, the Abbot left the table and headed for the soft drinks bar. Lucius and Paulo soon joined him to compare scores.

"Did you lead a heart against the club slam?" demanded the Abbot.

"Er . . . no, a diamond," replied Brother Lucius, "but . . ."

"Seventeen IMPs away," thundered the Abbot. "Lead a heart and the slam must go down, assuming declarer plays it properly."

"Does the lead make any difference?" asked Brother Lucius. "They were in seven clubs at our table. It's quite cold provided declarer takes the percentage play in trumps, finessing against East."

The St Titus team had lost their first match by a disastrous 19–1. Friar Trewin returned to have the result card initialled.

"I must say we didn't expect to win this one," he observed. "I shouldn't really tell you this, but . . ." he bent forward in secretive fashion, "Friar Leech has been running a small book on the event back at Edgeworth. Your team featured strongly in the betting. He made you 6/1, second favourites to St Hilda's Convent."

"What does he know about it?" snorted the Abbot. "Our man made us favourites at 7/2."

"Really?" replied Friar Trewin. "Well, Friar Leech used to run a betting shop before he joined us. Made quite a packet out of it by all accounts. It's not surprising he was nearer the mark."

3

Father O'Keefe's Complaint

As a result of their catastrophic defeat in the first round the Abbot and Brother Xavier found themselves on table 18 Blue at the start of the second round. This was an undignified situation in itself, but it was made worse, as far as the Abbot was concerned, by the knowledge that the only team they feared, St Hilda's Convent, was already on table one. Not only that, the convent's next opponents were none other than the incompetent Edgeworth Friary.

Still, nothing could be done about that, thought the Abbot. For the moment it was essential to extract a maximum against St Hubert the Innocent, reputedly an austere order from somewhere in the North of England.

"I always enjoy these Swiss events," said Father Berner, a miserable-looking man who scarcely seemed as if he could enjoy anything. "Great fun, aren't they?"

The Abbot gave a non-committal shrug and continued to sort his hand.

"What I like best about them," continued Father Berner, "is that however bad you are – and let's face it, our team is pretty bad – you always end up playing against people at the same level."

Brother Xavier caught a glimpse of the Abbot's reaction and hurriedly bit his lip to keep control of himself.

"It takes more than one round for the field to sort itself out," declared the Abbot blackly. "Shall we commence?"

This was the first deal.

East–West game, dealer North

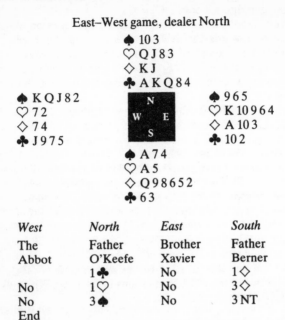

♠ 10 3
♡ Q J 8 3
♢ K J
♣ A K Q 8 4

♠ K Q J 8 2
♡ 7 2
♢ 7 4
♣ J 9 7 5

♠ 9 6 5
♡ K 10 9 6 4
♢ A 10 3
♣ 10 2

♠ A 7 4
♡ A 5
♢ Q 9 8 6 5 2
♣ 6 3

West	North	East	South
The	Father	Brother	Father
Abbot	O'Keefe	Xavier	Berner
	1♣	No	1♢
No	1♡	No	3♢
No	3♠	No	3 NT
End			

The Abbot led ♠ K against 3 NT and continued the suit. Father Berner won the third round, discarding a heart from dummy. Since he would still need at least one trick from the diamond suit even if the clubs divided, he next led a diamond to the king. Brother Xavier took his ace immediately, so that dummy's jack would block the suit, then returned ♡ K.

"Bad luck," declared Father Berner, "I'm afraid I have the ace."

Declarer could now count eight tricks. He was fairly sure that the spades were 5–3, so the obvious move seemed to be to duck a club trick to East, the safe hand.

When Father Berner led ♣ 3 the Abbot inserted the 9 from the West seat. Declarer won with dummy's ace and cashed two more club winners, East discarding a heart. Declarer's last shot was to overtake ♢ J with the queen, hoping that the 10 would fall. It was not to be. Brother Xavier took the last two tricks to put the contract one down.

"Well, I never," exclaimed Father Berner. "That ♡ K play didn't prove so expensive after all. In fact, wait a minute, I think I would have made the game on any other return."

"How amazing," replied Brother Xavier. "It just shows what a funny game bridge is, doesn't it?"

The sour-faced Father O'Keefe marked the score on his card, then leaned towards the Abbot. "I hope you don't mind me mentioning one thing, Abbot," he said. "We always confine ourselves to spring water at St Hubert's and our team was rather alarmed at the wide range of drinks being served in your buttery at this event."

"Quite so," agreed Father Berner. "Three different fruit squashes, fizzy lemonade and . . ." he paused to cross himself, "I understand ginger beer is available if you request it specifically."

The Abbot could not believe what he was hearing. If these abstinent fathers ever discovered what sort of drinks were normally imbibed in the St Titus buttery they would probably keel over and expire on the spot. "Yes, well, we had to make some allowance for the wide range of establishments competing this year," replied the Abbot. "I assure you that in normal circumstances it would be unthinkable to find a member of St Titus consuming a fruit cordial."

"I'm pleased to hear it," replied Father O'Keefe.

Meanwhile on table 18 Red, Lucius and Paulo were locked in battle with two of the oldest contestants in the room. This was the second board at their table:

North–South game, dealer South

```
                    ♠ 5
                    ♡ A 7 6 4
                    ◇ J 6 5 2
                    ♣ 9 7 6 3
    ♠ K Q J              N          ♠ 10 8 6 4 3
    ♡ K 10 9        W         E     ♡ 2
    ◇ K Q 8              S          ◇ 10 9 3
    ♣ K Q J 2                       ♣ 10 8 5 4
                    ♠ A 9 7 2
                    ♡ Q J 8 5 3
                    ◇ A 7 4
                    ♣ A
```

West	North	East	South
Father	Brother	Father	Brother
Cox	Paulo	Crocker	Lucius
			1♡
Dble	4♡	4♠	5♡
Dble	End		

[21]

Father Crocker, who liked to play a full part in the auction, sacrificed in four spades over four hearts. Placing partner with at most one spade, Brother Lucius advanced to the five level in pursuit of a vulnerable game. The white-haired Father Cox, deeming his hand worth a trick or two in defence, produced a firm penalty double. North passed and Father Crocker, sitting East, thumbed through his cards uncertainly. Perhaps partner was expecting a bit of defence from him after the four spades call. If so, he was going to be disappointed. It seemed well against the odds that any of his tens would score a trick. Yes, thought Father Crocker, it must be safer to take out into five spades.

"Is it my lead?" inquired Father Cox, hastily intervening.

"No bid," said Father Crocker.

The ♠ K was led and Brother Lucius won in hand. He then cashed ♣ A and led the queen of trumps, covered by the king and ace. Five black suit ruffs left declarer in his own hand with these cards still out:

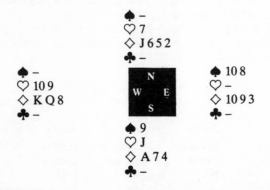

When declarer's last spade was led West could not afford to let dummy's small trump score. He ruffed with the 9 and returned the 10 of trumps to declarer's jack. Brother Lucius now led a low diamond from hand and West was endplayed to yield the eleventh trick.

"I can hardly believe that," declared Father Cox. "I had a 20-count, partner, and you'd bid at the four level!"

"Ah yes, it was difficult for you to read the situation," replied Father Crocker. "In fact I was *sacrificing*. That's an important part of the game at duplicate."

"Oh, I see," said Father Cox. "Even so, it's rather surprising that we came to only two tricks."

"Does it make any difference if ♡ Q isn't covered?" Brother Paulo asked his partner.

"I don't think so," replied Brother Lucius. "I come down to a similar ending where dummy holds ♢ J x x x and I hold a losing spade and ♢ A x x. I lead a low diamond and West, who has the master trump and ♢ K Q x, is endplayed just the same."

Father Crocker, looking somewhat dazed, sat back in his chair. If this was the standard of play at the bottom table, heaven preserve him from those nuns at the top table.

Both monastery pairs continued to do well. This was the last board of the match.

East–West game, dealer West

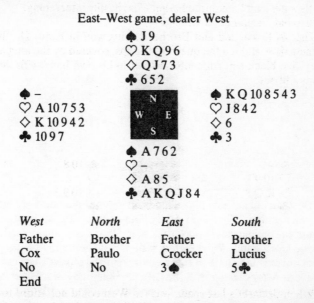

♠ J 9
♡ K Q 9 6
♢ Q J 7 3
♣ 6 5 2

♠ –
♡ A 10 7 5 3
♢ K 10 9 4 2
♣ 10 9 7

♠ K Q 10 8 5 4 3
♡ J 8 4 2
♢ 6
♣ 3

♠ A 7 6 2
♡ –
♢ A 8 5
♣ A K Q J 8 4

West	North	East	South
Father	Brother	Father	Brother
Cox	Paulo	Crocker	Lucius
No	No	3♠	5♣
End			

The ancient Father Crocker had never heard of the Rule of 500 and would have disapproved of it if he had. He opened three spades on the East cards and Brother Lucius overcalled five clubs, ending the auction.

West led the ten of trumps and Brother Lucius won in hand. After drawing trumps in two more rounds, he turned his attention to the red suits. How could he extract four tricks from them? West was quite likely to hold the two missing high cards in the red suits; if he had no more than four diamonds it seemed that he could be endplayed. Declarer would play ♢ A and a low diamond. If West went in with the king and returned a diamond, declarer could easily

[23]

succeed by winning in dummy and playing back ♡ K. If instead West held off ◇ K, declarer would return to hand with a heart ruff and lead a third round of diamonds towards dummy, achieving the same effect.

If West held five diamonds, though, he would be able to thwart the endplay – his fifth diamond would provide a safe exit at the crucial moment. The answer must be to play another trump or two, thought Brother Lucius, forcing West to weaken his holdings in the red suits. When Brother Lucius played a fourth and fifth round of trumps, West did in fact retain his five-card diamond holding, preferring to release two hearts. These cards remained:

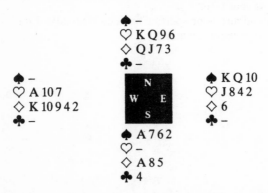

Brother Lucius now played ace and another diamond, dummy's queen winning. When East showed out on this trick, declarer had a count on the hand. He played ♡ K to West's ace and discarded a spade from hand. West exited with ♡ 10 to dummy's king, but declarer was now able to ruff a heart, removing West's last card in the suit. After cashing ♠ A, he led a low diamond towards dummy's jack. West won with the king but had to concede a tenth trick to the dummy.

"Quite unusual hand, partner" observed Brother Paulo. "Squeeze without the count at trick five, I think."

"Yes, and I had firepower in reserve," replied Brother Lucius. "Had I needed to apply more pressure I could have cashed ♠ A."

When the monastery team reconvened they found they had won the 8-board match by a massive 72 IMPs.

"What a tragic waste of IMPs," exclaimed the Abbot. "If we'd spread them more evenly over the two matches, we could have been in the lead by now."

Brother Lucius smiled at this. "Had we won our first match," he pointed out, "we might conceivably have played someone a little stronger in the next round."

The Mother Superior of St Hilda's passed by the table, obviously on her way to handing in a winner's result card. The Abbot, not keen to be spotted on table 18, bent forward in a desperate attempt to escape recognition.

"Afternoon, Abbot," said the Mother Superior. "Disappointing standard in the event this year."

Pretending he had just retrieved a fallen pen, the Abbot resumed an upright position. "I'm sure everyone is trying their best," he declared piously. "Most people don't take the event quite so seriously as your team, I dare say."

"We all admire your sporting attitude," remarked the Mother Superior, proceeding on her way.

4

The Abbot's Greek Encounter

With two rounds still to go in the St Francis of Assisi Swiss teams the St Titus team had pulled themselves up to table 3. Their next opposition was to be the Monastery of Aghios Gordios, a Greek Orthodox community from somewhere in North Wales. They had finished next to bottom in the event the previous year and the Abbot was expecting them to prove a most acceptable stepping-stone to table one.

"A good evening to you, Abbot," said the black-garbed Father Karlaftis, speaking in an incongruous Welsh accent. "Quite an occasion for our lads to face your illustrious team."

"We're certainly expecting a hard battle," replied the Abbot. "I see you have your strongest line-up."

"So it is, yes," replied Father Karlaftis. "We actually reached table one in the last round. Lost 15–5 to St Hilda's unfortunately. They play a hot game."

The Abbot winced. It would be embarrassing in the extreme if St Hilda's, the only female team present, were to win the trophy. He placed the first board on the table and reached for his cards with renewed determination.

East–West game, dealer North

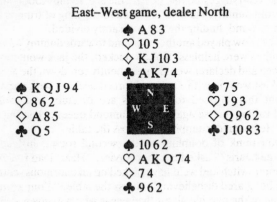

```
              ♠ A 8 3
              ♡ 10 5
              ◇ K J 10 3
              ♣ A K 7 4
  ♠ K Q J 9 4              ♠ 75
  ♡ 862         N          ♡ J 9 3
  ◇ A 8 5     W   E        ◇ Q 9 6 2
  ♣ Q 5         S          ♣ J 10 8 3
              ♠ 10 6 2
              ♡ A K Q 7 4
              ◇ 74
              ♣ 962
```

West	North	East	South
Father	Brother	Father	The
Karlaftis	Xavier	Delouka	Abbot
	1♢	No	1♡
2♠	No	No	3♡
No	4♡	End	

The Abbot was soon in four hearts and Father Karlaftis led ♠ K.

"How do you play your two spade overcalls?" demanded the Abbot.

"What, if it's a jump, do you mean?" said Father Delouka, stroking his jet-black beard. He glanced at his convention card. "We're playing ATV."

"I'm not familiar with the method," declared the Abbot. "ATV? What does that stand for?"

Father Delouka thought for a few seconds, then shook his head. "Do you know, I haven't the faintest idea," he replied. "We've had it on our card for years, but I never thought to enquire what it was. Sort of natural, I think."

"According To Vulnerability," explained Father Karlaftis, somewhat embarrassed at his partner's antics.

The Abbot won the spade lead in dummy and came to hand with the ace of trumps. Since he was short of entries to the South hand he delayed pulling any more trumps and led a low diamond immediately. West's call suggested that he held the ace, so the Abbot put up the king from dummy. He then returned to the king of trumps and drew a third round, finding the suit pleasantly divided.

The Abbot now played another diamond towards dummy's J 10 x. The defenders were helpless. If West ducked, the jack would force East's queen and declarer would subsequently ruff down the ace. In practice West went in with ♢ A and forced declarer with a spade. The Abbot then crossed to dummy's ace of clubs and took a successful ruffing finesse against the diamond queen, claiming the contract. He beamed triumphantly across the table.

"Did you think of doubling on the second round, instead of calling three hearts?" asked Brother Xavier. "Heart lead followed by a diamond switch and we'd have picked up an enormous score."

The Abbot glared disbelievingly across the table. "Your attitude reminds me of the parable about the beggar who was given a silver chalice," he declared. "The first thing he did was to complain that it wasn't gold."

"I don't recall that one," replied Brother Xavier, who prided himself on his biblical knowledge. "I must look it up when I get back to my cell. The Book of Job is a possibility."

At the other table Lucius and Paulo were facing a couple of earnest thirty-year-olds. The players sorted their cards for this deal:

North–South game, dealer East

♠ J 8
♡ 7 6
◇ K Q 7 2
♣ A Q 8 5 4

♠ 1 0 9 5 4 2
♡ 8 3 2
◇ J 1 0 8 4
♣ 6

♠ K Q 6
♡ K Q J 1 0 4
◇ 5
♣ J 1 0 9 3

♠ A 7 3
♡ A 9 5
◇ A 9 6 3
♣ K 7 2

West	North	East	South
Father	Brother	Father	Brother
Anapoulos	Paulo	Michaelis	Lucius
		1♡	No
No	2♣	No	2♡
No	3◇	No	3 NT
End			

Brother Lucius, who had a good fit for both his partner's suits, eventually opted for the nine-trick game. Hearts were led and continued, Brother Lucius winning the second round with the ace. What now? If either minor broke 3–2 the contract would be easy. There would still be chances if East held one of the minors. He wouldn't be able to guard everything when the winners in the other minor were cashed.

Brother Lucius began with the king and ace of diamonds, East discarding a spade. When a third round of diamonds was played, Father Michaelis was hard pressed to find a discard, despite it being only trick 5. If he threw another spade, dummy's jack would score. A club discard was obviously out of the question, so he had to release one of his winning hearts.

Brother Lucius now played king and another club, ducking in dummy when West showed out. East had only two winners to cash, so the game was home, dummy's long club providing the ninth trick.

[28]

"Christmas is arriving late this year, I see," observed Brother Paulo with a chuckle.

"I beg your pardon?" said Brother Lucius.

"Not a bad joke in English for an Italian to make," continued Brother Paulo, well pleased with himself. "You get it? Last hand was a delayed duck."

"Ah, I see," replied Brother Lucius, with a pained expression. "As you say, making jokes is difficult in a foreign tongue. Anyhow, over here we mostly eat turkey at Christmas."

Back at the other table the Abbot could scarcely conceal his delight at the way the match was going. "Where exactly is the Aghios Gordios monastery?" he enquired, sorting his cards in amiable fashion.

"On a hillside just north of Llanpwrrhyiogg," replied Father Karlaftis. "A beautiful location. We were fortunate to acquire it just after the first world war."

"Now, which Llanpwrrhyiogg is that?" continued the Abbot mischievously. "The one near Bradford, is it?"

"I didn't know there was more than one," replied Father Karlaftis. "Ours is on the Welsh coast, not far from Anglesey."

This was the last hand of the round:

Game all, dealer West

```
              ♠ J
              ♡ A 10 4 2
              ◇ A K 9 8 3
              ♣ K 5 4
♠ 9 7 6 2        N        ♠ A 8 5 3
♡ J 8 3      W     E      ♡ Q 7
◇ J 7 5          S        ◇ Q 10 4 2
♣ 10 9 7                  ♣ J 6 3
              ♠ K Q 10 4
              ♡ K 9 6 5
              ◇ 6
              ♣ A Q 8 2
```

West	North	East	South
Father	Brother	Father	The
Karlaftis	Xavier	Delouka	Abbot
No	1◇	No	1♡
No	3♡	No	4♣
No	6♡	End	

[29]

Father Karlaftis led ♣ 10 against six hearts and down went the dummy. The Abbot scanned its contents in alarm. What on earth had gone wrong with the losing trick count on this occasion? He had five losers facing a jump rebid and yet the slam was an appalling one. Still, at least he had escaped a spade lead. If clubs were 3–3 there might be chances.

The Abbot won the club lead with the ace and cashed the ace and king of trumps, everyone following. The first hurdle behind him, he paused to consider his continuation. If he played three more rounds of clubs immediately the defenders might be able to ruff the fourth round and force dummy with a spade. There would then be insufficient entries to establish the diamonds. No, it must be right to start on diamonds straight away.

"Ace of diamonds," instructed the Abbot, in a masterful tone.

"You're in hand, I think," said Brother Xavier.

"What difference does that make when I'm cashing an ace," grunted the Abbot. He crossed to ◇ A, ruffed a diamond and played three more rounds of clubs, discarding ♠ J. West refused to ruff this trick and the Abbot continued with ♠ K from hand. When West showed no interest in this card, following small, the Abbot decided to ruff in dummy and rely on a 4–3 diamond break. This line proved successful and twelve tricks were soon in the bag.

"If you lead a spade, reverend Father, he must go down," declared Father Delouka. "His only chance would be to find one of us with queen-jack doubleton of trumps."

"No, if you cash the spade I would try for a Devil's Coup," declared the Abbot. "Rather an ill-named play for a man of the cloth, of course, but I don't think that would have stopped me."

"Does the Devil's Coup work as the cards lie, Abbot?" enquired Brother Xavier innocently.

The Abbot tried unsuccessfully to recall the mechanism involved. "Er . . . I'd have to look into it," he replied. "I don't think the timing is quite right."

The round came to an end and the monastery team were soon busy comparing scores. Once again they found they had won by a handsome margin, 18–2 in victory points.

"Interesting hand, Abbot, that heart slam," remarked Brother Lucius. "If they take their spade trick early on, you can come extremely close to achieving a Devil's Coup."

"Yes, I reached the same conclusion," declared the Abbot.

"You would have to ruff two winning spades in dummy," continued Brother Lucius, "to shorten dummy's trumps."

"Understood, understood," said the Abbot.

[30]

"Then you come down to the famous position with dummy holding ♡ A 10 and a diamond and you holding ♡ K 9 x. Unfortunately East has the last diamond, rather than West, so you can't quite do it."

The Abbot nodded his head in agreement. "I was foolish enough to try to explain the technique to our opponents," he said, giving a short laugh. "It was quite beyond them, of course."

5

The Downfall of Brother Lucius

The St Francis of Assisi Swiss Teams had reached a fitting climax. The table one clash on the last round would be between St Hilda's Convent, who had led throughout, and the home team, the Monastery of St Titus. By the Abbot's reckoning a 14–6 win would suffice to lift the trophy.

"Evening, Abbot," said the Mother Superior, as the teams took their places. "I didn't expect it would be a full two days before we saw you at table one."

"Somewhat of a miracle that we reached here at all," replied the Abbot. "We had enough bad luck in the early rounds to last most teams a whole season."

The Mother Superior seemed unimpressed by this excuse. "Well, Sister Kristen," she said, "I think we should try to inflict a little more bad luck on these gentlemen. Shall we start?"

This was the first deal:

Love all, dealer South

```
              ♠ A K 9 6 5 3
              ♡ 5
              ◇ 9 7
              ♣ 10 7 5 4
♠ J 7 2                        ♠ Q 10 8 4
♡ K 10 8 2      N              ♡ Q J 9 4
◇ J 10 8 6 4  W   E            ◇ 2
♣ Q             S              ♣ J 9 6 3
              ♠ —
              ♡ A 7 6 3
              ◇ A K Q 5 3
              ♣ A K 8 2
```

West	North	East	South
Mother	Brother	Sister	The
Superior	Xavier	Kristen	Abbot
			1◇
No	1♠	No	3♣
No	3♠	No	3 NT
End			

[32]

Brother Xavier decided against showing his club support, leaving the Abbot in 3 NT. The convent pair attacked in hearts and the Abbot won the third round.

Even if diamonds broke 3–3 the Abbot would have only eight tricks because there was no entry to dummy. It therefore seemed that the club suit would be the key to the hand. If dummy could be reached on the fourth round of clubs, declarer would be able to enjoy the ace and king of spades.

The Abbot cashed ♣ A and was not pleased to see the queen appear on his left. If that was a singleton the dummy would be dead unless he could contrive some sort of endplay. The Abbot was fairly sure from the fall of the cards that hearts were 4–4, so his next move was to exit with his last heart. West won with the king and returned ◇ J. The Abbot won with the ace and cashed a second round of diamonds, East discarding a spade. These cards remained:

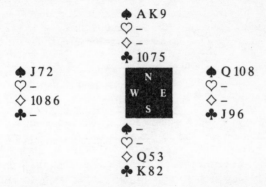

```
                    ♠ A K 9
                    ♡ –
                    ◇ –
                    ♣ 10 7 5
   ♠ J 7 2                          ♠ Q 10 8
   ♡ –          N                   ♡ –
   ◇ 10 8 6   W     E               ◇ –
   ♣ –            S                 ♣ J 9 6
                    ♠ –
                    ♡ –
                    ◇ Q 5 3
                    ♣ K 8 2
```

The Abbot played a club to the 7 and 9. When Sister Kristen returned a spade, he was able to cash two spades and take the marked finesse in clubs. Nine tricks were there.

"Perhaps I should have raised your clubs, Abbot," suggested Brother Xavier, scratching his head. "I suppose six clubs would have some play. On a 3–2 trump break, anyhow."

The Abbot waved aside this distraction from his fine play. "It may have escaped your notice," he said, "but we ended up doing very nicely in notrumps."

Brother Xavier sensed that some tribute was in order. "Yes, you played it brilliantly," he said.

The Abbot nodded. "No reason to expect a swing against such expert opposition," he declared heavily, "but . . . well, stranger things have happened in this game of ours."

Not far away the other convent pair were locked in battle with
Lucius and Paulo.

North–South game, dealer East

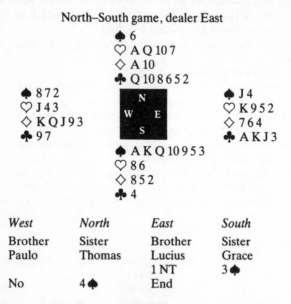

♠ 6
♡ A Q 10 7
◇ A 10
♣ Q 10 8 6 5 2

♠ 8 7 2
♡ J 4 3
◇ K Q J 9 3
♣ 9 7

♠ J 4
♡ K 9 5 2
◇ 7 6 4
♣ A K J 3

♠ A K Q 10 9 5 3
♡ 8 6
◇ 8 5 2
♣ 4

West	North	East	South
Brother	Sister	Brother	Sister
Paulo	Thomas	Lucius	Grace
		1 NT	3 ♠
No	4 ♠	End	

Brother Paulo led ◇ K against four spades and down went the
dummy. Sister Grace studied the cards laid out by her partner.
What was the best line? If she won the first or second diamond and
tried to clear a way back to her hand by leading a club, the defenders
would surely play back a trump to prevent her taking a diamond
ruff. Since ♡ K was marked offside by the opening bid, she would
then lose two diamonds, a heart and a club.

How about winning the second diamond and running the trump
suit immediately? Could she then endplay East? It seemed not,
unless East had started with only two diamonds.

Another plan occurred to Sister Grace. East was marked with the
king of hearts, but there was just room for West to hold the jack.
Yes, perhaps she could dispose of one of her diamonds on dummy's
heart suit. "Low, please," she said, letting West's ◇ K win the first
trick.

Brother Paulo continued with a second diamond, won by dummy's ace. Sister Grace now delivered her masterstroke. "Queen of
hearts," she said.

The defence was powerless. Brother Lucius, sitting East, won
with the king and cashed the king of clubs, drawing the 4 and the 9.

If he were to exit with a trump now, Sister Grace would simply draw trumps and finesse ♡ 10. Realising this, Brother Lucius attempted to cash ♣ A, just in case declarer had a 7–2–2–2 hand. Sister Grace ruffed with ♠ 10, drew trumps and claimed the contract. Her losing diamond would now go on dummy's ♣ Q.

"Jack of hearts onside?" enquired Sister Grace, in her usual gruff tone.

Brother Paulo nodded.

"Nothing you could do, then," declared Sister Grace. "3 NT would have been a better spot for us, of course."

"That may be," agreed the plain-faced Sister Thomas. "But I had no way of knowing that your spades were ready to run."

"Our lads are sure to be in four spades too," said Brother Paulo, entering the result in his scorecard.

"Yes, bound to be a flat board," observed Brother Lucius. "I can't see the Abbot missing that ♡ Q play. Can you, Paulo?"

A board or two later Sister Grace was in game once more.

Game all, dealer East

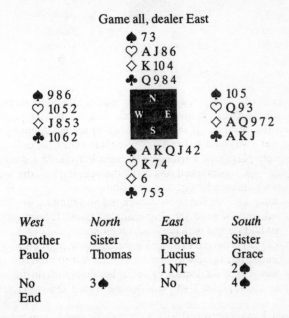

West	North	East	South
Brother	Sister	Brother	Sister
Paulo	Thomas	Lucius	Grace
		1 NT	2 ♠
No	3 ♠	No	4 ♠
End			

Paying little respect to Brother Lucius's vulnerable no trump opening, the convent pair reached a game in spades. Brother Paulo led the 9 of trumps, won by South, and declarer drew a second round, noting the fall of East's 10. Abandoning the trump suit for the moment, Sister Grace played a diamond to the 10. Brother Lucius won with the queen and found himself in an awkward situation. He marked time by cashing ♣ K, West signalling with the 2. To play on hearts or clubs now would in effect give declarer two tricks. Declarer would be able to return to hand with a diamond ruff, draw the last trump, then return to dummy to take a discard on the thirteenth card of the suit led.

After considerable thought Brother Lucius played ♢ A, ruffed by declarer. Sister Grace now ran the trump suit, arriving at this end position:

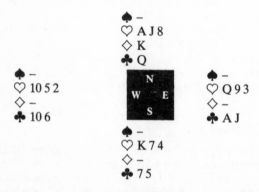

```
                    ♠ –
                    ♡ A J 8
                    ♢ K
                    ♣ Q
    ♠ –                             ♠ –
    ♡ 10 5 2          N             ♡ Q 9 3
    ♢ –          W         E        ♢ –
    ♣ 10 6           S             ♣ A J
                    ♠ –
                    ♡ K 7 4
                    ♢ –
                    ♣ 7 5
```

She crossed to ♡ A and cashed ♢ K, forcing a club discard from East. It only remained to throw East in with ♣ A. Brother Lucius's enforced heart return into the split tenace gave Sister Grace her tenth trick.

"Nothing I could do," declared Brother Lucius with a pained expression. "It seems that when I won that diamond trick I had three different ways of presenting declarer with the contract."

"Yes, poor lead, I'm afraid," apologised Brother Paulo.

"Once again 3 NT would have been better," remarked Sister Grace. "For that matter I suppose I might have doubled 1 NT." She turned towards Brother Lucius. "Six rounds of spades wouldn't help your hand very much."

Back at the other table the Abbot was reasonably happy with the way the match was going. His masterpiece of a 3 NT contract was already in the bag and Lucius and Paulo could usually be relied on for a swing or two.

This was the last board of the match:

North–South game, dealer North

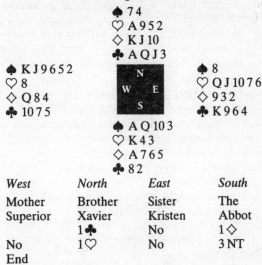

West	North	East	South
Mother	Brother	Sister	The
Superior	Xavier	Kristen	Abbot
	1♣	No	1♢
No	1♡	No	3 NT
End			

The monastery pair was given a free ride in the auction and soon arrived in a comfortable-looking 3 NT. The ♠ 6 lead was covered by the 7, 8 and 10. The Abbot then played a club to the queen, which was allowed to hold. Since West appeared to hold the spade length, the Abbot decided to play East for ♢ Q. He cashed ♢ K and ran the jack, losing to West's queen.

The Mother Superior switched to her singleton heart and the Abbot won in hand. When he repeated the club finesse, East won and returned the suit. The Abbot cashed dummy's ♢ 10, leaving these cards at large:

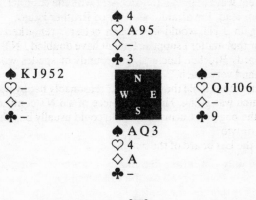

[37]

The Abbot had six tricks in the bag and three aces were on view. Was there any chance of an overtrick? It seemed unlikely. With nothing particular in mind, he led ♠ 4 from dummy. When East showed out, the Abbot paused to take stock. No spades had been discarded, so surely West had nothing but spades in her hand. Yes, that must be right. If he ran ♠ 4 to West, she would have to lead back into his spade tenace, giving him a possibly vital overtrick.

With an air of bored expertise the Abbot contributed ♠ 3 from hand. The Mother Superior followed with the 2.

The Abbot's mouth dropped. He was locked in dummy with no chance of reaching the two aces in his hand. What an unparalleled disaster! How *could* he have let his concentration slip like that?

"Three tricks to me?" said the thin-lipped Sister Kristen, displaying her cards to the Abbot.

The Abbot gave a resigned nod of the head, then swept up his cards and thrust them back into the wallet. Brother Xavier sought in vain for some words of consolation. Despite the many occasions when he had suffered from the Abbot's tongue, he felt genuinely sorry for the old buffer.

"Ah, here comes your other pair," said the Mother Superior, rising to her feet. "Thank you for the game, Abbot. I dare say I'll see you again before we leave."

The Abbot looked up at his incoming pair. "Any good?" he enquired.

"No," replied Brother Lucius. "Pretty hopeless. Did you do anything?"

"Not enough if you're bad," replied the Abbot. "We had one good board early on. Nothing that would win any brilliancy prizes since then."

The results were soon out. St Hilda's, with a 17–3 win in the final round, had won by a record margin. Brother Lucius gazed blankly ahead of him, apparently upset by the team's poor showing.

"Unlike you to be affected by a bad result," observed the Abbot.

"It's not us doing badly that I mind," replied Brother Lucius. "I lost heavily on it financially. I took over £100 worth of bets on St Hilda's."

"What?" exclaimed the Abbot. "Do you mean that members of our own community bet against us? I can scarcely believe it."

"Most of the bets were placed by members of the novitiate," continued Brother Lucius. "Where they get the money from, I really don't know."

"I'm certainly not letting the matter drop here," declared the Abbot blackly. "No, I shall want a full list of the traitors. On my desk first thing tomorrow morning."

PART II

Interlude in Mediaeval Nottingham

6

The Strange Tale of Witch Zelda

"An open and shut case, my Lord," declared Sir Guy of Gisburne, resplendent in his blue robe edged with ermine. "She has confessed to it all; she is condemned from her own mouth."

The Sheriff of Nottingham gazed at the ugly specimen of womanhood before him. Her grey hair was matted and her sackcloth garment bore traces of pig droppings. "Unusually tall for a witch," he observed.

"She has spent some time on Master Galvin's rack, my Lord," explained Gisburne. "Despite the evidence against her, the failure of her village's crop for three successive seasons, she was stubborn in the confession."

"Stubbornness is itself a mark of witchcraft," declared the Sheriff. He lifted his quill, preparing to sign the death warrant.

"Show mercy, my Lord!" cried the Witch Zelda. "Give this poor woman a chance to save her life."

The Sheriff sat back in his chair. An amusing idea came to him. "Do you play cards, you old hag?" he said.

"Yes indeed, my Lord," replied the Witch. "See, I have three cards here and one of them is the queen of spades. Now if your Lordship . . ."

"Be silent!" barked the Sheriff. "I'm not interested in your witch's tricks. Do you play bridge, the game of noblemen?"

"After a fashion, my Lord," croaked the old woman.

"I think you will like this, Gisburne," said the Sheriff, with an amused smirk. He turned once again to the Witch. "I will give you a chance, an undeserved chance, to save your life. You may compete in the annual Nottingham Goose Fair pairs championship."

"Thank you, my Lord," replied Zelda. "Your Lordship is truly a man of the highest . . ."

"Silence, you old faggot!" cried the Sheriff. "If you finish ahead of myself and Gisburne you will be reprieved. If not you will be burned one hour after the results are posted."

"Ah, very witty indeed, my Lord," said Gisburne, who was aware that the Sheriff had won the event for the past four years.

"As for a partner, you may take your pick from the layabouts and villains in the castle jail," concluded the Sheriff. "Take her away!"

Will Hearnley, a castle servant who had overheard this exchange, hurried to a dark corner of the castle battlements. He scribbled a note on a scrap of paper, fastened the missive to the shaft of an arrow and reached for his bow. He then sent the arrow flying over the houses of Nottingham. The arrow landed on the outskirts of Wykeham village, where it was quickly spotted and forwarded on towards the forest.

Zing . . . thud! The arrow imbedded itself in a thick oak near Robin Hood's camp. Little John, who had been standing in front of that very tree a few seconds previously, crossed himself in thanks for his narrow escape. He despatched a vituperative note of complaint in the direction from which the arrow had come, then carried the original message to his leader.

* * *

The following Saturday, play was about to start in the Goose Fair pairs. Witch Zelda was engaged in an earnest discussion with her partner, an old man with a grey beard. "And two of a suit is a weakness take-out when your partner opens 1 NT," she said. "You play that, Robin, don't you?"

The bearded man glared at her. "Don't call me Robin," he muttered. "I'm risking my life by being here." He scribbled on his convention card. "Right, weak take-outs opposite 1 NT."

Play was soon under way. This was an early board at Witch Zelda's table:

North–South game, dealer West

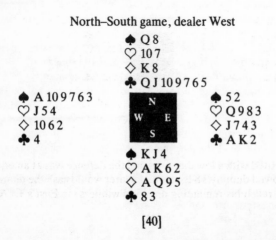

```
                    ♠ Q 8
                    ♡ 10 7
                    ◇ K 8
                    ♣ Q J 10 9 7 6 5
  ♠ A 10 9 7 6 3                      ♠ 5 2
  ♡ J 5 4              N              ♡ Q 9 8 3
  ◇ 10 6 2         W       E          ◇ J 7 4 3
  ♣ 4                  S              ♣ A K 2
                    ♠ K J 4
                    ♡ A K 6 2
                    ◇ A Q 9 5
                    ♣ 8 3
```

West	*North*	*East*	*South*
Henry	Witch	Piers	Robin
Bassante	Zelda	Holdegate	Hood
2♠	No	No	2 NT
No	3 NT	End	

Sir Henry Bassante spent most of his waking hours hunting and his approach at the bridge table was similarly cavalier. There were few hands on which he could not find an opening bid of some sort. On the present deal he opened a sub-standard weak two and Robin Hood arrived in 3 NT.

The ♠ 10 lead was won in the dummy and ♣ Q was allowed to hold the next trick. Robin Hood paused to consider this unwelcome development. Was it possible that the clubs were 2–2 and that the big honours would fall together on the next trick? Surely not. If East held a doubleton club honour, he would certainly have risen with it, intending to clear partner's spades.

It seemed pointless to continue clubs. Robin Hood's next move was ♡ 10 from dummy, ducking when East produced the queen. Back came a spade. Declarer contributed the king and, whether by design or accident, West ducked.

They defend well, thought Robin Hood. If the spade had been taken, East would surely have had no safe discard on the third round of spades. Hood exited with a club, won the heart return and played two more rounds of hearts, throwing East on lead again. These cards remained:

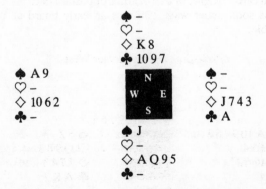

East exited with a low diamond and the defence was at an end. If West allowed dummy's 8 to score, declarer would cash the diamond king and reach his remaining diamond winners via East's ♣ A. In fact West played ◇ 10 and a subsequent finesse in the suit gave declarer a ninth trick.

"It's a better shot for you to lead the *jack* of diamonds at the finish," remarked Bassante gruffly.

Witch Zelda opened the scoresheet. "600 is worse than a parrot's puke!" she observed. "Everone else has made an overtrick." She glared malevolently at Robin Hood. "It is pairs, you know."

"They defended well against me," replied Hood. "Ten tricks are easy if they win the first round of clubs."

"Excuses, excuses!" cried the Witch. "Any more dummy play like that and I'll be a pile of ashes by this time tomorrow."

"You can play the next one," replied Robin Hood.

Meanwhile the Sheriff and Gisburne were facing a promising young pair, the twin sons of the Earl of Warwick.

Game all, dealer South

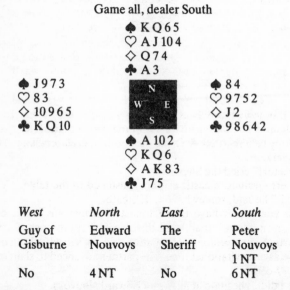

```
              ♠ K Q 6 5
              ♡ A J 10 4
              ◇ Q 7 4
              ♣ A 3
♠ J 9 7 3                      ♠ 8 4
♡ 8 3           N             ♡ 9 7 5 2
◇ 10 9 6 5   W     E          ◇ J 2
♣ K Q 10        S             ♣ 9 8 6 4 2
              ♠ A 10 2
              ♡ K Q 6
              ◇ A K 8 3
              ♣ J 7 5
```

West	North	East	South
Guy of	Edward	The	Peter
Gisburne	Nouvoys	Sheriff	Nouvoys
			1 NT
No	4 NT	No	6 NT

Gisburne made the somewhat dangerous lead of ♣ K and down went the dummy. Peter Nouvoys inspected its contents approvingly. Somehow he must try to combine the various squeeze chances with the possibility of dropping the ♠ J doubleton.

"Come on, come on," grunted the Sheriff. "You young players are all the same. Slow as a castrated tortoise."

"Oh, very droll, my Lord," exclaimed Gisburne. "I must note that one down."

"Small, please," said Nouvoys.

A club was continued and dummy's ace won. If East held the diamond length it seemed that a double squeeze would develop. West would have to guard the clubs, East the diamonds; no-one would therefore be able to guard the spades. When declarer tested the diamonds East threw a club on the third round. The ace and king of spades followed, but again no luck was forthcoming. The ♠ J refused to drop, leaving these cards still to be played:

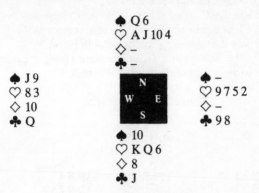

Declarer now played the ace, king, queen of hearts, ending in the South hand. The unfortunate Gisburne had no card to spare. Eventually he discarded ♣ Q and the youthful declarer claimed the remainder.

"Director!" cried the Sheriff.

Herbert Graines, a castle servant, hastened to the table. "Yes, my Lord," he said, somewhat out of breath.

"This young pair have taken a most improper advantage of a hesitation situation," thundered the Sheriff. "South opened 1 NT and North, after a prolonged hesitation, bid 4 NT in what I can only describe as an invitational tone. His partner advanced to slam on a barren 17-count."

"But I didn't hesitate at all," said Edward Nouvoys.

"Be silent!" cried Gisburne. "Are you calling my Lord Sheriff a liar?"

"Dear, oh dear; this is a serious offence," declared Graines. "What penalty do you suggest, my Lord?"

"Isn't it obvious?" replied the Sheriff. "The contract must be adjusted to 4 NT. The play would probably have gone differently, too. The non-offending side must be given the benefit of the doubt; it should be scored as 4 NT plus one."

"Quite so, my Lord," agreed Graines. "Your Lordship's knowledge of the rules is indeed remarkable."

Not long afterwards Friar Tuck and Will Scarlet found themselves at the Witch's table. This was the first board they played.

Love all, dealer East

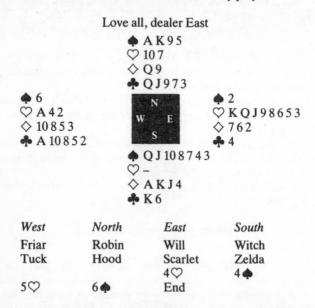

♠ A K 9 5
♡ 10 7
◇ Q 9
♣ Q J 9 7 3

♠ 6
♡ A 4 2
◇ 10 8 5 3
♣ A 10 8 5 2

♠ 2
♡ K Q J 9 8 6 5 3
◇ 7 6 2
♣ 4

♠ Q J 10 8 7 4 3
♡ –
◇ A K J 4
♣ K 6

West	North	East	South
Friar	Robin	Will	Witch
Tuck	Hood	Scarlet	Zelda
		4♡	4♠
5♡	6♠	End	

Will Scarlet made a disciplined pass over six spades and Friar Tuck, with two aces, decided to defend. Since ♡ A might well be ruffed, he led ♣ A at trick 1. This card drew the 3 and the 4, followed by the king from Witch Zelda, hoping to confuse the issue.

The lie of the club suit was quite obvious to Tuck. For one thing, the Witch had fumbled in her production of the club king, almost dropping it onto the floor. Also, if East had held 6–4 he would scarcely have contributed the 4 to the first trick.

Friar Tuck gave a sigh. Duty called. The only reason the outlaws were playing in the event was to attempt, by some miracle, to rescue the Witch. Gritting his teeth, he switched to ♡ A.

"Hah! Fooled you there!" cried the Witch, when the hand was over. "I had another club all the time; my king was a false card."

"Yes, you played it cleverly," replied Friar Tuck, who had never before realised that he was capable of such self control.

Robin Hood opened the scoresheet. "It's not bad for us," he informed the Witch, "but several other pairs made six spades."

The Strange Tale of Witch Zelda

"You're forgetting that I doubled," said Friar Tuck, in a martyred tone. "1210 to you."

"Ah yes, thank you," said Robin Hood, catching the Friar's eye. "I was forgetting the double; you're quite right."

Despite the outlaws' best efforts, the Sheriff held a commanding lead at the interval. His score was 68.3%, while Robin and Zelda were back in 6th position with 59.7%. Desperate action was called for.

Will Scarlet approached Graines, the tournament director. "Is your name Graines?" he said. "There's a young lady outside. Got a special message for you, she says."

Graines straightened his attire and left the hall with a silly grin on his face. A few seconds later he was viewing life from the inside of a sack in the North bell tower.

"My Lord and Ladies, pray resume your places for the second and final half of the Goose Fair pairs," bawled the Nottingham town crier, hired specially for the occasion.

Play restarted and Robin Hood was soon at the helm of a difficult spade game.

North–South game, dealer East

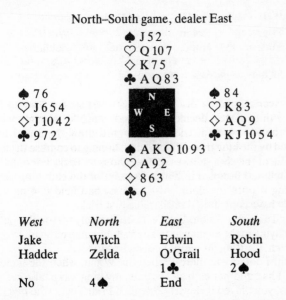

```
              ♠ J 5 2
              ♡ Q 10 7
              ◇ K 7 5
              ♣ A Q 8 3
♠ 7 6                        ♠ 8 4
♡ J 6 5 4      N            ♡ K 8 3
◇ J 10 4 2   W   E          ◇ A Q 9
♣ 9 7 2        S            ♣ K J 10 5 4
              ♠ A K Q 10 9 3
              ♡ A 9 2
              ◇ 8 6 3
              ♣ 6
```

West	North	East	South
Jake	Witch	Edwin	Robin
Hadder	Zelda	O'Grail	Hood
		1♣	2♠
No	4♠	End	

The ♣ 9 was led, won by the ace in dummy. The ♠ A and the 10 overtaken by the jack drew the outstanding trumps. Robin Hood then exited with ♣ 8, discarding a diamond from the South hand. East, perforce, won the trick.

O'Grail, a wool merchant from Bolton, paused to consider his return. It seemed that declarer had six trump tricks, the ace of clubs and the ace of hearts. Dummy's heart holding would yield a second trick in that suit, so it followed that East could not afford to return either minor; that would bring declarer's total to ten.

East returned ♡ 3 and West defended well by playing low, allowing dummy's 7 to win. Had West put in the jack, declarer would have scored three tricks in the suit.

Robin Hood now played the ace and queen of hearts, endplaying East once again. This time there was no escape. East played ♣ K, but declarer ruffed with the 9 and crossed to dummy's 5 of trumps to take a diamond discard on ♣ Q.

"You played it well," remarked Jake Hadder, who recognised a good piece of dummy play when he saw it. "I don't think we've met before. Do you play a lot?"

"No, not much duplicate," replied Hood. "I play a fair bit of rubber bridge in the local taverns – the *Bullock and Codpiece*, mainly."

"Can't say I've heard of it," replied Hadder.

The fifth round of the final session brought Friar Tuck to the Sheriff's table. "Ah, what have we here?" exclaimed the Sheriff, raising his voice for the benefit of the kibitzers. "I've never met a friar who played cards before. Is such frivolity not against your vows?"

"Indeed not, my Lord, in fact we are trying to encourage it," replied Tuck. "Our standard of play is poor at the moment, but we find the game an excellent discipline for the mind."

"Quite so," agreed the Sheriff, extracting his cards from the hand-carved wooden board. "I wish more churchmen would take up the game, instead of making fools of themselves meddling in politics."

This was the first deal:

East–West game, dealer West

```
              ♠ A Q J 5
              ♡ 9 4
              ◇ K Q J 8 2
              ♣ J 6
♠ 9 7 3                        ♠ 10 8 6 2
♡ A Q 10 6        N            ♡ J 8 2
◇ 10 9 4       W     E         ◇ 6 5
♣ 9 8 2           S            ♣ A K 7 3
              ♠ K 4
              ♡ K 7 5 3
              ◇ A 7 3
              ♣ Q 10 5 4
```

West	North	East	South
Friar	The	Will	Guy
Tuck	Sheriff	Scarlet	Gisburne
No	1◇	No	1♡
No	1♠	No	2 NT
No	3 NT	End	

Against 3NT Friar Tuck led ♣ 9, won by East's king. The outlaws normally led second best from four small, so Will Scarlet could tell that declarer had Q–10–x–x in clubs and there was no future in the suit. At trick 2 he switched smartly to ♡ J, covered by the king and ace. Tuck cashed ♡ Q and Scarlet unblocked the 8. A club to the ace allowed East to play ♡ 2 through declarer's 7–5 and the contract was two down.

An initial switch to the 8 of hearts would have put the contract only one down. West would win with the 10 and cross to the other club honour, but declarer would now cover East's ♡ J, promoting his 7–5 into a stop.

"You blundering idiot, Gisburne," exploded the Sheriff. "What was this 2 NT bid?"

"I had 12 points, my Lord," stammered Gisburne, "and Q 10 to four in the unbid suit. What would my Lord have me call?"

Ignoring the question, the Sheriff inspected the other results on the board. "A veritable harlot's bottom," he exclaimed, tossing the scoresheet across the table. "No-one else in the whole room went two down."

"But there was nothing I could do, my Lord," protested Gisburne.

"No, that's true," said Friar Tuck. "We took the first six tricks."

[47]

"If I require your opinion, I'll ask for it!" snapped the Sheriff, staring blackly at the Friar. "You are paid to pray for our salvation, are you not? In future you will be well advised to confine yourself to your abbey, instead of delving into areas beyond your compass."

The rounds of the second session ticked by. Eventually a handbell sounded from the far end of the hall. "My Lords, Ladies and gentlemen," boomed the town crier. "Be upstanding to move for the last and final round of the Goose Fair pairs."

"We go to North–South table 11," muttered Robin Hood to the Witch. "Remember we must reach six hearts on Board 25. Little John has planted a deal for us."

They took their seats and the table was soon completed by none other than the Sheriff and the unfortunate Gisburne.

"Ah, the Witch Zelda," exclaimed the Sheriff, pulling back the East chair. "Enjoy these two hands; they will be the last you play." He turned to inspect her grey-haired partner – a fair player, presumably, if their half-time position was anything to go by. "What is your name, old man?" he enquired.

"Rupert Hildebrande, if it pleases your Lordship," croaked the bearded figure, not looking up.

"Did you know that your partner has always wanted to be famous?" said the Sheriff, with a sideways look at Gisburne. "She has always had a burning ambition to perform before a crowd."

"Very witty, my Lord, as always," said Gisburne.

"Before sundown her wish will be fulfilled," declared the Sheriff, sorting his cards. He glared evilly at the Witch. "Unfortunately, however entertaining your performance, you will miss the applause at the end of it," he informed her. "Your call, Gisburne."

Robin Hood caught the Witch Zelda's eye. It was Board 25.

North–South game, dealer West

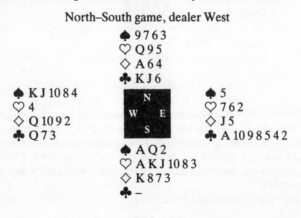

```
              ♠ 9 7 6 3
              ♡ Q 9 5
              ♢ A 6 4
              ♣ K J 6
♠ K J 10 8 4      N          ♠ 5
♡ 4          W       E       ♡ 7 6 2
♢ Q 10 9 2                   ♢ J 5
♣ Q 7 3          S          ♣ A 10 9 8 5 4 2
              ♠ A Q 2
              ♡ A K J 10 8 3
              ♢ K 8 7 3
              ♣ –
```

West	North	East	South
Guy of	*Witch*	*The*	*Robin*
Gisburne	*Zelda*	*Sheriff*	*Hood*
No	No	3♣	3♡
3♠	6♡	End	

Gisburne led ♣ 3 and down went the dummy. Hood winced as he viewed the flat 10-count. Was the Witch incapable of any subtlety? Why couldn't she have bid four hearts? Then he could have raised to six without arousing any suspicion. "Jack, please," he said.

The Sheriff played the ace and gave a pained expression in Gisburne's direction when declarer ruffed. Robin Hood played the ace and queen of trumps, West showing out on the second round. He then cashed ♣ K, discarding a spade, and ruffed dummy's last club.

Hood paused to consider his continuation. What was that fool Little John thinking of? Making twelve tricks in *four* hearts would be worth a top on this layout. Bidding six was a needless risk. Anyway, how did the cards lie? If West had a 6–1–3–3 distribution it seemed that nothing could be done. If West was 5–1–4–3, though, he would come under pressure when the trumps were run. Hood drew the last trump, leaving this end position:

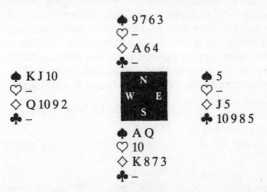

When ♡ 10 was led, Gisburne was in trouble. If he threw a spade, declarer would play the ace and queen of spades, establishing two extra tricks in the dummy. He chose instead to part with a diamond, but Hood then played ace, king and another diamond. Gisburne was endplayed, forced to lead into declarer's ♠ A Q. Twelve tricks were there.

"Director!" cried the Sheriff.

A tall figure loomed into view.

"I asked for the director, not a performing giant," snarled the Sheriff. "Where is Graines?"

"He was taken ill, my Lord," replied Little John. "I am his appointed replacement. What is the problem?"

The Sheriff reached for the North curtain card and tossed it on the table in front of Little John. "I opened three clubs. South made an overcall at the minimum level, three hearts, and over three spades from my partner the North player jumped to six hearts on that rubbish!"

Little John inspected the curtain card. "Well, I must say I would have asked for aces first," he observed. He turned to the Witch. "Are you not playing the Richmond 4 NT convention?"

"Are you blind, man?" thundered the Sheriff. "The hand is scarcely worth a raise to four. It is pitifully obvious that the Witch overheard someone discussing the hand, or stole a glance at someone's scorecard. The score must be adjusted."

"I'm afraid I can see nothing unusual in the call, my Lord," persisted Little John. "In a pairs event, though, I think I would have preferred 6 NT, to protect the clubs."

"I'm surrounded by imbeciles," grunted the Sheriff, giving up the struggle. "If they're not making ludicrous rulings, they're making damfool opening leads."

The Goose Fair tournament prided itself on its fast scoring. An army of scorers had been drafted and it was only some thirty minutes after play had ceased when Gisburne climbed the stairs to the Sheriff's state room, a sheet of paper in hand.

"Well?" said the Sheriff. "What was our score?"

"Er . . . 67.2%, my Lord," replied Gisburne.

"Excellent, despite your miserable efforts," replied the Sheriff. "Not quite as high as in 1195 when we won by four clear tops, but the standard is improving all the time."

"I'm afraid that er . . . we were second, my Lord," said Gisburne, almost choking over the words.

"What?" exploded the Sheriff.

"A very close second, my Lord," said Gisburne. "Only 3 matchpoints behind the winners."

"Don't stand there, you fool," commanded the Sheriff. "Go and re-score it. Fine the winners for slow play; use your imagination. Good God, man, for someone who fiddles our tax returns to King John, causing three or four matchpoints to vanish shouldn't be a problem."

"Very good, my Lord, but I believe the results have already been posted in the Great Hall."

"Already posted, I don't believe it," exclaimed the Sheriff. "Who in heaven's name beat us, anyway? It wasn't Warwick's brats, was it?"

"Er . . . no, my Lord," replied Gisburne. "Although it is very astute of your Lordship to suggest that they might be well placed. They were in fact fifth with a score of . . ."

The Sheriff strode towards Gisburne and tore the result sheet from his grasp. "The Witch won?" he cried. "If ever there were proof of witchcraft, this is it. A babbling half-wit, a mere female, partnered by some scum from my jail, finishes ahead of ME? This is the Devil's work; she will burn for this."

"Quite so, my Lord," said Gisburne, striding towards the door. "I will issue instructions immediately that she be recaptured."

"Recaptured?" said the Sheriff.

"Apparently she left the castle quite swiftly after the results were posted, my Lord," said Gisburne. "I asked where she was going, so that we could forward the green points, but she gave no answer. Her hearing is poor, I believe."

The Sheriff strode across the room and peered through one of the arrow slits in the outer wall. The sun was about to set and the outskirts of Nottingham were bathed in crimson light. "By the saints!" he exclaimed. "I believe that's her on the back of one of those horses heading for the forest. Take a look. Who rides with her on that horse, do you think?"

"From the green and brown jacket, I would say it was her partner in the pairs," replied Gisburne, peering through an adjacent arrow split. "He rides uncommonly well for his age. But, wait a moment. What a strange thing! He seems to have shaved off his beard, my Lord."

PART III

Deep in the African Jungle

7

Brother Tobias's Last Chance

Relations between the Bozwambi tribe and the neighbouring Zbolwumba tribe had been strained ever since the fatal spearing of Chief Hekke-Hazut, following a cheating scandal in 1934. Much to the Witchdoctor's annoyance, the Zbolwumbas had won the last two league matches between the tribes. Special action was called for.

"Hey, Mbozi," said the Witchdoctor, entering Mbozi's hut early one morning. "You awake?"

No sound came from the jumbled heap of goatskins on the bed.

"Mbozi!" cried the Witchdoctor, kicking the bed. "I's talkin' to you. You awake?"

A head emerged from the goatskins. "Wassamatter?" said Mbozi. He peered at the ancient alarm clock that Brother Luke had given him. It showed a quarter to six.

"Match against Zbolwumbas is next week," declared the Witchdoctor. "We mos' probably losin' again with pathetic white-Bwana in de team."

"Yeah, but can't do nothin' about it," said Mbozi, rising to his feet and stretching himself. "White-Bwana choosin' de team an' team-sheet always havin' his name on de top."

"Mebbe he could havin' small nasty accident," suggested the Witchdoctor. "Or mebbe bad-luck piece of food poisonin'. I got jungle chicken back in my hut what been dead over six months."

"Ain't worth de trouble," said Mbozi, ducking through his hut doorway into the early morning sunshine. "I tell Parrot-bird to nickin' all de contracts. Don' see why we shouldn't winnin' dis time."

The day of the big match soon arrived. This was an early board at the Witchdoctor's table.

Brother Tobias's Last Chance

Love all, dealer East

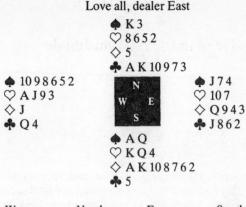

```
                    ♠ K 3
                    ♡ 8 6 5 2
                    ◇ 5
                    ♣ A K 10 9 7 3
♠ 10 9 8 6 5 2                         ♠ J 7 4
♡ A J 9 3          N                   ♡ 10 7
◇ J             W     E                ◇ Q 9 4 3
♣ Q 4              S                   ♣ J 8 6 2
                    ♠ A Q
                    ♡ K Q 4
                    ◇ A K 10 8 7 6 2
                    ♣ 5
```

West	North	East	South
Mahmed El Zhad	Mbozi	Zutto	Witch-doctor
		No	1◇
No	2♣	No	3◇
No	3♡	No	3 NT
End			

El Zhad, a fearsome warrior who was tall even by Zbolwumba standards, led ♠ 10 against 3 NT. After some thought the Witch-doctor won in hand with the ace. He then cashed the two top diamonds to see how that suit lay. If both defenders had followed he would have played a third round of diamonds, discarding dummy's ♠ K. The defenders would then have been able to clear their spades only at the expense of giving him an entry to his diamond winners.

In fact West showed out on the second diamond so the Witch-doctor turned his attention to the club suit. When the queen fell on the second round he drove out East's jack, claiming nine tricks.

"Hah! Dat one not too easy to make," proclaimed the Witch-doctor. "If I winnin' first spade trick with de queen, I can't doin' it."

"Ain't nothin' to shout about," said El Zhad fiercely. "Mos' contracts goin' down if you ballsin' up de entries."

In the other hut the Parrot and Brother Tobias were facing the Zbolwumba chieftain and his wife.

[53]

North–South game, dealer West

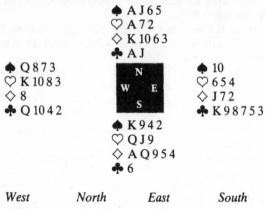

West	North	East	South
Chief	Brother	Mrs	The
Xhuba	Tobias	Xhuba	Parrot
No	1♠	No	2♦
No	4♦	No	5♣
No	5♡	No	6♦
End			

The Parrot concealed his four-card spade support, following Mbozi's instructions, and eventually became declarer in six diamonds. Chief Xhuba, who was wearing a heavy gold-embroidered raiment despite the heat, led ♣ 2.

The Parrot won with dummy's ace and drew trumps in three rounds. He cashed ♠ K, noting the fall of East's 10, then finessed ♠ J, East showing out. Returning to hand with a club ruff, he led ♡ Q, covered by the king and ace. These cards remained:

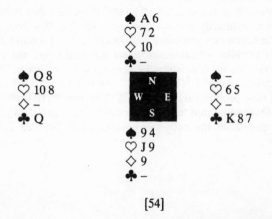

"Just the twelve," said the Parrot, facing his cards.

"How you playin' it?" demanded a suspicious Chief Xhuba. "I don' seein' no twelve tricks."

"I'm playing the jack and 9 of hearts," squawked the Parrot. "How else do you think I'm playing it? Alternatively, I can play ace and another spade; it makes no difference."

The Chieftain, none too pleased at being endplayed by a parrot, thrust his cards back into the wallet. "Write down 2 IMPs to us," he instructed his wife. "Six spades is easy make."

"You had four spades?" queried Brother Tobias.

"Er . . . yes," replied the Parrot. "But diamonds seemed safer. I had five of them."

When the board was replayed, a quite different auction resulted:

West	North	East	South
Mbozi	Zutto	Witch-doctor	Mahmed El Zhad
No	1 ♠	1 NT	Dble
2 ◇	Dble	No	No
Rdble	No	3 ♣	4 ♣
5 ♣	6 ♠	End	

When the Witchdoctor's 1 NT overcall received a vociferous double it was obvious to Mbozi that the call was a psyche, presumably based on a long diamond suit. He attempted to obscure the issue by removing to two diamonds on his own hand. Fielding psyches was a highly regarded part of the game in Upper Bhumpopo.

"What's dis two diamonds?" demanded El Zhad, sitting South. "You playin' transfers?"

The Witchdoctor shook his head and El Zhad turned to look disdainfully at Mbozi. "Pass," he said.

Mbozi paused to reassess the situation. It seemed that both his opponents were heavily armoured in diamonds. The Witchdoctor's call must be based on some other suit. Mbozi set the auction rolling again with an SOS redouble and the Zbolwumba pair bid competently to six spades. Twelve tricks were made for a score of 1430.

"You should passin' 1 NT doubled," the Witchdoctor informed Mbozi. "I mos' probably only five down. Just costin' 1100."

Only 2 IMPs separated the teams as the last set started. Nothing much happened on the first few boards. Then Brother Tobias picked up:

♠ 10 8 3   ♡ 9 7 6 3   ◇ −   ♣ A K Q J 8 2

Zutto, to his right, opened one spade and Brother Tobias overcalled two clubs. El Zhad raised to four spades and Zutto leapt to six
spades. This call was passed out, leaving Brother Tobias on lead.

He thumbed through his cards. Should he risk an underlead of the
clubs, hoping that the Parrot would hold the 10 and could give him a
diamond ruff? Or should he lead a wooden ace of clubs, hoping that
the bad diamond break might cost declarer another trick?

Normally Brother Tobias played a conservative game and would
have had his ♣ A on the table in quick time. But the recent
criticisms of his game had left their mark and he was determined to
regain his reputation. With a determined expression he reached for
♣ 2. This was the full deal:

Game all, dealer South

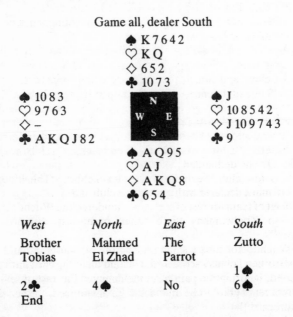

	♠ K 7 6 4 2	
	♡ K Q	
	◇ 6 5 2	
	♣ 10 7 3	

♠ 10 8 3		♠ J
♡ 9 7 6 3		♡ 10 8 5 4 2
◇ −		◇ J 10 9 7 4 3
♣ A K Q J 8 2		♣ 9

	♠ A Q 9 5	
	♡ A J	
	◇ A K Q 8	
	♣ 6 5 4	

West	North	East	South
Brother	Mahmed	The	Zutto
Tobias	El Zhad	Parrot	
			1♠
2♣	4♠	No	6♠
End			

Zutto inspected dummy's club holding with distaste. "Ten!" he
said.

The 9 appeared from East and declarer turned contemptuously
towards Brother Tobias. "Clever lead, Bwana," he said, laughing
openly. "Not many people findin' dat one."

Zutto next played the ace, queen and 9 of trumps, overtaking with dummy's king. Then came a diamond from dummy. The implications of Brother Tobias's McKenney signal of trick 1 were not lost on the Parrot. Praying that declarer would not draw the same conclusion, he contributed the 7 of diamonds, a mild false card. Zutto covered with the 8 and Brother Tobias showed out. Twelve tricks were there.

"What were your diamonds?" exclaimed Brother Tobias, leaning forward to see the Parrot's curtain card. "You had J 10 9? Can't you split your honours?"

"That would just give away the diamond position for the *second* time," squawked the Parrot. "He had two more entries to dummy, a heart and a spade. He can't go wrong if I put in a high diamond."

Zutto inspected the West curtain card. "I can makin' it another way," he declared. "Cash de hearts, then playin' four diamonds, throwin' a club. Parrot-bird have to givin' ruff-and-discard."

The final comparison was soon in progress and not going well for the Bozwambi team.

"De next board was FLAT!" declared the Witchdoctor in a threatening tone. "Four spades minus one. Dey playin' three rounds of clubs and fourth round for de trump uppercut. Quite OBVIOUS line of defence." He looked up at Brother Tobias.

"Yes, well, it didn't go quite that way in our room," replied Brother Tobias. "We lost 1430."

The Witchdoctor snatched Brother Tobias's scorecard and stared at it in disbelief. "Didn't it occurrin' to you to leadin' a club, holdin' de A–K–Q?" he demanded.

"I led a *low* club," explained Brother Tobias. "The bidding seemed to mark declarer with a singleton club and . . ."

"You out of team for rest of season," thundered the Witchdoctor. "Losin' to Zbolwumbas three times runnin' is disgrace to ancestors!"

The Witchdoctor took a small tinder from his waistband and set light to Brother Tobias's scorecard. He held on to the card until the last second, ignoring the pain from the flames. "For rest of season Bozwambi team goin' to be all black," he announced. "Black like your scorecard."

The Parrot coughed gently in the background.

"Well, black and blue and yellow, anyway," said the Witchdoctor.

8

The Witchdoctor's Research

"You comin' to watch de match tonight, Bwana?" enquired the Witchdoctor, strolling unannounced into Brother Tobias's hut. "Mhatpo Baptist team bottom of de league. Should be nice an' easy 20–0 win."

"Coming to *watch* the match?" exclaimed Brother Tobias, who was in the middle of shaving. "What the devil do you mean?"

"Parrot-bird needin' new partner," replied the Witchdoctor. "I suggestin' Mjubu, but Parrot-bird preferrin' Bwana Luke. Ain't much point in dat; he almost as bad as you."

Brother Tobias rinsed the shaving cream from his face and drew himself to his full height. "You seem to be forgetting that it was I who founded this mission," he declared. "I am also the senior churchman present, the most direct descendant of St Peter. As such, it is to be expected that I should play in the first team." He sat down on the wicker chair that had been specially reinforced for him by Mbozi. "I know what," he said. "You and I can play together, with the Parrot and Brother Luke at the other table."

"What! Drop Mbozi?" exclaimed the Witchdoctor. "Mbozi good player!"

"What in heaven's name do you think I am?" replied an exasperated Brother Tobias. "You've a very short memory. Have you forgotten that five clubs doubled I made against the Wahutsi last year?"

"What's in it for me?" said the Witchdoctor.

"I am making this request for the good of the mission," replied Brother Tobias, "To preserve my authority as spiritual leader here."

The Witchdoctor gazed at him, stony-faced.

"And er . . . for good measure," continued Brother Tobias, lowering his voice, "I'll throw in a bottle of Zbolwumba brandy and a 500-mpengo note."

"OK, for de good of de mission," agreed the Witchdoctor. "I ain't acceptin' none of dat poisonous 1-star stuff, mind you. I only drinkin' de 5-star."

That evening the match against the Mhatpo Baptists was under way. This was an early board at Brother Tobias's table:

Game all, dealer North

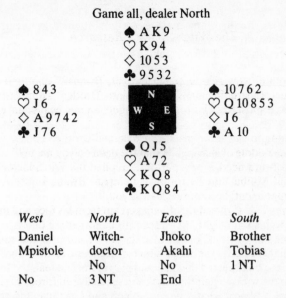

♠ A K 9
♡ K 9 4
◇ 10 5 3
♣ 9 5 3 2

♠ 8 4 3
♡ J 6
◇ A 9 7 4 2
♣ J 7 6

♠ 10 7 6 2
♡ Q 10 8 5 3
◇ J 6
♣ A 10

♠ Q J 5
♡ A 7 2
◇ K Q 8
♣ K Q 8 4

West	North	East	South
Daniel	Witch-	Jhoko	Brother
Mpistole	doctor	Akahi	Tobias
	No	No	1 NT
No	3 NT	End	

Mpistole led ◇ 4 against 3 NT and Brother Tobias found that he was faced with a crucial decision at the very first trick. If the lead was from the ace-jack, he should play dummy's 10. If it was from the ace-9, a low card would work better.

"Ten, please," said Brother Tobias.

When this card was covered by the jack, it was time to think again. There were five tricks in the majors and one in diamonds. To score another three in the club suit, Brother Tobias would need to find ♣ A with East. It followed that the best play in diamonds was to hold off the first trick. East's ◇ J won the trick and he returned his remaining diamond.

Mpistole won with the ace and returned the 2 of diamonds, a low card suggesting an entry in clubs. Akahi, sitting East, discarded ♣ A on this trick.

Brother Tobias took the third round of diamonds and had little option but to play on clubs. He crossed to dummy with a spade to lead a club towards his hand, just in case East had started with A–J doubleton; he could then have ducked the first round of the suit. It was not to be. West won the third round of clubs and cashed two diamond winners, putting the game one down.

"Good gracious, that was a smart defence," exclaimed Brother Tobias. "I thought your team was bottom of the league."

"Dat's when we havin' two white-Bwanas in de team," replied Mpistole. "After first three matches we doin' statistical survey of de contribution white-Bwanas makin'."

"Dat's right," said Akahi, taking up the story. "Turns out dey was costin' us 38 IMPs each per match, so we ditchin' 'em from de team and bringin' in nice sharp black pair."

"Yeah, we doin' similar survey here at Bozwambi," said the Witchdoctor, producing a sheaf of handwritten notes from his medicine pouch. "Ours costin' about de same. Now, where's de precise figure . . ."

"I think we can do without these racialist remarks," declared Brother Tobias. "Next board."

In the other room the Parrot and Brother Luke were facing stiff opposition in the shape of two middle-aged Africans, both wearing pointed beards in the style of an Assyrian warrior. This hand had just been dealt:

Love all, dealer East

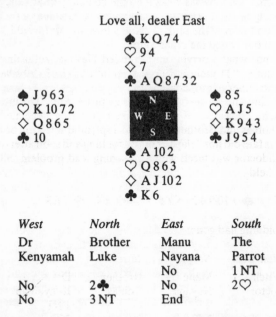

```
                    ♠ K Q 7 4
                    ♡ 9 4
                    ◇ 7
                    ♣ A Q 8 7 3 2
  ♠ J 9 6 3                         ♠ 8 5
  ♡ K 10 7 2          N            ♡ A J 5
  ◇ Q 8 6 5       W       E        ◇ K 9 4 3
  ♣ 10                S            ♣ J 9 5 4
                    ♠ A 10 2
                    ♡ Q 8 6 3
                    ◇ A J 10 2
                    ♣ K 6
```

West	North	East	South
Dr	Brother	Manu	The
Kenyamah	Luke	Nayana	Parrot
		No	1 NT
No	2♣	No	2♡
No	3 NT	End	

Facing a 12–14 1 NT, Brother Luke felt that his hand was not quite strong enough to offer a minor-suit game. He contented himself with Stayman and the Parrot ended in 3 NT. The chosen sequence would, for most partnerships, guarantee four spades in the responding hand. Dr Kenyamah, sitting West, nevertheless decided to lead a spade.

The Parrot inspected the dummy with a beady eye. It seemed that the contract was at risk only if East were to gain the lead in clubs and attack hearts from his side of the table. "King, please," requested the Parrot.

He continued with a low club from the dummy and East contributed the 4. With a superior expression the Parrot covered with the 6, won by West's 10. The defenders were now powerless. In fact West switched to a diamond, but the Parrot won in the South hand, unblocked ♣ K and took his nine top tricks.

"I can beatin' dis one," observed East. "Not easy, but ♣ J at trick 2 killin' it. I mus' gettin' de lead in clubs and an' I can firin' de ♡ J through."

The Parrot, who always welcomed the company of anyone who knew a thing or two about the game, gave his opponent a friendly smile. "Don't worry," he said. "I can't believe the ♣ J would occur to either of our two in the other room."

"Dat's not what worryin' me," replied Nayana, returning the Parrot's smile. "Trouble is I don' thinkin' de *six* of clubs would occurrin' to either of our lads."

At half-time the Bozwambi team led by just 3 IMPs. The interval refreshment consisted of cold smoked tree-frog, declined by Brother Tobias and Brother Luke, and a splendid selection of local fruits. This fare did not delay hostilities for long and soon afterwards the Witchdoctor was faced with an opening lead problem. Sitting West, he held

♠ J 10 9 4 2   ♡ K 7 2   ◇ 8 4   ♣ 7 6 3

and the bidding had gone:

West	North	East	South
Witch-doctor	Manu Nayana	Brother Tobias	Dr Kenyamah
			1 NT
No	2♣	No	2♡
No	3 NT	End	

Once again the auction appeared to mark North with a 4-card spade suit. Nevertheless the Witchdoctor decided that this was the most promising suit to attack. As for the choice of card, surely the 4 was correct. That might gain in various situations when partner held a useful doubleton such as Q–x. The Witchdoctor led ♠ 4 and down went the dummy.

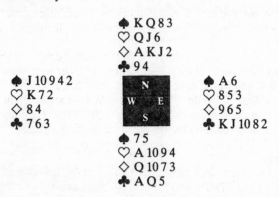

```
                    ♠ K Q 8 3
                    ♡ Q J 6
                    ◇ A K J 2
                    ♣ 9 4
    ♠ J 10 9 4 2                      ♠ A 6
    ♡ K 7 2          N               ♡ 8 5 3
    ◇ 8 4          W   E             ◇ 9 6 5
    ♣ 7 6 3          S               ♣ K J 10 8 2
                    ♠ 7 5
                    ♡ A 10 9 4
                    ◇ Q 10 7 3
                    ♣ A Q 5
```

"King, please," said Dr Kenyamah, who could scarcely afford to play low, letting East in to play a club.

Brother Tobias won with the ace and a close observer would have noted a glint of triumph in the Witchdoctor's eye. Provided East had a spade to return, the contract was doomed.

Brother Tobias returned ♣ J and declarer won with the ace. He then crossed to a diamond and ran ♡ Q into the safe hand. Ten tricks resulted, declarer eventually scoring his ♣ Q.

"You havin' two spades!" exclaimed the Witchdoctor, glaring malevolently across the table.

"Yes, but how could I read the spade situation?" replied Brother Tobias. "It seemed very likely that declarer would have 10 or 9 doubleton in the suit, and you might easily have held ace to three clubs."

"Where his openin' 1 NT bid in dat case?" thundered the Witchdoctor. "Waste of time makin' great openin' leads with you as partner."

Brother Tobias was unwilling to let the matter drop. "Don't be ridiculous," he said. "If we'd been sitting the other way round and I'd led ♠ 4, you would have switched to clubs just as I did."

"Damn right I would," snorted the Witchdoctor. "Ain't no chance of *you* findin' lead of de 4 from J 10 9 suit." He paused to scribble a small calculation on the back of his scorecard. "You already 3 IMPs over de white-Bwana cock-up quota," he announced.

When the match drew to a close the Bozwambi team found they had won by just 9 IMPs, an 11–9 win in victory points.

"Pathetic!" declared the Witchdoctor, after the visitors had departed. "Can't even scorin' 20–0 against bottom-of-de-table team."

"They played above themselves," said Brother Tobias, stifling a yawn. "Well, I'm off to bed. I have a busy schedule tomorrow, supervising Mbozi and the others repairing the grain-store roof."

"Dey doin' it bloody sight quicker without you supervisin' 'em," muttered the Witchdoctor. "Hey!" he shouted, as Brother Tobias moved off into the darkness. "Ain't you forgettin' somethin'? What about de brandy an' de money?"

"Shhh!" said Brother Tobias, reappearing from the gloom. "That is a private matter between the two of us." He beckoned the Witchdoctor to follow him to his hut. "It wouldn't do for anyone to find out you were so commercially minded, would it?" he said.

The Parrot's Grand Finale

It had not been a great season for the Bozwambi team in the league, but they had managed to reach the last eight of the Upper Bhumpopo Gold Cup. The final weekend was to be held at the Bhumpopo City Holiday Inn.

"We're playing El Kebir," observed Brother Tobias, studying the draw. "Probably some pig farmer from the swamps."

"I don't think so," remarked a cultured voice from behind him. "I believe he's a high court judge."

Brother Tobias spun round to see a middle-aged man, smartly attired in white desert costume. "Do you know the gentleman?" he said.

"I *am* the gentleman," replied El Kebir. "Presumably you are . . ." he leaned forward to consult the draw, ". . . Brother Toby-arse."

"Er . . . yes," replied Brother Tobias, "although it's pronounced Tobias actually. With the stress on the 'i' syllable."

The match had not been long under way when this board arose:

Love all, dealer East

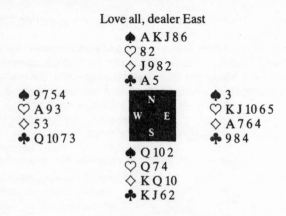

```
                    ♠ A K J 8 6
                    ♡ 8 2
                    ◇ J 9 8 2
                    ♣ A 5
  ♠ 9 7 5 4                        ♠ 3
  ♡ A 9 3            N             ♡ K J 10 6 5
  ◇ 5 3          W       E         ◇ A 7 6 4
  ♣ Q 10 7 3         S             ♣ 9 8 4
                    ♠ Q 10 2
                    ♡ Q 7 4
                    ◇ K Q 10
                    ♣ K J 6 2
```

West	North	East	South
The	N'hana	Witch-	Adel
Parrot	Wohda	doctor	El Kebir
		No	1 NT
No	2♡	Dble	2♠
No	4♠	End	

The Parrot, holding four trumps, decided to attack in hearts. Leading the ace was unlikely to succeed unless the Witchdoctor held both the king and queen, so the Parrot decided he might as well lead a low heart. This unorthodox play might gain if declarer held Q–x–x in the suit, or if dummy held K–x and declarer J–x.

The Witchdoctor won the first trick with ♡ K and, reading the position well, continued with ♡ J. El Kebir tried the queen, but the Parrot won with the ace and continued with a third round.

El Kebir ruffed in the dummy and cashed two rounds of trumps. This brought the unwelcome news that trumps were 4–1. East was likely to hold ◇ A on the bidding, so declarer could not afford to draw trumps at this stage. When he led a diamond the Witchdoctor ducked and the Parrot commenced a peter. The Witchdoctor took the next round of diamonds and gave the Parrot a ruff, putting the game one down.

"Good lead, partner," exclaimed the Witchdoctor. "Lucky I not playin' with fat Toby-jug on dis one."

El Kebir peered down his considerable nose at the Parrot. He had an impressive collection of falcons back home, but he had never seen a performing parrot before. "Yes, it was a very unusual lead," he observed. "The card was nearest your claw, I expect."

"Certainly was, certainly was," replied the Parrot, rocking from side to side. "I expect it will be again, next time there's a similar auction."

The scores were exactly level at half time and this board arrived soon afterwards.

Game all, dealer North

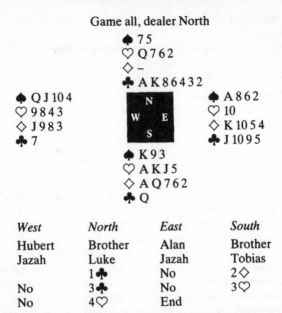

```
                    ♠ 7 5
                    ♡ Q 7 6 2
                    ◇ –
                    ♣ A K 8 6 4 3 2
  ♠ Q J 10 4                      ♠ A 8 6 2
  ♡ 9 8 4 3          N            ♡ 10
  ◇ J 9 8 3       W     E         ◇ K 10 5 4
  ♣ 7                S            ♣ J 10 9 5
                    ♠ K 9 3
                    ♡ A K J 5
                    ◇ A Q 7 6 2
                    ♣ Q
```

West	*North*	*East*	*South*
Hubert	Brother	Alan	Brother
Jazah	Luke	Jazah	Tobias
	1♣	No	2◇
No	3♣	No	3♡
No	4♡	End	

Hubert Jazah, slightly the balder of the Jazah twins, led ♠ Q against four hearts. Brother Tobias winced as the dummy was laid out. "A 5-loser hand?" he exclaimed. "Did you hear my jump shift?" He shook his head sadly. "I can just imagine what the Witchdoctor will say, not to mention the Parrot. You can explain this one to the others."

East won the spade lead and switched to his singleton trump. Brother Tobias won with the ace and cashed a second round with the king, West showing out. Twelve tricks were still there if the clubs broke 3–2, he noted, but if clubs were 4–1 twelve tricks might be out of reach after all. It would be a lucky escape for Brother Luke, who had no excuse for bidding his hand in such pusillanimous fashion.

Brother Tobias ruffed a diamond and attempted to cash ♣ A. West ruffed and returned his last trump to dummy's bare queen. Brother Tobias could cash ♣ K now, but nine tricks were the limit. He was one down.

"Ah yes, well played," observed Brother Luke. "You said you wanted *me* to explain this one to the others, didn't you?"

"No doubt they will be several down in six in the other room," replied Brother Tobias. "It was an excellent slam. No good pair would be out of it."

When the board was replayed, this was the auction:

West	North	East	South
The	N'hana	Witch-	Adel
Parrot	Wohda	doctor	El Kebir
	1♣	No	1◇
No	2♣	No	2♡
No	3♡	No	3♠
No	4♡	End	

El Kebir proceeded to show how the game could be made. The defence started in the same way, spade to the ace and a trump switch. El Kebir won in the South hand, ruffed a diamond and returned to ♣ Q for another diamond ruff. He then crossed to ♠ K and ruffed a third diamond with the queen. Only then did he play ♣ A from dummy, discarding a spade. West ruffed and returned a spade. El Kebir ruffed and drew the outstanding trumps, recording an overtrick when diamonds proved to be 4–4.

The Bozwambi team was trailing by 7 IMPs when the last set started. This proved to be the crucial board.

North–South game, dealer South

```
                  ♠ A 4
                  ♡ A K Q 7 2
                  ◇ A 5
                  ♣ Q 10 4 3
  ♠ J 10 9                      ♠ 6
  ♡ 10 8 4         N            ♡ J 9 6 3
  ◇ J 9 8 4 2   W     E         ◇ K 10 6 3
  ♣ 8 5            S            ♣ A K J 7
                  ♠ K Q 8 7 5 3 2
                  ♡ 5
                  ◇ Q 7
                  ♣ 9 6 2
```

West	North	East	South
Brother	Alan	Brother	Hubert
Tobias	Jazah	Luke	Jazah
			3♠
No	4◇	No	4♠
End			

"What was this four diamond bid?" enquired Brother Tobias, who was on lead.

"Mos' probably natural," replied Hubert Jazah, "or could be cue bid agreein' spades."

"How can you tell which?" persisted Brother Tobias.

"You makin' your lead an' we can seein' when de dummy goes down," replied Jazah impatiently.

If four diamonds was a cue bid, as seemed likely, dummy would have no club control. Brother Tobias therefore decided to lead his doubleton club. Brother Luke cashed three rounds of the suit and led a fourth round. This promoted a trump trick for West and the contract went one down.

"Four diamond bid *givin'* it away," complained the South player. "Even complete idiot would leadin' a club after dat bid." He turned towards Brother Tobias. "If he raisin' three spades directly to four, you would leadin' a trump, isn't it?"

"I doubt it," replied Brother Tobias. "That would be rather a waste of my only chance to lead through the strong hand."

This was the auction in the other room:

West	North	East	South
N'hana	Witch-	Adel	The
Wohda	doctor	El Kebir	Parrot
			3♠
No	4 NT	No	5◇
No	5 NT	No	6♡
No	7♠	Dble	End

West led ♠ J and the Parrot stared at the dummy in disbelief. Had the Witchdoctor finally lost his marbles? Not that he had ever had very many in the first place. "Thank you, partner," said the Parrot.

At least the club lead had been avoided, but it still seemed that thirteen tricks were some way off. A twelfth trick could probably be established in hearts but the subsequent squeeze possibilities were non-existent. The Parrot set off on another tack. He won the spade lead in dummy, cashed ◇ A and ran the trump suit. This was the end position:

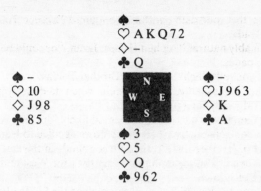

```
              ♠ —
              ♡ A K Q 7 2
              ◇ —
              ♣ Q
   ♠ —                      ♠ —
   ♡ 10          N          ♡ J 9 6 3
   ◇ J 9 8   W     E        ◇ K
   ♣ 8 5         S          ♣ A
              ♠ 3
              ♡ 5
              ◇ Q
              ♣ 9 6 2
```

On the last spade the Parrot threw a club from dummy. El Kebir, sitting East, fingered one card after another. A heart discard was out of the question and eventually he decided to throw his ace of clubs. The Parrot now cashed the established ♣ 9, squeezing East in the red suits. Thirteen tricks were there.

"What in heaven's name made you think that seven might be on?" screeched the Parrot, seemingly not mollified by the way the play had gone.

"You showin' one ace an' two kings," replied the Witchdoctor. "Ain't my fault if you an ace an' a king light."

The Parrot, restraining his temper with difficulty, handed his convention card to the Witchdoctor. "Five-ace Blackwood!" he squawked. "We agreed to play it after that absurd club grand you bid last month, don't you remember? And 5 NT asks for trump honours; my six-heart response shows two."

The Witchdoctor shrugged his shoulders. "You makin' it easily enough" he said.

The Bozwambi players were soon scoring the final set. It was neck-and-neck as they came to the final board.

"We end with a good one," declared Brother Tobias excitedly. "Plus 100! They bid four spades, of course, but I found the club lead to beat it."

"Yes, well don't blame me for this one," said the Parrot sourly. "The Witchdoctor forgot what sort of Blackwood we were playing."

"Just what we needed!" exploded Brother Tobias. "The best opening lead of the match wasted."

"We ended in *seven* spades," continued the Parrot, with a doleful shake of the head. "Doubled, of course. I played it as well as I could but, try as I might, the best I could do was to score 13 tricks."

"How many?" gasped Brother Tobias.

"Just the thirteen," said the Parrot, smirking disgracefully. "2470 to add to your 100!"

The opposing team approached the table and El Kebir stretched out his hand towards Brother Tobias. "Very close match," he said. "It all hinged on that spade slam that our other pair missed."

"It could happen to anyone," observed the Parrot. "I take it they weren't playing five-ace Blackwood?"

10

Chief W'haq's Headache

In the semi-final of the Upper Bhumpopo Gold Cup the Bozwambi players were not pleased to find they had been drawn against the all-international Bhumpopo Aces.

"Absolutely ridiculous that there should be no seeding," complained Brother Tobias to one of the tournament directors. "What sense is there in the two best teams playing each other?"

"We did seedin' de teams," replied the director, a tall man wearing a red and white striped djellabah. "De Aces seeded first an' your team seeded worst of de four."

"There must be some mistake," replied an exasperated Brother Tobias. "What basis was used for the seeding?"

"Me an' one of de other directors watchin' you an' Bwana Luke playin' in de quarter-finals," explained the tall man.

"Seeding shouldn't be anything to do with tournament directors," declared Brother Tobias. "It should be done by someone who understands a thing or two about the game."

The semi-finals started promptly at two o'clock. This was an early board at the Witchdoctor's table.

Game all, dealer North

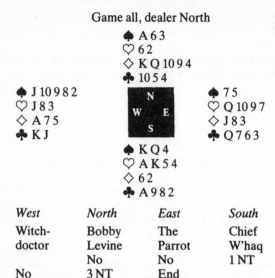

```
                    ♠ A 6 3
                    ♡ 6 2
                    ◇ K Q 10 9 4
                    ♣ 10 5 4
♠ J 10 9 8 2                          ♠ 7 5
♡ J 8 3                               ♡ Q 10 9 7
◇ A 7 5                               ◇ J 8 3
♣ K J                                 ♣ Q 7 6 3
                    ♠ K Q 4
                    ♡ A K 5 4
                    ◇ 6 2
                    ♣ A 9 8 2
```

West	*North*	*East*	*South*
Witch-	Bobby	The	Chief
doctor	Levine	Parrot	W'haq
	No	No	1 NT
No	3 NT	End	

The Aces reached 3 NT and the Witchdoctor led ♠ J. The South player, a wealthy chieftain who owned vast tracts of land in the East of Upper Bhumpopo, won the trick with the queen. A moderate player himself, he was sponsor of the Aces and had to play a minimum of half of the boards to qualify for the gold points. To stand any chance of making 3 NT he would have to make something of dummy's diamonds. At trick 2 he led a diamond and inserted dummy's 10.

The Parrot, sitting East, was ready for this. He followed smoothly with the 3, allowing dummy's 10 to win. Pleased with the way the contract was going, the Chieftain returned to his hand with a heart and led a second round of diamonds. The Witchdoctor again played low and declarer called for dummy's 9.

With a casual air the Parrot picked ◇ J from his wooden card-holder and tossed it onto the table with his beak. He then switched to a heart. The contract had no chance after this bright piece of defence and declarer ended two down.

"How in de Snake-god's name you findin' dat defence?" demanded the Chieftain, glaring at the Parrot. "How you knowin' your partner didn't havin K–J–10 to five spades? Holdin' up de diamond jack could costin' de contract in dat case."

"Agreed, agreed," smirked the Parrot, well pleased with himself.

"Somethin' suspicious goin' on here," persisted the Chieftain.

"You tappin' feet under de table to showin' de spade holdin'?"

"Hardly," replied the Parrot, proffering one of his claws for examination.

Bobby Levine, a professional rubber bridge player from Bhumpopo City, leaned forward. "They're playing strong 10 leads," he informed his partner. "The jack denies a higher honour, so he knew you had the king."

"If I needin' assistance from dumbo like you, I askin' for it!" thundered the Chieftain. "Don't forget who payin' de dollar packet in dis outfit."

"Sorry, Chief," replied Levine, sitting back in his chair. "My mistake."

A few hands later the Chieftain found himself in game once more.

East–West game, dealer South

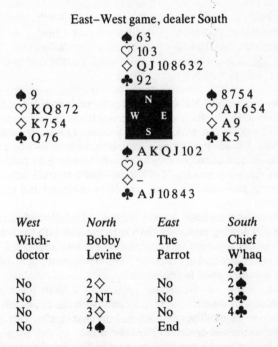

West	North	East	South
Witch-	Bobby	The	Chief
doctor	Levine	Parrot	W'haq
			2♣
No	2◇	No	2♠
No	2NT	No	3♣
No	3◇	No	4♣
No	4♠	End	

Chief W'haq reluctantly let the bidding die in four spades and the Witchdoctor led ♡ K. A second round of hearts followed and the Chieftain ruffed in the South hand. He drew one round of trumps, then played ace and another club. The Parrot won in the East seat and returned ◇ A, which South had to ruff. These cards remained:

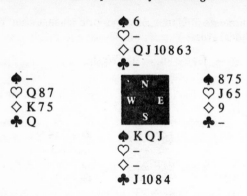

```
              ♠ 6
              ♡ –
              ◇ Q J 10 8 6 3
              ♣ –
♠ –                              ♠ 8 7 5
♡ Q 8 7       N                  ♡ J 6 5
◇ K 7 5    W     E               ◇ 9
♣ Q           S                  ♣ –
              ♠ K Q J
              ♡ –
              ◇ –
              ♣ J 10 8 4
```

Chief W'haq ruffed a club in dummy, establishing the suit. The Parrot knew better than to overruff, which would put declarer back in control of the hand. He discarded a heart, leaving declarer stranded in dummy. The Chieftain could now make no more than his three high trumps and ended two down. Levine said nothing, entering the score with a resigned air.

"What you sulkin' about?" said the Chieftain, glaring at his partner through snake-like eyes. "Ain't nothin' I can doin' about it on dat defence."

"No, they defended well," replied Levine. Of course, anyone entitled to call himself a bridge player would not have drawn that fatuous round of trumps before going for the club ruff. Holy Moses, the way things were going they would be 40 or 50 down by the time the Chief sat out. He and Sonny would have their work cut out repairing the damage.

"My two club openin' workin' like a dream," declared the Chieftain. "Takes a diamond lead to crackin' five hearts de other way. If I openin' one club, West comin' in with one heart."

"They won't go to the five level, vulnerable against not," replied Levine. "They might even double four spades; it could be a terrible one for us."

"Why's dat?" said the Chieftain. "Four spades can't be made."

"Oh, yeah," replied Levine. "I was forgetting that."

The Bozwambi team led by 29 IMPs at the half-way stage and Chief W'haq stepped down to allow his top four to make good the deficit. It was beneath his dignity to admit that the others played better than he did, but with his customary declaration that he felt a migraine developing he retired to his hotel room.

In the next set the two missionaries found themselves up against de Kuyper and Hogstaat, two South Africans with long term business commitments in Upper Bhumpopo. Exchanges had been even when this deal arose:

Game all, dealer West

♠ 6 4
♡ A 10 5
♢ Q 10 9 8 5 2
♣ K 7

♠ 10 7 2
♡ 8 7 4
♢ 7 6
♣ Q 8 5 4 3

♠ K Q 9 8 5
♡ K 6 3
♢ A 3
♣ J 6 2

♠ A J 3
♡ Q J 9 2
♢ K J 4
♣ A 10 9

West	North	East	South
Willi	Brother	Gustaaf	Brother
Hogstaat	Luke	de Kuyper	Tobias
No	No	1♠	1 NT
No	3 NT	End	

Brother Tobias arrived in 3 NT and Hogstaat led ♠ 2. From East's point of view the lead marked declarer with either A–10–x or A–J–x in spades. In an attempt to mislead declarer, de Kuyper played the king of spades on the first trick.

Brother Tobias gazed unhappily at this card. It seemed that West must hold Q–x–x and East K–10–x–x–x, but in that case what could be done? Holding up the ace for two rounds was no good, since the opening bid marked East with ♢ A. Ah yes, of course; he could block the spade suit by winning the *second* round of spades.

A shadow appeared over the table and Brother Tobias glanced round to see a tall figure observing the play. Look who it isn't, thought Brother Tobias. That blithering idiot who made such a pig's ear of the seeding. He paused to check his calculations. Yes, duck the first spade and win the second. If West decided to unblock the queen, the jack would become good.

Brother Tobias won the second round of spades and forced out ♢ A. De Kuyper won and cashed three rounds of spades to put the game one down.

"You had the king-queen of spades?" queried Brother Tobias. "Don't you normally play the queen from that combination?"

"I decided to ring the changes on this particular deal," replied East.

The tall director reached forward to put a fresh set of boards on the table. "Automatic false card in dat situation," he said.

Meanwhile the Parrot and the Witchdoctor were hard at work against the other Aces pair, Wise and Levine.

East–West game, dealer East

♠ 7 5 4 2
♡ K 7 6 3
♢ 6
♣ A K 9 4

♠ K 10
♡ Q J 10 8
♢ K 10 8 5
♣ J 6 2

♠ A 9 6
♡ 9 5 2
♢ Q 4 3
♣ Q 10 7 3

♠ Q J 8 3
♡ A 4
♢ A J 9 7 2
♣ 8 5

West	North	East	South
Sonny	Witch-	Bobby	The
Wise	doctor	Levine	Parrot
		No	1♢
No	1♡	No	1♠
No	4♠	End	

The Parrot arrived in four spades and West led ♡ Q. The Parrot surveyed the dummy, wondering why it was that the Witchdoctor never had any values to spare for his bidding. Now, how should he tackle four spades? It seemed that he would run out of steam if he played to set up the diamonds and draw trumps. When the defenders eventually won the lead with a high trump they would be able to force the life out of him. Perhaps he could play a cross-ruff? Yes, that looked a better idea.

The Parrot won the heart lead with the ace, crossed to ♡ K and ruffed a heart. He then cashed ◇ A and ruffed a diamond. Two high clubs and a club ruff, followed by another diamond ruff, left him in dummy. These cards were still to be played:

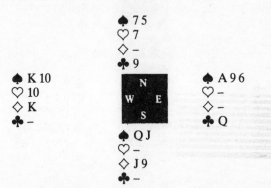

```
                    ♠ 7 5
                    ♡ 7
                    ◇ –
                    ♣ 9
  ♠ K 10                          ♠ A 9 6
  ♡ 10          N                 ♡ –
  ◇ K       W       E             ◇ –
  ♣ –            S                ♣ Q
                    ♠ Q J
                    ♡ –
                    ◇ J 9
                    ♣ –
```

West had made a mild attempt to disguise his distribution by playing the jack on the third round of hearts. The Parrot was not deceived; he played a heart from dummy, promoting a tenth trick for himself in trumps.

Levine gave a wry smile. "Spade king lead from you works well," he informed his partner.

"The Chief would have found it," retorted Wise. "King-one is his favourite lead."

"Don't I know it," replied Levine. "Cost us a game swing in the second set."

In the penultimate set, with the Bozwambi lead now down to 11 IMPs, the Parrot and the Witchdoctor came face to face with the South African pair. This was the most interesting board of the set:

Love all, dealer South

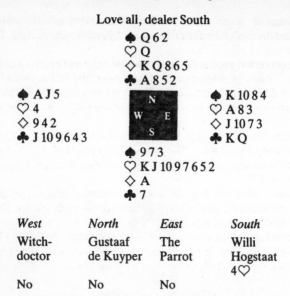

```
              ♠ Q 6 2
              ♡ Q
              ◇ K Q 8 6 5
              ♣ A 8 5 2
♠ A J 5                        ♠ K 10 8 4
♡ 4                            ♡ A 8 3
◇ 9 4 2                        ◇ J 10 7 3
♣ J 10 9 6 4 3                 ♣ K Q
              ♠ 9 7 3
              ♡ K J 10 9 7 6 5 2
              ◇ A
              ♣ 7
```

West	North	East	South
Witch-	Gustaaf	The	Willi
doctor	de Kuyper	Parrot	Hogstaat
			4♡
No	No	No	

The Witchdoctor led ♣ J against four hearts and down went the dummy. Hogstaat surveyed its contents with no great enthusiasm. West would obviously have led a spade if he held the A–K, so there seemed to be no genuine way to avoid three losers in spades and one in trumps. Unless . . . suddenly Hogstaat spotted an interesting possibility. "Small, please," he said.

The Parrot won with the king, rather than the queen, reversing the normal order to indicate a doubleton. He then returned ♣ Q, aiming to remove the entry to dummy. Hogstaat discarded ◇A, won the trick with dummy's ♣ A, and discarded two spade losers on ◇ K Q. He then knocked out the trump ace and claimed ten tricks.

With a muttered imprecation the Witchdoctor thrust his cards back into the wallet.

"Well?" squawked the Parrot. "Would *you* have switched to a spade on my cards?"

"Why you think declarer duckin' de club?" demanded the Witchdoctor. "Dat play stinkin' like pig in swamp. Only foolin' complete wally, I mus' say."

The Parrot blinked. Should he have found the spade switch? It seemed that a spade switch would gain only on the actual lay-out. Normally the Parrot reacted hysterically to any form of criticism, particularly when it was unjustified. On this occasion, though, he had no intention of jeopardizing his chance of being the first non-human to reach the Gold Cup finals. With an iron will he contorted his beak into a friendly smile. "Perhaps you're right," he replied.

With one set to go, the Bozwambi team's lead had been cut to just 3 IMPs. "You not in front yet?" thundered Chief W'haq, who had descended from his hotel room to check the situation. "You think I payin' you for twiddlin' de thumbs? I'd better playin' dis set. Sonny can sittin' out."

"Steady on, Chief," said Levine, not one to surrender a 20,000 mpengo win bonus easily. "We want to keep you fresh for the final. We don't want our star player tiring himself out. You leave it to us; we'll win OK."

"If you cockin' dis one up, I mebbe gettin' other players next year," announced Chief W'haq. "Mebbe signin' up dis Parrot-Bird. He seemin' quite useful player."

At Brother Tobias's table there was little action in the first few hands of the final set. It was obvious that the match was going to the wire. This was board 64, the last board of the match.

Game all, dealer West

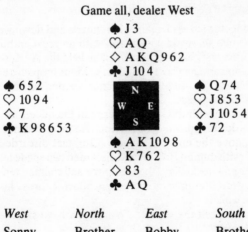

```
                    ♠ J 3
                    ♡ A Q
                    ◇ A K Q 9 6 2
                    ♣ J 10 4
  ♠ 6 5 2                           ♠ Q 7 4
  ♡ 10 9 4            N             ♡ J 8 5 3
  ◇ 7              W     E          ◇ J 10 5 4
  ♣ K 9 8 6 5 3       S             ♣ 7 2
                    ♠ A K 10 9 8
                    ♡ K 7 6 2
                    ◇ 8 3
                    ♣ A Q
```

West	North	East	South
Sonny	Brother	Bobby	Brother
Wise	Luke	Levine	Tobias
No	1◇	No	1♠
No	3◇	No	4 NT
No	5♡	No	5 NT
No	6◇	No	6 NT
No	7 NT	End	

Brother Tobias's 5 NT call confirmed that no ace was missing and

Brother Lucius advanced to the grand on the strength of his excellent diamonds. Wise, sitting West, led ♡ 10.

Brother Tobias, understandably weary after nine and half hours' play, surveyed the dummy. If the diamonds were running, he would have twelve tricks on top. He could then try to drop ♠ Q in two rounds, with the club finesse as a final throw.

Another line of play occurred to him. If in all probability he was going to end by relying on a finesse perhaps he should start by finessing in spades. If he could bring in that suit he would again have twelve tricks on top and excellent chances of a thirteenth, even if the diamonds broke 4–1.

Brother Tobias struggled to keep his eyes open. It was too late to indulge in some complex calculation of percentages. He was going to try the second line. He won the heart lead with dummy's queen and led ♠ J from dummy. Levine followed smoothly with a low card but Brother Tobias decided to persevere with his chosen line. He ran the jack and . . . saints be praised! . . . West followed with a low card. Brother Tobias waited a few seconds for his heart to stop pounding. He then cashed both red aces and repeated the spade finesse. Finally he ran the winners in the South hand, arriving at this end position:

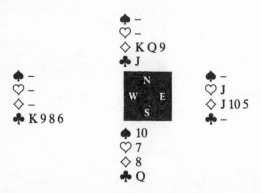

Brother Tobias led the last spade, knowing that if either defender held a diamond guard he would be squeezed if he held also the last heart or ♣ K. As the cards lay, East was squeezed in the red suits and thirteen tricks resulted.

"I'm glad I gave you seven," exclaimed Brother Luke, beaming at his pale but perspiring colleague. "It wasn't an easy decision."

Levine and Wise gazed blankly at each other. Could it be right to take that early spade finesse? Hogstaat or De Kuyper would surely never play it that way.

It turned out that the South Africans had played the board in seven diamonds, which had no chance on the bad trump break. The Bozwambi team took a huge swing on the board and won the match by 8 IMPs.

The winning four were soon in the hotel bar, enjoying a celebratory round of drinks. "Hah! Dat great play, makin' de grandie," congratulated the Witchdoctor, slapping Brother Tobias on the back just as he was starting his pint.

"Very kind of you to say so," replied Brother Tobias, wiping the beer off his cassock.

"I think we can justify another meal on the town tonight," said an exultant Brother Luke. "Why don't we go to that all-night Tandoori again? I don't believe that was dog meat we ate, whatever you say."

"Good idea," replied Brother Tobias. "I can't leave immediately, though. Chief W'haq wants to speak to me. Some sort of business proposition apparently. I can't imagine what."

11

President Mahunde's Intervention

The final of the Upper Bhumpopo Gold Cup was to be between the Bozwambi team and Chief Zokutto's team from the Alemwe tribe.

"Just play straight down the middle," Brother Tobias exhorted his colleagues. "We must be favourites for this one. The Alemwe Strong Club is notoriously unsound."

"They won the other semi-final by 72 IMPs," observed the Parrot, preening his blue and yellow plumage. "Seems like the Alemwe system might be quite a useful one."

"Yes, well, their opponents in the semi-final won't have put up the sort of intervention that we will," replied Brother Tobias. "It's the death of all one club systems, believe me. Don't forget the multi-coloured major defence that we discussed."

The first set of the final saw the two captains in opposition. This was an early board.

East–West game, dealer West

West	North	East	South
West	*North*	*East*	*South*
Chief	Brother	Hakah	Brother
Zokutto	Luke		Tobias
1♣	1♡	2♣	3♠
Dble	End		

"One club," said Chief Zokutto, first to speak on the West cards. This was the Alemwe Club, a conventional opening that promised at least 17 points.

"One heart," said Brother Luke. His partner knocked on the table to indicate that the call was conventional.

"Yeah?" grunted the East player, who wore a blue silk headband festooned with vulture feathers. "What dis meanin'?"

"It's the Tobias multi-coloured major convention," replied Brother Tobias proudly. "It shows either the red suits or the black suits."

"Two-suiter, you mean?" persisted the East player. "5–5 distribution at least?"

Brother Tobias permitted himself a smile. "At this vulnerability there should be at least seven cards between the two suits," he replied.

"Two clubs," said Hakah. In the Alemwe system this indicated a positive response with at least five clubs.

"Three spades," said Brother Tobias, looking pleased with himself.

"What dis meanin'?" demanded Chief Zokutto, eyeing his own splendid holding in the spade suit.

"He wants to play in three spades if I have the black suits,"

[83]

replied Brother Luke, "otherwise at the four level in one of the red suits."

"Double," said Chief Zokutto.

Brother Luke passed, indicating that he did indeed hold the black suits, and there was no further bidding. The play did not take long. Chief Zokutto opened his attack with four rounds of trumps. When he regained the lead with ♡ K he continued with ace and another club, covered by the 9 and 10. East cashed ♣ K, on which West discarded a diamond, and the defenders were able to ruff East's thirteenth diamond good. The play ended with Brother Tobias staring at just one trick turned his way.

"Appalling trump break," muttered Brother Tobias. "Who would believe we would go for 1500 when I had four-card trump support?"

Chief Zokutto flashed his superbly white teeth in Brother Tobias's direction. "White-Bwana forgettin' de new scorin' table," he informed him. "De penalty is 2000, or 'Big Twenty' as we callin' it in Alemwe tribe."

The two missionaries wore a somewhat apprehensive air as they commenced scoring the first set.

"Plus 1370 on de next one," declared the Witchdoctor triumphantly. "Parrot-bird makin' six clubs. De trumps was 5–0 but ace of clubs and finessin' de 8 doin' de business."

"Yes, well, it was fairly easy to cope with a 5–0 break in your room," replied Brother Tobias. "Not quite so easy in ours. 2000 away, that's er . . . 12 IMPs to them. Better news on the next one, though, I managed to make one heart."

"Two thousand away?" cried the Witchdoctor. "Dis some kinda joke?"

"No, it was a perfectly sound sequence, using the Tobias multicoloured major convention," replied Brother Tobias. "Plus 80 on the next one."

"How you think we winnin' de match if we losin' 12 IMPs every time Parrot-bird and me makin' a thin slam?" demanded the Witchdoctor, unwilling to let the matter drop.

"I think you're being very unfair," replied Brother Tobias. "Brother Luke and I have been playing the convention for over a year and as far as I can remember this is the first time we've ever gone for a 2000 penalty."

"Yeah, but we ain't played against any one-club players before," retorted the Witchdoctor.

Play eventually recommenced with the Bozwambi team some 17 IMPs in arrears. The Parrot's defence was tested on this deal.

Love all, dealer East

```
                ♠ Q 9 6 4 3
                ♡ 9 5
                ◇ 10 8 2
                ♣ J 5 4
  ♠ 7                          ♠ K 5
  ♡ 10 8 7 6 3 2      N         ♡ Q J 4
  ◇ 9 6 4 3      W       E      ◇ Q J 7
  ♣ 10 3             S          ♣ K 8 7 6 2
                ♠ A J 10 8 2
                ♡ A K
                ◇ A K 5
                ♣ A Q 9
```

West	North	East	South
Witch-	Hakah	The	Chief
doctor	Hakah	Parrot	Zokutto
		1♣	1 NT
No	2♡	No	5♠
No	6♠	End	

"You knockin' for de 1 NT?" queried the Witchdoctor, who was on lead.

"Game-forcin'," replied the North player.

"An' de two hearts?" continued the Witchdoctor, turning towards South.

Chief Zokutto looked scornfully at the Witchdoctor. "Transfer bid, of course," he replied. "I thought everyone playin' transfers opposite de 1 NT nowadays."

The Witchdoctor led ♣ 10, won by declarer's queen. There was no obvious entry to dummy for a trump finesse, so Chief Zokutto cashed two rounds of hearts and played ace, king and another diamond, putting the Parrot on lead in the East seat.

The Parrot tilted his head to one side, contemplating his next play. Declarer would clearly have reached dummy with a heart ruff if he held more than two in the suit, so a heart return would concede a ruff-and-discard. It seemed best to return a club, hoping that declarer held A–Q alone in the suit. What if declarer held A–Q–x though? He would then be able to let the club run to dummy, gaining entry for a trump finesse. There was one return that would cope with both situations. The Parrot stretched out a claw and flicked the king of clubs onto the table.

Chief Zokutto gave a resigned nod at the appearance of this card.

He won with the ace and played ♠ A from his hand. When the king did not drop he was one down.

"Hah!" exclaimed the Witchdoctor. "Great piece of defendin', partner."

The Parrot hopped up and down on his perch. "Obvious defence, obvious defence!" he squawked.

Scores were level as the players entered the last set before half-time. The two missionaries faced Bfartu and Naoli, two studious 25-year-olds.

Love all, dealer South

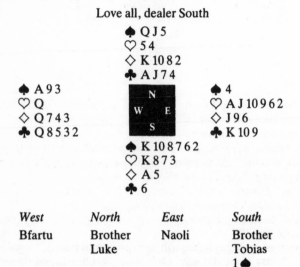

```
                    ♠ Q J 5
                    ♡ 5 4
                    ◇ K 10 8 2
                    ♣ A J 7 4
  ♠ A 9 3                            ♠ 4
  ♡ Q                 N              ♡ A J 10 9 6 2
  ◇ Q 7 4 3        W     E           ◇ J 9 6
  ♣ Q 8 5 3 2         S              ♣ K 10 9
                    ♠ K 10 8 7 6 2
                    ♡ K 8 7 3
                    ◇ A 5
                    ♣ 6
```

West	North	East	South
Bfartu	Brother Luke	Naoli	Brother Tobias
			1♠
No	2♣	No	2♡
No	2 NT	No	3♠
No	4♠	End	

Brother Tobias opened rather light and attempted to bail out in three spades over his partner's 2 NT call. He gave a resigned shrug when Brother Luke advanced to game. Surely three spades was a weak call? He would have called three diamonds to investigate the best spot on a stronger hand.

West made the rather wild lead of ♡ Q, won by his partner's ace. East returned ♡ 9 and Brother Tobias played the king. He could not believe his bad luck when this was ruffed by West. Back came the ace and another trump, leaving declarer with only one trump in dummy to deal with two heart losers.

Brother Tobias cashed ♣ A and ruffed a club. He then crossed to dummy with a heart ruff and ruffed another club. He cashed one more trump, leaving these cards still out:

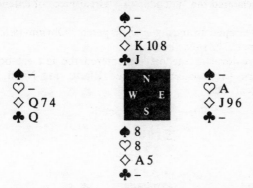

On the last spade West had to release a diamond. Dummy threw ♣ J and East had no card to spare. He eventually parted with ♡ A and declarer's ♡ 8 gave him a tenth trick.

"A double squeeze, as I live and breathe!" declared Brother Tobias, looking exultantly towards his partner. "If that's not worth a game swing, I don't know what is."

"Chief Zokutto South in de other room," said the bespectacled Naoli. "He ain't too good at de squeezes."

"Ah!" exclaimed Brother Tobias. "Then it will be an unfortunate board for him."

"He mos' probably holdin' off de heart king at trick 2," continued Naoli. "Easy make dat way. Only losin' two hearts and de trump bullet."

Brother Tobias, who was filling in the score, stopped in his tracks. Duck the heart? It had never occurred to him.

"I considered the play, of course," said Brother Tobias, "but it can hardly be right to throw away an overtrick worth 1 IMP just to guard against some 1% adverse distribution." He turned to address an elderly couple who were kibitzing. "Some of these so-called safety plays are plain bad bridge," he informed them. "I would never dream of making such a play myself."

At the other table the Alemwe Chieftain had just arrived in a slam.

North–South game, dealer East

```
                    ♠ A Q 5 4
                    ♡ A Q J 4 3
                    ◇ –
                    ♣ K 9 7 2
  ♠ K 8 7 2              N              ♠ –
  ♡ K 9 8 6 2        W       E          ♡ 7 5
  ◇ A 4                  S              ◇ K Q 10 8 7 5 3
  ♣ Q J                                 ♣ 10 6 4 3
                    ♠ J 10 9 6 3
                    ♡ 10
                    ◇ J 9 6 2
                    ♣ A 8 5
```

West	North	East	South
Witch-doctor	Hakah	The Parrot	Chief Zokutto
		3◇	No
No	Dble	No	4♠
No	6♠	No	No
Dble	End		

The Witchdoctor started with ◇ A, ruffed in the dummy. Declarer played a club to the ace and advanced ♡ 10. It would do the Witchdoctor no good to cover this card and in fact he decided to let the 10 pass. Still conveniently in the South hand, the Chieftain ruffed another diamond. He then cashed ♣ K and ♡ A, discarding his club loser. Heart ruff, diamond ruff, heart ruff, diamond ruff with ♠ A, left declarer staring at ♠ J 10 9. The Witchdoctor's ♠ K 8 7 was worth only one trick and the slam had been made.

"Lead a trump! Lead a trump!" screeched the Parrot, with an irritated flap of the wings.

"Any idiot can sayin' dat now," replied the Witchdoctor scornfully. "If de contract played de other way round, you not findin' trump lead in million years."

"Bloody difficult to lead a trump when you haven't got any," squawked the Parrot.

The Witchdoctor shrugged his shoulders. "Mos' probably bein' a flat board," he declared. "Anyone not doublin' on my hand would be complete wally, I mus' say."

There was little further action in this set and the Bozwambi team was soon comparing scores.

"Minus 1660 on de next one," said the Witchdoctor when they

reached the slam hand. "You gettin' doubled too?"

"Minus 1660?" queried Brother Tobias. "Which board are we talking about? I have +150 here."

The Witchdoctor rolled his eyes. "Board 29," he snarled. "De six spade hand."

"Ah yes, we did have a spade fit on that hand, I remember," replied Brother Tobias. "Anyway, West opened one heart and I'm afraid we passed it out. It was very awkward; I don't see how either of us can find a bid on the hand."

"You passin' out one heart when you got six spades on?" exclaimed the Witchdoctor, his eyes wide with disbelief. "Dat de mos' pathetic effort I ever hearin' of. Even for white-bwana."

"Quite so, quite so!" squawked the Parrot. "Mind you, it's always difficult when there's a pre-emptive barrage of one heart against you. We only opened three diamonds in our room."

The Bozwambi lead was down to just 4 IMPs at the start of the penultimate set. This was the first board of interest at the Parrot's table.

Game all, dealer South

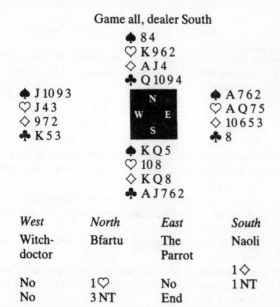

♠ 8 4
♡ K 9 6 2
◇ A J 4
♣ Q 10 9 4

♠ J 10 9 3
♡ J 4 3
◇ 9 7 2
♣ K 5 3

♠ A 7 6 2
♡ A Q 7 5
◇ 10 6 5 3
♣ 8

♠ K Q 5
♡ 10 8
◇ K Q 8
♣ A J 7 6 2

West	North	East	South
Witch-doctor	Bfartu	The Parrot	Naoli
			1◇
No	1♡	No	1 NT
No	3 NT	End	

The bespectacled Naoli opened one diamond on the South cards, following the Alemwe strong club system. He was soon in 3 NT and the Witchdoctor led ♠ J. The Parrot could tell that the Witchdoctor held no higher honour in the spade suit because he and his partner played 'Strong 10' leads. He put on the ace and declarer followed with the 5.

What next, thought the Parrot. South's 1 NT rebid had shown 15–16 points, so the Witchdoctor could hold at most one good card in the minors. It seemed that something would have to be made of the hearts. If declarer had J–x in the suit nothing could be done. What if he held 10–x, though? A low heart switch would then be good enough, provided partner had the wit to put in the 8 from J–8–x. He would then be able to return the jack later, pinning declarer's 10. Still, thought the Parrot, the chance of the Witchdoctor playing the right card from J–8–x was no more than 50–50. How about ace and another heart? No, that was no good. Declarer would simply hold up dummy's king for one round.

Suddenly the Parrot realised the solution to his problem. He returned the *queen* of hearts. Declarer won with dummy's king and ran ♣ Q. This lost to the king and the Witchdoctor's return of ♡ J gave the defenders three tricks in the suit. The contract was one down.

"Black magic, dat ♡ Q!" congratulated the Witchdoctor. "Don' know how you findin' it."

The Parrot gave a contended nod of the beak. Yes, even by psittacine standards, the ♡ Q had been a pretty good card.

Meanwhile, in the other room, Brother Tobias had just reached a vulnerable slam.

North–South game, dealer East

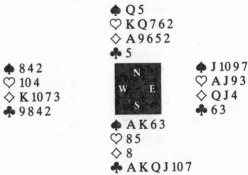

```
              ♠ Q 5
              ♡ K Q 7 6 2
              ◇ A 9 6 5 2
              ♣ 5
  ♠ 8 4 2            N          ♠ J 10 9 7
  ♡ 10 4        W       E       ♡ A J 9 3
  ◇ K 10 7 3        S          ◇ Q J 4
  ♣ 9 8 4 2                     ♣ 6 3
              ♠ A K 6 3
              ♡ 8 5
              ◇ 8
              ♣ A K Q J 10 7
```

West	North	East	South
Hakah	Brother	Chief	Brother
	Luke	Zokutto	Tobias
		No	1♣
No	1♡	No	1♠
No	2 NT	No	4 NT
No	5♢	No	6♣
End			

Hakah, whose feathered headband was drooping somewhat in the humid atmosphere, led a trump against six clubs. Brother Tobias surveyed the dummy. The trump lead had killed any chance of ruffing a spade, but the slam was still a good one. He won the lead and drew three more rounds of trumps, East after considerable thought discarding ♢ 4 and ♢ J. Brother Tobias followed with a heart to the king, which held the trick.

Brother Tobias paused to consider his continuation. It was tempting to return to hand with a diamond ruff to play another heart towards dummy. The snag with this was that if East held four spades and four hearts to the ace, as seemed very likely, he would be able to break the major-suit squeeze by returning a spade.

Brother Tobias nodded to himself. Yes, the only time it would gain to lead a heart *towards* dummy was when West held four hearts to the ace. This was most unlikely in view of East's apparent difficulty with his discards. Brother Tobias therefore led a low heart from dummy at trick 6. East won with the jack and returned a spade, won by dummy's queen. Declarer ruffed a heart, West showing out, and these cards remained:

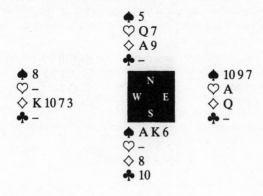

```
              ♠ 5
              ♡ Q 7
              ♢ A 9
              ♣ —
  ♠ 8                      ♠ 10 9 7
  ♡ —         N            ♡ A
  ♢ K 10 7 3  W   E        ♢ Q
  ♣ —             S        ♣ —
              ♠ A K 6
              ♡ —
              ♢ 8
              ♣ 10
```

When the last trump was cashed, dummy threw a heart and East a diamond. The ◇ A now squeezed East in the majors, giving declarer twelve tricks.

"Excellent card reading, Tobias," congratulated Brother Luke. "Even our friends in the other room will be impressed by that one."

"I wouldn't go that far," replied Brother Tobias, wiping his brow. "Still, one does one's best."

The Bozwambi team was exultant. With only eight boards to be played they led by 37 IMPs. Surely nothing could stop them from lifting the cup.

There was a sudden loud fanfare of trumpets and in swept President Mahunde, who some fifteen years previously had unanimously elected himself dictator of Upper Bhumpopo. Followed at a respectful distance by his entourage of soothsayers, bodyguards and musicians, he approached Brother Tobias.

"I understand you havin' only one set left in de final," he said, gold teeth flashing.

Brother Tobias rose respectfully to his feet. "Yes, indeed, your Excellency," he replied. "How kind of you to come and watch."

"Which team winnin'?" enquired the President.

"By good fortune we are 37 IMPs in the lead," replied Brother Tobias, "but it's not over yet, of course."

"Right," declared the President, "I playin' de last set in your team." He waved a dismissive finger at Brother Luke. "You can sittin' out de last set."

"Er . . . I don't understand," said Brother Tobias.

One of the President's military aides stepped forward. "His Imperial Excellence always joinin' de winnin' team to collect de gold points," he explained. "De constitution of Upper Bhumpopo say he only needin' to play eight boards to collectin' de gold points. Unfortunately for last three years de team leadin' with one set to play has always ended up losin'."

"Dat's right," confirmed the President, wedging himself into the seat vacated by Brother Luke. "Blitherin' idiots didn't knowin' first thing about de game." He turned towards Brother Tobias. "Now, you an' me playin' together," he said, flashing his gold teeth once more. "Is you familiar with de Modified Fa'had Relay system?"

The system, invented by the President himself, was notoriously unsound and played only by those in his immediate entourage.

"Er . . . not totally familiar, no," replied Brother Ṭobias. "I am aware of its er . . . excellent reputation, of course, but I much prefer to play Acol."

"You mos' easily pickin' it up," continued the President. "At de one level you open in de suit below de one you got. Also you respond in de suit below de one you got."

"I see," gulped Brother Tobias. "What happens after that?"

"Usually reachin' de right contract," replied the President. "Ah, here comes de opponents."

The Alemwe side, who had been looking somewhat crestfallen during the previous set, appeared to have perked up a bit. They had sent in their better pair to extract the maximum from any lapses the President might make.

On the first board Brother Tobias picked up these cards at Game All:

♠ K 5 2
♡ 8 4
♢ 7 6 3
♣ K J 9 7 5

President Mahunde opened one heart and the next player passed. Brother Tobias pulled his thoughts together. Right, one heart was equivalent to a one spade opening. His own hand was worth a raise to two spades but the first response had to be a transfer too. No problem so far. "Two hearts," said Brother Tobias.

"Three diamonds," continued the President, in a learned tone.

Heaven preserve us, thought Brother Tobias. Presumably, in the absence of any discussion, this must be a long suit game try. Three small in the key suit was hardly a helpful holding, so it must be right to sign off. "Three spades," said Brother Tobias.

The President raised an eyebrow. Obviously he had not been expecting this call. "Four spades," he said.

The next player doubled and three passes concluded the auction. This was the full hand:

Game all, dealer West

```
                    ♠ A Q 7 6 3
                    ♡ Q 10
                    ◇ K 9 2
                    ♣ A Q 2
  ♠ 10                               ♠ J 9 8 4
  ♡ J 9 7 6 5 3 2        N           ♡ A K
  ◇ Q J 4            W       E       ◇ A 10 8 5
  ♣ 6 4                  S           ♣ 10 8 3
                    ♠ K 5 2
                    ♡ 8 4
                    ◇ 7 6 3
                    ♣ K J 9 7 5
```

West	North	East	South
Bfartu	President Mahunde	Naoli	Brother Tobias
No	1♡	No	2♡
No	3◇	No	3♠
No	4♣	Dble	End

West led the diamond queen and Brother Tobias held off dummy's king for two rounds, Naoli won the third round with the ace and cashed his two heart winners. He then played a fourth round of diamonds, which West ruffed with the 10. Brother Tobias could not avoid two further losers in the trump suit and the contract was 1100 down.

"What's dis absurd three-spade bid?" thundered the President. "You chuckin' de match on purpose?"

"I had three small in the game-try suit," replied Brother Tobias. "I was signing off."

"Don't you even knowin' de system?" exclaimed the President. "To sign off, you mus' biddin' three hearts to transfer de contract to my hand. Three spades is cold from my hand. We scorin' plus 140."

"How was I meant to know that?" demanded Brother Tobias. "You said only the first response was a transfer. Anyway, if we weren't playing transfer openings in the first place I wouldn't need to transfer the contract back to your hand."

The President's eyes bulged. "It may escapin' your notice," he said, "but de opponents is cold for four hearts. Dat's de main point of de transfer openin's. Messin' up de other side's biddin'."

"Very commendable," replied Brother Tobias, looking somewhat overheated, "but since I've never played the system before, wouldn't it be wiser to revert to old-fashioned Acol, just for the last few boards?"

"Out of de question," replied the President. "Fa'had relay system much superior. Two professors at Qasradhan University have proved dis on computin' machine."

Brother Tobias reached wearily for his next hand. He picked up these cards:

> ♠ A Q 10 5 4
> ♡ K 4
> ◇ A J
> ♣ 9 7 6 4

President Mahunde opened one diamond and the next player passed. Here we go, thought Brother Tobias. One diamond shows a heart suit. I would normally have responded one spade, but the first response has to be a transfer. "One heart," said Brother Tobias.

This call concluded the auction and the President put down this dummy:

> ♠ K 8 3
> ♡ A Q J 9 2
> ◇ 9 7 2
> ♣ A 8

Spades were 3–2 and Brother Tobias collected five overtricks in his contract of one heart.

"I can't believin' my eyes here," cried the President. "How many points you havin'?"

"Er . . . fourteen," replied Brother Tobias.

"You passin' my openin' bid with 14 points?" demanded the President.

"I didn't pass," protested Brother Tobias. "I bid one heart to show my spade suit."

"By de Snake-God, I's playin' with complete imbecile here," declared the President. "You would have to biddin' one heart on complete Yarborough. With respondin' values and spades you mus' biddin' one spade. Dis two-way, either normal 1 NT response or spades."

"The whole system is absurd," replied Brother Tobias, throwing caution to the winds. "If I respond one spade how can you tell if I have spades or not?"

The President stared back in disbelief. "What do you think de whole point of 1 NT relay on de next round is?" he demanded.

"Look, I've never heard of any 1 NT relay bid," exclaimed Brother Tobias. "I've never played this system before in my life, neither do I ever intend to play it. It's cost us two huge swings already. Surely it's obvious, even to you, that we should switch to Acol for the last six boards."

There was a gasp from the President's bodyguards who were watching the game. If any of them had been so outspoken they would have been lucky to see the next dawn. The President, bearing in mind that some 64 gold points were at stake, chose to ignore the outburst.

After various further adventures of an unsavoury nature Brother Tobias picked up this hand on the final board of the match:

♠ A K Q J 6 3
♡ 5
♢ A Q 5
♣ A K 6

He groaned inwardly. The hand was worth an Acol two-club opening. All bids at the one level were transfers, so presumably he had to open 1 NT. If anyone deserved sainthood surely he did after enduring eight such important boards with someone who should have been committed to an asylum at birth. Or if not at birth, certainly when he invented his absurd system. "One notrump," said Brother Tobias.

"Two clubs," replied the President.

Presumably this was a transfer to two diamonds, a negative response. "Two spades," said Brother Tobias.

The President glared across the table. Clearly he had not been expecting this call. "Three clubs," he said.

"Three spades," continued Brother Tobias, rebidding his excellent suit.

"What a partner!" exclaimed the President. "Four clubs, I say."

If the President had a good club suit six spades would be easy, but Brother Tobias had a nasty suspicion that something had gone wrong with the auction. He decided to play safe. "Four spades," he said.

"I ain't never heard such poor biddin'," declared the President. "How on earth you gettin' to Gold Cup final?"

"Not by playing the Fa'had relay system, I assure you," retorted Brother Tobias. "It's your call."

"Pass," said the President slumping back into his chair.

This was the full deal:

North–South game, dealer South

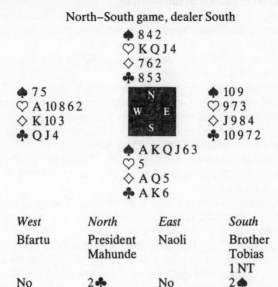

```
                    ♠ 8 4 2
                    ♡ K Q J 4
                    ◇ 7 6 2
                    ♣ 8 5 3
♠ 7 5                               ♠ 10 9
♡ A 10 8 6 2          N             ♡ 9 7 3
◇ K 10 3          W       E         ◇ J 9 8 4
♣ Q J 4              S              ♣ 10 9 7 2
                    ♠ A K Q J 6 3
                    ♡ 5
                    ◇ A Q 5
                    ♣ A K 6
```

West	North	East	South
Bfartu	President	Naoli	Brother
	Mahunde		Tobias
			1 NT
No	2♣	No	2♠
No	3♣	No	3♠
No	4♣	No	4♠
End			

"Why in heaven's name did you bid clubs so strongly on three small?" queried Brother Tobias.

"One notrump openin' showin' club suit, of course," replied the President. "You should passin' my two-club response. Ain't no such biddin' to go on callin' spades till de cows comin' home."

Brother Tobias won the opening ♣ Q lead and immediately played a heart. West went in with the ace and continued with the ♣ J, taken by declarer's king. When the ace of trumps felled the 10 from East, Brother Tobias paused to consider the likely lie of the trump suit. According to the Principle of Restricted Choice the 10 was more likely to be a singleton than to be from 10–9 doubleton. If West had started with three trumps to the 9, he could lead towards dummy's 8, gaining an entry to the heart winners. Brilliant! That would keep the President quiet for a while.

At trick 5 Brother Tobias led ♠ 3. The 7 appeared from West, covered by the 8 from the table. East won with the 9, cashed ♣ 10 and switched to ◇ 9. The diamond finesse failed and declarer was two down.

The President rose angrily to his feet. "You de mos' pathetic player I ever seen," he declared. "You playin' worse dan mos' of my wives!"

"I don't see that I played it wrongly," said Brother Tobias. "I had a guess to make in the spade suit."

"Play de ace-king of spades!" thundered the President. "Then you makin' twelve tricks easy as anythin'. Mos' probably they biddin' and makin' six in de other room. Your hand was *enormous*! Only complete banana-brain would openin' 1 NT on dat. Obvious to openin' Fa'had Multi two clubs, I mus' say."

Bfartu, the West player, leaned forward. "Couldn't you playin' 6 of trumps to de 8?" he suggested. "If dat losin' to de 9 you can crossin' to 4 on third round."

The President nodded his head in agreement. "Even a blind man seein' dat line of play," he declared. "How he gettin' to de final is complete mystery."

A few moments later the Parrot and the Witchdoctor returned to score the set. The Parrot was in jubilant mood. "We've won the cup," he sang, in a wavering tone, "We've won the cup. Ee-eye, tiddly-eye, we've won the cup."

"Quite impossible, I'm afraid," declared Brother Tobias blackly. "You've no idea what went on in this room. The Fa'had relay system is the biggest generator of minus scores yet to see the light of day."

"Our card is worth at least 50 IMPs," said the Parrot, still humming to himself. "They can't possibly have overtaken us."

Two recounts confirmed that the match now stood at an exact tie. The Parrot looked shell-shocked. The Witchdoctor was sitting in a corner, muttering to himself and rolling his eyes horribly. Eight more boards would have to be played.

The President lit a large cheroot and drew deeply on it. "Time to bring Brother Luke back into de team," he declared.

Brother Tobias breathed a sigh of relief. "Thank goodness," he said. "That's the first sensible thing you've said since you came in. You're back in, Luke!"

The President summoned Brother Luke to him. "Is you familiar with Fa'had relay system?" he said.

12

The Upstaging of Brother Tobias

"The Fa'had relay system?" said Brother Luke. "Yes, indeed. I've read your book on it; I found it very interesting."

"I don't believe it!" exploded Brother Tobias. "You let me suffer eight boards of purgatory, which cost at least 70 IMPs, and now you tell me you knew his system all the time?"

"Well, you never asked me," replied Brother Luke, taking his seat. "Now, your Excellency, I assume you play the Fa'had asking bids in the minor-suit slam sequences?"

"Quite so," declared the President. "With de epsilon extensions as well."

"Of course," replied Brother Luke.

This was the first board of the extra set:

Game all, dealer South

```
                    ♠ A 10 6
                    ♡ A K 9 6 3
                    ♢ K 10 4 2
                    ♣ 4
  ♠ 9 4 2                          ♠ 8 7 5
  ♡ J 10 8 5          N           ♡ Q 2
  ♢ A 8 7 6 3    W        E       ♢ Q J 9 5
  ♣ 10               S            ♣ K J 8 7
                    ♠ K Q J 3
                    ♡ 7 4
                    ♢ –
                    ♣ A Q 9 6 5 3 2
```

West	North	East	South
Bfartu	Brother Luke	Naoli	President Mahunde
			1 NT
No	2♢	No	2♠
No	3♢	No	4♣
No	4 NT	No	6♣
End			

"Now, what's dis biddin'?" enquired Bfartu, who was on lead. "1 NT showin' clubs, right? An' two diamonds showin' hearts?"

"Dat's right," replied the President.

"What's it meanin' when he rebiddin' de diamonds?" continued Bfartu.

"Fourth suit forcin', of course," said the President. "I thought everyone playin' dat nowadays."

"What was de 4 NT call?" persisted the West player.

"Dat Fa'had multiple exclusion cue bid," explained the President. "Mos' probably he got de major-suit aces an' at least one side-suit king."

West led ◇ A, ruffed in the South hand. The President crossed to ♠ 10 and finessed the queen of trumps, dropping the 10 from West. Declarer cashed ♠ K and crossed to ♠ A, everyone following. He then cashed ◇ K, discarding his last spade, and ruffed a diamond. Returning to ♡ A, he ruffed another diamond. A second round of hearts stood up, leaving these cards still out:

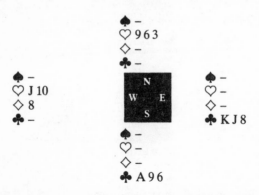

When a heart was led from dummy East ruffed desperately with the king. The President, his forehead gleaming from his exertion, paused to consider this. West was known to hold the J–10 of hearts and his other card was surely ◇ 8, unless East had been disgracefully devious with his plays in the suit. Yes, it certainly looked as if East held all three outstanding trumps.

His mind made up, the President underruffed with the 6. When ♣ 8 was returned, the President faced his last two cards with a triumphant flourish. "Finessin' de 9 for de contract," he announced.

"Brilliant play, your Excellency!" congratulated Brother Luke. "I must say I was reluctant to give you the 4 NT call with only one club. I should really have had at least two trumps in the system."

"Dat's true," grinned the President, "but one trump quite enough with big Pres' at de helm."

The President beckoned one of his aides to the table and instructed him to make a note of the hand. If the editor of Bhumpopo Popular Bridge Monthly knew what was good for him, he would doubtless feature the hand on his next front cover.

Meanwhile the Parrot and the Witchdoctor were hard at work, defending a tight spade game:

Love all, dealer East

♠ K 10 8 2
♡ Q 9 7
♢ Q 8 5
♣ A 9 4

♠ 9 6　　　　　　♠ 4
♡ A J 5 2　　　　♡ 10 8 4 3
♢ A 10 3　　　　 ♢ J 9 7 6 2
♣ K Q 10 8　　　 ♣ 7 6 3

♠ A Q J 7 5 3
♡ K 6
♢ K 4
♣ J 5 2

West	*North*	*East*	*South*
Witch-	Hakah	The	Chief
doctor		Parrot	Zokutto
		No	1♠
Dble	4♠	End	

The Witchdoctor led ♣ K, drawing the 4, 3 and 5. He stared thoughtfully at the Parrot's 3. Was it the start of an encouraging peter from J–3–2? Possibly, but it was more likely that declarer was hiding the 2, hoping to make the 3 look like a come-on signal. With a dismissive glance in the Chieftain's direction, the Witchdoctor switched to a trump at trick 2.

Chief Zokutto won in the South hand and led ♢ 4 towards dummy. West could not afford to rise with the ace or he would give declarer a discard for his losing club. He played low and dummy's queen won. Chief Zokutto returned to his hand with a trump and led ♡ 6 towards the dummy. Once again West could not afford to play the ace and dummy's queen won the trick.

The Chieftain now ran his trump suit, arriving at this end position:

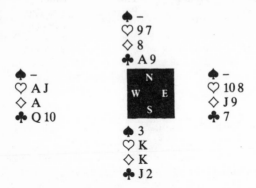

When the last spade was cashed West had only ♡ J to spare. He was then thrown in with ♡ A. After cashing ◇ A he had to lead into declarer's split club tenace and the game was home.

"Mos' excellent effort, partner," declared Hakah, the North player. "Two spear-plays on de same hand."

"Spear-plays?" queried the Parrot.

"Dat Alemwe name for when you stickin' small card through de ace," replied the North player. "Like stickin' poison spear through swamp-pig." He gazed impassively at the Witchdoctor. "Ain't much fun for de victim in either case."

A hand or two later the Alemwe Chieftain reached a dubious slam.

North–South game, dealer South

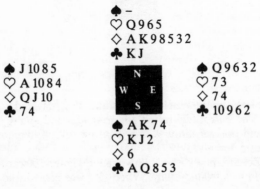

West	North	East	South
Witch-	Hakah	The	Chief
doctor		Parrot	Zokutto
			1♣ (1)
1 NT (2)	2♢	2♠	2 NT
No	3♢	No	3 NT
No	6♢	No	No
Dble	No	No	6 NT
Dble	End		

(1) Alemwe Club, 16+ points.
(2) Mhemhazzah defence, showing the majors.

The Witchdoctor made a foolish double of six diamonds, dislodging the Alemwe pair into 6 NT. He doubled this contract also and led the ♢ Q.

Declarer won in the dummy and cashed the king and jack of clubs, both defenders following. Declarer could visualise twelve tricks now – two spades, three hearts, two diamonds and five clubs, but it seemed there might be a problem disentangling them. At trick 4 he played a heart to the king. The Witchdoctor defended well by ducking. Chief Zokutto now ran his remaining club winners, arriving at this end position:

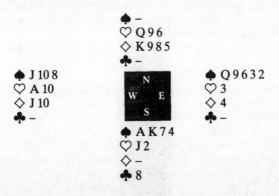

```
              ♠ –
              ♡ Q 9 6
              ♢ K 9 8 5
              ♣ –
♠ J 10 8                      ♠ Q 9 6 3 2
♡ A 10          N             ♡ 3
♢ J 10      W       E         ♢ 4
♣ –             S             ♣ –
              ♠ A K 7 4
              ♡ J 2
              ♢ –
              ♣ 8
```

On the last club the Witchdoctor, sitting West, decided to release a spade. The Parrot had raised him in spades and in any case his holding did not constitute a guard in the suit. A diamond was thrown from dummy.

Chief Zokutto now cashed his two spade winners, discarding two more diamonds from dummy. When ♡ J was played, the Witchdoctor decided to duck again. It brought him little joy. He had to win the next heart and exit with a diamond, giving the last two tricks to the dummy.

"Hold the spades, hold the spades!" shrieked the Parrot.

"I had to throwin' somethin'," declared the Witchdoctor. "If I throwin' a diamond he makin' de whole diamond suit in dummy. If I throwin' a heart he can gettin' to de long heart."

"Yes, but he can't make both spades," squawked the Parrot. "If you keep three spades, the bare $\heartsuit$ A and two diamonds, what can he do? If he cashes the top spades, we can make three spade tricks when you get in with $\heartsuit$ A. If he plays a heart without cashing both spades, you exit in diamonds and we must take a trick at the end."

The Witchdoctor gave a resigned nod. It was true; he had given them a vulnerable slam. Not that it was likely to affect the result. Luke and the President had probably had one disaster after another in the other room.

"Oh yes, and a BRILLIANT double of six diamonds, wasn't it?" continued the Parrot. "That would have had no play at all."

This was the auction when the board was replayed:

West	North	East	South
Bfartu	Brother Luke	Naoli	President Mahunde
			1 NT
No	2♠ (1)	No	2 NT
No	3♢	No	3 NT
No	4♣	No	4♡ (2)
No	5♢ (3)	No	6♣
End			

(1) Fa'had, 10+ points with diamonds

(2) Fa'had zeta bid.

(3) Three side-suit controls plus the ace or king of trumps.

President Mahunde arrived in six clubs, receiving a diamond lead. He won in the dummy and cashed dummy's two trump honours. Next he ruffed a diamond, establishing the suit. East's remaining trumps were drawn and declarer then played $\heartsuit$ K. West ducked, but the President was able to sense that he held the ace. When $\heartsuit$ J was ducked also, declarer overtook with dummy's queen and cashed the long diamonds, emerging with an overtrick.

It had been an anxious hour for Brother Tobias, who had been striding up and down the hotel foyer, unable to face watching the play. "Any good?" he said, as the Parrot and the Witchdoctor approached him.

"Hopeless," replied the Parrot. "We let through a no-play vulnerable slam and gained nothing on the others. With the disasters in the other room I expect we've lost by a mile."

Five minutes later Luke and the President joined them. "You don't look too happy," observed Brother Luke.

The Witchdoctor shook his head. "Already torn up de scorecard," he said.

"Well, don't give up hope," said Brother Luke. "The hands were ideal for the Fa'had system. I think our card should be worth quite a bit."

The President and Brother Luke had done just enough and the Bozwambi team had won by 5 IMPs. The eight teams that had contested the final weekend were soon gathered in the hotel ballroom, waiting for the presentations to be made by the UBBU chairman, Emanuel Lozeki.

"Mos' enthrallin' final dis year," declared Lozeki, who was wearing absurdly built-up heels. "Needin' extra boards for de first time. Eventually Bozwambi team winnin' by 5 IMPs. Please step forward, de winnin' captain, to receive de Gold Cup!"

Brother Tobias rose proudly to his feet. Rarely had more hurdles been placed in front of a team, but they had cleared each one and reached the finishing tape in glorious fashion. This was truly a moment to savour.

"Make way for His Excellency!" called a loud voice. President Mahunde elbowed past Brother Tobias, heading for the stage.

There was loud applause as the President received the cup and held it victoriously aloft. When the applause eventually died down he stepped forward to the microphone.

"Dis is de fourth year runnin' I reach de Gold Cup final," he declared, to further applause. "Mos' of de credit for winnin' mus' go to Fa'had biddin' system, played by myself and white-Bwana Luke. I would also like to thankin' our supportin' pair, de Parrot-Bird and Dr Mhemhazzah. Oh, yes, an' also de reserve player, white-Bwana Tobias, although, as I'm sure he agreein', he not in de best of form in dis match."

The Parrot looked round and saw Brother Tobias sitting somewhat disconsolately in a corner. He fluttered over and landed on Brother Tobias's shoulder. "It doesn't matter what that pompous idiot is saying," he declared. "We won the Gold Cup; that's the main thing."

"I suppose you're right," replied Brother Tobias. "It all seems such an anti-climax, the way things turned out."

"We won, though," continued the Parrot. "You can write a long letter to your Abbot about it. He'll be absolutely overcome when he hears the news."

A tired smile appeared on Brother Tobias's face. "You're right about that," he said.

PART IV

Return to the Monastery of St Titus

13

The Abbot's Mixed Fortunes

"Is the old buffer serious?" asked the Mother Superior. "He's never been very interested in fostering the relationship between St Titus and St Hilda's before."

"I don't suppose it's that," replied Sister Grace. "The Portland Cup attracts national green points, remember."

"He can't still be interested in green points, surely?" exclaimed the Mother Superior. "He reached Lifemaster years ago. He wrote four pages about it in the *Hampshire Chronicle*."

"Yes, but Lucius and Paulo came fifth in the National Pairs final last year," replied Sister Grace. "I dare say Lucius has moved ahead of him in the county ranking lists; he won't have liked that."

"Well, it's up to you, of course," declared the Mother Superior. "I don't know what you've done to deserve such a penance. Personally, I'd rather spend the weekend under a cold shower than partnering our friend Hugo."

Two or three weeks later play was under way in the Portland Cup, the British mixed pairs championship. This board arose halfway through the first session:

Love all, dealer East

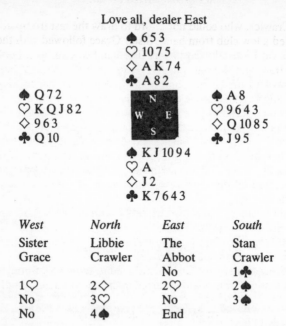

♠ 6 5 3
♡ 10 7 5
◇ A K 7 4
♣ A 8 2

♠ Q 7 2
♡ K Q J 8 2
◇ 9 6 3
♣ Q 10

♠ A 8
♡ 9 6 4 3
◇ Q 10 8 5
♣ J 9 5

♠ K J 10 9 4
♡ A
◇ J 2
♣ K 7 6 4 3

West	North	East	South
Sister	Libbie	The	Stan
Grace	Crawler	Abbot	Crawler
		No	1♣
1♡	2◇	2♡	2♠
No	3♡	No	3♠
No	4♠	End	

Stan Crawler, a small man wearing thick-lensed spectacles, arrived in four spades. Sister Grace led ♡ K, won with the ace, and
declarer crossed to ◇ A for a trump finesse. This lost to the queen
and another heart was returned, ruffed by declarer. When the
Abbot came on lead with the trump ace, he forced declarer again
with a third round of hearts. These cards remained:

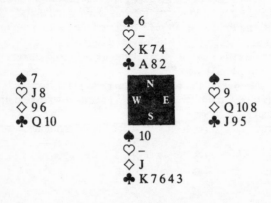

♠ 6
♡ –
◇ K 7 4
♣ A 8 2

♠ 7
♡ J 8
◇ 9 6
♣ Q 10

♠ –
♡ 9
◇ Q 10 8
♣ J 9 5

♠ 10
♡ –
◇ J
♣ K 7 6 4 3

Mr Crawler, who could not afford to draw the last trump at this stage, led a low club from hand. Sister Grace followed with the 10 and this card was allowed to win. The hand was an open book to Sister Grace and she was quick to return a fourth round of hearts. Stan Crawler ruffed in the dummy and took his best chance, playing the ace and king of clubs in the hope that the defender with the last trump would have to follow suit. It was not to be. Sister Grace ruffed the third round and the game was one down.

Libbie Crawler, a generously-sized woman in a purple two-piece, shook her head sadly as she opened the scoresheet. "Yes, a shocking one for us," she announced. "Several pairs stopped short of game, and all those who were in it must have remembered to draw trumps."

"Don't be silly," said Mr Crawler. "I couldn't draw the last trump before clearing the clubs."

Mrs Crawler proffered the scoresheet for her husband's inspection. "Everyone else managed it," she said.

The Abbot and Sister Grace continued to score well throughout the first session. This board occurred in the penultimate round:

East–West game, dealer North

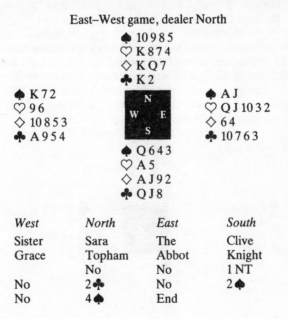

West	North	East	South
Sister	*Sara*	*The*	*Clive*
Grace	*Topham*	*Abbot*	*Knight*
	No	No	1 NT
No	2♣	No	2♠
No	4♠	End	

Sister Grace led ♡ 9 and the pretty young thing in the North seat laid out the dummy. "I've been a bit naughty on this one, Clivey," she said, adjusting her yellow designer scarf. "Only worth three, really, but you play them so divinely."

Clive Knight inspected the dummy. "See what you mean," he replied. Despite the combined 25-count it seemed that he would need to find a reasonable trump break with ♠ J onside. "King, please," he said.

When ♠ 10 was led from dummy, the Abbot rose with the ace and returned ♡ Q. Knight won in hand with the ace, crossed to a diamond and played a second round of trumps. The jack, queen and king appeared in quick succession and declarer soon had ten tricks in the bag.

"Not one of your brighter efforts, Hugo," said Sister Grace. "I had the 7 of spades."

The 7 of spades? The Abbot blinked. What was the old dear talking about?

"Play the jack on the first round of trumps and declarer has to cover with the queen," continued Sister Grace. "I win with the king and return a second heart, then I score a ruff with my 7 when you get in with the ace of trumps."

The Abbot thought this out. Somehow it had seemed funny to play the jack with the 10 9 8 sitting in the dummy. "Your heart lead might have been a singleton," he said finally.

Despite this setback the Abbot and Sister Grace scored 59.2% in the first session. This board arose midway through the evening session:

Love all, dealer South

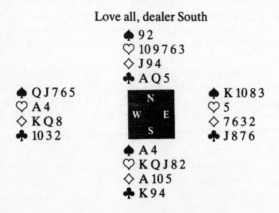

```
              ♠ 92
              ♡ 109763
              ◇ J94
              ♣ AQ5
♠ QJ765                      ♠ K1083
♡ A4           N             ♡ 5
◇ KQ8       W     E          ◇ 7632
♣ 1032         S             ♣ J876
              ♠ A4
              ♡ KQJ82
              ◇ A105
              ♣ K94
```

West	North	East	South
Sister	Sandra	The	Bob
Grace	Landhill	Abbot	Rowlocks
			1♡
1♠	3♡	3♠	4♡
End			

Sister Grace led ♠ Q against four hearts and the Abbot, after some thought, overtook with the king. The declarer, a tall thin man of impressively intellectual appearance, won the first trick with the ace and led the queen of trumps. Sister Grace went in with the ace and paused to consider her continuation. If she defended passively it was all too likely that declarer would be able to eliminate the hearts and clubs and force the defenders to surrender a second trick in diamonds. What was needed was a diamond lead from East. Judging that East would not have overtaken with the king at trick one unless he held the 10 also, Sister Grace decided to underlead her ♠ J. As she had hoped, the Abbot won with the 10.

Bob Rowlocks raised an eyebrow at this turn of events. This was the sort of defence he could do without. The Abbot switched to a diamond, won by Sister Grace's queen. When she exited safely with a club there was no way that declarer could avoid a second diamond loser. The game went one down, which proved to be an excellent result for East–West. "You did well to overtake with your king at trick one, Hugo," observed Sister Grace. "Otherwise this young man might have let my queen hold."

"Yes, I might just have found that play," muttered Rowlocks.

It was past midnight as the Abbot escorted Sister Grace to her overnight lodgings at the Hospice of St Clare the Benign.

"Good night, Hugo," said Sister Grace, pushing open the gate of the establishment. "A good final session tomorrow and we may be in the prizes."

What a fine woman Sister Grace was, thought the Abbot as he walked back to his own lodgings. Face like the back of a bus, it was true, but she certainly had a fine brain. He cast his mind back to some of the bids and plays that Sister Grace had made. Amazing! He might almost have been playing with another man.

14

Sister Grace's Obvious Defence

"Only just in the green points," observed Sister Grace, inspecting the overnight leader board. "With 60.9% I thought we'd have been higher than that."

"Well, there's a very mixed standard in this event," replied the Abbot. "Excuse the pun."

Sister Grace studied the scores of those ahead of them. "To get you a worthwhile haul of greens," she said, "it looks as if we'll need around 65% in the final session."

"You jest, presumably," replied the Abbot, with a short laugh. "Green points are hardly of interest to me; haven't been for a long time. You're a Life Master too, aren't you?"

"I don't recall," said Sister Grace. "At St Hilda's we pay little attention to such matters."

Play restarted and the Abbot's defence was soon put to the test.

Game all, dealer East

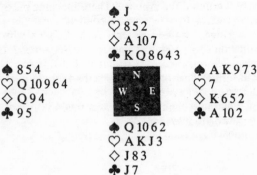

```
                    ♠ J
                    ♡ 852
                    ◇ A 10 7
                    ♣ K Q 8 6 4 3
   ♠ 854                              ♠ A K 9 7 3
   ♡ Q 10 9 6 4         N             ♡ 7
   ◇ Q 9 4          W       E         ◇ K 6 5 2
   ♣ 9 5                S             ♣ A 10 2
                    ♠ Q 10 6 2
                    ♡ A K J 3
                    ◇ J 8 3
                    ♣ J 7
```

West	North	East	South
The	Muriel	Sister	Jeremy
Abbot	Craddock	Grace	Hall-Beagle
		1 ♠	No
No	2 ♣	No	2 NT
No	3 NT	End	

"I have a six-timer for you," observed the ancient Muriel Craddock, painstakingly laying out the dummy a card at a time.

Sister Grace won the spade lead with the king. Dummy's club suit threatened and she lost no time in switching to a low diamond. Jeremy Hall-Beagle, a sprightly 60-year-old in a black blazer and a Cambridge rowing-blue tie, paused to assess the diamond situation. If he played low from the South hand, West's honour would force the ace and he would be left with ◇ 10 7 opposite his ◇ J 8; the defenders would always be able to stop him returning to dummy in diamonds. Feeling he was on the right track, Hall-Beagle went in with the jack of diamonds, covered by the queen and ace.

When clubs were played, Sister Grace won the second round and switched to a heart. Declarer captured with the ace and led ◇ 3, the Abbot following with the 4. "Try the 7, will you, Muriel," instructed Hall-Beagle.

The contract was now secure. Whether or not Sister Grace won the trick, declarer would score five clubs and two more tricks in each red suit.

"I go off if I don't put in that ◇ J," Hall-Beagle informed his partner. "I can't reach the club suit."

"Obviously," grunted the Abbot. "These blocking plays are so well known nowadays, they're almost second nature."

"Quite so, Hugo," agreed Sister Grace. "That's why I was surprised you didn't put in the 9 of diamonds on the second round."

"I say, what a clever wheeze!" exclaimed Hall-Beagle. "Did you follow that, Muriel? This gentleman here had the doubleton 9 of diamonds left; he could have . . ."

"Shall we play the second board?' intervened the Abbot. "You were rather slow on that first one."

A round or two later the Abbot had a chance to redeem himself.

Love all, dealer West

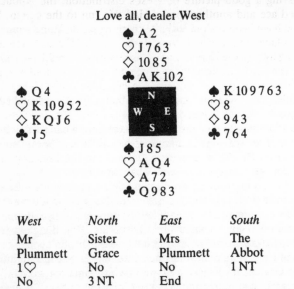

♠ A 2
♡ J 7 6 3
◇ 10 8 5
♣ A K 10 2

♠ Q 4
♡ K 10 9 5 2
◇ K Q J 6
♣ J 5

♠ K 10 9 7 6 3
♡ 8
◇ 9 4 3
♣ 7 6 4

♠ J 8 5
♡ A Q 4
◇ A 7 2
♣ Q 9 8 3

West	North	East	South
Mr	Sister	Mrs	The
Plummett	Grace	Plummett	Abbot
1♡	No	No	1 NT
No	3 NT	End	

The Abbot ended in 3 NT and West led ◇ K. Fearful of a spade switch, the Abbot won the first trick. He then led a low heart towards the dummy. West could not afford to put in the king or declarer would have three heart tricks. Dummy's jack won the trick and the Abbot proceeded to cash the club suit. West could discard one heart but no more. A spade discard would allow declarer's jack to score, so West's second discard had to be a diamond. These cards remained:

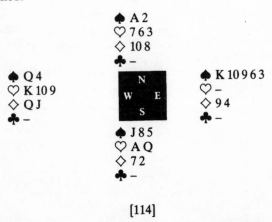

♠ A 2
♡ 7 6 3
◇ 10 8
♣ –

♠ Q 4
♡ K 10 9
◇ Q J
♣ –

♠ K 10 9 6 3
♡ –
◇ 9 4
♣ –

♠ J 8 5
♡ A Q
◇ 7 2
♣ –

[114]

Having a good picture of West's distribution, the Abbot now played ace and another spade. Had this run to the queen, West would have been endplayed; after cashing his diamond winners he would have had to lead into declarer's ♡ A Q. Mrs Plummett, a leading light of the Enfield Lady Conservatives, would have none of this. She rose smartly with the king on the second round of spades, swallowing her partner's queen. "A crocodile coup, Henry, if I'm not mistaken," she said, beaming proudly. She then switched to a diamond.

Mr Plummett looked distinctly less appreciative than his wife had hoped. After scoring his diamonds he had to lead away from the heart king. The Abbot therefore scored a total of three heart tricks as well as ♠ J, recording a somewhat unexpected +430.

"I don't think your king of spades was a very good idea, Eunice," ventured Mr Plummett. "We hold it to nine tricks if you play low."

"The only reason they made ten tricks was because you threw a diamond winner," replied his wife sternly. "In any case, if you wanted to hold them to nine tricks why on earth didn't you take your ♡ K at trick 2 and cash your three diamonds?" She leaned towards Sister Grace. "Typical of a man to try to blame the woman," she whispered, just loud enough for her husband to hear. "I never let him get away with it, of course."

The Abbot and Sister Grace were well pleased with their session as they extracted their cards for the final board of the event. This was the deal:

Game all, dealer East

	♠ K Q 8 4	
	♡ 8 6 3	
	◇ K 5	
	♣ Q J 10 2	
♠ A 5		♠ J 7 2
♡ 9		♡ A Q J 10 5 2
◇ Q J 8 7 6 2		◇ 9 3
♣ 9 6 5 3		♣ 8 4
	♠ 10 9 6 3	
	♡ K 7 4	
	◇ A 10 4	
	♣ A K 7	

West	*North*	*East*	*South*
Sister	Mrs	The	Stefan
Grace	Francis	Abbot	Szabranski
		2♡	Dble
No	3♡	No	3♠
No	4♠	End	

Sister Grace led ♡ 9 against four spades and the Abbot won with the ace. Back came ♡ Q, covered by the king. Sister Grace paused to consider her defence. It seemed that South held three hearts and therefore probably only four spades since a takeout double would not be an attractive proposition on a 5–3–3–2 shape. So, the Abbot was 3–6 in the majors. If he had a singleton in one of the minors, Sister Grace's winning defence would be to ruff the heart and switch to the suit where the Abbot was short. She could then give him a ruff when she won the ace of trumps. But if the Abbot had a singleton, wouldn't he have switched to it at trick 2? Surely that would seem more dynamic than a heart return, where declarer might well hold K–x.

Sister Grace was inclined to place the Abbot with 3–6–2–2 shape. In that case there was only one chance of beating the contract. Sister Grace ruffed declarer's heart king with the ace of spades.

Declarer won the trump return, pulled a second round of trumps, then turned to the club suit, hoping to dispose of his heart loser. The Abbot ruffed the third round of clubs with the jack of trumps and cashed a heart, putting the game one down.

Szabranski, one of London's top rubber bridge players, gazed curiously at Sister Grace. Was it conceivable that a grey-haired nun had actually known what she was doing, ruffing with the ace? One thing was certain – he was not going home without finding out.

"That was rather special defence," said Szabranski, who had never surrendered his Polish accent. "If you ruff low I easily make it. I can pull trumps without letting your partner in to take his heart winner."

"It was fairly obvious my partner was 3–6–2–2 when he didn't switch at trick 2," replied Sister Grace in a matter-of-fact tone. "I won't be the only one to ruff with the ace."

"You're the only one in this section, anyway," observed Mrs Francis, inspecting the scoresheet. "It's a top for you."

"Right, shall we be off, Hugo?" said Sister Grace, putting on a grey coat that had seen better days. "If your Morris Minor hasn't been wheel-clamped, that is."

"Wouldn't you like to wait for the results?" suggested the Abbot. "Not that either of us has the slightest interest in green points, of course."

Smiling her acquiescence, Sister Grace resumed her seat.

"I think the monastery finances might stretch to a couple of drinks from the bar," continued the Abbot. "Lemonade and lime all right for you?"

15

Brother Paulo's Contribution

The monastery team had one match to play in the county league. If they could win 17–3 against the team captained by Bill Maclean they would win the league and qualify to represent Hampshire in the Pachabo Cup.

The Abbot was pacing up and down the senior cardroom, awaiting the arrival of the opponents. "How does he pronounce his surname?" enquired the Abbot. "Macleen, like the toothpaste, or Maclain, like the author?"

Brother Xavier raised an eyebrow. It was unlike the Abbot to pay attention to such niceties. "It's Maclain," he replied. "Why do you ask?"

"I must get it right, mustn't I?" said the Abbot.

A few moments later the visiting team was ushered into the cardroom by Brother Zac, the monastery janitor.

"Ah, Mr Macleen!" exclaimed the Abbot. "You had a pleasant journey, I trust?"

"It's Maclain, actually," replied the visiting captain. "We followed the route you suggested but we ran into a terrible traffic jam on the Winchester bypass. That's why we're so late."

The Abbot gave a satisfied nod. He always recommended the Winchester bypass route. "It's hard to avoid the traffic nowadays," he said. "Shall we start straight away?"

Brother Paulo's Contribution

This was an early board at the Abbot's table:

North–South game, dealer South

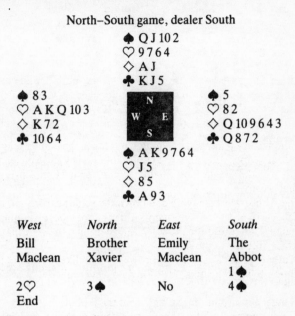

```
            ♠ Q J 10 2
            ♡ 9 7 6 4
            ◇ A J
            ♣ K J 5
♠ 83                          ♠ 5
♡ A K Q 10 3        N         ♡ 82
◇ K 7 2         W       E     ◇ Q 10 9 6 4 3
♣ 10 6 4            S         ♣ Q 8 7 2
            ♠ A K 9 7 6 4
            ♡ J 5
            ◇ 8 5
            ♣ A 9 3
```

West	North	East	South
Bill	Brother	Emily	The
Maclean	Xavier	Maclean	Abbot
			1♠
2♡	3♠	No	4♠
End			

Bill Maclean, who was almost as bald-headed as the Abbot, led
♡ A against four spades. East signalled with the 8 and West
continued with two more rounds of the suit, the Abbot ruffing the
third round.

Trumps were drawn with the ace and queen and the Abbot ruffed
dummy's last heart. He then played the ace and jack of diamonds.
East played low and West won with the king. A heart return would
give a ruff-and-discard so West had to exit with a club. The Abbot
played low from dummy; East played the 7 and the trick was won by
the 9.

The Abbot faced his cards, claiming the remainder. "Where was
the queen of clubs?" he enquired. "With my luck I expect it was
onside all along."

"No, I had it," Mrs Maclean informed him. "I knew you had the
ace, so there was no point in me playing the queen."

In the other room Lucius and Paulo were facing two students
from Southampton University. This was the auction when the board
was replayed:

[119]

West	*North*	*East*	*South*
Brother	Mark	Brother	Steve
Lucius	Butcher	Paulo	Marlowe
			1♠
2♡	4♠	End	

Brother Lucius led a top heart, noted his partner's 8, and paused to consider his continuation. This particular declarer was unlikely to play the 5 from J 5 2, so surely the hearts were 2–2. The defence needed two tricks outside the heart suit and East was marked with around 4 points at most. A black-suit ace would provide only one trick; that was no use. What if Paulo held the two minor-suit queens? That seemed to be the only chance. If East held those cards it must be right to switch to a diamond now, rather than assist declarer in setting up an elimination. Anyway, a second heart trick wouldn't run away.

At trick 2 Brother Lucius switched to a diamond. Declarer took the trick with dummy's ace, drew trumps and exited with a diamond. Brother Lucius won in the West seat and played two more rounds of hearts. Declarer ruffed and ran his remaining trumps, leading to this end position:

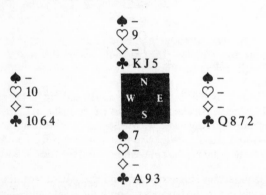

```
              ♠ –
              ♡ 9
              ◇ –
              ♣ K J 5
♠ –                        ♠ –
♡ 10          N            ♡ –
◇ –        W     E         ◇ –
♣ 10 6 4      S            ♣ Q 8 7 2
              ♠ 7
              ♡ –
              ◇ –
              ♣ A 9 3
```

On the last spade West had to release a club and dummy threw a heart. The young declarer now had to guess whether West was down to 10 x or Q x in clubs. With little to guide him, it was human nature to opt for the slightly more impressive play. He crossed to ♣ K and returned ♣ J, catching East's queen and pinning West's 10.

"Yes, well done," said Brother Lucius. "There's nothing we can do about it if you take the right view."

The first set was soon over and the monastery players were busy comparing scores. "Now, this one should be good," declared the Abbot. "Plus 620 on board 5."

"And minus 620," said Brother Lucius.

"I don't believe it," exclaimed the Abbot. "One of those young-sters found the elimination play?"

"No, I managed to break up the elimination," replied Brother Lucius, "But I was caught in the endgame. He pinned my ♣ 10."

The Abbot gave a wise nod of the head. "Yes, I thought that might happen," he said.

There was little action in the second set and the monastery team led by 12 IMPs at half-time. Play had scarcely restarted when the Abbot found himself in a borderline slam.

North–South game, dealer East

```
              ♠ J 4
              ♡ A J 9 7 6 2
              ◇ A 7 2
              ♣ 8 3
♠ K 10 7 6 5                    ♠ 9 3
♡ 8 4 3          N             ♡ 5
◇ Q 10 5 3   W     E           ◇ 9 8 4
♣ 5              S             ♣ K Q J 9 7 6 2
              ♠ A Q 8 2
              ♡ K Q 10
              ◇ K J 6
              ♣ A 10 4
```

West	North	East	South
Bill	Brother	Emily	The
Maclean	Xavier	Maclean	Abbot
		3♣	3 NT
No	6 NT	End	

Mr Maclean led his singleton club and the Abbot won the first trick. He could count twelve tricks if both the spade and diamond finesses were right, but East's pre-emptive opening made this a remote possibility. What was Xavier doing, jumping straight to 6 NT? A call of 4 NT or perhaps five hearts would have been nearer the mark.

The Abbot decided to play West for ♠ K. At trick 2 he led a low spade from the South hand. West played low and the Abbot was relieved to see dummy's jack hold the trick. The Abbot now cashed three rounds of hearts and played a second spade to the 9, queen and king. West was endplayed, forced to lead into one of declarer's tenaces. He chose a diamond and the Abbot claimed the contract.

"You put me on the rack there," exclaimed the Abbot. "If East had held the king of spades I would have gone six down vulnerable!"

"I'm not bidding less than six on my hand," replied Brother Xavier. "Anyway, you made it easily enough."

Some players were incapable of praising their partner, thought the Abbot. Since when did an avoidance play followed by a carefully planned throw-in qualify for "you made it easily enough"?

Lucius and Paulo had played a steady set and St Titus led by 28 IMPs with one set to go.

"Pachabo final, here we come," declared the Abbot. "We need just one more good one to get the 17 victory points we're after."

"Right," said Brother Paulo. "I'll see what I can do."

"There's no need to put your head on the block," grunted the Abbot. "Play down the middle and our superior skill will determine the matter."

On the penultimate hand of the match Brother Paulo, sitting South, picked up one of the finest hands he had ever held.

North–South game, dealer West

```
              ♠ 7 3
              ♡ K 10 6 4
              ◇ K J 8 5
              ♣ 8 3 2
♠ J                          ♠ 8 6 5 4
♡ Q J 9 8 5 2       N        ♡ 7 3
◇ 7 6           W       E    ◇ Q 10 9 4 3 2
♣ Q J 9 5           S        ♣ 10
              ♠ A K Q 10 9 2
              ♡ A
              ◇ A
              ♣ A K 7 6 4
```

West	North	East	South
Bill	Brother	Emily	Brother
Maclean	Lucius	Maclean	Paulo
2♡	No	No	6♠
End			

[122]

Mr Maclean led ♡ Q, won by the ace. When Brother Paulo drew a round of trumps the jack fell from West, ending any problems in that suit. Now, thought Brother Paulo, what position would he need in clubs? If the suit broke 3–2 all would be well. There was also the chance of an endplay if one of the defenders held a singleton ♣ Q. Declarer could pull trumps, cash ♢ A and exit with a low club. Yes, and this line might succeed if East held a singleton jack or 10 of clubs. West would have to leap in with a high honour to prevent his partner being endplayed.

Just in time Brother Paulo spotted a better chance. He drew two more rounds of trumps, cashed ♢ A, and continued with the ace and king of clubs. Although East had a trump left it was hardly tempting to ruff ♣ K and lead into one of dummy's red-suit tenaces. He discarded a diamond, but this only postponed the evil moment. On the next trick Brother Paulo exited with ♠ 2. East had no option but to win and concede three tricks to the dummy. Away went declarer's three losing clubs and the contract was made.

"I suppose you were playing me for three tricks when you bid the slam," said Brother Lucius with a smile.

"In my younger days I would have bid seven," replied the Italian.

The monastery team had won the match 19–1 in victory points and so had qualified for the Pachabo Cup.

"Will your car be up to the journey, Abbot?" enquired Brother Xavier, as the team enjoyed a celebratory drink afterwards. "You were having some problems with the steering last week, weren't you?"

"Yes, but that new novice, Brother Andrew, is meant to be handy with cars," replied the Abbot, re-filling his beer mug. "That's the only reason I admitted him to the monastery. He doesn't know one end of the pack from the other."

16

The Abbot's Loss of Memory

"Have you heard the news?" said Brother Aelred. "The Abbot and Brother Xavier have entered that tournament in Basingstoke on Sunday?"

"Well?" said Brother Michael. "What's so earth-shattering about that?"

"It's one of those 'No Fear' tournaments," replied Brother Aelred. "You know, the ones where conventions are restricted to Stayman and Blackwood and you have to be polite to everyone."

"Good gracious!" exclaimed Brother Michael. "The old boy won't last long in that atmosphere."

"You can say that again," said Brother Aelred. "I'm almost tempted to put us down for the event, just to see if any fireworks occur."

The following Sunday play was into the fourth round when an elderly couple arrived at the Abbot's table.

"Ah, good afternoon," said Bill Everard, resting his walking stick against the table. With some difficulty he took his seat. "I'm Bill Everard and this is my wife, Lilian. We're from the Andover Golf Club."

"Even then you can still beat it if you switch to a spade," declared the Abbot. "That knocks out dummy's ace and he's one entry short to establish the clubs."

Mr Everard gave a polite cough. "Bill and Lilian from Andover," he persisted, maintaining a pleasant smile.

"Ah yes, very nice to meet you," replied Brother Xavier. "I'm Xavier and this is er . . . Hugo."

Mr Everard leaned towards the Abbot. "You're supposed to introduce yourselves at the start of each round," he informed him. "Makes it that much more friendly."

The Abbot raised an eyebrow. There was hardly any need to introduce himself, surely?

"Right, let's get started, then," said Bill Everard. "It's game all and Brother Hugo to speak first."

Game all, dealer South

```
            ♠ A 8 6 5
            ♡ 9 7 4 3
            ◇ A J 9 6 2
            ♣ —
♠ 7                        ♠ 10 9 4 2
♡ A K 10 6      N          ♡ Q J 8 2
◇ K 8 5     W     E        ◇ 7
♣ K Q 10 8 3    S          ♣ 7 6 5 2
            ♠ K Q J 3
            ♡ 5
            ◇ Q 10 4 3
            ♣ A J 9 4
```

West	North	East	South
Bill	Brother	Lilian	The
Everard	Xavier	Everard	Abbot
			1◇
2♣	Dble	No	2♠
3♣	4♠	5♣	Dble
No	5♠	No	No
Dble	End		

The ♡ A was led and down went the dummy.

"I don't understand," said Mr Everard, turning towards Brother Xavier. "How could you double my two-club call when you have a void in clubs?"

The Abbot raised his eyes to the heavens. "It was a negative double," he replied. "Everyone plays them nowadays, surely? A double shows values in the majors on this sequence."

"I'm not sure that sort of thing's allowed in this event," said Mr Everard, giving the Abbot a pleasant smile. "Perhaps you had better call the director."

Brian Beamish, a retired dancing teacher who had been chosen to direct the event on account of his exceptionally pleasant demeanour, nodded his head as the facts of the matter were put before him. "Ah, yes. Well, there's nothing here to worry about too much," he declared. "Just play the hand in five spades doubled and if East–West get a bad board I'll . . . er . . . award an adjusted score."

The Abbot opened his mouth to contest this decision but Mr Beamish had already quick-stepped half-way across the hall, summoned to another table.

The heart ace won the first trick and West continued with the king, ruffed by declarer. The Abbot cashed the king and queen of trumps, West showing out on the second round. At trick 4 the Abbot led $\diamond$ Q, running it successfully when West declined to cover. He then cashed the club ace, discarding a heart from dummy, and continued with a diamond to the jack. East ruffed and returned a trump, leaving the Abbot a trick short.

"Yes," sighed the Abbot. "Five diamonds was our best spot. Even six diamonds is a make as the cards lie."

"Spades looked better at pairs scoring," replied Brother Xavier. "Anyway, can't you make five spades?"

"I took the best line available," said the Abbot stiffly. "Fill in the scoresheet, will you. There's another board to play."

"What happens if you play $\diamond$ 10 to the jack, instead of leading the queen?" said Brother Xavier. "Then you can ruff a heart, discard dummy's last heart on $\clubsuit$ A and play a diamond to the 9. East ruffs but you are in control. You can ruff a fourth round of hearts in dummy and draw the last trump."

The Abbot's reply was forestalled by the return of Brian Beamish. "Now, what happened on this board?" he enquired, putting a friendly hand on Mrs Everard's shoulder.

"No problem at all, thank you," replied Mrs Everard. "This gentleman went off in five spades doubled. We scored a nice top."

"Ah, well done," replied Mr Beamish. "I'm glad it worked out fairly in the end."

A few rounds later Brother Xavier found himself in a touch-and-go notrump game.

Love all, dealer South

♠ 8 3
♡ J 4
◇ Q 9 7 2
♣ A K Q 5 4

♠ A Q J 10 2   ♠ 7 6 5
♡ A 10 3   ♡ K 9 7 6
◇ 5   ◇ J 8 6 3
♣ J 9 6 3   ♣ 8 2

♠ K 9 4
♡ Q 8 5 2
◇ A K 10 4
♣ 10 7

West	North	East	South
West	*North*	*East*	*South*
Mrs	The	Mrs	Brother
Bagley	Abbot	Oakshot	Xavier
			1 NT
2♠	3 NT	End	

The aged Mrs Bagley led ♠ A against 3 NT and continued the suit. Brother Xavier won the third round with the king, discarding a heart from dummy. He then cashed the ace and queen of diamonds, followed by a finesse of the ten. On these last two tricks Mrs Bagley discarded ♡ 10 and ♡ 3, with a meaningful glance at her partner. On the fourth diamond she parted, less happily, with a spade.

It was clear to Brother Xavier that West was retaining a club guard. Instead of playing for an even club break, he exited with a heart. West won with the bare ace and cashed her remaining two winners in spades. These cards were still out:

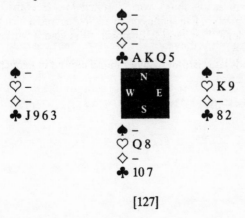

♠ –
♡ –
◇ –
♣ A K Q 5

♠ –   ♠ –
♡ –   ♡ K 9
◇ –   ◇ –
♣ J 9 6 3   ♣ 8 2

♠ –
♡ Q 8
◇ –
♣ 10 7

Mrs Bagley exited with ♣ 9, hoping that this cunning card would mislead declarer. Brother Xavier had no hesitation in running it to his 10 and the contract was made.

"Oh dear, partner," exclaimed the ancient Mrs Oakshot, "I still had the king of hearts at the end."

The Abbot opened the scoresheet and observed happily that +400 was a near top.

"Yes, keep a little heart and he must go one down," continued Mrs Oakshot. "Never mind, though."

"The trouble was, I had to hold on to the clubs," said Mrs Bagley. "Still, I dare say you're right."

"I think you and your partner are both missing the point of the hand," declared the Abbot. "It was easy enough to beat the contract. All you had to do was to exit with the *jack* of clubs at the end."

The two old ladies exchanged a glance. What an unpleasant man! What was he doing, playing in an event like this? He didn't look capable of saying a kind word to anyone, despite his monk's habit.

"Yes, lead the jack," continued the Abbot. "Declarer has to win in dummy and he must give you the last trick."

Mrs Bagley summoned her courage. "I hope you don't mind me pointing this out," she said, "but you're not meant to criticise your opponents' play in this type of event. That's why it's called a 'No Fear' tournament."

"That's right, my dear," agreed Mrs Oakshot, nodding her head several times. "You can criticise whoever you like in most duplicate events, but not in this one."

At half-time the monastery pair found they were lying 10th with a score of 53%. Since most of the contestants had never played duplicate before, this was scarcely the summit of the Abbot's expectations.

The monastery pair met with better fortune in the second half of the event and seemed to have some chance of finishing in a respectable position as they took their seats for the final round. The Abbot caught Brother Xavier's eye as two schoolboys joined them at their table. Surely two outright tops were not too much to expect when your opponents were barely out of short trousers.

The players extracted their cards for board 17:

Love all, dealer North

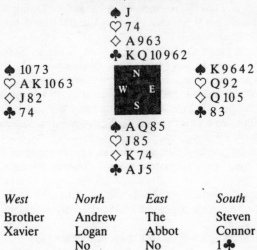

♠ J
♡ 7 4
◇ A 9 6 3
♣ K Q 10 9 6 2

♠ 10 7 3
♡ A K 10 6 3
◇ J 8 2
♣ 7 4

♠ K 9 6 4 2
♡ Q 9 2
◇ Q 10 5
♣ 8 3

♠ A Q 8 5
♡ J 8 5
◇ K 7 4
♣ A J 5

West	North	East	South
Brother	Andrew	The	Steven
Xavier	Logan	Abbot	Connor
	No	No	1♣
1♡	5♣	End	

Brother Xavier cashed the top two hearts and the Abbot followed with the 2 and 9. From Brother Xavier's point of view it was quite likely that declarer held three hearts to the queen. He therefore switched a spade at trick 3 in case the Abbot held the ace. This went to the jack, king and ace. The young declarer drew trumps in two rounds, cashed ♠ Q and ruffed a spade. He then ran dummy's trump suit, arriving at this ending:

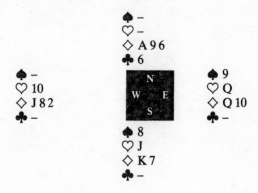

♠ –
♡ –
◇ A 9 6
♣ 6

♠ –
♡ 10
◇ J 8 2
♣ –

♠ 9
♡ Q
◇ Q 10
♣ –

♠ 8
♡ J
◇ K 7
♣ –

[129]

The Abbot, sitting East, was hard-pressed to find a discard when the last club was led. He eventually discarded ♡ Q, hoping that Brother Xavier held the jack. Steven Connor faced his hand, claiming the remainder.

The Abbot gazed at declarer's cards in disbelief. Surely this impertinent youth, without having the faintest idea what he was doing, had just executed a three-suit squeeze of some sort.

The Abbot turned towards the young declarer. "I was squeezed," he informed him. "If I throw ◇ 10 you can score three diamond tricks. Do you see? You can cash ◇ K, dropping my queen, then finesse dummy's 9."

"That's right," agreed Connor. "It was a guard squeeze. We had a similar hand in our match against Norway in the Junior European."

The Abbot's mouth dropped. Junior European? What in heaven's name were a couple of junior internationals doing in an event of this type?

The afternoon's play drew to a close with board 18:

North–South game, dealer East

```
                    ♠ 6
                    ♡ A J 10 8 5 2
                    ◇ K 3 2
                    ♣ A 9 8
  ♠ A 4 3                            ♠ Q J 8 2
  ♡ K 6 3          N                 ♡ Q 9 7
  ◇ Q 8 7 4      W   E               ◇ J 9 6 5
  ♣ J 6 5          S                 ♣ Q 4
                    ♠ K 10 9 7 5
                    ♡ 4
                    ◇ A 10
                    ♣ K 10 7 3 2
```

West	*North*	*East*	*South*
Brother	Andrew	The	Steven
Xavier	Logan	Abbot	Connor
		No	1♣
No	1♡	No	1♠
No	2♢	No	2♠
No	4♣	No	4♢
No	6♣	End	

Brother Xavier was faced with an unattractive lead against six clubs. Since the opponents had reached a slam and he held a 10-count himself, it seemed that the Abbot must have a near Yarborough. Reluctant to lead from any of his major honours, Brother Xavier eventually placed a small trump on the table.

"Nine, please," said Connor, not overjoyed at the dummy his partner had put down.

The ♣ 9 was covered by the queen and king. Declarer crossed to ♡ A and ruffed a heart. He then finessed ♣ 8 successfully and ruffed another heart, establishing the suit. Finally he drew the last trump with dummy's ace and ran the heart suit. This end position resulted:

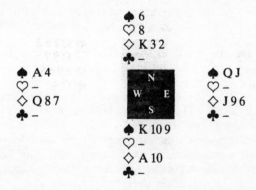

The last heart was now led from dummy. The Abbot, sitting East, could not afford to release a spade or declarer would be assured of a trick in that suit. He threw a low diamond and declarer discarded a spade. Brother Xavier decided to retain his diamond guard. He threw ♠ 4, baring the ace.

Connor now led a spade from dummy and the jack appeared from East. Declarer paused to consider his play from the South hand. East would surely not have thrown from a potential diamond guard just to retain ace-jack doubleton in spades. It was just possible that he held A Q J in the suit, but in that case he would probably have overcalled one spade on the first round of the auction.

Connor decided to play the Abbot for the queen and jack of spades. He ducked from the South hand and West's bare ace appeared. Against all the odds twelve tricks had been made.

"Now I've seen everything," exclaimed the Abbot, slumping back in his chair. "That trump lead was suicidal, partner. There's no other word for it."

"It can still be beaten, can't it?" said the blonde-haired North player. "Even after a trump lead."

"Of course not," replied the Abbot. "If I throw a spade honour at the end, declarer can't go wrong. How can the contract possibly go down after such a poor lead?"

"Sorry, I shouldn't be commenting on the opponents' play in this type of event," said the North player, rising to his feet. "Please excuse me."

"No, no, come on," exhorted the Abbot, unwilling to let his young opponent off the hook. "You said there was a way to beat it. Let's hear it."

"Well, I don't think it can be done if you hold off your queen of trumps at trick one," said Logan. "Isn't declarer one entry short to establish the end position?"

The Abbot had heard enough. He had not patronised this event merely to suffer two absolute zeros from a couple of under-nourished schoolchildren. He rose to his feet and headed across the hall towards David Perry, one of the event's organisers.

"Ah," said the Abbot. "I see you have two chairs on the stage, ready for the experts' discussion of the hands."

"Yes," replied Perry. "We've been quite lucky there. Eric Crowbar has agreed to take part. He didn't play in the event of course, but he watched quite a few boards."

"Excellent," said the Abbot. "I'm sure I'll get on very well with him."

"We were a bit pushed to find anyone else," continued Perry, "but I managed to twist Ken Beale's arm. He can be quite amusing, particularly if he's had a drink or two. I just bought him a couple of whiskies at the bar."

The Abbot's convivial smile vanished in an instant. "In that case we will need a third chair on the stage," he declared.

The experts' analysis of the hands was soon under way. "Right," said Eric Crowbar, his white hair as unruly as ever. "I think we should start with boards 17 and 18, easily the most interesting of the afternoon. Would you like to kick off, Abbot, while Ken finishes his drink?"

"Yes, indeed," replied the Abbot. He leaned towards the microphone and consulted his hand record sheet, searching for the boards in question. "Ah, here we are, board 17." There was a pregnant pause as the hundred onlookers turned their eyes towards the Abbot, waiting to hear how these great players had performed. "I er . . . don't seem to recognise these boards," said the Abbot. "No, my partner and I must have sat out for that round. What did you do on them, Ken?"

17

The Abbot's Unproductive Duck

The monastery team had made a late arrival in Birmingham, where the Pachabo Cup would be contested.

"Isn't this parking space reserved for invalid drivers?" queried Brother Xavier, leaning forward from one of the back seats of the Abbot's car. "There's a white wheelchair sign painted on the road."

"I don't think that applies at weekends," grunted the Abbot. "Anyway, the event starts in ten minutes."

He levered himself from the car and, for the benefit of any onlookers, affected a severe limp as he headed towards the Grand Hotel.

In the Pachabo final each team played a 3-board match against the other contestants. Scoring was mainly point-a-board (2 VPs for a win, 1 for a tie, plus another 3 VPs based on the aggregate margin). The monastery team's first match was against Shropshire, one of the less formidable teams.

North–South game, dealer South

```
              ♠ 9 4 3
              ♡ K Q 6 4 3
              ◇ Q 10
              ♣ Q 10 3
♠ A 8 6 2                      ♠ K 10 5
♡ 8 5 2          N            ♡ A 10 9 7
◇ K J 8 7 5 2  W   E          ◇ 3
♣ –              S            ♣ 9 8 6 4 2
              ♠ Q J 7
              ♡ J
              ◇ A 9 6 4
              ♣ A K J 7 5
```

West	North	East	South
Brother	Bernard	The	Enid
Xavier	Slythe	Abbot	Slythe
			1♣
1◇	1♡	No	2 NT
No	3 NT	End	

The Abbot, who had resigned himself to a diamond lead from his partner, was pleasantly surprised to see ♠ 2 appear on the table. He won with the king and fired back ♠ 10. Declarer played the queen, which was allowed to hold. The Abbot ducked ♡ J and declarer crossed to ♣ Q to play another high heart. This time the Abbot won and returned a third round of spades. West cashed two winners in the suit but declarer claimed the remainder. The ♣ 10 would act as an entry for dummy's heart winner.

"Not too bad," observed the Abbot. "On a diamond lead declarer has an easy ten tricks. We should win the point-a-board."

"A diamond return from you works well, oddly enough," replied Brother Xavier. "The game goes one down, I think."

The Abbot stopped in mid-gloat. A diamond return?

"Yes, that's right," intervened Mrs Slythe. "If I run the diamond, your partner can win with the king and return a low spade, and if I put up ◇ A I must lose two diamonds, two spades and a heart."

"As it happens," agreed the Abbot, recovering his poise. "It would have been an *absurd* defence to play, though."

Despite this setback the monastery team won their first match 5–4. Their next opponents were two dons and two students, representing the county of Oxford. Brother Lucius did well on this board:

Love all, dealer South

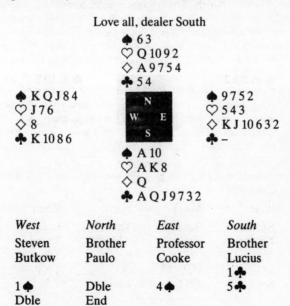

```
              ♠ 63
              ♡ Q 10 9 2
              ◇ A 9 7 5 4
              ♣ 5 4

♠ K Q J 8 4                    ♠ 9 7 5 2
♡ J 7 6            N            ♡ 5 4 3
◇ 8            W       E        ◇ K J 10 6 3 2
♣ K 10 8 6        S            ♣ –

              ♠ A 10
              ♡ A K 8
              ◇ Q
              ♣ A Q J 9 7 3 2
```

West	North	East	South
Steven	Brother	Professor	Brother
Butkow	Paulo	Cooke	Lucius
			1♣
1♠	Dble	4♠	5♣
Dble	End		

Brother Lucius won the spade lead and played the ace of trumps. As feared, after West's double, the trumps were 4–0. The only chance was to dispose of the spade loser on dummy's hearts. Brother Lucius played three rounds of hearts and West followed all the way. On the fourth round of hearts declarer threw his spade loser and West ruffed with the 8. Brother Lucius ruffed the spade return, leaving these cards still out:

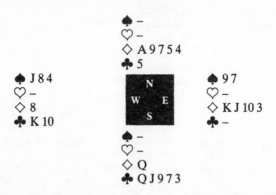

Brother Lucius had ♣ Q half-way out of his hand when he paused to count West's distribution. He had five spades, presumably, and had shown up with four clubs and three hearts. That left him with a singleton diamond. So, it would be disastrous to play ♣ Q at this stage. West would exit with his singleton diamond and subsequently score his ♣ 10.

Brother Lucius smiled to himself. He had nearly thrown the contract away. He led ♢ Q to the ace and only then did he play another round of trumps. The contract was now secure.

"Yes, a Dentist's Coup," observed Professor Cooke, nodding respectfully in Brother Lucius's direction. "Extraction, you see. Nothing we could do."

At the other table of this match the undergraduate declarer had just arrived in 6 NT.

Game all, dealer North

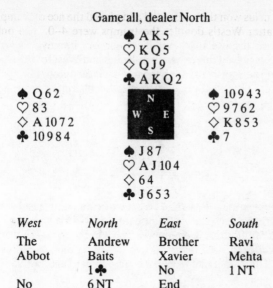

♠ A K 5
♡ K Q 5
◇ Q J 9
♣ A K Q 2

♠ Q 6 2
♡ 8 3
◇ A 10 7 2
♣ 10 9 8 4

♠ 10 9 4 3
♡ 9 7 6 2
◇ K 8 5 3
♣ 7

♠ J 8 7
♡ A J 10 4
◇ 6 4
♣ J 6 5 3

West	North	East	South
The	Andrew	Brother	Ravi
Abbot	Baits	Xavier	Mehta
	1♣	No	1 NT
No	6 NT	End	

The Abbot, on lead, studied the students' convention card. "Precision Club, is it?" he said. "How strong is the 1 NT response?"

"Eight to ten," replied the North player, who had a multi-coloured college scarf round his neck.

The Abbot led ♣ 10 and down went the dummy. The Abbot performed some mental arithmetic. Yes, Xavier was marked with at most two points. All the queens were on view, so the most he might hold was a couple of jacks. The Indian declarer won the club lead in the dummy, East playing the 7, declarer the 5.

"Queen of diamonds, please," said the young Indian, without pausing for thought.

Brother Xavier played low, not wishing to set up a possible finesse against West's 10, and so did the Abbot. With a diamond trick in the bag, declarer now cashed three rounds of clubs, followed by four rounds of hearts. This was the end position:

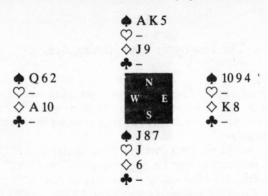

```
              ♠ A K 5
              ♡ -
              ◇ J 9
              ♣ -
♠ Q 6 2                      ♠ 10 9 4
♡ -          ┌─────────┐     ♡ -
◇ A 10       │    N    │     ◇ K 8
♣ -          │ W     E │     ♣ -
             │    S    │
             └─────────┘
              ♠ J 8 7
              ♡ J
              ◇ 6
              ♣ -
```

The Abbot, sitting West, had no good discard on the last heart. If he threw ◇ A, declarer would discard a spade from dummy and establish a twelfth trick in diamonds. The Abbot's actual choice was ◇ 10; declarer threw a diamond from dummy, then exited with a diamond. The Abbot had to lead away from ♠ Q and twelve tricks resulted.

"Why on earth did you play it like that?" exclaimed the North player. "You had twelve tricks on top, just by knocking out the ace of diamonds! You might have gone down the way you played it."

"No, no, I am not having diamond king," replied the Indian, flashing his white teeth. "This was only way I am making this contract."

The Abbot reached for his opponent's curtain card. "Just a moment," he said. "Your partner said you would have 8–10 points. There are only 7 here."

"Ah yes," replied the young Indian learnedly, "but A J 10 combination undervalued by point count. I am counting six and a half points for this holding."

"I expect it will be a good board for you," declared the Abbot stiffly. "Our other pair doesn't play Precision."

18

The Tale of the Two Missing Aces

The first session of the Pachabo Cup was over. Monastery finances would not permit an excursion to one of Birmingham's gourmet restaurants, if such existed, so the St Titus team repaired to a local fish-and-chip shop.

"I hope we have better luck tonight," declared the Abbot, shaking some vinegar onto his bag of chips. "That Oxford team hadn't the first idea. Heaven knows how they beat us 8–1."

Brother Paulo peered inside his chip bag. "They aren't seeming to like Italians here, Abbot," he observed. "I have only half as many chips as you."

"Yes, portions are a bit small in this part of the country," replied the Abbot. "Fortunately I had the foresight to order a double portion."

The evening session started with a match against Gloucestershire. The Abbot's opponents were two young men of sporty appearance.

Love all, dealer East

```
                    ♠ A 10 9 7 6
                    ♡ Q 5
                    ◇ Q 8 7 2
                    ♣ 9 4
   ♠ 3                              ♠ K
   ♡ J 9 7 2          N            ♡ K 8 6 3
   ◇ J 10 9 6 3    W     E         ◇ K 5 4
   ♣ J 10 5           S            ♣ K Q 7 6 2
                    ♠ Q J 8 5 4 2
                    ♡ A 10 4
                    ◇ A
                    ♣ A 8 3
```

West	North	East	South
The	Philip	Brother	John
Abbot	Croke	Xavier	Lang
		1♣	1♠
No	4♠	No	6♠
End			

Against six spades the Abbot led ♣ J, won by South's ace. It seemed to the Abbot that the declarer was far from overjoyed at the assets laid out in the dummy. There was nothing in his own hand to suggest that the cards were lying favourably for declarer, so there seemed to be every chance of a big swing in the right direction.

Declarer cashed ♢ A and crossed to the spade ace, felling East's king. A diamond ruff was followed by a trump to the 10 and a second diamond ruff, bringing down another king from the East hand. A trump to the 9 allowed declarer to dispose of a club on ♢ Q. These cards remained:

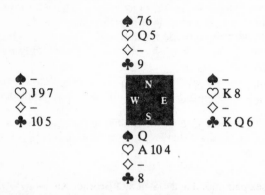

When declarer called for dummy's ♣ 9 Xavier bravely played low, letting the trick run to the Abbot's 10. The Abbot came off lead with a low heart but declarer took the right view, running it to his hand. Twelve tricks were there.

"Lucky to escape a trump lead," observed the jubilant declarer. "That leaves me one entry short, I think."

The Abbot glared at his opponent. "I suppose you would have led a trump from my hand?" he said.

"It's usually safest, against a slam," came the reply. "Still, I suppose a club could have been right."

The monastery team lost this match 6–3 but fared well in their next few encounters. In the last match of the evening they faced Sussex, captained by lady international Sandra Landhill. This was the first deal:

Game all, dealer East

```
                  ♠ A K Q 8 2
                  ♡ A 10 5
                  ◇ 7 3
                  ♣ A 9 2
  ♠ 9 7                           ♠ J 10 5 3
  ♡ 9 8 4 2          N            ♡ 7 6
  ◇ J 10 9       W     E          ◇ Q 6 5 4
  ♣ K J 5 3          S            ♣ 10 8 7
                  ♠ 6 4
                  ♡ K Q J 3
                  ◇ A K 8 2
                  ♣ Q 6 4
```

West	*North*	*East*	*South*
Brother	John	The	Sandra
Xavier	Ellery	Abbot	Landhill
		No	1♡
No	2♠	No	2 NT
No	3♡	No	4◇
No	6♡	End	

The Sussex pair ended in a 4–3 fit and Brother Xavier led ◇ J.

"Thank you, John," said Landhill, studying the dummy through an impressive pair of spectacles. "Small, please."

Landhill won with ◇ A and immediately ducked a round of spades, won by East. When the Abbot exited passively in diamonds, she won with the king and ruffed a diamond with dummy's ace. She then drew trumps in four rounds and returned to the spade suit. Twelve tricks were there when the suit divided 4–2.

The Abbot turned to survey Landhill. How was it possible for a woman to play the dummy that well, he wondered. And the bidding hadn't been too bad either. It looked as if 6 NT might be in difficulties.

The next hand was played in a part score. On the final hand of the 3-board match the Abbot, sitting East at adverse vulnerability, picked up these cards:

♠ A   ♡ J 9 4   ◇ 3   ♣ K Q J 10 9 7 5 2

"Two diamonds," said Ellery, to the Abbot's right.

The Abbot consulted Ellery's convention card. Yes, they were playing the multi. Three clubs seemed the obvious call, but that might make it too easy for the next player. "Four clubs," he said.

"Four diamonds," said Landhill.

"Four notrumps," said Brother Xavier.

Ellery passed and the Abbot stared at his hand once more. Four notrumps? That was Blackwood, surely. He was beginning to regret his four-club venture. Xavier would doubtless expect more in the way of high cards than this. Yes, it seemed best to deny the ace and keep the bidding low. If Xavier did hold two aces and some means of disposing of the heart losers, that was too bad. "Five clubs," said the Abbot. Landhill passed.

"Seven clubs," said Brother Xavier.

The Abbot's heart sank. Seven! Was Xavier on some kamikaze suicide mission? The awful truth dawned on the Abbot. His five-club response had shown 0 or 3 aces. Xavier, with one ace, had read him for the remaining three. There was nothing to be done. He would just have to take his medicine.

Suddenly the Abbot realised that Ellery was still thinking. Miracle of miracles! He was obviously thinking of bidding seven diamonds.

"What was the 4 NT call?" enquired Ellery, turning towards the Abbot.

"Blackwood," replied the Abbot. "We like to keep it simple."

". . . and the five-club response?" continued Ellery, turning to his right.

"Nought or three aces," replied Brother Xavier.

Ellery surveyed his cards once more. The Abbot would have given quite a bit to see how Sandra Landhill, with two aces in her hand, was taking the situation. He dared not look up, though.

"Seven diamonds," said Ellery.

"Double," said the Abbot.

"Pass me my cigarettes," growled Landhill.

This was the complete deal:

East–West game, dealer North

```
                    ♠ Q 10 8 7 6 2
                    ♡ 8 3 2
                    ◇ K 9 5 4
                    ♣ –
♠ J 3                                   ♠ A
♡ K Q 10 7 5          N                 ♡ J 9 4
◇ Q 7            W         E            ◇ 3
♣ A 8 4 3             S                 ♣ K Q J 10 9 7 5 2
                    ♠ K 9 5 4
                    ♡ A 6
                    ◇ A J 10 8 6 2
                    ♣ 6
```

West	North	East	South
Brother	John	The	Sandra
Xavier	Ellery	Abbot	Landhill
	2◇	4♣	4◇
4 NT	No	5♣	No
7♣	7◇	Dble	End

Brother Xavier led ♡ K, won by declarer's ace.

"Sorry, partner," muttered Ellery.

"There's another one to come!" barked Landhill.

The monastery team had climbed into sixth place by the end of the evening session. They were in a satisfied mood as they drove back to their overnight accommodation.

"You see?" exclaimed the Abbot. "I told you I wouldn't get a parking ticket."

"They probably took pity on you," replied Brother Lucius. "With a car as old as this, they must have thought you wouldn't be able to afford the fine."

"Outside appearances aren't everything," declared the Abbot, crunching into third gear. "They don't make cars like this nowadays."

19

London Bridge is Falling Down

The monastery team was in a respectable sixth position overnight in the Pachabo final. The sun was shining through the guest-house windows as they took their breakfast.

"Play starts at 11 o'clock," observed Brother Lucius, pouring himself some cornflakes. "What time do you think we ought to get there, Abbot?"

"Oh, about 10.15, I suppose," replied the Abbot. "It's always enjoyable to talk to the other teams beforehand."

Not always, thought Brother Lucius. Last time they had reached the Pachabo final they had been 26th out of 28 teams overnight. If memory served him correctly, they had narrowly escaped a fine for late arrival.

The monastery team's first match on the final day was against Derbyshire. Both tables reached the spade game on this board.

North–South game, dealer East

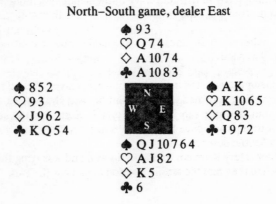

```
                    ♠ 9 3
                    ♡ Q 7 4
                    ◇ A 10 7 4
                    ♣ A 10 8 3
    ♠ 8 5 2                        ♠ A K
    ♡ 9 3              N           ♡ K 10 6 5
    ◇ J 9 6 2      W       E       ◇ Q 8 3
    ♣ K Q 5 4          S           ♣ J 9 7 2
                    ♠ Q J 10 7 6 4
                    ♡ A J 8 2
                    ◇ K 5
                    ♣ 6
```

West	North	East	South
Brother	John	The	James
Xavier	Barker	Abbot	Heape
		1 NT	2♠
No	3♠	No	4♠
End			

Brother Xavier led ♡ 9, won by declarer's jack. The Abbot captured ♠ Q with the king and paused to consider his defence. Since he and Xavier led second best from poor suits, West's ♡ 9 had to be from a doubleton. Declarer's shape must therefore be something like 6–4–2–1. He must have at least one of the minor-suit kings, so the only chance of beating the contract was to score a heart, a heart ruff and two trump tricks. How could that be done?

With a masterly air the Abbot returned the *king* of hearts at trick 3. Declarer won with the ace and played a second round of trumps. In with the ace of trumps, the Abbot gave Brother Xavier a heart ruff. West exited with ♣ K and East's ♡ 10 now stood sentinel over declarer's 8. There was no way declarer could avoid the loss of a heart trick and he went one down.

"The only way to beat it, if I'm not mistaken," declared the Abbot. "Not a defence that would occur to many."

Brother Xavier returned his cards to the board. "A small heart at trick 3 is just as good, isn't it?" he said. "You can play the king on the third round, pinning dummy's queen."

The Abbot gave an irritated wave of the hand. "As it happens," he replied, "but the king of hearts at trick 3 is the more elegant play."

In the other room Brother Paulo reached the same contract and again ♡ 9 was led.

"Queen, please," said Brother Paulo.

The queen was covered by the king and ace, leaving the defenders powerless. East returned a heart when he won the first round of trumps, but declarer ran it to dummy's 7. East won the second round of trumps and gave his partner a heart ruff but that was the last trick for the defence.

The monastery team continued to do well and was lying third or fourth when they met the strong London team near the end.

Game all, dealer South

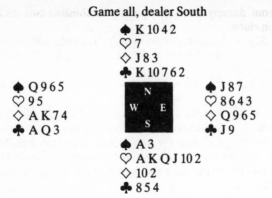

West	North	East	South
Barry	Brother	Peter	Brother
Rigour	Lucius	Davies	Paulo
			1♡
Dble	No	2♢	3♡
No	4♡	End	

Both monastery players bid boldly and a dubious heart game was reached. Barry Rigour, sitting West, cashed two rounds of diamonds and continued with a third round. Brother Paulo ruffed and played four rounds of trumps. West was in difficulty in this end position:

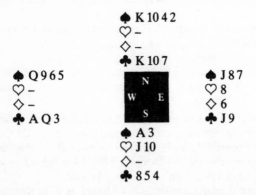

When ♡J was led West had no satisfactory discard. If he threw a spade, declarer would discard a club from dummy and ruff a spade good. West's actual discard was a club, but Brother Paulo threw a

[146]

spade from dummy and subsequently established two tricks for himself in clubs.

Barry Rigour, looking none too happy, reached for his scorecard.

"Low club at trick 3 beats it, I think," came a Welsh voice from across the table.

"Yes, I *had* noticed," replied Rigour heavily. "Kind of you to point it out, though."

In the other room the Abbot and Brother Xavier faced David Bryce and Chris Duckweed. The Abbot had been hard-pressed to conceal his irritation that the opponents were both smoking incessantly. No-one would have guessed from his intolerant attitude that he had once been a 40-a-day man himself. This board had just been dealt.

North–South game, dealer West

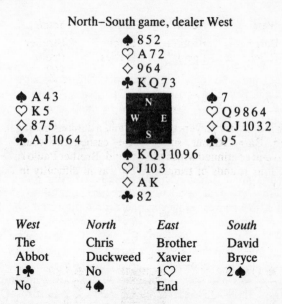

West	North	East	South
The	*Chris*	*Brother*	*David*
Abbot	Duckweed	Xavier	Bryce
1♣	No	1♡	2♠
No	4♠	End	

The Abbot, who had pointedly moved his chair back a couple of feet to avoid the smoke, stretched out an arm to place ♡ K on the table. Bryce peered down his impressive nose at the dummy. No point in playing the ace, he thought. They were bound to score a heart ruff if he did that. "Small, please," he said.

The Abbot continued with another heart, won in the dummy. Bryce crossed to the diamond ace and led a club. The Abbot ducked and dummy's king won. Next came a trump to the king. The Abbot, defending well, ducked again and Bryce continued with a second round of clubs towards dummy. The Abbot went in with ♣ A and exited safely with a diamond. These cards remained:

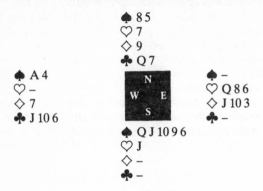

```
                  ♠ 8 5
                  ♡ 7
                  ◇ 9
                  ♣ Q 7
     ♠ A 4              N              ♠ –
     ♡ –         W           E        ♡ Q 8 6
     ◇ 7              S              ◇ J 10 3
     ♣ J 10 6                        ♣ –
                  ♠ Q J 10 9 6
                  ♡ J
                  ◇ –
                  ♣ –
```

Bryce had noted East's 7 on the first round of trumps. East would have no reason to peter from two small and if by any chance he held the ace of trumps he would get in to cash his heart winner anyway. No, thought Bryce, it must be right to play West for the two outstanding trumps. West was bound to duck again if a trump honour was led. The only chance was to slip the 6 past the ace, reaching dummy with the 8. His mind made up, Bryce led ♠ 6.

The Abbot edged to the front of his chair and leaned forward to inspect the dummy's cards. Now, what small spades were still out? It escaped him which card Xavier had played on the first round of the suit. Not that he would have had much chance of spotting it through these clouds of smoke. How was one expected to think clearly in such an atmosphere?

The Abbot pulled his thoughts together. The spade pips were irrelevant, he concluded. Declarer surely had a 6-card suit for his jump overcall. The Abbot won the second round of trumps with the ace and exited once again in diamonds. There was no entry to dummy and Bryce had to surrender the last trick to East's ♡ Q. He was one down.

Bryce looked apologetically at his partner. "I should have eliminated the diamonds," he said. "Ace-king of diamonds, club to dummy, diamond ruff and another club. That does it."

Duckweed nodded and reached for another cigarette.

"West can exit with a third round of clubs when he takes the club ace," continued Bryce, "but I can play low in the dummy, ruff in my hand and then lead a high trump on the second round."

"True," agree Duckweed. "If he holds up the ace of trumps again you can throw him in on the third round. He has to give dummy the lead with a club."

"That's the line I was afraid of," said the Abbot.

"Sorry," said Bryce, drawing deeply on his cigarette. "Do you smoke?" he added, proffering his pack of Benson and Hedges to the two monks in turn.

"Not willingly," replied the Abbot, waving away the smoke as he rose to his feet.

With one match to go the monastery team led the field by 3 VPs. A 6½–2½ win would guarantee them the trophy. The Abbot looked over to where their last opponents were sitting. He could not believe his eyes. Two elderly mixed couples awaited them.

"Do you see what I see?" said the Abbot, giving Brother Lucius a nudge. "The cup is as good as ours."

20

The Abbot's Glimpse of Heaven

The monastery's opponents in their last match were two elderly married couples, representing Hertfordshire. This was the first board at the Abbot's table.

Love all, dealer South

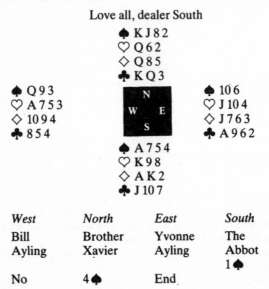

```
              ♠ K J 8 2
              ♡ Q 6 2
              ♢ Q 8 5
              ♣ K Q 3
♠ Q 9 3              N        ♠ 10 6
♡ A 7 5 3                     ♡ J 10 4
♢ 10 9 4      W       E       ♢ J 7 6 3
♣ 8 5 4              S        ♣ A 9 6 2
              ♠ A 7 5 4
              ♡ K 9 8
              ♢ A K 2
              ♣ J 10 7
```

West	North	East	South
Bill	Brother	Yvonne	The
Ayling	Xavier	Ayling	Abbot
			1♠
No	4♠	End	

The Abbot arrived in four spades and won the diamond lead with the ace. What next? Everything would be easy if he could pick up the trumps. If a trump finesse failed, though, he would probably lose two hearts and a club as well.

Another plan occurred to the Abbot. He could eliminate the minor suits and cash the ace and king of trumps. If the queen failed to drop, he could exit with a trump and force the defenders to open up the hearts. Yes, that must be better. It would succeed whenever the spade queen was doubleton and at least half the time when it was tripleton.

At trick 2 the Abbot led a club to the king, taken by East. The diamond return was won in the dummy and the Abbot cashed two rounds of trumps, everyone following. The remaining minor-suit winners were cashed, leaving these cards still to be played:

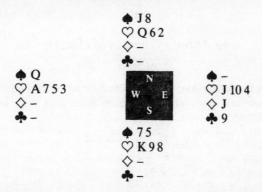

The Abbot now exited with a trump. Mr Ayling won with the queen and returned a low heart to the jack and king. Declarer's 9 and 8 of hearts now gave him a choice of plays; he could play West for either the ace or the 10 of hearts.

The Abbot, who had no intention of making a hurried decision at this crucial stage of the event, sat back in his chair. An expert East, holding both the jack and 10 of hearts would doubtless choose at random between the two cards. The Principle of Restricted Choice would then make West a 2–1 favourite to hold the 10 of hearts. Surely in the present circumstances the odds were even better. Mrs Ayling looked like the sort of person who would always play a true card, the 10, from a J 10 combination.

His mind made up, the Abbot ran ♡ 9. East won with the 10 and the contract was one down.

The Abbot winced. "The trump finesse would have worked," he said.

"Quite so," agreed Mr Ayling. "Mind you, I have every sympathy for the way you played it. The queen of spades is often doubleton."

Mrs Ayling smiled pleasantly at the Abbot. "I couldn't believe it when I made my ♡ 10," she said. "I was sure you would go up with dummy's queen. You make it then, don't you?"

The Abbot refrained from caustic reply. "I placed your partner with ♡ 10," he said. "In that case the 9 would force your ace."

"But I didn't have the ace," declared a puzzled Mrs Ayling. "You had it, Bill, didn't you?"

It was a foregone conclusion that the point-a-board had been lost on this hand. The 3 extra VPs for the aggregate difference were also likely to vanish unless a large swing could be engineered on one of the two remaining boards. Hoping for some distributional hand with swing potential, the Abbot extracted his cards for the next board. This collection met his eyes:

♠ 82　♡ A J 5 4　♢ Q 10 2　♣ K J 9 5

The Abbot's heart sank. A flat 11-count. What magic could be wrought from that? One might as well give Michelangelo a block of reinforced concrete.

"Two clubs," said Brother Xavier, setting the auction in motion.

The Abbot's spirits rose somewhat. He did not believe in responding 2 NT on this type of hand. An initial negative response would leave more room. "Two diamonds," said the Abbot.

Brother Xavier rebid three diamonds and the Abbot consulted his cards once more. It was time to spring into action. He could raise to four diamonds, but it would be more descriptive to make an immediate cue bid, announcing his slam intentions.

"Four hearts," said the Abbot.

Brother Xavier paused for a while. "No bid," he said finally.

For a second or two the Abbot looked as if someone had stabbed him in the back. What in the name of the saints was Xavier thinking of? A jump from three diamonds to four hearts must be a cue bid. What else could it be?

"My lead?" enquired Mr Ayling. "Now, tell me, what did this four-heart bid mean?"

"Well, it doesn't come up very often," replied Brother Xavier, "but in Acol a negative response followed by a jump shows a one-loser suit."

Mr Ayling led ♣ 7 and down went the dummy. This was the full deal:

East–West game, dealer West

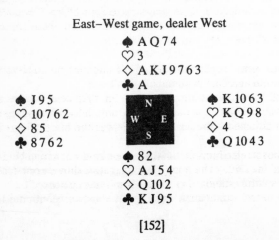

♠ A Q 7 4
♡ 3
♢ A K J 9 7 6 3
♣ A

♠ J 9 5　　　　　　　　♠ K 10 6 3
♡ 10 7 6 2　　　　　　♡ K Q 9 8
♢ 8 5　　　　　　　　♢ 4
♣ 8 7 6 2　　　　　　♣ Q 10 4 3

♠ 8 2
♡ A J 5 4
♢ Q 10 2
♣ K J 9 5

of play. If he could ruff three hearts in the South hand he would still arrive at ten tricks.

The Abbot crossed to ♡ A and ruffed a heart. He then re-entered dummy with a diamond and ruffed another heart. He returned to the North hand with ♣ K, leaving these cards still to be played:

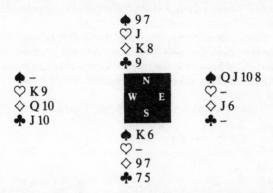

```
                ♠ 9 7
                ♡ J
                ◇ K 8
                ♣ 9
♠ –                           ♠ Q J 10 8
♡ K 9              N          ♡ –
◇ Q 10         W     E        ◇ J 6
♣ J 10             S          ♣ –
                ♠ K 6
                ♡ –
                ◇ 9 7
                ♣ 7 5
```

When the Abbot led dummy's last heart, East was helpless. If she discarded a diamond, declarer would score his 6 of trumps and make two more tricks. Mrs Ayling decided to ruff with the 8 of trumps and the Abbot discarded a diamond. The trump return was won with the king and the Abbot was now able to ruff a diamond in the South hand for his tenth trick.

"A small something retrieved from the wreckage," declared the Abbot, flopping back in his chair. "I don't expect it will be enough, with three teams breathing down our neck."

Lucius and Paulo soon returned. "Minus 460 on the first one, I'm afraid," said Brother Lucius. "Heart lead against 3 NT."

"And minus 50," said the Abbot.

"You played in six?" queried Brother Lucius.

"No, one off in four spades," replied the Abbot. "We had K J to four opposite ace to four, you remember? It was one of the best played hands of the weekend. Very unlucky."

"Plus 50 on the next one," continued Brother Lucius after a slight pause. "They played in 6 NT, going for the good point-a-board. Six diamonds was cold, of course."

"Heavens be praised!" exclaimed the Abbot. "We stopped in game. I thought it would be a bad one for us. Plus 420." The Abbot's eyes shone brightly. "And I think you'll like our last one, too," he said. "Plus 620! I managed to make four spades."

"Yes, flat board," replied Brother Lucius.

"They made four spades?" gasped the Abbot.

"She took three ruffs in the South hand," said Brother Lucius. "Told us that she always enjoyed 'ruffing in'. There was nothing we could do."

"What did we score, anyway?" said the Abbot. "A two and a one on the point-a-board. The aggregate was level, so that's another one and a half."

"Yes," agreed Brother Paulo. "Four and a half altogether. We were three ahead of the London team, so they will need to win 8–1 to beat us."

"Have you heard the London score?" said a bald-headed man, arriving at their table. "It was 9–0!"

"I don't believe it," thundered the Abbot. "Are you sure about that?"

"Yes, I watched them score the boards," replied the bald man. "They must have overstretched, trying to catch you up. They didn't score a single point."

A triumphant smile came to the Abbot's lips and he raised his eyes heavenwards. So, there was justice in the world after all. Forty years of hard toil at the green baize had finally been rewarded.

"What an exhilarating win," declared Brother Lucius. "I must say, I never thought we would do it."

"I was quietly confident," replied the Abbot. "With Xavier and me playing such a steady last set, the result was never in doubt."